Scott Oden's lifelong fascination with Egypt and the ancient world began in 1976, when his third-grade teacher showed his class slides from the travelling Tutankhamen exhibition. Oden went on to study history and English at Calhoun College and the University if Alabama (Huntsville) before leaving school to pursue his dream of becoming a writer. Over the years, he has worked the usual variety of odd jobs: delivering pizza, driving a truck for a printing company, and clerking at a video store, just to name a few. Now a full-time writer, Oden lives in rural North Alabama, near Huntsville, in a house that is sadly lacking in cats.

www.scottoden.com

MEN OF BRONZE

scott oden

BANTAM BOOKS

LONDON · TORONTO · SYDNEY · AUCKLAND · JOHANNESBURG

MEN OF BRONZE
A BANTAM BOOK : 0553817914

Originally published in the United States by Medallion Press

First publication in Great Britain
Bantam edition published 2006

1 3 5 7 9 10 8 6 4 2

Copyright © Scott Oden 2005

The right of Scott Oden to be identified as the author of this
work has been asserted in accordance with sections 77 and
78 of the Copyright Designs and Patents Act 1988.

All the characters in this book are fictitious, and any resemblance
to actual persons, living or dead, is purely coincidental.

Condition of Sale

This book is sold subject to the condition that it shall not, by way
of trade or otherwise, be lent, re-sold, hired out or otherwise
circulated in any form of binding or cover other than that in which
it is published and without a similar condition including this
condition being imposed on the subsequent purchaser.

Set in 11/13pt Sabon by
Kestrel Data, Exeter, Devon.

Bantam Books are published by Transworld Publishers,
61–63 Uxbridge Road, London W5 5SA,
a division of The Random House Group Ltd,
in Australia by Random House Australia (Pty) Ltd,
20 Alfred Street, Milsons Point, Sydney, NSW 2061, Australia,
in New Zealand by Random House New Zealand Ltd,
18 Poland Road, Glenfield, Auckland 10, New Zealand
and in South Africa by Random House (Pty) Ltd,
Isle of Houghton, Corner of Boundary Road & Carse O'Gowrie,
Houghton 2198, South Africa.

Printed and bound in Great Britain by
Cox & Wyman Ltd, Reading, Berkshire.

Papers used by Transworld Publishers are natural, recyclable
products made from wood grown in sustainable forests.
The manufacturing processes conform to the environmental
regulations of the country of origin.

For my parents, Arthur and Polly Oden,
who taught me that reading was the door to a
thousand possibilities, and for Laura Hipps,
my first librarian, who made sure I
opened the right doors.

ACKNOWLEDGEMENTS

I owe a tremendous debt of gratitude to the men and women of Egyptology, Archaeology, and related disciplines, whose passionate pursuit of understanding has given generations of novelists a skeleton on which to hang the imperfect flesh of fiction. Any historical veracity to *Men of Bronze* exists because of their scholarship; any mistakes are my own.

A very special thank you to my incomparable agent, Rebecca Pratt, who became a tireless champion of the work despite the neuroses of her client. Equally important to me has been the support, advice, and encouragement of my Medallion Press family: Helen Rosburg, my publisher; Leslie Burbank, Medallion's Vice President; and Connie Perry, COO and Author Liaison. Their patience made the process of shepherding a project from cluttered manuscript to finished book look easy. I cannot thank them enough.

I place a terrible burden on those people around me, readers and writers, when I foist pages off on them and monopolize their time. I thank them for their graciousness and expertise: Darren Cox, Jason 'Who' Hatfield, Sarah Hocutt, Abe Johnson, Adam 'Bean' Johnson, Edna Leo, Tanja Lewis, Wayne Miller, Nancy Morris, Kristie Oldaker, Josh Olive, Kris Reisz, and Rob Reser.

Finally, thanks to James Byron Huggins, friend and author, who blazed a trail that's been easy to see yet hard to follow.

CONTENTS

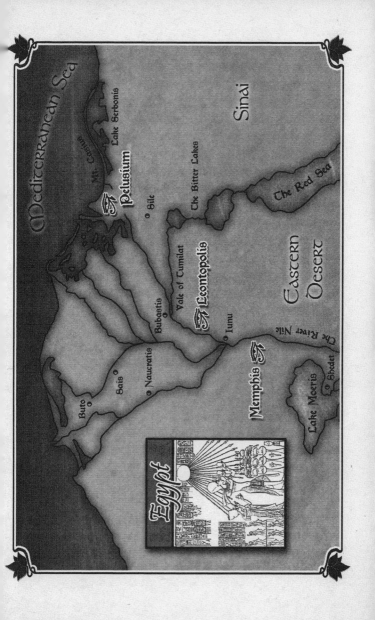

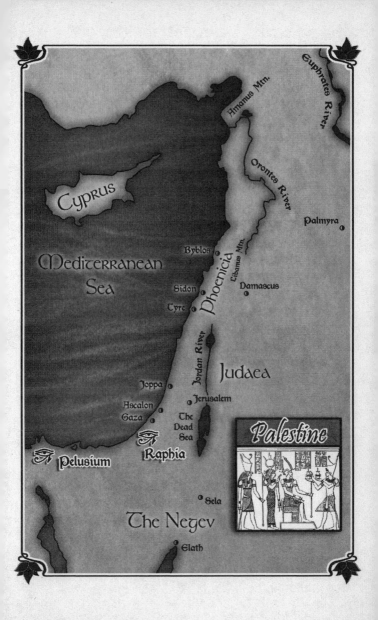

'There was another thing which helped to bring about the Egyptian expedition. One of the Greek mercenaries of Pharaoh, being dissatisfied for some reason or other, escaped from Egypt by sea with the object of getting an interview with Cambyses. As this mercenary was a person of consequence in the army and had very precise knowledge of the internal condition of Egypt, Pharaoh was anxious to stop him . . .'

Herodotus, *The Histories*

PART ONE

Year Forty-four of the reign of Khnemibre Ahmose
(526 BC)

1

THE CITY OF LIONS

In the blue predawn twilight, a mist rose from the Nile's surface, flowing up the reed-choked banks and into the ruined streets of Leontopolis. Remnants of monumental architecture floated like islands of stone on a calm morning sea. Streamers of moisture swirled around statues of long-dead pharaohs, flowed past stumps of columns broken off like rotted teeth, and coursed down sandstone steps worn paper-thin by the passage of years. As the sky above grew translucent, streaked with amber and gold, a funerary shroud settled over the City of Lions, a mantle that disguised the approach of armed men.

From the desert came two score and ten dark shapes, clad Greek-fashion in leather cuirasses and studded kilts, Corinthian helmets perched atop their foreheads. Bowl-shaped shields hung from their shoulders by gripcords of plaited hemp, freeing each man to wield a short, recurved bow. They moved in earnest, silent, a company of phantoms drifting through the fog.

The Medjay had come to Leontopolis.

Medjay. The soldiers bearing this appellation were the most savage of Pharaoh's mercenaries. They were a cadre of outcasts, criminals in their own lands, who banded together under Egypt's banner to dedicate their lives to the gods of violence. The emblem painted on their shield faces, the *uadjet,* the all-seeing Eye of Horus, symbolized their task as guardians of the eastern frontier. Pharaoh paid them to be vigilant, to crush any intruders before they could reach even an abandoned ruin such as Leontopolis, and he paid them well. This time, though, the Medjay had failed their royal paymaster.

To a man, they froze as the rasp of metal on stone drifted through the mist; instinctively, their eyes sought out the massive silhouette of their commander. Phoenician by birth, Hasdrabal Barca ruled the Medjay with the tigerish strength of a born killer. Spear, arrow, torch, and sword, all this and more had touched his flesh, leaving behind the indelible scars of a lifetime spent waging war. He disdained a helmet; long black hair, shot through with grey, fell over his face as he stood with head bowed, straining to hear.

The clatter came again, followed by sibilant cursing.

Barca looked up; his eyes turned to slits, like splinters hacked from the iron gates of Tartarus. He motioned, and a young soldier, a Libyan, edged up to his side. The Phoenician dragged his index finger across his throat in a chilling pantomime. Nodding, the soldier handed his bow and shield off to another, removed his helmet, and drew a curved knife from the small of his back. Beneath a thatch of sandy hair, plastered with sweat, the young Medjay's eyes shimmered with anticipation as he crept off to do Barca's bidding.

Raids like this were nothing new. The desert folk of Sinai, the Bedouin, encroached on Egypt's borders every season, fleeing tribal feuds or seeking relief from generations of drought. The Medjay turned most back at the Walls of the Ruler, a line of ancient fortifications stretching from Pelusium on the coast, along the Bitter Lakes, to the Gulf of Suez. A few, though, slipped through the Medjay's nets to plunder the border villages. Such was the fate of Habu, south of the vale of Tumilat, on the shores of the Great Bitter Lake.

Habu lay on the patrol route between Sile and Dedun, on the Gulf; it was a small village of two dozen mud brick huts clustered around a brackish well whose inhabitants mined salt in the nearby hills. The Medjay, following the Bedouin's trail, found Habu in ruins. Barca recalled the mound of severed heads in the village square, the corpses left to rot in the merciless sun. The men were killed outright, the women raped and mutilated. Even the children . . .

Barca's scout returned as quietly as he had left. He made a show of wiping his knife on a Bedouin headscarf.

'You were right,' the scout, Tjemu, whispered, 'they are the Beni Harith.'

'How many?' Barca's voice did not carry past the Medjay's ear.

Tjemu nodded back the way he had come. 'Maybe twice our number, camped in a square some hundred yards beyond a causeway of crouching stone lions. Their pickets are asleep. Careless bastards.'

'They're not expecting us.' Barca's jaw tightened; deep in his soul he felt the Beast stir, flexing its claws. *Even the children.* 'Fan out!' he ordered, raising his fist. Sinew creaked as the Medjay bent their bows.

The Bedouin camp stirred and came alive. The younger men fetched water from the Nile's bank while their elders sat in council before the camel-hair tent of their *shaykh,* Ghazi ibn Ghazi. Four of his brothers, an uncle, and seven nephews reclined on their blankets, talking in low voices about this last stage of their journey. Spear butts and sheathed swords clattered on the cracked paving stones; tethered camels bawled, as unhappy about the claustrophobic mist as their masters were.

Ghazi ibn Ghazi plucked a date from a wooden bowl and popped it into his mouth. Age, sand, and sun had left his face fleshless, seamed, an uncured hide stretched tight over a frame of bone. His eyebrows and beard were grey and sparse, his shoulders stooped, calling to mind a wizened shoemaker rather than a Bedouin war leader.

'This place is accursed!' the man on his right said, with all the frustrated weariness of one who had not slept soundly in days. He wore clothing similar to his Bedouin companions – robes of grimy brown wool and a once-white head scarf held in place by a leather band – but his accent and manners marked him as a Persian. 'It is fit for jackals, perhaps, or Bedouin, but it is no place for a man of refinement.'

Ghazi grinned. 'Where are your balls, Arsamenes? Have you Persians become so civilized that you can no longer stomach the hard road?'

The Persian, Arsamenes, leaned forward, helping himself to the dates. His eyes, small and dark, flickered up to the Bedouin's face. 'We could have been done with the hard road, and in Memphis already, had you not stopped to glut yourself on that flyspeck of a village.'

At this, the other Bedouin ceased their own conversations. This was not the first time the Persian had broached that topic.

'I told you before,' Ghazi said quietly, 'Habu is none of your concern.'

'Will the Medjay not notice the slaughtered villagers? Will they ignore the spoor of a hundred camels leading in country from Sinai? You fool! Everything about this mission is my concern! You have jeopardized it, and I want to know why!'

The old *shaykh* sighed. From other tents, he heard voices, muffled laughter, and the *slish* of blades on oiled stone. 'It was an old debt,' Ghazi said, finally. 'In my youth, a man of Habu shamed a girl of the Harith. We could not pass them by without exacting our vengeance.'

Arsamenes' face darkened; his close-cropped beard bristled. 'You put the honour of a two-shekel desert slut over the interests of the King of Kings?'

Ghazi's lips curled into a sneer. 'The Harith are not slaves to your king, not like the Medes or the Parsi. We paid Cyrus his due because we respected him, but you would do well to remember not even your great king could conquer the People of the Sands.

'I have given the son of Cyrus my word to escort you to Memphis. After that . . .' With a speed his years belied, Ghazi drew his knife and put it to Arsamenes' throat. The Persian gasped, his body going rigid. 'After that, you live at my pleasure, understand?' Arsamenes' eyes blazed. Without the slightest hesitation, he reached up and pushed Ghazi's hand away. 'Cambyses will have your head.'

'Finding it will not be difficult, eh?' Ghazi grinned, sheathing his blade. 'Since it will be buried between the thighs of Pharaoh's daughter!' Raucous laughter erupted from the Bedouin; even Arsamenes smiled, though his eyes lost none of their fire. The tension broken, Ghazi's kinsmen stood and stretched, eager to be away from this desolate place, with its leonine statues and in-human sphinxes. The *shaykh* gave orders for the tents to be struck, the small fires doused, and the sentries recalled.

Ghazi did not have the gall to call this gathering of his kin an army, though by Bedouin standards, it was a veritable host. He had seen true armies in his youth, armies drawn to the standards of Nebuchadnezzar of Babylon. In comparison, his five-score would have been as a single grain of sand in the desert. Yet, he doubted the Chaldeans were more loyal to their king than his Harith were to him. They would ride to the gates of Hell, if he asked it of them. Pride swelled Ghazi's chest. With a thousand Bedouin, he could make Sinai a power to be reckoned with; with a hundred-thousand, he could make the world an Arab playground. Someday, Ghazi told himself, someday . . .

Ghazi uncorked a skin of wine. He made to raise it to his lips, but stopped in mid-gesture, his head cocked to the side. The hairs on the back of his neck stood up as he sensed unseen eyes on him.

'What is it, *shaykh*?' Others, too, muttered their concern.

Ghazi's frown deepened. 'Quiet. Listen.'

Though he had seen no sign of it, Ghazi knew in his marrow the Medjay were in relentless pursuit, driven by that devil of a man, the Phoenician. If they were out there, this fog would work to their advantage. *We should not have tarried here*. Ghazi glanced around, his eyes coming to rest on his sister's son, Tajik. An unspoken question passed between them.

'Sounds like locusts,' Tajik said. The young

Bedouin craned his neck and died as a bronze-tipped arrow split his skull.

A deadly hail rained down through the mist, punching through flesh and bone, shattering on stone. Arsamenes twisted with an agonized scream, clawing at the black-fletched shafts that sprouted from his back. Ghazi's frayed robe flared out behind him like misshapen wings as he leapt the fallen Persian and took cover in the lee of a massive lion-headed statue. All around, his Bedouin crumpled and died.

'Move!' he shouted, drawing his sword. 'Move, you bastards! The Medjay are upon us!'

Baying like human wolves, the Medjay charged into the Bedouin camp, Barca at the head of a loose wedge of fighters. They cast their bows aside, drew their swords, and unslung their shields; men grabbed the flared cheek pieces of their helmets and tugged them down, transforming flesh-and-blood soldiers into the faceless cogs of a bronze killing machine.

The Bedouin did not stand idle. Though disarrayed by the sudden arrow storm, Ghazi's cry rallied their spirits. 'Move, you bastards! The Medjay are upon us!' Young men and old snatched their weapons up and answered the Medjay's threat with the undulating shriek of the desert folk.

Time grew hazy, indistinct. Seconds took on the

aspect of hours. In this last elongated heartbeat between life and death, a man's senses became painfully acute. Hereditary enemies stared at one another across the shrinking interval, teeth bared in snarls of hate, grimaces of fear. Thoughts of distant homes, long-lost loves, and forgotten embraces vanished beneath the adrenalin-laced pulse of blood lust. Neither side called for terms; none sought guarantees of mercy. This fight would be as savage and brutal as it would be short.

Muscles tensed. Weapons glittered. Lips prayed. Shields balanced.

And suddenly . . .

Medjay and Bedouin collided in a grinding of flesh and bone, underscored by the crunch of chopping blades and the screams of the dying. Swords flickered like lightning, crashing on shield and helmet, rasping on enemy blades. Men strained breast-to-breast, helmet-to-turban, a vicious mob fighting for purchase on the blood-smeared stones. The wounded collapsed, shrieking as they were trampled underfoot, dragging the living down with them. Iron punched and shattered, and blood flowed like wine at Hell's banquet. No time to issue orders or ponder tactics, Barca ploughed into the heart of the fight and trusted its outcome to the gods. The massive Phoenician roared and struck from side to side, dropping a man with each blow. A soldier of the Medjay stumbled against him, a spear buried in his neck. His killer's cry of triumph became a death-rattle as Barca's scimitar licked out and sheared through his turbaned skull. The Bedouin called the captain of the Medjay *al-Saffah*, the Blood-letter; with each killing stroke, Barca demonstrated the truth of that sobriquet.

The Bedouin redoubled their attack. Bearded faces pressed in from all sides, visages radiating hatred and bloodlust. Frothing lips hurled curses as knotted fists hurled blows. Bedouin grew reckless, sacrificing their own lives in an effort to bring Barca down. A knife blade scored the flesh of his forearm; a sword rebounded from his shield. The Phoenician snarled. With a chilling cry, Hasdrabal Barca unleashed the Beast.

The Greeks called it *katalepsis* – demonic possession in the heat of battle, rendering a man insensate to the flesh, his own or his foes. A berserk fury boiled up from the depths of Barca's soul, from a place only he knew. A fury stoked by memories that had haunted him for more than twenty years . . .

Moonlight pierced the darkness, caressing her thigh, her breast. A night breeze ruffled the gauzy curtains as she crawled to where her lover sat, arching her back like a cat in heat. He was Greek, perfumed and pomaded, a soldier in name only. 'Neferu,' he whispered with a smile, stripping off his linen kilt and leading her eager mouth to him . . .

Faces welled and ebbed around Barca. Dark features half-glimpsed, hands that grasped and tore. In that press of humanity, the Phoenician's body itself became a weapon. The hard bones of his forehead sent a Bedouin reeling; his elbow crushed a man's throat like a mace; his sandalled heel shattered a kneecap. Blood sprayed as his scimitar wove a web about him, a silvery cocoon as beautiful as it was lethal. Still, the Beast howled and gibbered in his brain . . .

The Greek rutted between her thighs, their sweat mingling, their cries of pleasure echoing in the darkness. Neither of them noticed the door opening. They did not see the anguished eyes of her young husband, nor did they see as that anguish turned to a white-hot rage. Wordless, he moved to where the Greek's sword lay . . .

Through the red haze of *katalepsis*, Barca caught sight of Ghazi ibn Ghazi. The old Arab hammered a Medjay shield aside and slashed at the soldier's exposed neck. The man fell, spewing crimson. With a moment's respite, Ghazi's eyes gauged his Bedouin's odds as the armoured Medjay scythed through them. His casualties were mounting. He spotted al-Saffah, and the look of pure hatred in the Phoenician's face struck Ghazi like a physical blow. He staggered, blood draining from his features and taking with it his courage. Ghazi ibn Ghazi spun and fled, leaving his kin to die beneath the blades of the Medjay.

Barca, with a bellow of rage, gave chase.

The battle became a rout; the rout, a slaughter. Memories of the burning huts of Habu, of the children left to rot in the sun, sealed the Bedouin's fate. Barca's soldiers ranged the field with vengeful purpose, mutilating the dead and slaying the wounded, despite their cries for succour. As the rising sun crested the distant hills, searing away the mist, silence came again to the City of Lions.

Tjemu, his back against a crumbling obelisk, snatched a bloodied turban off the ground and knotted it around his punctured thigh. 'Sand-fuckers!' he hissed. He had made it through the battle with only cuts and scrapes until the very end; until an injured Bedouin lurched up and rammed a broken spear through his leg. The blade missed the great artery, though a savage twist left him with a hole the size of a child's fist. The Bedouin who speared him, a beardless boy barely out of his teens, lay crumpled at his feet, the Libyan's sword still wedged in his skull. Tjemu spared him a single pitiless glance.

The ebb and flow of battle carried Tjemu to the edge of the square, its stones littered now with the detritus of war: broken and discarded weapons, hacked shields, bodies and parts of bodies, all of it stewing in pools of blood and bowel that gathered in the low places. He recognized friends among the slain. Gambling partners, drinking companions, and sword brothers lay supine now, staring at the azure sky with glazed eyes. The Libyan felt a pang of regret which lasted only a few heartbeats before he succumbed to the satisfaction of being alive. The Medjay, finished with their murderous rampage, saw to their wounded. Some bound their cuts; others sat very still, sipping water or wine. In the shadow of a leonine statue of the goddess Sekhmet, he saw the old Canaanite, Ithobaal, crouching over a corpse. Of Barca, he saw no sign.

Tjemu limped to Ithobaal's side. 'What did you find, old man? Loot, I hope.'

'Trouble,' Ithobaal said, gesturing to the body. Tjemu frowned at the corpse, trying to look past the waxen skin and skewed limbs, past the trio of arrows that ended the thread of his life, to see what Ithobaal saw. Tjemu toed aside the blood-grimed head scarf and looked more closely at the dead man's face.

'Amon's balls! A Persian!'

Ithobaal tugged a leather dispatch case from inside the dead man's robe. 'And a courier, to boot. We'd best find Barca.'

Tjemu looked around. An eerie silence gripped the battlefield, sending an involuntary shudder through the Libyan. In his gut he knew they would not find Barca until the devil in his soul had sated its lust.

𓂀 𓏺 𓊖 𓀀 𓊹

Ghazi's breath came in sharp gasps. His heart hammered in his chest as he flattened himself against a crumbling retaining wall and listened for sounds of pursuit. Nothing. The old *shaykh* exhaled. The swords of the Medjay left his robes

31

in tatters, and he bled from a score of lacerations. Ghazi glanced down at the scimitar in his clenched fist, its crimson blade dull, notched from the fighting. Sunlight shredded the morning mist. Before him, running parallel with the wall, lay a flat plain that sloped down to the Nile's edge, broken now and again by heaps of shattered stone, solitary palm trees, and scrubby acacias. Knee-high grasses swayed in the light breeze. He could see the reedy bank and the sluggish water beyond. Perhaps a boat lay near?

'Al-Saffah!' he said, wringing the sweat from his eyes. 'Al-Saffah! The gods take you!' At Kadesh, the oasis of the Beni Harith, Arsamenes had warned him about the Medjay and their implacable captain. Warned him, a child of Sinai, that no good could come from tweaking the devil's beard! *Why didn't I listen?* Five-score of his men, his kin, paid for his arrogance, his foolishness. They were dead and Ghazi was trapped, the breadth of Egypt between himself and safety. He could still reach Memphis. From there, he . . .

The crunch of a hobnailed sandal on stone shattered Ghazi's reverie. He glanced around, sword ready. The noise repeated itself. Fear-bile welled up in the *shaykh's* throat. Where? Dust trickled across his face, feathery light. Suddenly, a shadow stretched out before him.

They're above me!

Ghazi glanced up. Atop the wall, like one of the Furies in blood-splashed armour, crouched al-Saffah. His features were twisted into a mask of hate, and his slitted eyes burned with a baleful fire.

'Bastard!' Barca hissed, his jaw clenching spasmodically.

Ghazi paled. A high-pitched scream burst from his lips as he dropped his sword and bolted for the river. He thought of nothing save the promise of succour to be had in the Nile's muddy swirl. Terror lent his ageing limbs speed. If only he could reach the river's edge . . .

Pain blossomed in Ghazi's left shoulder. A fist-sized chunk of masonry, hurled with all the strength of Barca's arm, splintered the bone. The force of the blow sent the Arab cartwheeling. He struck the ground hard. Breath whooshed from his lungs, and his agonized shriek choked off in a tide of vomit. Ghazi fought for breath. He fought to drag his body, one arm useless, to the Nile's dark breast. A long shadow fell across him. The Arab craned his neck, eyes wide with panic.

Al-Saffah leapt from the wall and stalked through the grass, a ribbon of blood drooling from the blade of his scimitar.

Ghazi wept. 'M-Mercy! P-Please, al-Saffah! Please . . .'

Barca's scimitar flashed down, crunching through the old man's head, shoulder and into his chest. 'Did you bargain with the women and children of Habu?' he hissed, hacking at the flailing Bedouin. Again and again he struck until the thing under his blade grew unrecognizable even as human. With its hunger slaked, the Beast relinquished its grip on his body, leaving his limbs cold and trembling. Barca reeled away, his sword falling from his grasp. He stumbled backwards; leather scraped stone as he struck the wall and slid to the ground. He cradled his head in his hands . . .

He struck as their moans reached a crescendo, driving the sword point-first between the Greek's shoulder blades. Vertebrae splintered as he leaned on the hilt. Beneath her lover, the young man's wife screamed, a piercing shriek that ended when the sword crunched through the Greek's body and into hers. Blood exploded from her nostrils. Cold, betrayed by his own rage, the young husband fled, leaving the lovers joined forever in death.

'Neferu,' he whispered.

Tjemu spotted him first, walking through the windrows of the dead like a farmer in the wake of harvest. Barca paused beside knots of wounded Medjay, clapping their shoulders and laughing. In his presence groans ceased; grimaces of pain turned to triumphant smiles. The Libyan nodded to Ithobaal. 'I cannot tell who loves him more, gods or men. Look at him. Barely a scratch. You've been with him longer than I have. What's his secret?'

Ithobaal, who could claim kinship with King Achish of conquered Gath, shaded his eyes with a spade-like hand. Blood spattered his greying beard. At sixty, he was the old man of the Medjay, the voice of temperance and reason, the wise old wolf in a pack of killers. Blood-grimed fingers toyed with an amulet around his neck, a lapis *uadjet* on a leather thong.

'Secret?' Ithobaal said, his voice like the tolling of a bell. 'He has no secret. When death holds no terror for a man, little brother, what does he have left to fear?'

Ithobaal watched Barca's mood darken as he approached. In all his years of soldiering, he had never met a man quite like the Phoenician. He had seen his share of veterans humbled by the aftermath of battle. Champions who tearfully thanked the gods for the gift of another day; princes who puked their guts up as fear caught up with them; kings who needed a moment alone to compose themselves. He'd seen men become so overawed by the recognition of one's own mortality that came on the heels of violent confrontation that they would never fight again. But not Barca. Never Barca. Without fail, the captain of the Medjay assumed the air of a man who had been cheated, a man who had been guaranteed a rendezvous with Death only to have it denied him.

'Wine!' Barca snapped as he strode up to where the two men waited. Ithobaal tossed him a leather flask. He upended it, pouring the contents into his mouth, much of it sluicing down his chin and armour. 'How many dead?'

Ithobaal grimaced. 'Twenty-two. Another eight may not make it.'

'Send runners to the villages here about. We'll need supplies.' Barca sat on the stump of a column. 'These Bedouin were tougher than they looked. Wonder what drove them to strike this deep into Egypt?'

'Not what, who. Found a dead Persian among them.' Ithobaal handed the dispatch case to Barca. 'He had this on him. I think the Bedouin might have been his escort.'

The case was a flat satchel of thick dark leather, stiffened with the messenger's blood and battered from innumerable handlings. Thongs held the flap in place, and a bulla of clay, impressed with the dragon-seal of Babylon, ensured that its contents remained inviolate. 'Escort to where?' Barca said.

Tjemu peered over the Phoenician's shoulder as he broke the seal. Frowning, Barca drew out a heavy sheet of vellum. Tjemu grunted. The Libyan could not read, but his eyes marvelled at the delicate Aramaic script filling the page. 'What does it say?'

Barca said nothing for a moment, his eyes sharpening to points. 'It's addressed to the commander of the garrison at Memphis. It acknowledges some prior communication and . . . those sons of whores . . . it offers terms for their defection to Persia!'

Tjemu whistled. 'Amon's balls!'

'Defection? You think it's genuine?' Ithobaal said. The threat of mutiny proved a powerful weapon in the long-standing war between mercenary and paymaster. Soldiers, especially hired swords, were a petulant lot, and only trustworthy while a campaign netted them slaves and spoils. An unhappy mercenary attracted offers from rival generals as a lodestone attracted iron filings.

'The garrison is Greek,' Barca said, a snarl twisting his features. 'Greeks are fed treachery with their mother's milk!'

Ithobaal shook his head. 'Think about it, little brother. A mutiny? In Memphis? Word of such a thing should have spread the length and breadth of the Nile. Rumours would have reached the ears of Pharaoh himself if there were discontent among his pet Greeks.'

'True,' Barca said. 'But, some rumours can be silenced with promises, others with gold. The rest . . .' Barca trailed off, tapping the hilt of his sword. The Phoenician stood. All around the square, his Medjay cared for their dead. They stripped them of their armour, laid them out with reverence; their shields and personal effects would be taken back to Sile and enshrined in the temple of Horus Sopdu. The Bedouin dead, they ignored. Barca turned to face Ithobaal and Tjemu. 'It will take at least three days for a rider to deliver this letter to Pharaoh at Sais. I want to be in Memphis by then, to see how things are for myself. How's the leg, Tjemu?'

'A scratch,' the Libyan replied, grinning.

Barca nodded. 'Good. Bury our dead, then

shepherd the wounded to one of the nearby villages and make for Sais. Let no man dissuade you from giving the letter to Pharaoh directly. Ithobaal, you're with me. Gather those men with the scantiest wounds . . .'

Ithobaal shook his head, then hawked and spat.

'What?' Barca folded his arms across his chest.

'Our place is guarding the border, not policing the Greeks.' The Canaanite was a careful man, calculating and precise – a merchant in the guise of a soldier. 'Don't give in to impulse, little brother. In my heart I agree with you: traitors should be run to ground. But instinct tells me this is unwise. If anything, we should make for Sais ourselves, warn Pharaoh, and await his orders. Going off like this, on a whim—'

'*Our place?*' Barca checked his temper. 'Our place is between Pharaoh and his enemies, wherever they may be. This is not an invasion. We'll go quietly, poke our noses where they don't belong, and be away before the Greeks know what happened.' Barca started to turn away, stopped. 'But if you plan to second-guess me at every turn, Ithobaal, perhaps you should return to Sile. I need men for this, not old women!'

Ithobaal took a step toward his commander, his hand dropping to his sword hilt. 'You son of a Tyrian whore! I was fighting Pharaoh's enemies while you were still wallowing in your own shit!'

Barca grinned and tugged the old Canaanite's beard. 'There's fire still in your belly, then,

Ithobaal? Thank the gods! You had me worried.' The Phoenician turned away and held the diplomatic pouch aloft, using it to gesture at the scattered Medjay. 'Gather round, brothers! We're not going back to Sile, not yet!'

2

MEMPHIS

The sky above Saqqara burned white-hot, baking the sprawling necropolis like clay in the kiln of Ptah, the Creator. Stone and soil absorbed the heat, radiating it back in a dull imitation of the sun. Few things could survive in this waterless waste. Scorpions and beetles crawled through sand thick with yellowed bone, shards of pottery, and scraps of crumbling linen. Jackals slept the day away in the shade offered by the stair-stepped pyramid of Djoser. Falcons soared over the Serapeum in search of prey, riding that same bellow's-breath of air that rattled the leaves of acacias and sycamores yet provided little respite from the intolerable heat.

Through this inferno a runner came.

He was no ordinary man, this runner, but a Greek, born into a cult of personal glory and prowess that elevated him beyond mere mortals. Failure. Mercy. These were not words he used often, if at all, for to speak them would be to acknowledge them, to give them weight. Phanes of Halicarnassus acknowledged nothing save his own superiority.

Physically, that superiority was plain to see: a perfection of face and form that seemed somehow a blending of mortal and divine. Broad of shoulder with lean – almost feminine – hips, his powerful frame carried a layer of iron-hard muscle forged on the anvil of war. Dark eyes set deep into an angular face glared at the wasteland before him as though it were an enemy ripe for conquest.

He followed a vestigial road past crumbling pyramids, smaller than the monoliths at Giza, to the north, but impressive nonetheless. But if Phanes felt even the slightest twinge of awe at these constant reminders of Egypt's unfathomable age, he did not show it. For him, such glories of architecture, and their appreciation, were better left to the sophists.

Phanes ran with a loping stride that ate up the miles, sweat sluicing down his naked torso, soaking the scrap of cloth twisted about his loins. He darted around a plodding oxcart carrying chunks of limestone down to the stone-cutters' market in Memphis. A grizzled old man and a lad of twelve eyed him as he passed. The boy made to wave, a smile cracking his brown face, but a harsh word from his grandfather aborted the gesture. The old man wore a look of tolerant disgust. They were a proud folk, these Egyptians, Phanes could not deny that. Proud, strong, and courageous, but lacking the all-consuming thirst for freedom that separated Greek from barbarian.

Phanes crested a final ridge, the sun at his back, and beheld the panorama of the Nile Valley below. The sapphire ribbon of the river and the green of the cultivated fields stood in stark antithesis to the naked sand and rock of the desert's edge. More striking, though, was the city rising like a mirage from the Nile's bank.

Memphis. The City of Menes. Situated on a broad plain eight miles long and four miles wide, and protected from the annual Nile floods by a complex system of dykes and canals, the foundations of Egypt's capital were laid even as Phanes' ancestors crept from their caves to ponder the riddle of fire. It was a bustling metropolis before Herakles endured his twelve labours; impossibly ancient on the eve of Illium's fall. With each successive dynasty, Memphis grew in power and size, earning the appellation *Ankh-Tawy*, the Life of the Two Lands. By the year of Phanes' own birth, the generations who had lived and died in Memphis could be tallied in the hundreds.

Dominating the cityscape was a sprawling complex of temples dedicated to the gods of the Memphite triad: Ptah, Osiris, and Sokar. According to ancient tradition, it was Ptah, the Egyptian Hephaestus, who created man, conjuring him by thought and word. For that gift, the gift of life, Egypt repaid the Chief Artificer by building for him an earthly palace of unrivalled splendour. The Mansion of the Spirit of Ptah was a collection of open-air courts, shaded colonnades, hypostyle halls, chapels, shrines, sacred groves, and pools. Every pharaoh since the second Rameses – great Ozymandias – felt duty-bound to glorify the Creator by adding another ornamental pylon, another obelisk, another statue, until the whole became as chaotic and jumbled as the Labyrinth of the Cretan king, Minos. North of Ptah's temple, at the end of an avenue of human-headed sphinxes, lay the enclosure of hawk-headed Sokar, protector of the necropolis; south, near the edge of the city, lay the solemn and brooding precinct of Osiris, the Lord of the Dead. Other, smaller temples radiated out from these.

By the time Phanes reached the outskirts of Memphis, the sun was a ball of molten copper on the western horizon. He slowed his pace, drawing superheated air into his lungs in gulping breaths. The broad, dusty road swarmed with traffic. Men caked in grime trudged home from the quarries. Carts and wagons rattled over the hard-packed earth, laden with produce bound for the evening market in the Square of Deshur. Donkeys brayed and struggled. Oxen stumped along, led by brown-skinned children armed with frayed reeds. All around, flies rose in thick plague-like clouds, seemingly fuelled by the combined stenches of rotting fish, dung, and rancid oil.

This portion of Memphis, abutting Saqqara, was given over to the industry of death, and by Phanes' reckoning it was a thriving industry. His Greek forebears were pious folk, god-fearing and mindful of tradition. They buried their dead with dignity, said a few prayers over the graves, and went on with their lives. Compared with the Egyptians, though, his ancestors were a disorganized pack of heathens. Phanes had never seen a society so enamoured of death, and their fascination was reflected in the number and variety of merchants lining the street, hawking every conceivable amenity, from incense and unguents to palm wine and cedar resins. Potters sold canopic jars for the deceased's viscera; sculptors turned blue-glazed faience into small *ushabti* figurines; carpenters crafted coffins of palm-wood and cedar; jewellers worked gold, silver, lapis lazuli, and a whole host of semi-precious stones into amulets and fetishes; weavers made fine linen; scribes offered meticulously lettered copies of the *Book of the Dead*.

Phanes passed a public well alongside the road in the shadow of a stand of palm trees. The canopy of green fronds crackled in the light breeze. A Nubian slave, nearly naked in the blistering heat, worked the creaky arm of a *shadouf*. His efforts filled the basin one bucket at a time. Men and women clustered around the stone-lined pond, some washing off the day's dust, others filling pottery jugs. A toddler squealed as his father splashed water over him. But, as the Greek ambled by, their laughter, their chatter, ceased. Even the children stopped, staring, fearful in the sudden silence. Phanes felt the hostility in their collective gazes.

They did not hate him for his foreign blood. Indeed, two generations of Greek mercenaries had honourably served the kings of Sais, their heavy armour shaping a political landscape ravaged by years of Assyrian rule. No, they hated him because, instead of serving Pharaoh as mercenaries should, Phanes and his men strutted about like conquerors, taking what they wanted, and who. None were safe. Not the priests in their temples or the merchants in their stalls. Not their daughters or wives. Not their sons. The Greek garrison strangled Memphis with a noose of arrogance and greed, tightening it daily. Phanes sneered at their impotent rage.

Ahead, a chariot cut through the human sea like the prow of a ship. Pedestrians scurried aside; the driver plied his whip to remove any stragglers from his path. Phanes grinned. The man who worked the reins was Greek, as well, though burned dark as an Ethiop by the relentless sun. His height, combined with lean muscles and a long jaw, gave Phanes the impression of a racing hound, a thoroughbred. He wore a short Egyptian kilt of bleached linen, belted at the waist. Phanes raised a hand in greeting as the chariot drew abreast.

'A true man,' the driver said, curbing the horses, 'would have made that run in full *panoplia*.'

'A true man,' Phanes said, 'or a Spartan?'

'They are one and the same.'

'You are Spartan, Lysistratis, yet I see no sheen of sweat on your brow. Did you sprout wings and fly to the Serapeum?'

'If I did, who then would look after your affairs in Memphis while we're off puttering in the desert?' Lysistratis said. 'Come. You've a guest. That fool Callisthenes has returned from Delphi.'

Phanes' grin widened, a wicked gleam in his eyes. He leapt up into the chariot beside Lysistratis. 'Praise the gods! That bastard's been away so long I feared he'd made off with our offering.'

'Why you would trust a fat and lazy merchant of Naucratis is beyond me,' Lysistratis said. 'I would have gone.'

'Only you would suspect good Callisthenes, jolly Callisthenes, of treachery. What was the oracle's answer?'

The Spartan shrugged. 'Wouldn't say. Says her message is for you, alone.'

Phanes expected as much. It wasn't superstition or piety that drove him to seek guidance from the gods, but tradition. Since hallowed antiquity, the Greeks undertook no expedition, nothing, without first consulting the proper oracles. Heroes sought divine wisdom in their dealings. Kings sought answers to thorny problems. Even the lowliest sheep herder beseeched the gods for guidance in raising worthy flocks and worthier sons. With that in mind, Phanes sent offerings to the temples of Zeus at Dodona, Gaia at Olympia, and Dionysus at Amphicleia. Thus far, the answers to his enquiries had been cryptic yet affirmative. The last, and the one he anticipated most, was the answer of the priestess of Pythian Apollo at Delphi.

Lysistratis hauled on the reins, his horses disrupting the flow of traffic along the Saqqaran Road like a stone dropped into a fast-moving stream. Egyptians scrambled aside as the Spartan's whip cracked above their heads.

Phanes openly leered at several of the women on the street, their linen skirts sheer, their bare breasts slick with sweat. 'I'll not miss this slag-heap of a land, Lysistratis, but I will miss its women. Egyptian women are so . . . liberated.'

'I've heard the women of Persia are more beautiful.' Lysistratis raised his voice to be heard over the clatter of the chariot's wheels. 'Think Cambyses will share his seraglio with us?'

Phanes grinned. 'We give him Egypt, and I imagine he'd let us rut his sisters out of gratitude.'

From the Saqqaran Road, they crossed the broad, red-paved Square of Deshur at the western entrance of the Mansion of Ptah, where the Alabaster Sphinx glowed in the setting sun. Around this recumbent image, the evening market swirled. Men and women employed by the wealthier households bustled between stalls selling produce, bread, meat, and beer, haggling over prices, and arranging delivery to their masters' kitchens. Priests of the temples stood aloof as their factors inspected lambs and sheep, seeking those of the finest quality to serve as the next morning's offering to the gods. One such priest turned his head as Phanes' chariot passed; the Greek was unsure whether the sneer curling the priest's thin lips was intended for him, or for the bleating lamb his agent held between his knees.

Phanes' eyes narrowed. 'No matter what the oracle's answer may be, it's time we started culling the herd,' he said, indicating the Egyptians with a nod of his head. 'Use the Arcadians. Leon's men. But keep them under strict discipline, Lysistratis! I don't want a repeat of last summer's little orgy of violence. We're not the *krypteia*, and these aren't helots we're terrorizing.'

The Spartan glanced sidelong at his commander. He had been responsible for giving Leon's men a free hand during last summer's troubles, and though he found their methods deplorable – whole families executed to the last child – they were effective. The Arcadians were experts at rooting out discontent among the populace. 'Where should they start?'

'I leave it to you.'

The chariot rattled over a stretch of broken pavement before plunging down the great north-south avenue, called the Way of the Truth of Ptah. Lysistratis said, 'There's a gaggle of wealthy men, old bureaucrats for the most part, who have been trying to get letters through to Pharaoh. Petenemheb showed them to me. Mostly, they complain at great length about the "arrogance of the Hellenes", and beg Pharaoh's intercession. I suspect they would organize any resistance the Egyptians might mount against us.'

'Who leads them?'

'Most of the letters came from a man called Idu,

48

son of Menkaura. A merchant, of all things,' Lysistratis said, with a moue of distaste. His Spartan heritage gave him a healthy disdain for those who made their lives off the needs of others. 'A dealer of wine.'

Phanes grunted. 'Menkaura?'

'You know him?'

'There was a general from Memphis in the army of old Pharaoh Apries, during the Cyrene campaign. They called him,' Phanes barely suppressed a grin, 'the Desert Hawk.'

'If he's the same man, then his son does not share his martial pretensions,' Lysistratis said. The chariot passed beneath the twin colossi of Pharaoh flanking the gates leading into the fortress enclosure of Ineb-hedj, the White Walls. Hoplite sentries snapped to attention, their spear-butts grinding against the flagstones. Bronze flashed in the fading sunlight. Ahead, on a manmade acropolis, the citadel walls reared above the city it professed to guard.

'Use this Idu as an example,' Phanes said, his face diabolical in the thickening shadow. 'Menkaura, too. I want these Egyptians to bleed for me as I bled for them, Lysistratis. I want them to fear me before I pillage their peaceful little world.'

Callisthenes of Naucratis paced in a tight circle, his stubby fingers twittering with a finely carved jasper scarab that lay on his breast. Lamplight gleamed on his shaven skull, and the green malachite outlining his eyes – an Egyptian trick to lessen the sun's harsh glare – gave Callisthenes a sinister cast incongruous with the colourful linen robes draping his fleshy frame.

The antechamber of the throne room at Memphis recalled the glory of an age long past, an epoch when Pharaoh's shadow stretched across the known world. Under incised and painted murals depicting the battle at Qadesh, dark-bearded emissaries of the Hittite king would have felt outrage at the portrayal of their lord as coward. Dark-skinned Nubians, accounted the tallest men on earth, would have been made to feel small and inconsequential beneath the mammoth columns that supported the ceiling, their shafts like stalks of papyrus hewn from cold white limestone. Messengers from Palestine would have found the bound figures etched into the stone tiles to be a source of distress: at every step, they would grind their captive ancestors beneath their bare feet. The effect the chamber had upon foreigners who came to Memphis, whether a tribute bearer or princely ambassador, was to remind them of their place by reinforcing the splendour and majesty of the Lord of the Two Lands.

An effect wasted on the two hoplites standing nearby.

They were part of the squad tasked with holding inviolate the inner throne room. In rotating shifts they ground their spears outside the sealed gold-sheathed doors, bronze statues who would spring to murderous life should an intruder dare even to touch jamb, threshold, or lintel. Unlike their brothers walking sentry on the ramparts, the door wardens' vista never changed: cut and fitted stone, painted plaster, gilt, leaf, and inlay; a landscape of opulence that jaded their senses. Callisthenes stalked past them, lost in thought.

'Slow down, lad,' said the elder of the pair, a tough shank of whalebone, his face seamed by sun, wind, and the indelible march of time. He spoke a rough patois, Ionian Greek leavened with words drawn from Egyptian and Persian. 'You're making my head ache. Take a seat and rest. The general's coming as quick as he can.'

Callisthenes ignored him. He stopped and stared at the lifesized statues of ancient pharaohs lining the walls, their stony faces in sharp relief: the powerful visage of Ramses the Great; hawkish Thutmoses, savage warrior-king who brought Palestine to its knees; stern Horemheb, who was general before he was pharaoh. The olden kings stared back with cold, accusing eyes.

Beneath their gaze, Callisthenes experienced a sense of loathing for his Greek heritage. How could his own people engender such revulsion in him? His Hellenic cousins possessed a fighting spirit without equal, but they cheapened it through an overweening sense of pride. Kings could buy their loyalty like a prostitute's wares, and still they called others barbarians.

Callisthenes was a child of two cultures, two philosophies, two religions; as drawn to the quiet precepts of the sage Ptah-hotep as he was to the blood and thunder of Homer's epics. Among his countrymen at Naucratis, he was anathema, a traitor to his people; at Memphis, he was an interloper, a Greek masquerading as an Egyptian. To whom did he owe his allegiance? A complex question, and one that, since departing for Delphi four months ago, had never left the forefront of his mind.

Callisthenes' journey to central Greece for Phanes of Halicarnassus came at the behest of his father, a merchant and politician of Naucratis. Old Rhianus could smell a chance for profit the same way a hound smelled blood. 'Egypt is rotting,' he would say to Callisthenes on his infrequent trips home. 'A cancer is gnawing away at Pharaoh's guts, and when he dies the country will die with him.' Rhianus wanted his son in a position to benefit from Egypt's illness; never had he asked Callisthenes what he wanted. Perhaps that was a godsend, since his desires were nebulous, hazy. The only thing Callisthenes knew for certain was the world at large should let his adoptive homeland alone. Let the Egyptians go about their business; let the Nile rise and fall as it had for a thousand generations.

Red-orange light flooded the antechamber as an exterior door opened and shut again, bathing the room in the brilliant gleam of dusk before plunging it back into artificial night. The hoplite guards snapped erect. A mask of politesse slipped easily over Callisthenes' face, impenetrable, flawless, transforming him into a young man so taken by tales of valour that he would do anything to be viewed as an equal in the fraternity of war.

Phanes strode across the antechamber, the Spartan in his wake calling for one of the hoplites to fetch water and a robe for their general. Callisthenes flashed an amiable smile. He inclined his head and was preparing to launch into a litany of greeting when Phanes shattered decorum by sweeping the merchant up into a rib-splintering hug.

'Zeus Saviour! You are a welcome sight, Callisthenes! Waiting for your return smacked of the punishment of Tantalus, and I've found it not to my liking! Great gods of Olympus! I am pleased to see you!' Phanes grinned as he loosed Callisthenes. The merchant staggered and righted himself with as much dignity as he could muster.

'And I you, general. Forgive my delay. We had unfavourable weather after reaching Athens. We were forced to sacrifice to Uadj-ur and the four winds before we could make good our departure by sea.'

Phanes eyed him critically. 'I imagined a trip to the heart of Hellas would have broken you of this Egyptian affectation. Still, Delphi seems to have agreed with you. How fared Naucratis in the Pythian Games?'

The merchant smiled. 'Half the world, it seems, turned out to see my own cousin, Oeolycos, take the prize of valour in the pentathlon; the other half came to see the new temple of Apollo. A splendid structure. Your donations were well spent.' Callisthenes stroked the scarab hanging around his neck. 'Forgive me for being brusque, general, but I am weary. Shall we finish this?'

A servant bustled up, bearing a bronze ewer of water and a linen mantle. Phanes waved him away. The general vibrated with suppressed excitement; his eyes were glassy and bright, feverish, as if the juice of the opium poppy surged through his veins. 'On to business, then.'

From inside his robe, Callisthenes withdrew a tube carved from a branch of olive-wood, its surface burnished from years of use. Lead sealed its ends, the metal impressed with the symbol of the oracle at Delphi. 'I gave your original inquiry to the *prophetai* and left it in their care. When I returned after the proscribed time, I received this. I pray it provides you with the insight of Apollo.' Callisthenes made to leave, but a gesture from Phanes forestalled him.

'Stay,' he said. The general savoured the moment, as a groom on his wedding night eager to make that first taste of pleasure last. Accepting Lysistratis' knife, he used it to pare away the seal at one end of the tube, then handed it back. Phanes removed a small roll of vellum, opened it with trembling fingers, and read aloud:

'*Many are the dreams of the Hellene, as grains of sand on the beach. And their passions and hatreds run deeper than the depths of Oceanus.*

Take heed, child of Halicarnassus! Take heed, for long have you toiled. In sand and sea for a master cold as stone. Yet despair not, for guile, craft, and bronze are the tools by which thrones are toppled.'

Phanes looked at Lysistratis and grinned.

'Oracles,' Lysistratis said, shaking his head. 'Can they never answer plainly? What does it mean?'

'It means the gods favour us in this. "Despair not", it says, "for guile, craft, and bronze are the tools by which thrones are toppled".' Phanes handed the vellum to the Spartan, who only laughed.

'If you say so, then it must be. I think wine is in order, a libation to Apollo.'

'Do not celebrate our victory just yet,' Phanes said, his brows furrowed. 'We'll proceed as planned. Instruct the *polemarchs* to be ready to deploy in Memphis by week's end. As of now I want campaign discipline. No carousing, no fraternizing. I want the men ready to pull out in an hour's notice.'

'I'll see to it personally.' Lysistratis bowed and took his leave.

'What of me?' Callisthenes said. 'I've been away for months; there's no telling what damage that half-wit Akhmin has wrought in my absence. Am I to be privy to your plans now, or will you discharge me like a servant who has reached the end of his usefulness?'

'You wound me, Callisthenes,' Phanes said. 'I

promised Rhianus you would be kept safe and well-cared for. War is coming; it is as certain as the rising of the sun at dawn. Unlike the Egyptians, we have the luxury of deciding what stance to take – to rise or fall, to side with the victors or be counted among the slain. We're going to give Cambyses what he wants, and in return he'll give us what we want.'

The warm blood flowing through Callisthenes' veins turned sluggish, a glacial brine. Despite this, the merchant's face remained neutral. 'If war is, as you say, a virtual certainty, then only a fool would want to be on the losing side. How can you be so sure Cambyses and his Persians will conquer Egypt? The Assyrians tried, to the ruin of their empire.'

Phanes smiled, a gesture lacking compassion or humour. 'The Assyrians didn't have a phalanx of Greeks at their disposal. When the time comes, we will strike right here, in Egypt's heart. We'll raze Memphis, then fade away into the Western Desert to raid the oases there. We will hand Cambyses the jewel of his empire. You are welcome to come along, of course.'

Callisthenes, his fingers stroking the scarab at his throat, resumed pacing. 'Not every Greek is receiving this courtesy, are they?'

'No. Only an elite few.'

'Why me?'

'Because,' Phanes said, his tone matter-of-fact, 'you understand these Egyptians. You know what they fear, what moves them. You're a master at gathering *social* intelligence – at dissecting their circles and cliques and defining who moves in and out of them. It is information Cambyses will need. Beyond that, you have wisdom, Callisthenes,' Phanes gripped the merchant's shoulder, 'and that is a rare gift these days. I sleep better knowing you serve with me, rather than against me. We will talk more of this later. Go, rest and see to your business.' With that, Phanes turned and vanished through an interior door, servants flocking around him like a covey of sparrows.

Callisthenes watched him go, the mask of politesse sloughing away like a snake's skin. His eyes glittered dangerously in the wan light. Blood throbbed at his temples, filling his ears with the whirr of kettle drums, the clash of bronze. He glanced up at the statue of great Ramses, Ozymandias of legend, warrior, conqueror, statesman. Granite eyes flashed in imperious wrath at what his stone ears had overheard.

To whom did he owe his allegiance? 'Pythian Apollo be damned!' Callisthenes hissed in Egyptian. Stopping Phanes would be a deadly game, the merchant reckoned, one pitting both sides against the middle, and his life would be forfeit should he lose. Still, he knew full well how Egypt would fare under the heel of a foreign tyrant.

Egyptians should rule the Nile valley. The statues lining the antechamber's walls, the images of the pharaohs of old, appeared to nod in unison in the flickering lamplight.

Now, Callisthenes thought, gathering his robes about him, *all I need is an ally.*

South and east of the fortress of Ineb-hedj, along the banks of the Nile, lay the district of Perunefer. A bustling naval yard in ancient times, Perunefer diminished over the years into a small and insular enclave of fishermen. Even so, signs of its former glory abounded. The canting beams once used to support the hulls of Pharaoh's warships now served as drying racks for hundreds of nets. Stone stelae, their commemorative hieroglyphs faded by time and neglect, paved the grassy sward where each day's catch was gutted and strung for drying. Middens rose at every hand, artificial hills of fish bones, scales, and entrails towering over the drab huts of the fisher-folk. A rutted dirt path wound through this festering maze. It descended through stands of palm, willow, and sycamore, following the natural slope of the shoreline until it dead-ended at a quay of age-blackened limestone. Water lapped against the hulls of skiffs tied to corroded mooring rings.

Overhead, twilight hastened into night. Stars flared to life, casting their thin light on the dark waters of the Nile. The two men who walked along the quay had no need of other illumination; their business was best concluded without it. Flakes of stone crunched underfoot as the smaller of the pair, his weight resting on a gold-shod staff, turned to his companion and hissed, 'Are you positive it was him, Esna?'

The man called Esna nodded. He wore a kilt of muddy brown linen and a broad leather belt, trimmed in copper scarab and ankh amulets that clashed with each step. One long-fingered hand rested lightly on the ivory hilt of a knife. 'Beyond doubt, lord,' Esna said. 'The Phoenician is no easy man to forget. I saw him at Sile once, perhaps three years ago. Then, this afternoon, I saw him again on the road from Iunu, leading a train of camels and men. A score of them, foreigners all. I hurried back as quick as discretion allowed.'

Music filtered through the trees, from Perunefer, the sound of flute, sistrum, and lyre punctuated by crude laughter and snatches of song. Esna glanced up toward the tree line, aware of how exposed they were here on the quay. His companion, though, was oblivious, his brows knitted in a look of brooding consternation.

Ujahorresnet, First Servant of Neith in Memphis, tapped the butt of his staff on the stones, a metronomic rhythm that kept time with his thoughts. The priest was small for an Egyptian, thin to the point of emaciation, with shoulders unbowed despite the sixty-four years that weighed upon them. His skull was shaven and his blunt features concealed a mind sharper than the claws of Amemait, the Devourer. 'What business has he here?'

'Of that I have no knowledge, lord,' Esna said. 'He has few allies in Memphis, and none among the Greeks. I want to know his movements, Esna. Have your people locate him, keep him in sight at all times. Also, set a man to watch the house of the Judaean, ben Iesu. He has served as the Phoenician's informant in the past.'

'Your will shall be done, lord.' Esna bowed deeply and withdrew.

Ujahorresnet remained still. He stared into the rippling waters of the Nile, lost in thought. The Phoenician. He had spent the last twenty years watching him from afar, chronicling the highs and lows of his career, cataloguing his countless sins against the lady Ma'at, until he knew the man better than he knew himself. The Phoenician was, above all things, a creature of habit. Rarely did he leave the windswept deserts of eastern Egypt; rarer still did he travel to the populous heartland of the Nile valley. What prompted this visit? The priest did not chide himself for not placing a man inside Sile, among the Medjay. To do so would have meant relying on a foreigner. *A foreigner!* The thought was like bitter oil on the priest's tongue. *Never again!*

Ghosts from the past shimmered and danced in the water. He could yet recall every detail of her face – the flaring of her thin nostrils, the cosmetics lining her eyes, how her lips curled into an angry pout. The day had been one of unaccustomed clarity, with only a light haze obscuring the view from the roof of his villa. Pharaoh's palace glittered in the distance.

'*I am your father, Neferu! You will do as I*

command!' The fury in his voice sent his servants running, scattering them like a flock of birds. But not Neferu. Not dear Neferu. In a gesture so reminiscent of her mother, she had drawn herself up, straight and tall, her eyes flashing in the afternoon shadows.

'*I'm not one of your slaves!*' she said. '*I'll choose the man I am to marry!*'

The family of Ujahorresnet was of pure blood, untainted, their lineage unbroken since the time of Amenhotep the Golden. As a daughter of princes, Neferu's future had lain in the inner chambers of Pharaoh's palace, as wife to his heir, mother to the sons of his son. Instead, without thought or word, she threw it all away so she could go off and serve as whore to the son of a foreign merchant. Ujahorresnet tasted gall.

Though he served as high priest of Neith in Memphis, Ujahorresnet made lavish sacrifices to the shrine of the lady Sekhmet, goddess of vengeance. Once invoked, Amon himself could not sway the Mistress of Plagues from her destructive task. He'd given the goddess blood; would she give him satisfaction?

'How?' Ujahorresnet said, staring at the water. 'How do I stop a man whose name has become a byword for violence?'

For an instant the Nile turned like glass and Ujahorresnet saw the heavens reflected there, one cluster of stars brighter than the others: the constellation of Sah, the Fleet-footed, the Longstrider, called Orion by the Greeks.

Ujahorresnet sighed and closed his eyes. *The Greeks.* His answer had been there all along, written in the stars. *He would need the foreigners.*

'You teasing little whore.' Phanes laughed, slapping the young woman's bare buttocks. The motion caused warm water to slosh over the rim of his bath. Her body, perched precariously on the tub's edge, writhed in pleasure as she continued exploring herself with her fingers.

'Come here, Sadeh,' Phanes said, reaching for her.

The woman, Sadeh, a sloe-eyed Egyptian beauty barely half the Greek's age, slithered close to him and pressed her naked breasts against his chest. Her nimble fingers kneaded the hard ridges of muscle rippling down his abdomen as she lowered herself onto his erection. She arched her back, grinding her pelvis against him in the first of many orgasms. Phanes grinned.

The bathing chamber was spacious, lit by several oil lamps whose light the floating clouds of steam diffused and scattered. Paintings from myth and legend adorned the walls. Dionysus, Priapus, Aphrodite, and the Naiads all frolicked through an Elysian paradise in pursuit of the same pleasure Sadeh received. Her damp hair hung like a veil about her face; Phanes reached up and caught a handful of it, thrusting mercilessly into her as she ground down upon him. He made not a sound as she shivered and moaned.

Phanes glanced up as Lysistratis ambled into the bath. Sweaty, covered in dust, the Spartan looked as though he had just finished a footrace. He made a curt gesture, indicating the woman should leave. Sadeh, pouting and still unfulfilled, made to disengage herself from Phanes, but the Greek took her by the hips and forced her back into position. Sadeh gasped, her eyes glazing.

'Your lechery knows no bounds,' Lysistratis said, grinning. 'Does she speak Greek?'

'No. You look troubled. Is there news?'

'Only a worrisome rumour,' Lysistratis said, 'about the Medjay. I'm told Bedouin came down out of Sinai and razed the village of Habu. In itself, that is nothing extraordinary, but these Bedouin pushed on instead of returning to their mountain fastness. A company of Medjay tracked them through the waste to the Nile's banks and slaughtered them in the ruins of Leontopolis. I've sent a charioteer to survey the site, though in my bones I know what he'll find.' The Spartan stripped off his tunic and eased himself into the far end of the tub.

'And what will he find?'

'A dead Persian. Arsamenes should have set out from Babylon a fortnight ago, which explains why the Bedouin pressed on to the Nile. They were escorting him to Memphis. I knew you were teasing the Fates by using Bedouin in the first place,' Lysistratis said, shaking his head. 'The

Medjay are too canny not to notice such a large force crossing the border.'

'What's done is done,' Phanes replied, trapping Sadeh's hardened nipples between his thumb and forefinger. He twisted them gently, sending her into spasms of pleasure. 'The hand of Apollo has blessed us.'

'The blessing of Apollo's not proof against failure,' Lysistratis said. 'Barca himself leads these Medjay and he's not a man to be trifled with. He stands high in Pharaoh's counsel. That alone makes him a dangerous opponent.'

Phanes said nothing for a while, his tongue engaged in a duel with Sadeh's. Though Memphis had countless prostitutes and courtesans – women of Syria, Greece, Libya, and Nubia – Phanes limited his sexual encounters to young Egyptian women of the upper class, chosen as much for their looks as their parentage. Under Phanes, Sadeh would learn to embrace her primal side, her innate lasciviousness. He would use her, treat her no better than a common whore, then cast her aside like so many who had come before her. The thought sent a ripple of pleasure through his loins.

He broke their kiss, leaving Sadeh breathless. 'Barca! Phoenicians should keep to the sea, where they belong! Meddlesome bastard!'

'*Bar-ka*,' Sadeh panted in Egyptian, recognizing the name. 'He is a goblin the matrons of . . . of Sais use to frighten s-small . . .' Her voice faltered as she shook through the throes of yet another orgasm.

'Mind your business, girl,' Lysistratis said, 'lest we put your mouth to better use.' Then, to Phanes, 'Look, Barca is notorious for being a thorn in the side of Pharaoh's enemies. He has two choices: he can go to Sais and warn Amasis, or he can come to Memphis and attempt to interfere. Granted, he's one man, but—'

'If he comes here, Lysistratis, I want him dead. Before he can cause problems,' said Phanes. 'Double the guards on the eastern shore and send out additional patrols.'

'I'll see to it tomorrow.' Lysistratis floated up behind Sadeh, cupping her breasts as he kissed her. She stretched her hands above her head, her nails digging into the Spartan's neck. Her moans redoubled.

'Ah,' Phanes said, his hands spreading Sadeh's buttocks to allow the Spartan to enter her, 'if only the rest of Egypt could be plundered as easily as you, my dear.'

3

OLD FRIENDS

A desultory breeze rustled through the forest of reeds growing along the Nile's eastern bank. The night was quiet save for the soothing clamour of frogs and insects, and the hiss of water spooling through the shallows. Well back from the river, hillocks rose from the rich, black soil. Atop them, farming villages sat like stately country squires, their lights dim and clouded, their finery diminished with age. Between the river and the villages, lay the fields that fed the teeming masses of Memphis.

Barca and Ithobaal stood at the edge of a muddy embankment, just inside a tangled copse of sycamores, and watched the lights of Memphis glittering across the dark waters of the Nile. 'I'm going in tonight. Alone,' the Phoenician said.

Ithobaal's knees creaked as he crouched and scooped up a handful of loose soil.

'Alone? Are you mad?' He heard a cough, explosive in the silence, and glanced toward the noise. The Medjay sat in the darkness beneath the trees, too weary to prepare a fire or unsling their bedrolls. Eighteen faces stared at nothing; splashes of light from a sickle moon gave them a ghoulish cast, like wandering souls unburied, unmourned. Soil trickled between Ithobaal's fingers. 'This forced march has exhausted the men. It's exhausted you. Why not bide the night here and rest until dawn? We made good time from Leontopolis. What difference will another day make?'

The city across the river consumed Barca's attention. His answers were there, in the inscrutable darkness that thrived where the small circles of light failed. He continued as if Ithobaal had never spoken. 'Get some sleep and enter Memphis at dawn, on the first ferry. Find lodging around the Square of Deshur and wait for me. I'll get word to you when I have something useful. If any should ask, tell them you're guards for a caravan out of Jerusalem.'

Under casual scrutiny the Phoenician could easily pass for an itinerant caravaneer. Clad in a threadbare tunic and sandals, a knife thrust into his belt at his back, he had shed his armour and shield and ordered his men to do the same. Their telltale *uadjets* would draw too many curious stares. A troop of Medjay in Memphis would place the Greeks on their guard. Barca needed stealth; he needed freedom to move about with as much anonymity as possible.

Ithobaal stood. His nerves were stretched thin, close to breaking. 'How, in the name of horned Ba'al, will you get across the river, little brother?

The ferries have ceased for the night, unless you're Greek. You plan to swim the Nile?'

Barca clapped the Canaanite on the shoulder. 'Have faith, Ithobaal. There's more than one way into Memphis.'

'Then, why go alone? At least let a few of us accompany you. The odds . . .'

Barca shook his head. 'The odds worsen with every passing moment. If twenty men follow me in, that's twenty chances that the Greeks will get wind of us. We're already playing against time. Once the Greeks hear about what happened to their messenger at Leontopolis, do you think they'll sit idle? I don't. I think they'll set their plans in motion as fast as they can. Tonight, I'm going to find Matthias ben Iesu. If anyone knows what's been happening, he will.'

'If the old Jew still lives,' Ithobaal muttered as he turned and walked back to the loose circle of Medjay. 'I may be old, but I'm not daft, little brother. You've come to kill Greeks, and the gods preserve any who get in your way!'

Barca dismissed the Canaanite with a wave of his hand as he descended the embankment and headed south, following the curve of the river. Mud squelched underfoot. He forged a treacherous path around boulders and gnarled roots, risking a twisted ankle or worse should a slick rock turn under his weight. Papyrus stalks rattled in a faint breath of wind.

Barca withdrew into himself, his senses alert, his body moving over and around obstacles.

Ithobaal was right. Exhaustion gnawed at him. His bones and muscles ached; his joints felt like they were spun from glass. Rest would have been a godsend, had it been at all possible. Deep down Barca could feel the Beast stirring, flexing its claws in anticipation. This dormant bloodlust was akin to having another living being inside his skin, a lean wraith whose hunger flogged him to action, despite pain or weariness. Barca knew he had come to Memphis to aid Pharaoh. No one could argue otherwise. Yet, the truth of Ithobaal's condemnation stabbed like a white-hot knife of guilt. Had he also come to Memphis to gorge the Beast on Greek blood?

A short time later, a cluster of shanties emerged from the darkness: a mud-dweller's village. Despised by their agricultural neighbours, the mud-dwellers were the poorest of the poor, a gypsy folk who drifted with the currents, who eked whatever living they could from fishing, scavenging, and outright theft. Their villages were barely habitable. Tumbledown huts of cast-off mud brick, roofed with reed mats and dried palm fronds, clung to the shore like barnacles to a ship's hull. The village would vanish with the next inundation, and the mud-dwellers would vanish with it, scattered by the Nile's indomitable will.

Barca plunged through the maze of huts. An open sewer cleft the village square, allowing slops and human waste to drain into the river. The Phoenician stepped over this fetid trench. Through curtained doorways he could hear the sounds of men snoring, the hard crack of a fist on flesh, laughter. In the distance a dog howled in pain.

Ahead, a ramshackle jetty sprang from the river muck, a leprous finger of wood prodding at the Nile's breast. Small boats scraped the pilings, their oars shipped, sails furled. Barca crept out onto the jetty and peered into each boat. He found what he sought in the last one. A village boy lay curled around the base of the mast, his head cradled on a cushion of rope. He was young, ten years old at most; hard years if the long puckered whip scars lacing his shoulders and back were any indication. In one fist he clutched a small horn, chipped and worn from rough use, while the other held a knife made from a shank of corroded copper. No doubt he was charged with standing guard over the boats tied to the jetty.

Barca knelt. Gently, he prodded the young sleeper with the tip of his sheathed sword. The boy groaned, swatting at the intrusion. Barca poked him again. 'Wake up, lad,' the Phoenician said. 'I have a task for you.' At the sound of Barca's voice, the boy's eyes flew open. He scrabbled across the bottom of the skiff brandishing his makeshift knife, his horn held out like a shield. The boat thumped against the rotting pilings of the jetty. The boy glared at Barca, his mouth open in a soundless scream.

He was tongueless.

Barca held his hands out, palms up, in a gesture meant to be friendly. 'Is this your boat?' he said, his voice low and even. The boy shook his head, nodding back toward the village. It belonged to his father, then. Or an uncle. Likely the same person who whipped him without mercy and cut out his tongue. A slow rage boiled in Barca's veins. 'Can you sail it?'

A vigorous nod. The boy stared at Barca's sword, his initial fear replaced by curiosity. He pursed his lips and extended a trembling hand. His body tensed; he expected to be slapped away, beaten for his presumptions. Barca surprised him by letting him run his fingers along the edge of the sheath.

'Like swords, do you?'

The boy grinned. He clambered to his knees and puffed out his chest, his little knife held aloft. Whatever he mimicked must have come from a Greek story. The Egyptians were dismissive of heroic tales. Their heroes' deeds were for the good of Egypt rather than glory's coarse rewards.

'You'll make a fine Achilles,' Barca said. 'But you'll need a better blade.' Barca reached around and tugged the knife from the small of his back. It was a superb weapon, the curved iron blade inlaid with a tracery of gold vines and set in a hilt of yellowed bone. Avarice gleamed in the boy's dark eyes.

'I'll give you this,' Barca said, 'if you take me across the river.'

The boy chewed his lip. He looked from the knife to Barca's face and back again. The Phoenician could see nothing naive in the boy's manner.

If caught filching the boat, his elders would administer fresh beatings, perhaps even deprive him of more than his tongue. The knife, though . . . in his world a knife like that could save his life. Barca reckoned the boy no fool. After a moment's thought the youngster agreed and gestured for the Phoenician to hurry. Barca climbed down into the skiff, untied their moorings, and shoved away from the jetty as the boy raised the patchwork sail.

They drifted slowly toward the centre of the river, a night breeze tugging at the sail as the boy used an oar to keep them on course. Like an old sailor, the lad navigated against the current, following Barca's hand gestures. The wind drove them south, past the mouth of the canal that led to the royal quays, past clusters of ships tied for the night to mooring posts. Barca discerned the Mansion of Ptah, with its soaring ramparts backlit by the countless torches left burning throughout the night. Past the temple, trees lined the rising bank, screening slums and villas alike. A short time later, the Phoenician caught sight of his goal.

'There. Get me as close as you can.'

His destination was the Nilometer, an angled stone staircase cut into the high bank of the Nile. Steps chiselled with hieroglyphs measured the level of water from season to season. Life in Egypt, all life, depended upon the rhythms of the river, on the annual inundation of the Nile. Low floods were harbingers of famine; high floods promised ruin. A perfect inundation meant granaries full of emmer, cisterns full of beer, and a year of prosperity for all.

The boy inched the nose of the skiff into the Nilometer until the hull scraped stone. Barca clambered out of the boat and gripped the prow. Cool water lapped at his ankles. He paused before handing the lad his knife. 'Forget you saw me,' he said. The boy nodded, flashing a gap-toothed smile. He accepted his prize as if it were given for valour. Barca gave the boat a shove, watching it spiral out into the river. Satisfied the boy would find his way home, the Phoenician turned and ascended the algae-slick stairs of the Nilometer.

The mouth of the Nilometer lay inside the walled enclosure of the temple of Osiris, on the southern edge of Memphis. Through a dark veil of palm trees, Barca saw the glimmer of white stone marking the ceremonial entrance of the temple; to his right lay a scattering of chapels and out-buildings. Though the sanctuary was dedicated to Osiris, the temple grounds housed countless other gods, along with shrines to the deified pharaohs and tombs of high-ranking priests.

The folk of Egypt, Barca reckoned, were relig-ious to the point of excess. Ritual and magic permeated their lives. Mothers taught their daughters prayers to ensure bread would not burn, milk would not spoil, and children would sleep through the night. Fathers passed along to their sons the words of power that would make crops grow, arrows fly true, and crocodiles look the other way. The wealthy knew dozens of incantations that would keep their gold safe; the poor knew just as many to make that gold safe to the touch. This unquestioned faith in the unseen, in the divinity of Pharaoh, and in the gods, was the force that bound Egypt into a unified whole.

Barca slipped out of the Nilometer and followed the circuit of the wall. He came to a small side gate that opened on one of the city's infamous winding alleys and stopped, listening. No priests stirred about at this late hour; no suppliants came to beg lord Osiris for succour in the next world. The only sounds came from the wind rustling through the trees and the commotion of the nearby Foreign Quarter. The Phoenician drew the wooden bolt and slipped out the gate.

He felt a momentary flash of claustrophobia. Accustomed to the wide-open sky of the Eastern Desert, Barca felt surrounded by those ancient mud brick walls. A thin strip of starlight overhead mocked him. Clenching his teeth, stifling the fear that somehow the buildings would collapse on him, Barca set off at a trot.

He headed west, crossed a broad lane lined with human-headed sphinxes, and plunged into the tangled warren of the Foreign Quarter. Barca's informant lived on the southern edge of this turbulent district, on the Street of the Chaldeans, in the shadow of a solitary obelisk known as the Spear. At least, Barca hoped Matthias ben Iesu still dwelt there. Five years had passed since his last visit; five years could encompass a lifetime in a city such as Memphis, a city in a state of constant flux. Barca chided himself for not maintaining contact with the aging Judaean. If he had, perhaps he could have squashed this potential crisis months ago.

Barca ghosted down the alley, past doors and windows, past mud brick crevices and jagged chasms that yawned like the gates of Hades. The heat, coupled with the stench rising from a thin runnel of sewage, made his lungs ache. Sweat drenched his tunic; stinking muck caked his sandalled feet. It was like moving through the bowels of a stone leviathan. After an hour, he knew he must be closing in on his destination.

The alley turned sharply and widened, becoming a small irregular square. To his right, gleaming like an alabaster spike above the skyline, Barca caught sight of the Spear. The obelisk belonged to an ancient temple façade, its stone cannibalized during one of the interregnums of pharaonic power. Now it stood isolated, a reminder of darker times. Barca glanced around the square. He wasn't alone. Shapes huddled in the corners; he heard muttered curses, smelled the raw stench of human waste. From the shadows at his feet, a filth-encrusted hand plucked at the Phoenician's tunic.

'Mercy,' a voice wheezed in Egyptian, densely accented. 'Mercy for an old soldier?'

Barca brushed the hand aside. A few other pitiful forms leaned out and importuned him, begging for coin. Like the mud-dwellers, the beggars of Memphis were a caste unto themselves, an indigenous population who slipped through the cracks of Egypt's rigid society. They were the insane, the infirm, the solitary, cast aside and forgotten as their usefulness waned. *This could be my fate*, Barca thought, feeling a glacial abscess in the pit of his stomach. He glanced down at the beggar. 'A soldier, you say?'

'Aye,' the beggar said, crawling to his knees. A cloud of flies rose from his filthy nest. 'Much younger, I was. Carried spear and shield in the company of Lord Huy of Bubastis.' The beggar exhaled, a wheezing chuckle that reeked of rotted onion.

'I'm a soldier, as well, and I need to know if a man still lives nearby. A Judaean . . .'

'The astrologer!' The beggar pawed at Barca's belt. His fingers brushed the Phoenician's sheathed scimitar and jerked away as if burned. 'You're Phoenician . . . yes, he told us to be expecting you. He told us you'd be seeking the Jew.'

'Who? Who told you?'

'The man with the copper bangles.'

One of the other beggars hissed. 'Not 'pose to tell 'im, fool!'

'We're soldiers, he and I! Brothers! Not like you other dogs! You'd sell your mothers for a jug of beer!'

Barca crouched. 'The man with the bangles, was he Greek?'

The beggar shook his head. 'Egyptian. Tall as a palm trunk. Wanted us to tell his mate, over by the Spear, if we saw you. These other curs might. Not me. Too tired to fight. Too tired . . .' The beggar's head drooped. None of the others moved, either; even the one who hissed a warning curled up in an old shawl and fell asleep muttering to himself.

'My thanks, brothers,' Barca whispered, rising. Someone had spotted him, but how? How? With a savage growl, Barca moved to the alley mouth, flattened his body against the wall, and peered out into the street.

The Street of the Chaldeans was not a well-planned thoroughfare. Some buildings thrust out beyond their neighbours or sat at odd angles, as if the architect suffered from a malady that made him incapable of straight lines. At one end of the street, a grove of palm trees rose around the base of the Spear. At the other, a small wine shop still did a brisk custom at this late hour, catering to foreign merchants and caravan guards. The house of Matthias ben Iesu lay halfway down the street, toward the obelisk, its dilapidated façade recessed into shadow.

Movement under the palm trees caught Barca's eye. A man waited there, just as the beggar had said. The figure stood, stretched, then crouched down again, barely visible in the darkness. His attitude spoke of wariness, patience, as if he were waiting for something. Or someone. Barca's eyes narrowed. No matter. He knew another way in.

Matthias ben Iesu wrote by the uneven light of an oil lamp. Failing eyes forced his body into a question mark over the sheet of papyrus, his back bowed like the Hebrew slaves of legend who toiled beneath the vicious eyes of Pharaoh. Matthias paused, scraping the tip of his reed pen across a moistened cake of ink, then continued:

Memphis is a cruel city, cousin. Cruel and unforgiving. In Babylon they respected my art; it was sought after by prince and pauper alike. Here, in Egypt, they revile me as a charlatan. I have no hope. That is the crux of this letter, dear cousin. I wish to return, to have my banishment lifted so at the very least I can die with dignity.

'Dignity.' Matthias set his pen aside and straightened, flexing his cramped fingers. With his grey-black beard and fringe of hair ringing his bald scalp, Matthias ben Iesu could have passed for a desert patriarch. He stared into the wavering flame of the oil lamp, his eyes lost amid the lines and folds of his face. 'Is that too much to ask, O Lord of Hosts?'

Matthias glanced up as a breeze redolent of smoke and Nile mud stirred the scrap of papyrus under his fingers. He sat beneath a loggia that partially enclosed his roof, forming a three-walled room he jokingly called his observatory. He could see very little beyond the circle of light cast by his oil lamp. A pair of potted plants stood just outside the loggia, a woven reed mat on the ground between them. The moon's thin illumination gave a sheen of silver to the surface of the knee-high brick wall ringing his roof.

Something moved in the deeper shadow near the edge of the roof A cat? No, it was too large. Matthias frowned. He had been out most of the evening, dining at the wine shop down the street in hopes of overhearing bits of gossip, idle chatter, anything scandalous he could use to his advantage. Had someone followed him home, mistaking him for a man of means rather than the vagabond he had become? Annoyed, he rose and stepped out onto the rooftop terrace. 'Is someone there?' he said.

An arm shot out of the gloom. The Judaean's eyes goggled as a hand clamped over his mouth. 'Silence, Matthias,' a voice exhorted, softly. A voice Matthias knew. 'Forgive my rude entry, but men watch your house and unless I'm wrong, they watch for me.'

'Barca?' He gaped. 'Hasdrabal Barca? How . . . how did you . . . ?'

Barca grinned. 'I scaled your wall. Mud brick is like a ladder to a Phoenician.'

'Merciful God of Abraham! What are you doing here?' The Judaean clasped Barca's arm.

'It's a long, dry tale.' Barca cocked his head to one side, listening. 'Have you any wine, Matthias?'

'Look at me,' Matthias said, 'I have the manners of a swineherd. Come.' He led Barca beneath the loggia. 'It has been . . . what? . . . five years since we last crossed paths? It must be something momentous to draw you from your haunts in the East.' From a shelf Matthias took down two terracotta bowls, chipped and burnished with age, and an amphora of deep russet pottery emblazoned with the symbol of the vineyards of Naxos. He poured a measure of resin-thickened wine into one bowl, then paused.

'You still take it unwatered?'

'Is there another way?' The Phoenician propped his hip against the desk.

Matthias chuckled and filled the other bowl, handing it to Barca. He set the amphora on the desk between them.

'What's happened, Matthias? Last I heard you were making gold like fabled King Midas. Now . . .' He indicated the shabby condition of the house.

Matthias shrugged and sat. 'Would you frequent an astrologer who couldn't discern his own fortunes? I wouldn't. No, my friend, I'm a victim of my own arrogance. These Egyptians, these astrologer-priests, they have forgotten more about the heavens than I'll ever know. I thought my years of study in Babylon would stand me in good stead among them. And for a while it did.' The Judaean laughed bitterly. 'But, when I wouldn't grovel on my belly before the First Seer of Amon – that heathen idolater! – they branded me a charlatan, a fraud. What wealth I had evaporated, and now the only custom I have comes from the dregs of the Foreign Quarter.'

Barca looked disapprovingly at the old Judaean.

'You should have come to me, Matthias. If it's money you need . . .'

Matthias shook his head, smiling. 'I would not accept it. The measure of my god's ill will is mine, and mine alone, to bear without complaint or charity, Phoenician. But, my thanks for the offer. You must tell me, before my curiosity gets the better of me, why have you come to Memphis?'

Barca drained his bowl and held it out for a refill. Matthias obliged. He stared at the Phoenician, unable to read the inscrutable look in his eye. Barca took his bowl back and, in a paucity of words, recalled the past few days: the battle at Leontopolis, the dead Persian, the letter. 'Cambyses offered the garrison a king's ransom to switch their allegiances, and I fear Phanes has agreed.'

'I am not surprised.'

'What have you heard, Matthias?'

The Judaean smoothed his beard like a learned Pharisee. 'It is not so much what I've heard as what I've seen. The Greeks rule Memphis like gilded tyrants, Barca. They do as they please with the blessing of the governor, Petenemheb. Those who speak out against them do so only once.'

'What of the garrison? How many men does Phanes have at his disposal?' Barca said. Matthias had never served in the army; indeed, Barca reckoned he had never picked up a blade in anger, but the Judaean's keen eyes and ears made him an invaluable source of intelligence.

'He has maybe two thousand hoplites and

another five hundred mercenary peltasts, archers mostly, men of Crete and the Aegean. His *polemarchs* are a capable lot, veterans of those little civil wars the Greeks hold so dear. A Potidaean called Nicias commands the heavy infantry, the backbone of the garrison. Hyperides of Ithaca commands the light troops. Far more dangerous, though, is Phanes' second-in-command, Lysistratis, an exiled Spartan. There's a man Yahweh didn't bother wasting a soul on. He's brother to the serpent; as deadly as the scorpion underfoot. His men swear he is Patroclus to Phanes' Achilles. Surely, though, now that you know what's happening, your Medjay can stop the Greeks from defecting?'

'We could, but to send for them would leave the border undefended. Cambyses' envoys have stirred up the Bedouin. No, we have enough problems without having to repulse an invasion from Sinai,' Barca said. 'I've sent a man on to Sais. Once Pharaoh is informed, he can muster the regiment of Amon and the Calasirian Guard and be en route inside a week.'

'If your man gets through.' Matthias emptied his bowl and set it aside. The wine seemed tasteless now, oily. 'And if he does, will Pharaoh even care?'

Barca frowned. 'What do you mean?'

'We've all heard the rumours, Barca. Amasis is not the man he once was. He's become a drunkard, more interested in his harem than in governing. Even if only a fraction of the innuendo

82

is true, well, it does not inspire me to confidence. Your man's warnings may fall prey to sheer apathy.'

Weariness crushed Barca's bones to dust. 'What's happened to Egypt's fear of Persian ambition?'

'Time has lessened it. Time and the aristocracy's hatred of Pharaoh. Amasis is a usurper. Though it's been forty-four years since the deed was done, Egypt's nobility has a long memory.' Matthias flashed a weak smile. 'I cast my horoscope this evening. It spoke of titanic change. I should show it to that priggish idolater in Amon's temple and demand vindication. Have you a plan, Barca?'

The Phoenician stared into the depths of the lamp burning on Matthias' desk. A plan? The Greeks were entrenched in the soil of Memphis like the roots of a gnarled tree. It would take a major campaign to tear them out. A campaign that would cost the lives of many good men. Barca's eyes narrowed. 'Tell me, Matthias, how does a tree protect itself against rot?'

'Against rot?' Matthias said, scowling. 'Why, a tree will harden its exterior, adding new layers of bark to protect the heartwood from infection. What does that have to do with us?'

Barca stood. 'That's what we must do. We must thicken Memphis against rot. No matter how cosy the nobles get with him, the average Egyptian will never trust Phanes. I have to play on that, and I have to trust that my man will rouse Pharaoh to action. It's our only hope.' Barca stroked his stubbled jaw. 'Help me and, if we make it out of this, I'll speak to Pharaoh on your behalf. I'll make sure everything the priests of Amon stole from you is returned, with interest.'

Matthias clapped him on the shoulder. 'Ah, Barca. You know me better than that. I'll help you because you're my friend.'

'No,' Barca said, shaking his head. 'A friend who only seeks your company when it's convenient is a poor friend. I am not deserving of your kindness.'

The Judaean smiled, a gesture of infinite patience. 'The road to Sile runs in both directions. Do not shoulder the lion's share of the burden, Phoenician. Especially when it's not yours to shoulder. Now, tell me what I can do to help.'

Barca walked out on the rooftop terrace and stared at the star-flecked sky. He said nothing for a long moment, then turned suddenly. 'We need a diversion. Something that will delay whatever plans the Greeks may have and buy us time. I need men who have served before, either in the army or the temple guard, and a figurehead to fire their blood.'

Matthias tugged his lip between thumb and forefinger. 'I know someone who might fit your needs. He was a soldier, once. A general . . .'

4

CONSPIRATORS

The home of Idu, son of Menkaura, lay near the temple of Osiris, on a winding lane shaded by well-tended sycamores. A low sandstone wall bounded the property, creating a haven of isolation amid the hustle of the city. Willow trees, grapevines, and rose shrubs thrived in the thick black soil, while beds of asphodel, thyme, and mint grew near the stone-curbed lotus pool. Frogs trilled amid the manicured reeds.

Inside the front gate, a woman rattled the wooden bolt and checked the oil in the reservoir of the night lantern. Normally, this would have been the door warden's task, but master Idu had dismissed him, and the other servants, for the night. The fewer witnesses to his dealings, the better. Satisfied that the gate was secure, the woman turned and made her way back to the house. Her anklet of blue faience beads jingled with each step. The sound roused a heron from its perch beside the pool; it fled from her, lofting into the night on outstretched wings, cursing her in its shrill tongue. The woman gave a start, then laughed at her own nervousness.

Though in manner and dress the woman could pass for Egyptian, her features marked her as foreign. Cascades of dark hair framed her high cheekbones, and her sharp nose and pointed chin were of such perfect proportion as to instil envy in the breast of Egypt's artisans. Deep-set eyes the colour of smoke expressed more with a single look than a thousand words could convey, and they told a tale, for those who cared to read them, of a life spent in servitude.

The woman, Jauharah, was a slave.

Slave. The word did not sting as it once had. She had learned its meaning at the hard and calloused hands of her father. By her tenth year, he had beaten and raped into her the bitter truth of life: a woman was no better than an animal, good for bearing sons and cooking, but little else. The next year, after being traded to an Edomite slaver for two goats, that truth was reinforced by the cunning application of a rawhide whip. Jauharah endured a succession of brutal lords before master Idu bought her from a lecherous old merchant in Jerusalem. Rescued her, more like.

Ahead, the white-plastered walls of the villa glimmered in the darkness. That flat-roofed, rambling structure could have easily become a prison had Idu been cut from the same cloth as her previous masters. Nothing cruel or mean-spirited existed in him. Never had he raised a hand in anger, or assumed she could serve him best in his bed. For Jauharah, a slave's life in

Egypt held far more promise than the life of a free woman in her native Palestine. Here, Idu taught her, even a slave had rights. She could marry, own goods and property, and even buy her own slaves, provided she could maintain them. In time, she might even scrimp and save enough to purchase her freedom. Ten years had passed since she left Jerusalem, and in that time Idu's kindness healed many of Jauharah's scars, binding her to the family with shackles far stronger than bronze.

On cat's feet, Jauharah mounted the steps to the portico and slipped into the villa. From the vestibule, it would be a small matter to check in on the girls, Meryt and Tuya, then sneak off to the kitchen for a cup of beer and a honey cake. Her path, though, carried her close by the tightly-shuttered doors of the east hall. There, she paused. Voices resonated inside. Jauharah crept closer, listening.

'. . . understand your concern, but your father was right, Idu. We can't fight the Greeks with rhetoric and good intentions!' Jauharah peered through a crack in the door. Five men clustered in a circle; three of them nodded in agreement with the speaker, a stately fellow with close-cropped hair gone white with age. A sixth chair stood empty.

'What would you suggest, Amenmose?' Idu said, his voice growing sharp with anger. 'That we take up sticks and rocks and storm the garrison? That would be foolhardy, and you know it! My father knows it, as well! I will not let impatience force us into an action we cannot win!'

Idu, a thick-set man, squat and round, had a pockmarked face and gentle eyes that belied his ferocious sense of justice. In height, in temperament, in desires, in all ways, he stood in antithesis to Menkaura. With nothing in common, father and son kept clear of each other's social circles, coming together only for business. Tonight, the business was sedition. From what Jauharah could gather, at the noon hour tomorrow, a granary in the shadow of the fortress, Ineb-hedj, would burn as a sign of growing unrest. Menkaura preached stronger action. Violence against holdings first, Idu countered, against men later. Menkaura's furious exodus prompted Jauharah to check the gate.

She heard Idu sigh. 'I know you all want something more, something dramatic, but the time is not yet ripe for that. If we confront the Greeks openly, they will shed Egyptian blood. I cannot, in good conscience, support such a disastrous course of action. No, we must bide our time and occupy ourselves with such small victories as a burned granary.'

Reluctantly, even Amenmose could see the wisdom in that. It took only a few more moments to solidify their plans, and then the conspirators scattered into the night, leaving Idu alone with his thoughts. Quietly, Jauharah entered the columned east hall and began gathering up the goblets and platters. Idu looked up and handed his empty goblet to her. 'The family?' he asked.

'They have gone to slumber.'

Idu pursed his lips, thinking. He glanced sidewise at the woman. 'What is your opinion on this matter, Jauharah? On the things you heard this evening? Don't try and deny it since I know your hearing is sharper than a cat's. Do you think we are doing the right thing?'

'I have no opinion save what you tell me, master.'

'Have you no rancour for the Greeks? Does it not boil your blood to see them strutting like peacocks through the streets?'

'I am a slave, master. What I like or dislike is of little consequence. I exist to serve you and your family as best I can. The world outside this house, I leave in the hands of those more capable than I. If you think burning a granary is best, then it must be best.'

Idu shook his head. 'I did not teach you to read and write so you could play the fool, Jauharah. It does not become you. You have an opinion about everything. Tell me what you think.'

Jauharah sighed. After a moment, she said, 'Burning a granary is like swatting a viper with a roll of papyrus – no damage is done beyond angering the viper. The Greeks will react the only way they know how: with violence.'

Idu chewed his lip. 'I see how people might arrive at that conclusion, but I don't believe they would risk violence yet. They will issue more edicts and pitch a child's tantrum.'

'Master,' Jauharah said, choosing her words

with care. 'Is it wise for you to get so involved in this? If something happens to you, what will become of mistress Tetisheri and the children? The Greeks will not sit idle once they discover who leads this insurrection.'

'And I cannot sit idle while my kin and my friends embark on an unwise course of action, Jauharah. You heard them. Without me, they would charge off and get themselves killed. My father is a good man, don't misunderstand, but he's always been a hothead.' Idu sighed. 'Thothmes worships him. Hekaib is terrified of him. Ibebi and Amenmose would defer to his judgement because they respect his age, his accomplishments. No, Jauharah, I must be involved in this, if for no other reason than to provide balance.'

Jauharah bowed her head. A familiar sense of helplessness welled up from deep inside her. 'Would that I had been born your son, and not the daughter of a filthy Asiatic shepherd,' she said, her voice no louder than a whisper.

Idu took her hand. 'You would second-guess the gods, Jauharah? They make us who we are for a reason, for a purpose. Their plan is inscrutable to us, but I would not change it for all the world. You are like a wellspring of strength to me, no matter your heritage.'

Tears sparkled on Jauharah's cheeks. 'Thank you, master.'

Idu stood and stretched, his bones creaking. 'The girls are ecstatic about going with you to the bazaar tomorrow,' he said. Jauharah laughed, wiping her eyes.

'They begged me to teach them how to roast a goose,' she said. 'Meryt wants a white one, thinking the meat will be softer, but Tuya thinks white geese are sacred to Isis. They've been squabbling about it all afternoon.'

Idu smiled. 'Knowing Tuya, she'll see the goose and wish to rescue it, then our ducks will have a graceful companion while we go hungry.' He shuffled toward the suite of rooms he shared with his wife and children.

'Mistress Tetisheri said much the same thing,' Jauharah said. 'Is there anything you need before retiring?'

'No, Jauharah. That will be all. Good night.'

'Master.' Jauharah hugged herself. 'Be careful tomorrow.'

'It is only a granary, dear girl,' he said. 'Only a granary.'

⸎ 𓏤 𓊝 𓀀 𓏺

Barca checked his surroundings, wondering if Matthias could have sent him to the wrong street. The neighbourhood did not meet the Phoenician's expectations of where a former general should dwell. Even the house, a small, single-storey affair of plastered mud brick with an awning tacked on above the door almost as an afterthought, fitted more into the mould of a retired labourer's home. No lights burned in the windows. Indeed, the place looked deserted. Perhaps Matthias had been mistaken?

The Judaean begged off coming himself, claiming his age made it unlikely he could slip out unseen by those who watched his house. Instead, Barca trusted him with a different matter. 'At dawn, my men will be entering the city. Intercept them and tell Ithobaal everything you've told me.' Matthias agreed and laid out the simplest way of reaching this man he thought could aid them.

As Barca watched, an old Egyptian shuffled up the street, muttering under his breath. He carried a round loaf of bread and a stoppered jug.

'Old man,' Barca said, stepping into view. 'Is this the house of Menkaura?'

The fellow gave a start, his eyes narrowing. 'Who are you, and what do you want?'

'I seek Menkaura.'

'You've found him, boy. Now, what the hell do you want?'

Barca blinked. This Menkaura, the man Matthias swore was a general, looked more like an aged stonemason, his scalp wrinkled and hairless, his once-thick frame gone to gristle. That the old man's leathery skin bore the white tracks of ancient scar tissue was the only indication of his former occupation. Even his pleated kilt hearkened back to an earlier age. 'I am Hasdrabal Barca, commander of the Medjay.'

Menkaura grunted in surprise. 'I've heard of you. You're a far piece from the frontier, boy. Have you quit the desert for gentler climes? In my day dereliction of duty was punishable by death. Apries counselled me once to practise restraint with deserters. I was young then, green, but I told him restraint was what made the men desert in the first place. They needed a hard hand . . .'

Barca cut him off. 'I'm not a deserter. But the Greeks will be unless you help me.'

Menkaura eyed him, scrubbing the back of his hand across his nose. 'Help you? Are you daft, boy?'

'It's best if we discuss this off the street,' Barca said.

Menkaura mulled it over, grunting, muttering under his breath. Finally, he agreed and led the way into his home.

A lamp flared, and light bathed their faces. As far as Barca could tell, the house was a single room, tiled in rough stone and strewn with multi-coloured rugs. Despite its exterior, the place looked immaculate. Crockery bowls and plates were stacked above a barrel of fresh water, clothes hung from pegs, even the sleeping pallet was squared away, blankets folded beneath a wooden head rest. Though not the home of a general, Barca could tell a soldier dwelt here.

Menkaura set his jug and loaf on a low table and motioned for Barca to take one of two antique campaign chairs. 'What's this blather about the Greeks deserting, and me helping you stop them?'

Barca sketched out everything he knew, from the battle at Leontopolis to his plans to delay Phanes until Pharaoh could muster the army. 'But, in order to make such a diversion work I need a man who has the ear of the people. That's where I need you. You were a general . . .'

'A man might be a priest, boy, but that doesn't make him pious,' Menkaura said bitterly. 'Look around you. Is this the home of a man with the ear of the people? Doesn't look like it to me. It's the home of a man who has been humbled. Whatever currency I had with the common man, I lost at Cyrene, and later against Ahmose. No, my son Idu is the one you should be talking to, though I daresay you and he would hardly see eye to eye on what should be done. He has aspirations of leading the sons of Horus in a rhetorical rebellion. He believes the Greeks will slink away, chastised, after he gives them a fine tongue-lashing!'

Barca squinted at the old Egyptian. 'Consider this, then. I've been in Memphis only a handful of hours, and already I know who stands opposed to Phanes. Do you think the Greek is any less informed? I would wager my life that he is well aware of your son's activities and will move to silence him, should he become too vocal. You, with your military background, are likely already marked for death.'

Menkaura snorted. 'Your handful of hours in Memphis have given you infallible insight, eh?'

'I know this because it's what I would do,' the Phoenician said, his voice hard. 'For the love of the gods, man! Has age made a dotard of you? If

Phanes is half as smart as they say he is, he'll make an example of your whole damn family!'

The old man grumbled, rubbed his nose. 'What do you want from me, Phoenician?'

'Gather together your kin, your friends, every man you know of who has fought or served in the army, in +the temples, even those who have guarded caravans. Divide them into groups, and give each group a mission – a man to kill, a house to burn, something. Denounce the Greeks on every street corner and in every pleasure house. Can you do that?'

Menkaura hemmed and hawed, shifting his weight from foot to foot. Barca could not tell why he was so loath to agree to such a thing. Did he prefer living under Greek rule? Maybe the defeat at Cyrene had stripped his confidence from him?

'Amon's balls!' Barca said at length. 'I offer you a chance to lead an armed rebellion, to reclaim the glory of Egypt, and all you can do is grouse and grumble! Take me to your son, then. Perhaps Idu's stones haven't yet shrivelled to the size of chickpeas!'

๏ ⸱ ⸲ ⸳ ⸴

Jauharah woke with a start. She lay on her pallet, a thin linen coverlet draped across her upper body, her legs exposed to the cool night air. She blinked back sleep. She had heard a sound in the night, something that should not have been there. Or had she? Perhaps her imagination . . . ?

The sound repeated, the stealthy scuff of a foot on stone.

Jauharah rose and went to her door, frowning. Which of the children wandered the halls at this late hour? Perhaps it was master Idu? Carefully she opened her door and peered out. Her room lay off the central hall, near the servants' entrance, and on the opposite side of the house from the main family chambers. Small clay night lamps cast pale circles of light that barely relieved the darkness. Something moved across the hall, a shadow slinking toward Idu's chambers. Jauharah's heart leapt into her throat.

A man.

Then another.

A third followed in their wake; each wore a voluminous black cloak, and naked knives glittered in their fists. Three more joined them outside Idu's door. Six. Six men armed and disguised. When she heard their harsh whispers, Jauharah recognized them for what they were.

Greek soldiers.

'Searched the grounds,' one said. 'No sign of stragglers.'

'Do it quick. The whole family, Lysistratis be damned.' They nodded to one another and reached for the door.

Jauharah did the only thing she could think of. She bellowed at the top of her lungs. 'Master!'

Time froze. The echoes of Jauharah's scream hung in the air. The men stared over their shoulders at her; she stared back. For an eternity this tableau held, unblinking, unwavering, until at last one of the Greeks hissed an order chilling in both brevity and intent.

'Kill her!'

At that same instant Idu's door opened. 'Merciful Amon! What . . . ?'

'Master! Look out!' Jauharah rushed forward.

The assassins reacted with military precision. Two grabbed Idu and hurled him to the floor. Three vanished into the suite of rooms. One turned and stalked Jauharah.

She skidded to a halt, her eyes wide with fear. The Greek's curved knife glimmered in the wan light as it slashed toward her belly. Jauharah shied away from him, her hand brushing a stand holding a dozen of her master's carved walking sticks. Instinctively, her fist closed on one.

The Greek lunged. With a dancer's grace, Jauharah sidestepped and ripped the walking stick from the stand. It whistled through the air like a sabre, cracking over the Greek's shoulders and neck. The assassin careened into the stand, stunned. His knife clattered on the floor.

Chilling screams came from her master's bedroom. Jauharah spun, her face pale.

She knew she would remember those screams until her dying day, more so the cruel silence in their wake, as clearly as she would remember the struggle taking place before her eyes.

Idu was on the ground, crawling across the threshold leading to the bedroom. His hands clawed at the stone tiles as the pair of assassins straddled him, plunging their knives into his back. The blood . . . 'J-Jauharah!' Idu roared. 'Find help!'

His voice galvanized her. She heard curses as the fallen Greek struggled to his feet. Whirling, Jauharah planted a foot in his groin and sprinted for the side door. She had to find Menkaura.

Jauharah's nightmarish flight through the dark streets of Memphis left her bathed in sweat. Her heart hammered in her chest; her ears rang with the sound of children screaming. She felt her pursuers closing in, as sure as the itch between her shoulder blades presaged the tip of a knife being driven into her back. The Greeks would follow. She was a witness to murder, and they would not suffer her to live.

Find Menkaura!

But, what could he do? Idu's father was an old man.

Find Menkaura!

Gods! They were dead already! What use could come from getting others killed, as well? Adrenalin surged through her system. No! They weren't dead! They couldn't be dead! The thought of the girls, Meryt and Tuya, in peril sent a fierce shockwave through her body.

She would kill – or die – to save them!

The quickest route from her master's villa to where Menkaura lived meant traversing the

Foreign Quarter. Normally, the thought of broaching those tangled streets sent a thrill of fear down her spine. What could happen to her in there that would rival her terror of the Greeks? If anything, the Foreign Quarter would hide her movements.

Jauharah darted through the open-air shop of a coppersmith. The glow of the banked forge striped the shadows with tendrils of angry red. An apprentice watched her, his eyes dull, lifeless, as he plucked at a loaf of bread. She stopped to get her bearings, then sprinted up the street, scattering a quartet of cats fighting over the carcass of a Nile perch.

Here, the buildings grew close together, the air heavy and hot, as stifling as a woollen blanket around her throat. She passed doorways where prostitutes lounged between customers, windows where harsh foreign laughter crackled in the night. A dizzying array of smells and sounds assailed her. Jauharah's head spun. She rounded a corner . . .

. . . and crashed against a muscular torso. Her feet slithered out from under her, sending her sprawling to the ground. A figure loomed in the darkness. She had the impression of a strong jaw, aquiline nose, and dark eyes before the sheathed sword in his fist consumed her attention. Defiant, she glared up at the man, expecting her death blow. Instead, his free hand reached out and helped her to her feet.

'Be careful, girl,' the man rumbled, his Egyptian lightly accented.

Another man, coming behind him, cursed. 'Damn you, woman! Get out of the way! We have . . .'

Jauharah recognized the voice.

'Master Menkaura!' she sobbed, clutching at the old man's belt. 'Your son, master Menkaura! The G-Greeks . . . !'

'Who is she?'

'Idu's serving woman.' Menkaura took Jauharah by the shoulders. 'What's happened, girl? What's happened?'

'It's master Idu! They . . .'

The other man cut her off, his voice cold and hard. 'Take care of her, Menkaura.' He stared at something behind her. She heard the sound of runners slowing, the rasp of metal on leather. Jauharah twisted.

Behind her, six Greeks shed their cloaks and spread out, blocking the street.

'Fortune smiles on us, brothers,' said the leader of the Greeks. He moved forward, his men flanking him. Blood speckled their arms and faces. 'Here we have the estimable Menkaura, the Desert Hawk of Cyrene. I am Leon, son of Philon, and my father was a commander in the army that dealt you such a grievous blow years ago. Ironic that his son will be your executioner.' Leon glanced at Barca. 'A sad day for you, friend. We only wanted Menkaura and the girl.'

A dangerous edge stiffened Menkaura's voice. 'Give me your sword, Barca!'

'Stay back!' the Phoenician growled. He drew his scimitar and walked toward the Greeks. 'You want them? Come, take them.'

'Barca, is it? Of the Medjay?' Leon glanced at his companions. Palms grew sweaty; the six men shifted nervously. They had heard of Barca, of his reputation as a killer. They were journeymen in the craft. Here, they faced a master. 'Give them up, then, and be on your way with our blessing.'

Barca smiled, his eyes like stone chips. 'I am one. You are six. Come, take them if you can.'

The Greeks advanced cautiously, on the balls of their feet. Leon exhaled, his lips framing a curse, a prayer, an order.

Barca was in motion before Leon could finish. The Beast tore loose from his soul, driving him into their midst. His blade struck left and right, weaving an intricate pattern of carnage. Blood showered the stones like a red rain. Three assassins went down, their lives spilling across the street, and a fourth reeled away, his hands full of his own entrails. In a heartbeat, six had become two. The remaining Greeks panted like cornered hounds. In desperation, they charged. A sword thrust at Barca's gut; he caught the fellow's wrist and spun him around, kicking his legs out from under him. The man struck the ground hard, stunned, his breath exploding from his lungs. Only the man called Leon remained standing. With wild eyes, the Arcadian slashed overhand.

Barca's scimitar turned it with practiced ease and his riposte tore through Leon's jugular. The fallen Greek watched in horror as Leon sank down beside him, gobbling as his life spurted through scarlet fingers. The man struggled to rise.

'Give my regards to Polydices,' the Phoenician snarled as he struck the Greek's head from his shoulders.

Sheer awe kept Jauharah rooted to the spot, unable to tear her eyes away from the deadly scene before her. The man, Barca, moved with an uncommon grace; never a wasted movement, a false step, his sword an extension of himself. Jauharah had never seen anything like it.

Neither had Menkaura. Jauharah noted the look of shock on the old man's face. That a general who had fought in countless battles, a man inured to the horrors of war, could register such surprise left a cold knot in the pit of Jauharah's belly.

She heard the Phoenician speak, but the voice was not the same one she had heard minutes earlier. It was hard, guttural and full of rage: 'Give my regards to Polydices!' Then, as suddenly as it began, the fight ended.

Barca stepped away from his handiwork, from the six Greeks he had sent to Hades' realm. He crouched, cleaning his sword on one of the dark cloaks the would-be assassins had cast aside. All was perfectly still. In the distance, Jauharah heard the barking of a dog, the harsh grate of voices.

'We'd best get off the street,' Barca said, rising. 'Unless you want to be seen standing over six Greek corpses.'

'Merciful . . . !' Menkaura's voice faltered. Jauharah blinked, staring at the Phoenician's bloodstained hands without realizing he was speaking. 'What of my son?'

'If he's dead there's no use going on any further.'

'T-The children,' Jauharah said, choking back tears. 'We should see t-to the children.'

After a long silence, Barca agreed. 'Bring the girl.'

Silence. Barca paused at the gate of Idu's villa and scanned the garden. A light breeze sprang up, ruffling the palm-leaves and grasses. He led the way down the path to the front steps. Menkaura and the girl made to push past him, but he barred their way. 'Wait here. The Greeks might have left a rear guard.'

'There were only six of them,' the woman said, an hysterical edge creeping into her voice.

'Wait here.'

The Phoenician ascended the steps and went in alone. The naked blade in his hand seemed out of place against the vibrant pastoral scenes adorning the walls. He crept through the vestibule and into the spacious west hall. Here, Idu's family would have taken their evening meal, basking in the warm red glow of the setting sun. His foot brushed a wooden paddle doll, its coloured yarn hair awry.

Barca stopped. His nostrils flared. The stench of fresh blood hung in the still air.

Lotiform columns separated the west hall from the central hall. Flames flickered in small clay lamps. He could make out a scattering of chairs and cushions in the dim light. After the evening meal, Idu and his family would have retired to the central hall. Did he discuss his day with his wife? Tell stories to his children? Or did he sit and listen to his wife sing while she played the small harp that usually lay on a side table? Barca slipped into the central hall and stopped.

A corpse lay in the doorway leading to the master bedchamber, seeming to float in a pool of blood. Idu. The Greeks had done their job well. Their knives had ripped open the flesh of his back and neck. Barca peered through the doorway and into the bedchamber. A woman was sprawled on the floor; in the bed were two small, bloody shapes, half covered by linen sheets.

The Greeks had done their job too well.

Barca turned and left the villa. He walked slowly down the front steps, to where Menkaura and the girl awaited him.

'The children?' Jauharah sobbed. Barca caught her before she could move past him.

'No,' he said. 'You don't want to remember them this way.'

Menkaura groaned and leaned against the steps. Jauharah shook her head. 'N-No! You're w-wrong! No!' she said over and again. Barca stared down into her eyes. Horror, agony, and guilt warred for control. 'No,' she whispered. Suddenly, her body went limp, her legs buckled. She collapsed into Barca's arms.

The Phoenician glanced at Menkaura. 'Can I count on your help, now?'

The old general could do nothing but nod.

5

LORD OF THE TWO LANDS

They called it *Ta-Meht*, the Delta, the ancient kingdom of Lower Egypt, a verdant, watery fan bounded by deserts to the east and west. Here, the Nile branched into seven tributaries, each winding serpentine into the emerald surf of the Mediterranean. Jungles of papyrus camouflaged deep pools where the hippopotamus and the crocodile lurked. A network of dykes and embankments, like strands of a web still damp with morning dew, converged on a solitary flat-topped hill.

Sais, the seat of power of Pharaoh Khnemibre Ahmose, rose from this moist loam like the mound of creation itself. Though smaller than Memphis or Thebes, Sais eclipsed them both in prestige, if not in ancestry. Monumental pylons of granite, stark white against the rich green of the Delta, gleamed in the first flush of dawn. A haze of smoke from cooking fires, forges, and foundries drifted on the light northerly breeze. Broad, straight streets led from the outskirts of the city to its centre, terminating at the great plaza fronting the palace of Pharaoh. Before those cedar doors, soldiers of the Calasirian Guard stood like stone monuments, spears ground at attention, eyes forward, their manner unfazed by the sight of a horse and rider crossing the plaza. The people gathering there, the merchants and scribes, sycophants and servants, all hoping for an audience with Pharaoh, stopped and stared.

Blood drenched the rider's thigh and his horse's flank.

Tjemu swayed, sweat pouring off his ashen forehead. He had ridden without pause from Leontopolis, eating in the saddle and catching what rest he could on the boats that ferried him over the different branches of the Nile. To his fevered perception, it felt as though a week had passed since the battle. It had been three days.

Tjemu drew rein. His head swam. His legs felt rubbery and unsure as he clambered off his horse; the right one ached beyond measure as he put his weight on it. He staggered up the palace steps.

'You,' he growled at one of the immobile guards. 'Fetch your commander! I bear grave news for Pharaoh!' The guard said nothing, his eyes never moved, his spear remained ground at rest. 'Are you deaf? Fetch . . .'

'No need to shout,' said a man behind Tjemu.

The Libyan hobbled about to face the newcomer. He was Egyptian, impossibly tall with a lean, almost feline, musculature that rippled beneath skin the colour of dark copper. Beneath a short wig, banded in gold, his sharp face bore a passing similarity to images of the god Horus. He wore a kilt of white linen. Incongruous to this, a faded leather belt supported a sheathed knife, the ivory hilt worn from use. He patted the horse's neck and allowed it to nibble from a rind of melon.

'I am Nebmaatra, captain of the Calasirian Guard. Give me your message. I'll see that Pharaoh gets it.'

Tjemu gritted his teeth. His vision swam. 'The only person I'm giving this message to sits on a throne in yonder palace. C-Conduct me to . . .' The Libyan stumbled. Nebmaatra caught him before he could fall. A gesture from the captain brought a pair of guards running. They supported the Libyan's weight as Nebmaatra knelt and lifted the sodden edge of the bandage.

'Unless we get this bleeding stopped,' Nebmaatra said gravely, 'the only person you'll be giving your message to is Lord Osiris.'

☥ 𓀭 𓀀 𓀗 𓏏

'Sons of buggering whores!' Tjemu roared, swatting at the priest-physician stitching his thigh. Nimbly, the man ducked, then went back to his ministrations. The Libyan glared at Nebmaatra. 'I didn't kill two horses getting to Sais just so I could be pampered and petted! When can I see the Pharaoh?' No one had been able to pry the

108

diplomatic pouch from Tjemu's fist; the last attempt brought him uncomfortably close to murder.

'Calm yourself, Libyan,' Nebmaatra replied, looking up from a papyrus scroll.

He sat on a divan, a scribe at his elbow holding a palette and a reed pen. The small side chamber where his men brought the Libyan lay on the first floor of the palace, beneath the balcony called the Window of Appearances. Here, Pharaoh greeted the masses on festival days, showering them with small gifts and trinkets in the manner of the ancient kings. 'Pharaoh is a man of ritual. Before he tackles the affairs of state, he must first see to the affairs of the gods.'

Nebmaatra laughed to himself. He had spoken that lie so often he almost believed it. A man of ritual? God-fearing? Ahmose was many things, but neither of those could be counted among his attributes. He was a common soldier thrust into an uncommon position. A general in the army of his predecessor, Haaibre Apries, Ahmose gained the throne by dint of his popularity with the native troops. Now, Pharaoh spent his mornings wrestling with the affairs of state, and the balance of his days wrestling with wine jugs and his own impending mortality. He was a fair ruler, Nebmaatra reckoned, wise in his own way and a shrewd statesman, but nothing like the god-kings of the elder days.

The physician bandaged Tjemu's thigh with fresh strips of linen, then rose and gathered his things. Nebmaatra handed the scroll back to the scribe. 'He'll live?'

The physician nodded. 'The spear missed the artery. It should mend well, so long as he keeps it clean and dry.'

'Good. Now, Medjay, let's see about getting you an audience with . . .'

Without warning a man swept into the room, his austere white robes rustling about him, his face dark, lined, severe. His eyes burned with an imperious fire. The physician and the scribe bowed low; Nebmaatra came to his feet with a warrior's grace and inclined his head.

'Vizier.'

The vizier, Sethnakhte, ignored Nebmaatra and fixed his gaze on Tjemu. His lips curled back in a perfect, haughty sneer. 'You are the . . . messenger?'

'I am,' the Libyan growled, bristling.

'Your message, then. Quickly!' Sethnakhte said.

'I have only seen Pharaoh from afar, but I am positive you are not him,' Tjemu said. 'If you cannot pave a way for me to see him, then stand aside. I tire of this game you call bureaucracy.'

'Impudent wretch!' Sethnakhte roared. He moved quickly. One manicured hand lashed out like a leather strap, striking Tjemu across the mouth. 'Speak thus to me again, and I will see you flogged!'

Murder danced in Tjemu's eyes as he lurched to his feet, hand on his sword hilt. Nebmaatra interposed himself between the two men.

'Control yourself!' the commander said. He turned to the vizier. 'This man has ridden two days and nights with a wound that would leave most men bedridden. He bears important news from the frontier, from Hasdrabal Barca. The quicker we secure him an audience with Pharaoh, the quicker he can discharge his duty.'

'Barca, eh? I can only imagine what message *he* would send.' The vizier spun and stormed from the room. Nebmaatra watched him with eyes narrowed to slits. Doubts about the vizier's loyalty were ever at the forefront of his mind. Rumour placed him in opposition to the throne, in collusion with the Theban aristocracy who favoured replacing Pharaoh. Another scandal had Sethnakhte plotting with the Persians for the double-crown. Unfortunately, rumour and innuendo had a way of sliding off the vizier like oil off mud. To catch him, Nebmaatra knew he would need something far more substantial.

'I apologize for that,' Nebmaatra said, helping Tjemu along.

'He's one pleasant son of a whore,' Tjemu muttered, rubbing his jaw.

'Sethnakhte believes when he looks in a mirror, he beholds the face of a god. As such, it is difficult for him to show humility and courtesy around this flock of mere mortals.'

'God or not, he touches me again,' Tjemu said, 'they'll find his body floating face down in the Nile.'

A gesture from Nebmaatra brought a pair of

servants to Tjemu's side. They eased him into a chair, hoisted it, and bore the wounded man along at a quickened pace. Morning sunlight streamed through windows high in the walls, casting a warm golden glow over scenes of Pharaoh smiting hordes of his enemy. Petitioners of noble blood lined their path. Their voices, though not above a whisper, buzzed with indignation at being superseded by a grimy foreigner.

The guards flanking the entrance to the throne room snapped to attention at the vizier's approach. Door wardens, feathered Nubians in leopardskin cloaks, levered the gold-sheathed portals open. Tjemu swallowed. He felt his throat go dry; his tongue became a shank of old leather. Beyond those doors dwelt the Son of Ra. His chair-bearers put him down; Nebmaatra offered him his arm. Tjemu shrugged him off. He would make it the rest of the way on his own.

The great valves swung apart, revealing a smaller room dominated by four columns. Between them, atop a dais of black marble, rested the golden throne of Pharaoh. A man stood at the base of the royal dais – a young, vigorous figure in an elaborately woven black wig. He wore a fine linen kilt and a pectoral of faience and carnelian and lapis lazuli. His frank gaze spoke of a keen intellect.

'That is Prince Psammetichus, Pharaoh's heir and First Servant of Neith,' Nebmaatra whispered. 'A good man, though hampered by the advice of imbeciles.' He looked pointedly at the vizier.

If Tjemu heard him, he gave no indication of it. His eyes were drawn upward, his whole being consumed by the man who sat upon the dais. Pharaoh Khnemibre Ahmose, Lord of Upper and Lower Egypt, Divine Son of Ra, called Amasis Philhellene by the Greeks, sat easily on his throne, a man born to rule. Forty-four years had passed since he usurped the crown, since he evolved from mortal general into living god, and he wore those years heavily. His shoulders were square, and the muscles of his arms and chest, though loose with inactivity, had not yet turned to gristle. He wore the *nemes*, the striped head-cloth, offset by a golden cobra writhing at his brow. The crook and flail, twin symbols of kingship, lay in his lap. Wide-set eyes above a falcate nose regarded the men, and a hint of amusement tugged at the corners of his mouth.

The three men bowed deeply and approached the throne.

'You look positively vexed, Sethnakhte.'

The vizier bowed again. 'I am beset by petty, self-important men, great Pharaoh.'

'Are you, indeed? I understand this one bears a message for me?' he said, nodding to Tjemu. 'Speak, then. Tell me your message.'

The Libyan swallowed hard. 'O Pharaoh, I have been sent by Hasdrabal Barca, who commands the Medjay in your name. Barca instructed me to relay this to your royal person, and only to your royal person.' Tjemu held out the diplomatic pouch taken at Leontopolis.

'Approach, then.'

Tjemu hobbled forward and ascended the dais. Nebmaatra moved opposite him, in case he should fall. Tjemu began to prostrate himself, to show deference to the divinity of the king, but Pharaoh waved him off.

'With that leg you'll never get up again, son. An arrow?'

'Spear,' Tjemu said, placing the pouch in Pharaoh's hand. 'Bedouin spear.'

Pharaoh frowned. 'Are we at war with the Bedouin, again?' He pried open the flap of the diplomatic pouch, the leather stiff with dried blood. He tugged out the vellum and began to read. With each sentence, a change came over Pharaoh. His eyebrows met and formed a 'V'; his brow wrinkled; his lips peeled back from his teeth in a savage display of naked rage. He handed the vellum to Psammetichus.

'Tell me,' Pharaoh said, his voice flat, 'from the beginning.'

Quickly, Tjemu relayed the tale of Habu, of Leontopolis, of finding the dead Persian envoy. 'Barca led the rest of the men on to Memphis to scout out the landscape and learn what he could of the Greeks' disposition.'

Sethnakhte stepped forward. 'With your permission,' he said, taking the vellum from the Prince. He scanned it, then laughed aloud. 'It's a forgery, Golden One. A plot by Cambyses to sow discord among us. Phanes is a loyal soldier; I've seen it with my own eyes. If we accuse him of treachery, then you may as well place my head on the block, too!'

'Maybe we should!' Tjemu said, his voice a dangerous purr.

The vizier rounded on the soldier. 'Impertinent fool! I will have your skin flayed off your back and your miserable body staked out for the flies to feast on! This is nothing more than Barca's way of casting your disfavour on the garrison at Memphis. It is no secret that the Medjay envies their position. Perhaps . . .'

Tjemu's hand wrapped around the hilt of his sword. 'Speak ill of Barca one more time, you pompous ass, and there won't be enough left of you to feed the maggots!'

'Enough, both of you!' Pharaoh said. 'What say you, Psammetichus? Were you Pharaoh what would your decision be?'

The Prince stood silent for some time, his head bowed, his arms folded over his chest. Pharaoh's heir had gleaned a reputation at Sais as a patient, concise thinker. He weighed his words like gold. 'Phanes has served you loyally since the fall of Lydia, father. Thrice you've awarded him the gold of valour. Unlike the vizier, I do not count Phanes as my friend, and I would give everything I own to renounce the Libyan as a dog and a liar.'

'Yet, you wouldn't.'

'No, Father.'

'Why?' Pharaoh felt pangs of pride deep in his chest.

115

'Because I know Phanes' reputation,' Psammetichus said. 'Glory is the hot-clefted slut who stirs his passions. He's tasted it all his life. Among Greeks, glory, once sampled, is never forgotten.'

Ahmose nodded. 'My mind says much the same thing. Leave me, all of you. There is much to ponder. I will make my decision before the sun strikes its zenith.' He gestured to the Prince, who nodded and led the way.

Silently, the men bowed and filed from the room. The Nubians closed the doors. Outside, sunlight seared the hypostyle hall, heating the stones like an oven. Nebmaatra led Tjemu to a bench where the Libyan could rest his leg. He scowled as Sethnakhte took hold of Prince Psammetichus' elbow and guided him away, out of earshot. They conversed heatedly.

'One day,' Nebmaatra muttered, watching the vizier. 'One day he will make a mistake, and I will be right there.'

'Honestly,' Tjemu said, 'I do not understand why Pharaoh dawdles. I say dispatch a regiment or two and order them to bring back that bastard's head.'

'Life is simpler in the desert, Libyan,' Nebmaatra replied. 'Many of the Pharaoh's enemies will use this turn of events to promote their own careers. Powerful as he is, Ahmose is not the god-king of ancient times. Common men put him on the throne, and those selfsame common men can remove him just as easily. And, the common man of Egypt has been taught to fear Greek ambition.

Ahmose has worked hard to allay those fears, but this incident may well destroy us all.'

'The politics of Sais,' Tjemu spat.

'No, the reality of life.'

Alone in the throne room, Ahmose sagged. One liver-spotted hand tugged the *nemes* cloth off his head; the other massaged his scalp. His chest ached, and he could feel congestion pooling in his lungs with every deep breath. These were the moments when this gilded prison made him long for simpler times, for a life of anonymity far away from the intrigues of court. Phanes, a traitor? He sighed. As much as he loved the culture of the Hellenes – its art, its vigour – he often had to remind himself that they were a bloodthirsty people whose ambitions rivalled those of the arrogant Persians.

Is this how it began with his old allies? A rumour here, an insinuation there? What started as a grand alliance between Egypt, Babylonia, and Lydia had barely lived through its infancy. Croesus of Lydia fell first, outwitted by that Persian swineherd Cyrus. Nabonidus of Babylon held out longer, but he, too, eventually succumbed to the Medes, a victim of his own indifference. After the fall of Babylon, the lesser members of the grand alliance vanished like smoke. Now, only Egypt remained.

Psammetichus spoke true. Yet, he left out how a rebellious subject lent credibility to the rumours that the Land of the Nile was consumed by the cancer of corruption. Once it became known that a man like Phanes, a man with detailed knowledge of the inner workings of the military and ambition beyond ability, was unhappy, Persian spies would crawl from every rat-hole in Memphis. Ahmose sighed again. He would have to take Phanes down a notch, show him who ruled and who served.

Ahmose heard the silky grate of oiled stone hinges and looked up. A section of the palace wall swung outward; a woman stepped through. Her long cotton gown flared out behind her as she crossed the throne room. Pharaoh smiled.

'You heard, I take it?'

'Heard? The palace is all a-twitter! Are you seriously considering sending troops to Memphis?' Her voice echoed the concern etched on her brow.

'Not send. Lead. Ah, Ladice. What choice do I have? In all my years, I've learned one lesson quite well: If I show weakness, I'll not be long for the throne.' Ahmose gazed at her, felt the soothing effect her presence had on him. He could have stared at her for an eternity.

In her youth Ladice had been an incomparable beauty, one of those rare few the gods had gifted with a symmetry of form and a keenness of intellect. Poets from Cyrene to Byzantium composed verses in her honour. Sculptors begged to immortalize her in stone and bronze. Indeed, had Ladice been born a man, all of Greece would have had a new demi-god to worship, a new warrior to emulate, a new philosopher to follow.

As a man she would have conquered nations; as a woman, she conquered hearts. Yet, even though her thirtieth year had passed, Ladice's allure faded but little. She retained the beauty of a Spartan queen tempered with the magnetism of wisdom and maturity.

Ladice knelt by the throne and clasped Pharaoh's hand. Dark, liquid eyes stared up at him. 'My heart cares more for your safety, husband. I've heard this Phanes embodies the worst aspects of my people – ruthless, ambitious, and cruel. As a tool, you could ask for none better, but as an adversary . . .'

'What would you counsel?'

Ladice sighed; her shoulders slumped. 'I think you must do this, if for no other reason than to show the nobles of Egypt that you fear no man.'

He stroked her cheek. 'I should free you from your bondage, child. Let you return to your home in Cyrene. I have kept you overlong as a slave of my harem.'

The woman laughed. It was a light, silvery sound that brought a smile to the old Pharaoh's face. 'Child? You are as adept at flattery as you are at statecraft. Do I toil under your overseer's lash, my husband? Am I a silky plaything pining away in your seraglio? I think not. I live in the shadows by your side, giving you my love and my strength, should it be your desire.'

Ahmose kissed her gently. 'If Phanes embodies the worst in your people, then you, favourite of my wives, symbolize what I fell in love with.' He

119

broke their embrace. 'Time grows short. Be off with you.'

'Shall I come to you tonight?' she said, her fingers tracing the line of his jaw.

Ahmose smiled. 'Surely you do not wish to lie with a dried-up old man?'

'Now you presume to tell me my own mind,' Ladice said, taking the *nemes* from him and arranging it perfectly. She placed the *uraeus,* the golden circlet wrought in the image of the divine cobra, on his forehead. 'Let me come to you, if only to lie together and whisper.'

'After a dozen years,' Ahmose said, 'you still surprise me.'

'I will take that as a yes.' Ladice kissed him quickly and hurried from the room. Pharaoh took up the crook and flail and tried to gather his thoughts, his purpose hindered by teasing images of his favourite wife. He laughed like a man twenty years his junior.

'Guards!'

'I do not understand,' Tjemu said for the thousandth time. The man who shared his bench was a *hem-netjer*, a god's servant; he threw his hands up in defeat. 'You tell me tales that openly conflict with one another, and say that it does not matter? It does matter.'

'No,' the *hem-netjer* closed his eyes, 'all that matters is that we enact the rites and observe the festivals that mirror the perfection of divine order, and acknowledge and hold sacred the gods as represented by their animal forms.'

Tjemu looked lost. 'So, when you worship the crocodile, you're not actually worshiping the crocodile, but the spirit of Sobek?'

'Exactly!'

Tjemu shrugged. 'It makes no sense . . .'

The priest started to open his mouth, but Nebmaatra interceded. 'It would be easier, Pure One, to explain the subtleties of Egyptian religion to yonder statue.' A soldier of the Guard caught Nebmaatra's eye and nodded. 'It's time.'

The guards at the palace doors snapped to attention as servants levered the gold-sheathed portals open. Nebmaatra helped Tjemu to his feet. Courtiers trickled in according to their social stature, lesser making way for greater. Nebmaatra and Tjemu fell in behind the vizier.

'. . . kept waiting like common courtiers!' Sethnakhte growled to one of his sycophants. 'This is preposterous! I am vizier! I should be the one who counsels him! Who does he think . . .'

'School your tongue if you would remain vizier!' Nebmaatra warned. They were of comparable height, but the soldier's thick frame made him seem all the more daunting. 'The ground you tread can just as easily become your grave! Keep this in mind: should you attempt to walk the path that your friend Phanes has embarked on, then I will become your enemy. And my enemies tend to die violent deaths.'

The vizier's thin nostrils flared. He bared his teeth in an animal-like snarl. 'You are nothing to me! A peasant! For reasons known only to himself, Pharaoh favours you, but that favour will not last many more years. I will accept your lack of respect for now, but there will come a day when no one will stand between us. No one!'

'When that day comes, I'll not be hard to find!'

Sethnakhte made a subtle spitting gesture and turned away from Nebmaatra, rejoining his clique.

'Why does Pharaoh tolerate him?' Tjemu whispered.

Nebmaatra exhaled. 'His arrogance notwithstanding, Sethnakhte is good at what he does. You'll find that Pharaoh has boundless patience when it comes to men of that sort.'

'Snakes, you mean?'

Nebmaatra smiled.

Pharaoh held up his hand, and every tongue was stilled; every eye turned toward him. Psammetichus mounted the royal dais. Ahmose spoke.

'I rule this land, and my word is the word of the gods, yet no man rules in a vacuum. To rule effectively, I must listen to those I trust. I have learned to trust Hasdrabal Barca's judgement. His instincts have never led him astray. But, I also trust my own instincts.

'The safety of Egypt rests in more than her military might; it rests in her people, as well. If we abandon them in times of strife, would they not abandon us in times of prosperity? Men say I am a wine-sot, that I am a philanderer, but let no man say I am fickle! Prepare the royal fleet. Muster the regiment of Amon and the Calasirian Guard. I intend to set Memphis aright, as it should be. Psammetichus, I leave Sais in your hands.'

'Sire,' Sethnakhte said, 'in spite of the preponderance of circumstantial evidence I must protest! At the very least, do we not owe Phanes the benefit of the doubt? Send for him! Make him explain himself!'

'Protest to your heart's content, vizier, but see that my will is made known.' Pharaoh rose. 'I am going to Memphis. If Phanes is loyal, he will greet me as his king. But, if he wishes a fight, then by all the gods of the Nile, a fight he will have!'

6

DESHUR

The same sunlight warming the palace at Sais barely penetrated the tangle of streets at the heart of the Foreign Quarter of Memphis. An elongated square of dusty gold brought unnatural colour to the faces of the dead Arcadians.

'Ah, Leon,' Phanes whispered, crouching over the assassin's corpse. 'Finally met your match.' The Greek's practised eye swept over the slain men, noting their positions, their wounds. In his mind he recreated the carnage, willing the dead to rise again and fight, watching them die in painfully slow motion. The men who did this . . .

Phanes picked up Leon's sword, an antique weapon, its leaf-shaped blade fitted with a worn ivory hilt. A deep notch scored its edge. Phanes stood as Lysistratis approached. A small crowd had gathered, kept at bay by a hedge of hoplite spears.

'Whatever else happened,' Lysistratis said, his voice low, 'they accomplished their objective. Idu and his family are dead.'

'What of Menkaura?'

'No word yet. You don't think an old man did this?' The Spartan glanced down at the corpses.

'Oh no, this wasn't Menkaura's doing.'

Lysistratis frowned. 'Who, then? Idu's cronies?'

'My guess . . . Barca.' He tossed the notched sword to Lysistratis. 'Leon fought briefly with someone wielding a heavy iron blade, probably a scimitar. The Medjay use scimitars with blades of Carchemish iron.'

'If the Medjay are here, they made good time. How can we confirm it?'

'Assume Barca will make his presence known in due time. Have you doubled the guards and stepped up patrols?'

'I have,' the Spartan said.

One of Phanes' hoplites, his crested helmet perched on his forehead, gestured back to the perimeter. 'The merchant, *strategos*.'

Callisthenes crossed the street, confusion writ plainly across his face. He glanced from Lysistratis to Phanes to the corpses. His face paled. 'Merciful gods!'

'They are, indeed, my friend,' Phanes said. 'I'm sorry to rouse you this early, but I'm in need of your counsel.'

Callisthenes hovered at the fringe of the slaughter, unwilling to approach any closer. 'You should have sought my counsel before you loosed your dogs.'

Phanes, a grim smile on his lips, nodded. 'Advise me, then, Callisthenes. In honesty.'

'In honesty?' Callisthenes stroked the scarab

amulet. 'I would say this bit of foolishness did your cause little good. By making martyrs of Idu and his family, you've given the rabble an ideal to aspire to. Were I in your place, I would salvage this blunder by finding a scapegoat – a business rival, a scorned lover, someone. Make arrests and show the people the truth of Greek justice.'

'You're a ruthless man, Callisthenes,' Phanes said. 'I admire that trait in my associates.'

One of the hoplite guards approached Phanes with a note in his hand, a square of papyrus. He whispered something and nodded back the way he had come. A boy stood along the perimeter, a scribe's apprentice in a stained tunic.

Phanes read the note, crumpled it in his fist.

'What is it?' Lysistratis said.

'Our confirmation, it seems. The Medjay have been spotted in the Square of Deshur. Take three squads. If they are indeed there, arrest them. If they resist, kill them.' Phanes said, grinning. 'Scapegoats.'

'What about me?' Callisthenes said.

Phanes turned. 'You and I must see a priest.'

Menkaura closed the door and walked over to the narrow window. The house they had fled to lay nestled in a palm-grove on the southwestern edge of Memphis. A breeze fluttered through the window, carrying the scent of damp earth and barley off the open fields. Menkaura's shoulders slumped as he leaned against the window casement, his face long beyond belief. Barca handed him a crockery juglet of beer, one of two their host provided. He drank without tasting.

'How is she?' Barca said, sitting heavily on a divan. Menkaura shrugged.

'She's sleeping. Jauharah's a strong girl, for an Arabian.'

Their host, a pinch-faced old scribe Menkaura had addressed as Weni, backed out of the room and left them alone.

'He was with me at Cyrene,' Menkaura said, nodding after the scribe. 'Many of my old followers live in Memphis, in near poverty, their service to Pharaoh all but forgotten. I truly don't know how I can help you, especially now. I have funerals to oversee.'

'If you try to claim their bodies, the Greeks will kill you. It's what they are betting on,' Barca said. 'You said many of your old followers live in Memphis. Do you think you can organize them and their kinsmen into an effective irregular force?'

Menkaura rubbed his leathery skull. 'Possibly. I owe it to them to try, at least. Idu and I were not close, but he was my son nonetheless. But their burials . . .'

'Let the girl handle them,' Barca offered.

'The girl?' Menkaura's voice dropped to a hiss. 'Did you not hear me? She is Arabian, a Bedouin. I would as soon leave Idu unburied as to trust his eternal *ka* to a foreign slave!'

Barca shrugged. 'Then your son and his family died for nothing. I cannot fight the Greeks alone. I need help. I need you, Menkaura. But, I understand. The dead come before the living. Such is the Egyptian way.'

Menkaura said nothing, his brow creased in a troubling scowl. He stared out the window. In the distance, dark-skinned workers in loincloths grubbed a boulder out of the ground on the edge of the field. The sounds of their voices, their tools, did not reach the house. Finally, he spoke: 'Tell me again how you would handle this thing. This diversion.'

'We operate independently of one another. While you inflame the people, my Medjay will wage a war of attrition. We need to sow chaos in their ranks, keep them off balance. That way, once Pharaoh arrives, the task of rooting them out will be less dangerous.' Barca stretched out full-length on the divan, his sword inches from his hand.

'You're sure Pharaoh is coming?'

'Depend on it, Menkaura.'

'Rest, then.' The old man sighed. 'I will consider your plan.'

'You do that,' Barca said, his eyes closing. He fought the inexorable pull of sleep. So much to do, so much to plan for, but his exhausted body overruled everything else. Slowly, he drifted off. 'You do that.'

By the second hour after dawn, an endless stream of humanity choked the Square of Deshur. Merchants, both Egyptian and foreign, erected stalls in the long shadows cast by the walls of Ptah's temple. All manner of bread, fruit, and meat could be found heaped on woven-straw platters. Women, matrons and their daughters, filed past mounds of old faience beads destined to find new life as jewellery. Their husbands and brothers clustered around temporary rope paddocks, haggling over the prices of sheep and cattle. Under awnings of striped linen, sculptors honed their craft on chunks of diorite and granite as their representatives bawled their praises to the crowd. Naked children darted and played underfoot. Voices blended with smells: cones of fat infused with fragrant oils, strings of sun-dried fish, fresh onions, sweat, and offal. Motion, sound, and smell wove together, forming a hypnotic haze that overwhelmed the senses.

Matthias moved through the crowd like a man twice his age, his body leaden and heavy. What little sleep he had, if it could be called such, had been restless. The excitement of Barca's arrival, his revelations about Phanes, drove away the cloud of despair that had gripped him. He hurried past the Alabaster Sphinx, ignoring the pack of older children who had claimed it as their own and were hurling taunts down on the swelling mob. His destination lay in the lower corner of the square, where taverns and inns existed in profusion. There, if he understood

Barca correctly, he would find the Medjay. The Judaean cursed himself for not rising before dawn to intercept them at the ferry.

Ahead, in a stall erected near the wall of the Mansion of Ptah, Matthias caught a glimpse of an arm bearing a tattooed *uadjet*. Eyes accustomed to picking details out of the crowded heavens spotted others, too, in a variety of forms: amulets on thongs, bronze and gold buckles, lapis inlays. Their owners were milling about, studying the crowd, reconnoitring. As he drew closer, a voice rose above the clamour of the bazaar.

'You don't understand! I don't want to buy your whole shipment! Just enough for my men!'

An exasperated Egyptian voice answered. 'No! It is you who do not understand! I sell *amphorae* of wine, not *bowls*! There are taverns aplenty down the street!'

The sight of the small merchant in his starched white kilt, his beaded collar flashing in the morning sun, striking a defiant pose against the lean and dusty Canaanite, Ithobaal, nearly sent Matthias into spasms of laughter. He could tell the greying old Medjay had about exhausted his boundless stores of patience. As Matthias approached, Ithobaal's hand had strayed toward his sword hilt.

'Peace, Ithobaal! Peace! Do not kill him, for he knows not what he does! Were I you, master merchant, I would reconsider selling a few juglets

130

of your wares. I have seen the Medjay stake a man out in the sun for a lesser insult.'

Ithobaal glanced at Matthias, a twinkle in his eye.

The merchant paled, sweat popping out on his brow. 'M-Medjay?'

'Indeed,' Matthias said, touching the golden symbol inlaid in the obsidian pommel-stone of Ithobaal's sword. 'This is not the mark of a priest of Horus.'

'I . . . How much wine do you need?'

Ithobaal grinned. 'Enough for twenty men.' The merchant scurried off to locate a fitting vintage. Ithobaal drew Matthias aside. 'It is good to see you, friend Matthias. Still an adherent of the grape, I hope?'

Laughing, the Judaean nodded, clasping Ithobaal's hand. 'Only if you're still the voice of reason.'

'Precious little reason in our being here,' Ithobaal said. 'Where's Barca? Have you seen him?'

'Not since last night, though I doubt it not that the six men slain in the Foreign Quarter a few hours gone is his handiwork. He's got it in his head to organize the resistance against the Greeks.'

Ithobaal's face darkened. 'Damn it! I told him this would happen! I told him we were stepping into a nest of scorpions!'

'Before he left, he asked that I find you and offer you sanctuary in my home.'

'You're generous, friend Matthias, though unlike Barca, I would not deign put you at risk.'

The merchant returned and plucked at the Judaean's robe. 'S-Sir? The price is . . .'

'Price? These are soldiers of Pharaoh. Submit your cost to the Overseer of the Army and you will be reimbursed, as always.' Matthias glanced at Ithobaal. The Canaanite, lost in thought, tugged at his lower lip with his thumb and forefinger. 'Is that not correct, Ithobaal?'

Ithobaal glanced up. 'Forget the wine.'

The merchant breathed a sigh of relief. Ithobaal continued.

'He's playing with our lives this time, Matthias. I'm ordering the men to split up, to find somewhere and stay out of sight. I'll accompany you, and together we'll await Barca.' He turned to gesture to the Medjay when a distraction at the far end of the square caught his eye. Matthias followed his gaze.

A squad of hoplites entered the bazaar from the north end, using their brightly polished shields to part the crowd. Their helmets were lowered; their faces blank, expressionless bronze. Not even their eyes were visible.

'I don't like this,' Ithobaal said.

The Medjay fanned out.

The Greeks mimicked their manoeuvre, shields ready, spears cocked over their right shoulders. Bleats of terror rose from the men and women who packed the bazaar. They stampeded away from the hoplites. A child screamed.

Ithobaal drew his sword. 'The die is cast now, brothers! They're on to us! We'll have to cut our way free!'

Matthias stammered, colour draining from his face. 'Ithobaal?'

'Get clear if you can!' the Canaanite said, jaw clenched. 'I'm sorry, Matthias!'

A man stepped to the front of the Greek line. He jacked his helmet back, revealing a long, sinister face. 'I am Lysistratis,' he said. 'I'm placing you men under arrest for the murder of Idu, son of Menkaura, and for being in league with the Persians! Do you yield?' A murmur of disbelief rose from the onlookers.

'Liar!' Ithobaal snarled. 'We've only just arrived in Memphis. If you would find murderers and Persian sympathizers, it would be wise to look among your own ranks!'

'Then, you plan to offer resistance?'

'No, I plan to tear your lying heart out!' Ithobaal held his sword ready. All along their ragged line, the Medjay readied their weapons. The proud Horus-eye symbols they wore gave the hoplites a moment's hesitation as they recalled the reputation of the desert-fighters. The air crackled with tension.

'Good,' Lysistratis smiled. 'I hoped you would have some fight left in you. Archers!'

From rooftops on each side of the bazaar Ithobaal saw dozens of figures rise up, men of Crete in soft felt caps and leather tunics. Bronze-heads glittered in the sun. He had a sinking feeling in the pit of his stomach. 'Damn you, Hasdrabal Barca!'

At a gesture from Lysistratis, the peltasts opened fire.

The hypostyle hall of the temple of Neith stayed cool in the rising heat, the gloom pierced by thin shafts of sunlight that gave the carved columns a haunting depth. A lesser priest closed the door in their wake, leaving Phanes and Callisthenes alone in the cavernous hall.

'I am confused,' Callisthenes said. Phanes arched an eyebrow. The merchant continued. 'Why would Barca risk his life for an old man like Menkaura? It makes no sense.'

'Actually, it is an almost flawless strategy,' Phanes said, stepping close to a column to inspect a row of deeply cut hieroglyphs. 'Barca doesn't have the manpower to interfere with my plans, so what does he do? He seeks out those who already stand opposed to me. Who is Menkaura?'

'An old man?' Callisthenes said, brows knitting. 'A holdover from an earlier time?'

'No, my friend. You're thinking too traditionally. Menkaura is a legend, the Desert Hawk of Cyrene. As a general under Apries, he was dealt his most shattering defeat by Greeks. That makes him a legend with an old score to settle. He is a *symbol,* Callisthenes.'

'I agree, general.' A figure stepped from the shadows.

Phanes' eyes narrowed. 'Ujahorresnet, isn't it?'

The priest nodded, his golden pectoral glittering in a shaft of sunlight. He wore the traditional long kilt and over this, draped across his shoulders, the gold-fringed leopard skin of a high priest. His staff cracked imperiously on the tiled floor. 'If anyone can inflame Memphis against you, it is Menkaura. Barca knows this. He's raising an army against you.'

'An army?' Phanes said, sneering. 'A rabble of artisans, more like! Faugh! Let him waste his time recruiting malingerers and malcontents. What I wonder, priest, is what interest is it of yours?'

Ujahorresnet smiled thinly. 'It is well known but little spoken that you covet the crown of Egypt; barring that, you'd readily serve the Persians as satrap of the Nile valley. I want to help you in your quest for power, general. I will give Cambyses the tacit approval of the temples of Neith, Amon, and Ptah. We will stand behind his bid for the throne by not hindering him. Once the Persian is firmly ensconced, I and my fellow priests will elevate him to Pharaoh: titulary, ritual, everything. The people will see that his rise was the will of the gods, and that is the road to being accepted by all of Egypt. For arranging this, his debt to you would be phenomenal.'

Phanes grunted. 'You would do this? Guarantee it?'

'It will have the permanence of stone.'

'Why?' Callisthenes said. 'Why would you aid Cambyses? And what price will we have to pay for it?' His mind reeled. A coalition of priests in league with the Persians? Though it taxed his skill, his bland expression did nothing to betray the turmoil that raged inside.

'There are times when weak rulers, weak dynasties, need to be invigorated by foreign incursions,' Ujahorresnet said. 'My people need the fire and pride of the Persian. His people need the piety and simplicity of the Egyptian. As for you and I, Phanes, I think we can both benefit from an alliance such as this. For myself, I ask a small favour. I want Hasdrabal Barca.'

'Better to ask for the sun or the moon,' Callisthenes muttered.

Phanes looked sidelong at the priest. 'Why do you want him?'

'That is personal. It is none . . .'

'None of my business?' Phanes snarled. 'I disagree. Should I decide to capture Barca, it will cost some of my men their lives. I'll not send them down to Hades for no reason. Answer the question.'

Ujahorresnet met his gaze coolly and evenly. 'You're familiar with Barca's past?'

'Only in passing,' Phanes said, frowning. 'A merchant's son from Tyre, I think. His father was high in Pharaoh's favour before his death.'

'Yes. Death is the central theme of Barca's existence, general. As with any tragedy, there was a girl, a lively and impressionable young woman of the finest blood. She fell under the charm of his foreign ways, and they were married soon after.' The priest's face grew dark, his eyes clouded. 'His young bride was a woman of immense . . . *appetite*. After Barca inherited his father's business, his interests kept him away many nights. Naturally, the girl took a lover. He was a Greek soldier in service to Pharaoh. Their dalliance grew passionate and heated, and I believe there was some talk of a future that did not include her young husband. Such is the fickle nature of women. Anyway, Barca grew suspicious of his bride and contrived to slip home one night when he was not expected. He caught her in the Greek's embrace and, in a fit of rage, slew them both.'

Phanes whistled, glancing at Callisthenes. 'So, he is only a man, after all.'

'He is a man,' Ujahorresnet said, 'but a man steeped in blood. Slaughter has become second nature to him. After all, if a man can murder his own wife, then taking the life of a stranger is of little consequence.'

Phanes turned and strolled around a column, studying the detail. 'Fine story. Still, it's not an answer. I grow impatient, priest. Why . . .'

It was Callisthenes who answered. 'The girl.'

'Yes!' the priest said, trying to contain the passion in his voice, the anger. 'She was my daughter!'

A slow smile crept across Phanes' face. He could see the hand of Pythian Apollo in all this. 'Then the blood-price for her life will be nothing less than the throne of Egypt. Callisthenes, see if you can locate Barca. He's in Memphis, so I trust your spies can weed him out.'

Callisthenes nodded. A kernel of an idea took root in the back of the merchant's mind. Embryonic, but well worth exploring. Allies, he reckoned, could be found in the least likely of places.

'No need,' Ujahorresnet said. 'Mine have already found him. Barca entered sometime during the night and immediately sought out a familiar face, a Judaean astrologer named Matthias ben Iesu. The two have had contact in the past. Barca dwells on the Street of the Chaldeans, under the Judaean's roof.'

'What if he won't be taken alive?' Callisthenes said. 'From what I've heard, this Barca is not one to submit willingly. What if he leaves us no other choice?'

'What about it, priest? If Barca is killed, will you renege on your word?'

Ujahorresnet smiled. 'Dead or alive, I will honour my end of our bargain. I would prefer alive, but if you must kill him, then kill him slowly.'

Barca awoke with a start. The room was quiet; the sounds of late afternoon trickled through the narrow window: voices raised in greeting and laughter, the clatter of a chariot. From somewhere, he heard the staccato *plop* of water. The smell of roasting meat reminded him he had not eaten since the day before.

Barca rubbed his eyes. *How long have I slept?* He stretched and flexed, working the muscles of his arms and back. His joints felt like someone had split them open and poured bronze filings into the sockets. He stood and glanced out the window. The workers were gone and long shadows striped the distant fields.

By now, Matthias should have his men sequestered someplace safe. He could imagine the look of disapproval on Ithobaal's face, his head tilted forward, brows beetled, when he heard the tale of the night before. Barca was positive he would be forced to endure a new round of groaning and griping.

The door opened. Barca turned, expecting to see the pained face of his host, Weni. Instead, Jauharah entered the room. She averted her eyes, but Barca could tell they were red and swollen. She balanced a tray on her hip, a tray heaped with bread, meat, and beer.

'I-I thought you might be hungry,' she said.

'I am. Thank you,' Barca said, taking the tray from her and returning to the divan. He tore into the food with unaccustomed relish. 'Where's Menkaura?'

'He left some hours ago, and he said it would be best if no one knew where he had gone. He told me to tell you that I would be overseeing . . .' she choked, her voice thick with emotion. Jauharah shifted, tears welling in her eyes. 'He . . . He asked me t-to . . .'

'To see to the funerary arrangements for his family?'

Jauharah nodded. 'He said you would understand.'

Barca said nothing, his eyes fixed on something only he could see. He understood completely. An old soldier, Menkaura put his duty to country above his own personal obligations. He would organize, and he would fight. It was more than Barca had hoped for, and yet . . .

Jauharah cleared her throat. 'I know something is about to happen. Something violent. I . . . I want to help. Is there anything . . . ?'

Barca eyed her critically. 'You can listen to those around you, those you come into contact with. Learn what they know. Anything, even something trivial, could be used as a weapon against the Greeks.'

'Listen?' She stared at the floor, her jaw tight. 'While the men march off to fight? Men who have lost nothing?'

'It's no easy thing to lose a family. I understand this. You must understand that whatever we undertake here will not be done out of a desire for revenge. This is not a personal crusade, no matter what you may think.'

'Tell me it's not personal after they kill someone you love!' The vehemence in her voice startled her. She blinked back tears and struggled to get herself under control. 'T-The sage Ptah-hotep wrote that a person should only speak when invited. I have worn out my invitation. With your leave, I will go. I have much listening to do.'

Barca held up a hand. 'I understand your anger, but it's misplaced on me, as is your role of a petulant slave. If you don't like my opinion, then tell me. If you have pressing business, then go to it. You need not wait for my permission to speak or to leave.'

'I'm sorry,' she said, bowing slightly. She opened the door, stopped with one foot across the threshold. 'Thank you for everything,' she said, her voice frosty, and then she was gone.

That woman had fire, Barca had to admit. Fire and strength on a magnitude that surprised even the Phoenician. Enraged, she would be a match for any man. Barca hoped she had the self-control not to go out and do something foolish. He sat in the fading light and thought about another spirited woman, a woman twenty years dead.

𓂀 𓏏 𓊖 𓀂 𓏺

It was a massacre. Phanes walked among the bodies, Lysistratis at his side. A smile twisted his perfect lips. 'So, these were the feared Medjay,' he said. 'How easily they were disposed of.' He spotted movement: an old soldier clawing toward the hilt of his sword. Arrows pierced his limbs and stood out from between his ribs. Phanes reached his side, kicking the Medjay's sword out of reach. 'Your leader,' he said. 'Where is he?'

Eyes filled with a terrible hate, Ithobaal raised himself on his elbows and spat blood at the Greek's foot.

Phanes gestured, and the Spartan slit the old man's throat.

'Kill the rest of their wounded.'

'Who is this Judaean you seek?' Lysistratis said, wiping blood from his knife on the Medjay's kilt.

'A man of little consequence who knows far too much for his own good.'

'Think he's here?' Lysistratis glanced around. A few bystanders had been hit along with the Medjay. A sobbing child crawled to his mother, her body riddled with arrows. Others were being pulled to the fringes of the bazaar. In all, the losses were acceptable. 'Had I known . . .'

'You did well, Lysistratis. Not a man under your command suffered so much as a splinter. Excellent. As for the Judaean, he is here. Servants of our new-found ally followed him from his home.'

Hands clasped behind his back, the Greek stepped over the dead and dying to enter the stall of a wine merchant. An Egyptian lay face down across his wares, an arrow standing out a hand's breadth from the back of his skull. Another man lay on the ground.

Phanes smiled. It was the Judaean.

An arrow gored his hip; a second shattered his kneecap. Fear clouded his eyes as he stared up at Phanes. Fear and pain.

142

'Greetings, Matthias ben Iesu. I have some dire questions that need answers.'

At dusk, Barca slipped from Weni's home and ghosted through the streets. An odd sense of expectancy tinged the air, a feeling of oppression and fear. He wondered how the Greeks reacted to finding their dead. Had they put some sort of curfew in place?

Corners that should have thronged with people were deserted; houses were dark and silent. It was as if Memphis held its breath and waited for the axe to fall.

Barca returned to the Judaean's without incident. At one time a garden thrived at the rear of the house, a holdover from a time when this part of Memphis boasted numerous mansions and villas. He paused at the base of a low wall of flaking stucco, listening. Hearing nothing, the Phoenician bounded up, caught the crumbling stone coping, and swung himself over the wall as lightly as a man mounting a horse. He dropped to the earth, scimitar half-drawn, and took in his surroundings with a glance.

A willow tree scrabbled through the hard-packed earth, gleaning a twisted existence from the dead black soil. Pottery shards crunched under foot as Barca crept past empty stalls of mud brick and wood that once housed a collection of potted plants. A skeletal grapevine hung from an arbour like an unburied corpse. Nothing moved; the air, warm and thick, bore the stench of decay. A light burned in an upper window of the house. The lack of sound disturbed Barca, as did the lack of movement. Even if his men lurked inside, Ithobaal would have posted sentries on the roof or in the garden, yet Barca saw no one.

Frowning, the Phoenician pushed open the rear door, the crack of its warped wooden hinge-pins explosive in the silence. From his left, ambient light filtered down a flight of mud brick stairs, built as an extension of the wall. In the heyday of his wealth, Matthias had surrounded himself with opulence, with rugs and hangings, with furniture hand-carved from precious woods, and with vessels of alabaster and gold. Now, Barca found the extent of his friend's poverty heartbreaking. Matthias kept this part of his house sparse, the floor bare save for a scattering of cushions and a low table strewn with the scraps of papyrus and ostraka scrounged from temple refuse heaps.

Where were his men?

A strange smell permeated the house. It floated down the stairs, tickling Barca's nose. It reminded him of seared meat, though subtly different. The Phoenician padded to the stairs. The upper floor was as bleak as the rest of the house. The only sign that the place was occupied at all came from Matthias' bedchamber. A curtain covered the doorway; light spilled out from around it. Eyes narrowing to slits, Barca used the tip of his blade to push the curtain aside. The Judaean's sleeping place reflected his love of the heavens. A riot of loose papyrus, ostraka, and clay tablets depicted the night sky from every point of the compass. That stench . . . Its strength increased as the Phoenician crossed the threshold of the bed-chamber.

The skin between Barca's shoulder blades prick-led; the hair stood up on the back of his neck. He spun to his left, sword extended, and felt his stomach tighten.

A man hung against the wall, his body held erect by thick bronze spikes driven through his wrists and ankles. His crucified form had been savagely tortured, his limbs broken, his face and eyes ruined. Flames had seared away his hair and beard, and a mixture of blood and liquified fat seeped through ruptures in his charred skin. There was something familiar about him. Realization struck the Phoenician, a hammer that cracked his soul.

The thing on the wall was Matthias ben Iesu.

'Who did this to you?' Barca whispered, staring at the body of his friend. The Greeks, Barca reckoned. They must have discovered Matthias was aiding the Medjay and tortured him for information. *But how?* Barca could not fathom it, but they knew he was in Memphis. Phanes would hunt him, a lethal game of cat and mouse. By all the gods! If that was the game he wanted, Barca would oblige him.

Sickened, the Phoenician turned away, looking for something to cover the body with. He would have to pry the spikes out with his sword. After that, he would find Ithobaal and . . .

'Barca!' bellowed a Greek voice from the street.

The Phoenician sprang from the bedchamber and peered out of one of the windows overlooking the Street of the Chaldeans. Torches flared, reflecting off the polished armour of a squad of hoplites. More were pouring from the adjacent buildings. One man stood apart from the rest, his armour silver-inlaid.

Phanes.

'Your friend, the Judaean, was a man of remarkable valour. I couldn't tell if he spoke the truth when he said you had twenty more men with you. I only counted nineteen corpses in the bazaar. Oh, well. I'm afraid I had to get a bit . . . rough with him, in the end. I offer you one chance to save yourself. Swear allegiance to me, pledge your blade to my service, and you just might walk out of this with your hide intact! Time grows short! What is your answer?'

So, that was it, then? Ithobaal and the others were dead, too. Dead because they trusted him. Barca bowed his head. In the after-world, twenty new souls occupied the Scales of Justice, swinging the balance farther toward the jaws of damnation. Twenty new souls cried out for vengeance.

To answer their call, Barca needed a way out. Anticipating his arrival, the Greeks removed the wooden stairs that led up to the rooftop terrace, leaving behind fragments only. The windows were too narrow for him to squeeze through. The back door?

'Barca?'

A quick glance revealed soldiers streaming toward the front of the house. Damn them! The Phoenician bolted down the stairs and hurtled for the back door, for the garden and the tangled alleys beyond. The sound of splintering wood brought him skidding to a halt. Over his shoulder, he watched as the front door exploded inward.

Hoplites, silhouetted by the orange glow of torches, poured through the breach. There were four of them in the vanguard, shields held at eye level. Others crowded at their backs. They were armed with hardwood clubs instead of spears.

Phanes wanted him alive.

'It's over!' a hollow voice said. 'Throw down your sword! We . . .' The hoplite never finished; he never knew what killed him.

Something bloody, vengeful, and utterly inhuman raged from the dark recesses of Barca's soul, filling his veins with a lust for rich, frothy gore. The thing that seized control of his body, the Beast, thrived on pain. It thrived on carnage and chaos and bodies torn asunder. Its strength flooded his limbs. Barca loosed a savage howl as he threw himself on the hoplites. Their armour, their training, their discipline, all amounted to nothing in the face of the Phoenician's elemental fury. His blade licked out, slashing through bronze and bone. A head leaped skyward, riding a fountain of blood. In the tight confines of the doorway, the Greeks could not bring their clubs to bear; their shields clanged against the door frame, against one another, useless. Men staggered and fell back.

Without losing stride, Barca turned from the thrashing hoplites and hurled himself at the rear door. He ducked his head, his body knotting into a compact mass of muscle and sinew as he struck shoulder first. The aged, dry wood blew apart under the impact, and Barca rolled cat-like to his feet, cursing.

Soldiers were scaling the garden wall.

There were too many of them. Barca whirled to his right. If he could make it to the top of the wall, he could snag the lower edge of the window and use it as a ladder up to the roof. Once atop the house, the Phoenician could escape across neighbouring rooftops. A desperate gamble . . .

Greeks pounded toward him. Shouts and cries grew in volume. A half-dozen steps and Barca bounded into the air, swinging onto the wall. He crouched there for a split second, ape-like, before flinging his scimitar up onto the roof. Powerful muscles drove his body after it. Barca leapt, twisting, catching the window sill with his fingertips. He tottered there for an instant before the mud brick of the window casing crumbled under his weight. Arms flailing, Barca plummeted, unarmed, into the midst of the Greeks.

The game was over. It was time to die. Barca resolved not to sell his life cheap.

Men went down under his weight. He grabbed

a helmet crest and slammed a bronze clad skull into the ground. A knee shattered under his crushing heel.

'Back!' a voice roared above the din. 'He's mine!'

Barca sprang to his feet. Like well-trained dogs the hoplites backed away, forming a circle. Lysistratis stepped forward, sheathed his sword, and methodically stripped off his armour.

'I've heard of you, Phoenician! You're rumoured to be the best fighter in Egypt, bar none. Faugh! A reputation gleaned fighting desert rats is no reputation at all! I'm willing to match my pure Spartan blood against the thin eastern piss flowing through your veins any day! Come!'

Without bluff or bluster, Barca hurled himself at Lysistratis. Here were two savage fighters: one the scion of a warrior culture, the other born to it naturally, both evenly matched in height and size. Fists hammered flesh as the two danced together, then sprang apart, their long shadows alien in the wan torchlight.

In that instant of contact, Lysistratis encountered something that left him chilled and shaking. He encountered a man stronger and faster than himself. A flurry of punches rocked the Phoenician's head back; Barca's riposte shattered the Spartan's nose and very nearly broke his neck.

Back and forth they went. Sweat and blood poured down the Spartan's face; his eyes burned with hate. No blow, no matter how powerful, could slow Barca's assault. He fought in a single-minded frenzy that would not abate until one of them lay broken and bleeding on the ground. It was not like fighting a man – it was like fighting a creature of elemental rage.

In desperation, Lysistratis drew a knife from his belt.

The timbre of the fight changed, then. No longer did Barca dart in and out, fists cocked and flying. He circled, wary, his weight shifting to the balls of his feet. His eyes narrowed to slits and murder danced in their dark depths.

The end came after a moment's respite. A heartbeat passed as the two men glared at one another across the intervening space. Then their bodies were in motion once again. Jab. Block. Backpedal. Momentum carried them against the wall. Lysistratis slashed at Barca's face, a feint the Phoenician had to twist to avoid. The Spartan saw his opening and lunged.

A slower man would have been impaled, but Barca wrenched his torso, drawing the Spartan into a close embrace. Lysistratis watched his blade rip through the Phoenician's side. In the same instant, Barca's iron-hard fist streaked toward his temple. That blow had the whole of Barca's weight behind it, and it connected with a sound like an eggshell crushed underfoot.

It was the last sound Lysistratis of Sparta would ever hear. He flopped to the ground with the side of his head caved in. Barca drew a breath, clutching his side . . .

. . . and reeled as something smashed into the

base of his skull. He went to his knees. Greeks swarmed over him. A foot lashed out, catching him under the chin. The sky wheeled as the ground rushed up to meet him. Barca struggled at the edge of the abyss. A ring of faces, cold and merciless, watched as the Beast fled, watched as the darkness rose up to envelop him . . .

7

CITY OF THE DEAD

Torchlight danced, striping the walls of the tomb orange and black, animating the exquisite carvings. The spacious burial chamber, a sign of great wealth, held only a granite sarcophagus. Grave goods should have littered the floor: furniture, statuary, jars of precious oils and wines, jewellery, cosmetics, figurines of servants and scribes. Everything the deceased needed to continue a pleasurable existence in the afterlife would have been provided. But, the allure of such wealth lying unguarded proved too much for some men to bear. Over the centuries, robbers took everything they could carry, leaving only the sarcophagus and a few shards of broken pottery.

And the carvings on the walls.

Three men sat in conclave, watching Menkaura in rapt silence. The old man strolled the perimeter of the chamber, studying the reliefs, the true wealth of the tomb. Scenes from the *Book of the Dead* were mixed with details from the life of the man interred here, an architect of some note.

With a finger, Menkaura traced the hieroglyphs: *Homage to thee, Osiris, Lord of eternity . . .*

One of the men cleared his throat, a nervous gesture amplified by the close confines of the tomb. Menkaura turned and met their curious stares.

'Why have you called us here?' said Ibebi. He was a tall man, broad of shoulder, with skin the colour of dark copper. His duties as master of the royal wharfs kept him impossibly lean and fit for a man of his years. He glanced around at his companions. 'It could mean our heads if the Greeks find us!'

'We have lived in the shadow of these Hellenes for far too long,' Menkaura said. Torchlight played across his features, giving his age-worn face a merciless cast. 'They strut through the streets as if they rule Egypt, not serve her. Their arrogance sickens me, and tonight it comes to an end.'

Word of the massacre had reached Menkaura, who bided his time among the tombs and monuments of the necropolis at Saqqara. The word, borne by his young kinsmen, was one of outrage. The Greeks had shot arrows into the crowded bazaar! A seething wave of righteous anger rolled through Memphis. Men clamoured for insurrection, shook their fists and spat at the mention of the Greeks.

'What of the Phoenician?' Menkaura asked.

Ibebi shook his head. 'They captured him alive.'

'We must do this alone, then.'

'What are you saying?' This from Hekaib, who served as supervisor of the royal building projects. He was a squat fellow, spindly-legged with a grotesque swag-belly. 'We're no match for the Greeks!'

'Hekaib is right. We're old men, Menkaura,' said the merchant, Amenmose. He wore his wealth like a badge of honour: golden pectoral, kilt of the finest linen, gemstones glittering in the hilt of his knife. Despite this display of cultured softness, his scarred body yet retained its strength, its flexibility. Thick silver eyebrows, flecked with black, knotted in a troubled scowl. 'Our days of glory are long past. The Greeks have superior arms, superior training, and superior numbers. Even in my prime I would have been hesitant . . .'

'In your prime, I watched you cut through the men of Cyrene like a scythe through grain!' Menkaura said. 'And you, Hekaib, did you not fight in the vanguard at Sardis? And was it not you, Ibebi, who led the first wave of marines against the Libyan pirates of the Plinthine Gulf? Yes, we are old men, but tales of our doings still stir the blood of our younger kin – our nephews, our cousins, our sons. They watched the massacre in the Square of Deshur. Look in their eyes, and you'll see a desire for justice. With us or without us, they will fight. Without us, they will die.'

Menkaura let that sink in.

'My son's wife,' Ibebi hissed, 'was in Deshur. She took an arrow in the back. She likely won't live through another night. Her brothers are ready to fight, as are my sons. Menkaura's right. They need hands guiding them that have felt spear shafts and sword hilts before.'

Hekaib frowned. 'At Sardis, we fought to preserve an alliance I did not understand. We were willing to die for the homes of our allies. Can I do less for my own home?' He nodded at Menkaura. 'I will do what I can.'

Amenmose dismissed them with a wave. 'Given time, the Greeks will go away, just as the Assyrians did.'

Menkaura shook his head. 'No, my friend. Given time, the Greeks will destroy all we hold dear.'

'Can you be sure of this, Menkaura, or do you give voice to your grief?'

The old general bowed his head. 'My grief is boundless, Amenmose. My son, your friend, did not deserve to die, not like that. Though as expansive as my grief is, my outrage will not be denied.'

Amenmose hedged. 'What chance do we have without the Phoenician? If they can take him – him! – what chance would a gaggle of old men have?'

'True, the Phoenician is a killer like no other. He saved my life, I owe him that, but he saved me for his own purposes. If death is his portion, then so be it. I will mourn him. Yet, the Phoenician is one man. We,' Menkaura's gesture encompassed the tomb and beyond, 'are a nation. Two thousand

Greeks cannot stop a nation, Amenmose. The choice is yours. Will you stand with us?'

Amenmose folded his arms across his chest, his head bowed in thought. 'If we do this thing and fail, we will be hunted men, or dead. I have not worked my entire life only to lose everything at the end.'

'When the Greeks take everything, Amenmose, will you be better off, or worse?' Menkaura leaned across the sarcophagus, towering over the merchant. 'When they drag your daughters off to slake their lusts, will you be better off, or worse? When your grandsons are castrated and sent to service a Greek tyrant, will you be better off, or worse? There are no guarantees in this, Amenmose. None. We all stand to lose our lives, and more. But what do we stand to lose under Phanes' thumb?'

Amenmose smiled wearily. 'You've not lost your gift for the game, have you, my old friend? I will stand with you, though I do so with a heavy heart.'

Menkaura straightened. His eyes shone like glittering onyx. 'Then it is decided. Return to your homes and spread the word, but silently. Ibebi, we will need weapons; spears, swords, whatever you can get your hands on. Hekaib, from you I need intelligence, anything your long ears can discover about the Greeks – their names, their families, their whores. Amenmose, you and I will recruit fighters from the young men, from the old veterans, and from those who have had their fill of Greek arrogance.'

Menkaura knelt behind the sarcophagus. He moved aside a sand-coloured canvas, revealing a cache of swords, antique sickle blades gleaming in the torchlight. He tossed one to each man. Ibebi ran an appraising hand over the tarnished bronze. Hekaib caught his sword with more grace than his stunted frame implied. He stared at it like a long-lost friend. Amenmose shook his head sadly and laid his across his knee. They looked to Menkaura.

'Let them fear us for a change!'

👁 ⌇ ▯ 𓀙 𓏤

At first, there was nothing but darkness . . . His senses returned slowly, in small increments, like a blind, deaf mute inching his way from oblivion's edge. He was aware of voices, of the smell of charred wood, and of a fiery pain lancing through his side. Something rattled in the darkness, and he winced as a cool rag touched his fevered brow. He tasted blood; his limbs felt like granite.

Faces welled and ebbed in the darkness. Matthias, tortured and screaming. Ithobaal, writhing in gut-shot agony. Each of his men in turn, eyes rolling back in their skulls, tongues swollen and protruding. Barca, they howled. Barca, they cursed. Barca, they pleaded.

'Barca.'

Neferu, clad in gauzy silks, floated through the blackness. Her face, thin and pointed, bore a look of indescribable ecstasy. Dark hair floated around her like the snaky locks of a Gorgon. Ruby lips parted; her tongue darted out. Barca, she panted. Barca, she moaned. Barca, she screamed.

'Barca!'

Hasdrabal Barca stirred, feeling dried reeds crunch under his naked shoulders. His eyes fluttered open. He squinted. The light from a guttering torch knifed through his brain.

'Ah, the sleeper awakes!'

The voice came from nearby, distorted, hollow. He tried to struggle into a sitting position but could not move. His arms and legs were like wood. He tried to remember.

Tried . . .

'M-Matthias . . . ?' he grunted, his tongue thick. He rolled to the side and spat blood.

Derisive laughter. 'No, not Matthias. I'm afraid your Jew didn't make it.' A pause. 'Help him up.'

Barca felt hands under his shoulders, levering him into a sitting position, his back against a wall. The room was hazy, indistinct. Colours swam before his eyes. He clenched his teeth and tried to focus.

Slowly, the room came into view.

In the dim torchlight, Barca could make out few details. The walls were yellow sandstone, undecorated, the blocks rough and unfinished. Reeds carpeted the dirt floor. A door lay across from him, its stout timbers bound in green and pitted bronze, and cool air flowed from its barred grate. A man stood on either side of him; a third sat to the left of the door, his cuirass glittering in the uneven light. The smile on his lips dripped mockery. Phanes.

'I'm surprised you didn't kill me,' Barca croaked. 'If our situations were reversed, you'd be waking up in hell right now, like that Spartan bitch of yours.'

Phanes gestured magnanimously. 'That's where we differ, Phoenician. In my eyes it's not personal. Only conflicting senses. Your sense of duty conflicted with my sense of ambition. Ambition won, it's as simple as that. Lysistratis,' Phanes sighed. 'Lysistratis was a victim of your duty, my ambition. He will be missed.'

Barca glared at the Greek. 'You've not won,' he said, 'so long as I have breath in my lungs.'

Phanes chuckled, propping his chin on his fist. 'When I see you, I'm reminded of a dog my father had when I was a boy, on our farm in Halicarnassus. It was a scruffy, little black hound; easily the most stubborn beast I have ever seen. It had this patch of ground on a hilltop, at the base of an ancient oak, where it liked to take naps. Zeus have mercy on any poor soul foolish enough to want to sit in that hound's spot. Its hackles would rise, and it would howl and bay as though you'd put the bronze to it.

'Anyway, one summer my father allowed a band of mercenaries to set up shop on the crest of that hillock, to make the Carians think again before raiding our lands. They built their mess area right there under the oak. That dog, it went mad. Day and night it would harry those soldiers, growling, barking, gnawing at their legs when they got careless. They tried throwing stones at that dog. They tried burning it, whipping it – one even tried catching it in a rabbit snare. Nothing. That mangy cur became the bane of their existence. Finally, after they had all they could stand, the mercenary captain put an arrow through that dog's skull. It died for a patch of land no larger than a hoplite's shield.

'You're like that pup, Barca. A stubborn bastard who's willing to die over a piece of land . . . land that's not even yours! You're not Egyptian, so do you truly care who pays you to guard Egypt's borders?'

'I gave my word,' Barca said truculently.

'Your word?' Phanes laughed. 'By the gods! You sound just like Lysistratis! You would die for your word?'

'In this life, all a man has is his word. Not gold, not power, those are all fleeting, all illusions. The only real, tangible thing a man has is his word.'

'You truly believe that, don't you?' Phanes said. He shook his head sadly. 'This cult of honour . . . I'm afraid I'll never grasp it.'

'Grasp this, boy-fucker! You murdered my men, my friends! When I am free, I will hunt you down, wherever you hide! If it takes a thousand years, then so be it!'

'I concede,' said Phanes, 'that you would be far less trouble dead. But, I have struck a bargain with a gentleman highly placed in the Egyptian priesthood. In exchange for you, he will legitimize my new employer's bid for the throne. A small price to pay, really.' Phanes rose and opened the door to the cell. His men filed out. 'He's yours, priest. Do with him as you will.'

A figure stepped into the cell, robed, a dark cowl hiding his features. He walked over to Barca and stared. Barca saw the glimmer of teeth. Suddenly a foot lashed out, catching Barca in his wounded side. The Phoenician roared in agony as waves of pain coursed through him.

'I have been waiting to do that for twenty years, you son of a bitch!'

Barca's lips peeled back in a primal snarl. He knew the voice; hearing it again clarified many things, least of all how Phanes learned he was in Memphis. 'I'm surprised you have the stomach for this, Ujahorresnet!'

'You remember me? Good.' The priest drew back his cowl.

'How could I forget? You raised a cheating whore for a daughter!'

Phanes laughed. 'While I would love to stay, to witness such a heartfelt family reunion, I have much left to do. You're no fool, Barca, so I won't insult your intellect by asking if you sent word on to Sais. Amasis is coming, and I have no desire to be caught unawares. You are still planning to honour our bargain, aren't you, priest?'

'You have upheld your end in good faith,' Ujahorresnet said. 'Should your Persian master's bid for the throne meet with success, I will uphold mine.'

Phanes sketched an exaggerated bow. 'So be it. Shall I leave a squad of my men behind to ensure your safety?'

Ujahorresnet smiled. 'No need for that. Esna!'

The priest's agent entered the cell at his master's command, pulling a gauntlet over his right fist. He rubbed his hand across the polished bronze studs. Phanes turned to Barca.

'Farewell, Phoenician. You would have made a worthy adversary.' With that Phanes and his soldiers left the two Egyptians alone with their captive.

Barca snarled, straining against the ropes biting into his flesh.

'Shall we begin?' Ujahorresnet said.

Callisthenes moved quietly through the balmy night, clutching at his scarab amulet for protection. His eyes darted. Every noise sent a thrill down his spine; every shadow held menace. It was not a good night to be out, if you were Greek. Only the gravest necessity could have driven him from the safety of his villa.

He needed to speak to Menkaura.

Callisthenes had an inkling of where the old general might be hiding, but there existed a protocol in these matters. If he simply played his hunch and barged in, dawn would find a fresh Greek corpse steeping in the mud of the Nile. No. He had to do this the traditional way, which meant finding one of Menkaura's kinsmen with a sympathetic ear.

To get to Menkaura, he first had to get to Thothmes.

Lengths of coloured linen draped from pylons, fluttered from cedar poles. These bright festive touches stood in stark contrast against the grim mood of the people. Callisthenes passed pleasure houses and wine shops where men talked in hushed voices, fortifying their resolve with crock after crock of beer. Eyes watched him from darkened windows, and he heard sibilant curses hurled at him from open doorways. He had to find Thothmes . . .

Thothmes was an artisan, a painter of tombs for the temple of Ptah. His home reflected his prosperity. It was located in a peaceful quarter of the city, north of the great temple, on a street normally reserved for servants of the god. A low wall circled the grounds, and through the open gate, Callisthenes could see a well-kept garden, paths of crushed rock, and a stone-rimmed pool decorated in glazed blue tiles. The scent of lotus and jasmine spiced the cool night air. Callisthenes exhaled slowly, then plunged through the gate and up the path.

Before he had gone halfway, he saw a slave moving toward him, a thick-shouldered Egyptian in a heavy black wig, a knotted club in his fist. He glared at the Greek as if he were offal left at his master's door. 'Who are you, and what business do you have here?'

The merchant felt his anger rising. 'I am Callisthenes, and my business is none of your concern! Fetch your master, dog!'

The slave sketched a mocking bow, turned and made his way back to the house. Minutes drifted by. Callisthenes' nerves crackled; he felt like the whole of Memphis watched him. He was about to give up and go in search of another of Menkaura's kinsmen when the slave reappeared. Something about the fellow's toothy grin made Callisthenes uneasy.

'Out the gate and down the alley,' he said, 'follow the circuit of the wall until you reach a small, bronze-girt door. Rap thrice and wait. Thothmes will receive you there.'

Wordless, Callisthenes spun and did as he was instructed. Damn them! Time grew short. These games served no purpose. The alley narrowed; he had to twist his body in order to negotiate it. Time and the elements had eaten away at the mud brick walls, making them jagged and rough. Callisthenes cursed as he stumbled, abrading his hands on the pitted walls. Soon, though, the alley widened out and he found the door. He balled his fist and drew back to knock.

The crunch of a foot on sand gave him pause. He half-turned as a pair of figures sprang from the darkness. Callisthenes had time for a terrified bleat before their fists clubbed him to his knees.

'P-Please . . . !'

Calloused hands wrenched the Greek's head back, and he felt the icy touch of a knife blade at his throat. Callisthenes squeezed his eyes tight, knowing when he opened them again it would be as he crossed the river Styx.

The small door in the wall opened.

'What do you want, Greek?' a voice demanded. Callisthenes blinked.

Thothmes towered over the cowed merchant.

Tall and lanky, Thothmes possessed that quality in his eyes so often associated with artists; keen, penetrating, and tinged with madness. Immobile, his arms folded across his chest, the Egyptian glared at Callisthenes. 'What do you want?' he repeated.

Callisthenes swallowed, feeling the knife scrape his throat. 'I must speak with Menkaura.' He saw other men behind Thothmes, young and old, each sharing the same angry, hate-filled stare.

'What makes you think I know where Menkaura is?' Thothmes said. 'And if I knew, what makes you think I would tell you?'

'You know me, Thothmes!' Callisthenes pleaded. 'You know I would not have come to you if it weren't important!'

'Important for who?'

'For your people!' Callisthenes hissed. 'Damn it, man! I may be Greek, but I'm not in league with Phanes! I oppose all he stands for, though I'm not strong enough to do it openly. The Persians are coming, Thothmes! Menkaura will need every edge he can get to keep the garrison from ravaging Memphis! I have a plan that may benefit you, your people, and your country! But I must speak with Menkaura!'

'Are we too stupid to do our own thinking? Kill him, I say!' an old man said, jabbing a gnarled finger at Callisthenes. 'Arrogant bastard doesn't deserve to breathe!'

Thothmes rubbed his jaw with pigment stained fingers. 'You're a fool, Callisthenes. I do know you, which is all that is keeping you alive right now. Until today I had no quarrel with you. But, Sethos is right. All Greeks should be staked out in the desert and left to die! Why should you be treated any differently? Because you speak our tongue, wear our robes, sacrifice to our gods?'

'Take me to see Menkaura! If I'm playing you false, then kill me!' Callisthenes said with more valour than he felt.

Thothmes touched the knife at his belt. 'Do not tempt me. You are stupid as well as a fool if you presume Menkaura needs aid from a fat Greek merchant.'

'He doesn't need my aid, Thothmes,' Callisthenes said, 'but he does need Barca's, and I know where he is being held.'

'That's no great secret! The Phoenician's in the belly of Ineb-hedj, and if he yet lives, it is only because your brothers wish it!'

Callisthenes smiled, some small measure of his self-control coming back. 'He lives, and he is not in the White Citadel. The priest, Ujahorresnet, has him in the compound of the temple of Neith.'

'You jest!' the old man, Sethos, interjected. 'The priest . . . ?'

'There is a personal grudge between the two. In return for the Phoenician, Ujahorresnet has guaranteed the priesthood won't oppose Cambyses, should he seize the throne. Menkaura has seen this Phoenician fight. He knows what he is, and he knows you will need him for the coming battle,' Callisthenes said. 'Aid me in freeing him!'

Thothmes stared through the merchant, his eyes distant, clouded. 'The priest,' he grunted. 'We will have to deal with him, too. Abetting the enemy is a crime punishable by death. But, his punishment must come later. Our fight is with Phanes. With your kinsmen, Callisthenes. For all his skill, Barca is but one man, and one man is not enough to sway the course of a battle. If he dies, we will bury him with all due respect and honour. If he lives, we will free him when we apprehend the priest.'

'He saved your cousin's life!' Callisthenes said. 'Or have you forgotten?'

From his belt, Thothmes drew a knife and tossed it at the merchant's feet. 'Take this,' he said. 'If you oppose Phanes as you say, then smuggle this to the Phoenician. No doubt he will know how to use it. That is all the aid I can offer.'

Callisthenes stared at Thothmes, then scooped the knife up and spun. The slave moved to block his way, but a gesture from Thothmes stopped him.

'Let him go.'

Callisthenes stopped. 'Should I assume it would

be futile of me to seek out another of your brood in hopes of talking with Menkaura?'

'None will aid you, I swear it.'

'What if he tells Phanes about us?' Sethos said. The others at his back murmured their assent.

Callisthenes sighed, his brows furrowed. 'Don't worry, old man. I'll not divulge anything I know to Phanes. I did not lie when I said I opposed him. If it were in my hands, the commander's days in Memphis would be numbered.'

It was enough for Thothmes. 'Then go in good faith and do what you must. We will do what we must.'

With that, the Egyptians filed back through the small gate. The burly slave sneered at Callisthenes as he slammed it closed, punctuating the night with a sense of finality. The merchant stared at the knife in his fist. He would have to aid Barca on his own.

Callisthenes of Naucratis felt his knees go to jelly.

෴ ⚕ ▯ 𓀀 𓏺

The crack of leather on flesh echoed through the temple of Neith.

In the cell, which had begun its existence as a granary, Ujahorresnet watched dispassionately as Esna adjusted his gauntlet. The studded leather glistened in the wavering light. On the floor, Barca had drawn himself to his hands and knees, curling his body to protect his wounded side. He bled from a score of gashes; one eye was swollen shut. Ujahorresnet marvelled at his endurance. He fought on despite his wounds. Despite his pain.

'I cannot sleep,' Ujahorresnet said, 'without seeing my daughter's body as you left her, violated and exposed. Were you a father, you would understand the suffering you put me through. You would understand why I want you to suffer, in return. What she did was wrong, I admit. But that has been the way of women since the beginning of things. Did she deserve to be murdered?'

'Hades take you!' Barca spat. Esna leaned in and slammed his fist into the Phoenician's jaw. Barca's head rocked back; blood drooled from his split cheek. The fires of hate smouldering in his eyes flared brighter. 'Is that all you have, little man?' he said to Esna. 'On the border those little love taps would get you bent over a barrel and rooted senseless!'

Esna growled, punching Barca twice more in rapid succession.

When the Phoenician looked up, there was something different about him.

Ujahorresnet watched as a physical transformation washed over Barca. His face grew hard, like a bust carved of stone, and his eyes shrank to mere slits. His nostrils flared, and he grinned a death's head grin that sent chills down the priest's spine. Something inside him fought to get free. If it did loose itself, Ujahorresnet had little doubt it would paint the walls of the cell red with their blood. Perhaps the time had come to

169

end this session. There would be other days, other tortures.

The priest reached out to restrain Esna as Barca exploded.

Muscle and sinew creaked, straining against the biting ropes as Barca thrust upward. He rammed Esna with his shoulder, driving him against the cell door, then turned and hurled himself on Ujahorresnet.

Stunned, the priest could not move.

Barca struck him full in the chest, and they fell in a welter of thrashing limbs. Barca tucked his knees up, using the momentum of their fall to drive the breath from the Egyptian's lungs. There was enough slack in the rope for Barca to lever his hands apart, and enough space between his hands for him to wrap his fingers around Ujahorresnet's throat. The priest felt the life being squeezed out of him. Blackness, shot through with red, ringed his vision. The Phoenician cackled like a madman, bloody spittle and froth dripping from his jaws . . .

Esna loomed over them, pounding his gauntleted fist again and again into the side of Barca's head, driving his knee into his ribs. Barca sagged, his fingers losing their strength, and slumped to the floor.

'Merciful Neith!' Esna said, his chest heaving. He helped Ujahorresnet to his feet. The priest gasped for breath, his windpipe bruised, as he staggered to the door. Esna stared at Barca's prostrate form with a fear that bordered on the supernatural. 'Seth possesses him, lord. He is too dangerous to keep prisoner. Let me finish him!'

'No,' Ujahorresnet said, rubbing his throat. 'We must weaken him. Bring him not a scrap of food, Esna, and only half a cup of water a day. And beat him. Beat him until he begs!'

'This is madness, lord! Did you not see his eyes? Why tempt the gods so?'

'I want him to beg!'

Esna looked down at the Phoenician. His instincts screamed; he knew in the pit of his stomach he should grab an axe and hack the bastard's head off, vengeance be damned. This man was feral, a rabid dog. Toying with him was an invitation to disaster.

The priest must have read it in his eyes. 'If you cannot do it, Esna, I'll find another who can!' Ujahorresnet spun and reeled from the cell, leaving Esna standing alone with the Phoenician. His hand dropped to his knife hilt. No amount of gold was worth dying over.

8

INSURRECTION

The copper disc of the sun rose in the eastern sky, and with it came the spectre of Ares, of war. The shadow of the great god loomed over bazaar and bedchamber, casting a pall of despair despite the brilliant morning light. Phanes could feel the apparition at his shoulder as he walked the battlements of the White Citadel. He could feel it, and he drew strength from it.

'We must decide,' Phanes said. He stopped, turning to face the three men who attended him. Two were his *polemarchs*, Hyperides and Nicias; the third, Petenemheb, served as governor of Memphis. The Egyptian's sallow features bore the stamp of unending debauchery – spider veins on his cheeks and dark circles beneath his eyes – that not even thick cosmetics could hide. His fingers toyed with a pleat in his bleached white kilt. Phanes continued, 'Barca's meddling has brought an Egyptian army within striking distance of Memphis. Do we stay and fight, or do we cleave to our original plan and make for the western oases? We can put the decision off no longer. What say you . . . fight or flight?'

The men stirred. Pennons snapped and rustled in the breeze. One of the *polemarchs*, Nicias of Potidaea, a squat and ogrish veteran who wore his scars with pride, ran a hand through his tangled mass of hair. 'The men would prefer a fight, but the odds are stacked in Pharaoh's favour,' he said. 'His ground forces, alone, stand at twice our number if the scouts are to be believed. A mixed force of chariots and infantry. Add marines from the Nile fleet and the tally could easily triple.'

'A Hellene is more than a match for any three Egyptians,' said Hyperides of Ithaca, nicknamed *Kyklopes*, tilting his head to the left to stare at Phanes with his one good eye. A crock of flaming pitch, slung by a Tyrrhenian marine at Alalia, had ruined his once-handsome face. Patches of hair clung to the leprous tissue, giving the lean Ithacan a monstrous appearance.

'Against infantry, aye,' Nicias said, 'but the phalanx is powerless against a concerted charge of chariotry. I say we put Memphis to the sword and make for Siwa oasis. From there, we can strike all along the river until Cambyses arrives.'

'Kyklopes?'

Hyperides shrugged. 'Lead us to Tartarus, if you will, and I'll spit in Hades' eye.'

'Fight or flight,' Phanes muttered. He walked to the corner of the battlement, his commanders in tow. Ineb-hedj stood on a man-made hillock some fifty feet above the surrounding city. The white

173

limestone walls rose another forty feet above the crest of the hill, giving Phanes a panoramic view of the landscape. Below, traffic streamed along the Way of the Truth of Ptah. Artisans and tradesmen, field hands and fishermen, scribes and priests trudged past statues of Proteus and Rhampsinitus, Apries and Amasis, unaware that their fate lay on a knife's edge. 'If I were Amasis,' Phanes said, tapping the embrasure with his fingertip, 'I would try to land troops inside the temple, to use the enclosure wall to my best advantage. At the same time,' he turned, pointing west toward the pyramids of Saqqara, 'my chariot corps would approach from the opposite direction. The desired effect would be as two hands clapping together.

'But what if Amasis were unable to land infantry because we're in control of the quays? That would force them to dismount from their chariots and fight in the streets. Deshur would see another blooding.' Phanes turned, his eyes agleam. Nicias and Hyperides dangled on his next words. 'What do we have to lose by fighting? Our homes? Our lives? Faugh! All men die, but how many men have a chance to author their own destinies? If we do this thing, if *we* conquer Pharaoh, our reward will be more than the riches of Memphis, more than the gratitude of Cambyses. We will be masters of Egypt!'

Nicias whistled. 'That would stick in the Persian's craw.'

Petenemheb could hold his tongue no longer.

He gave a strangled cry and lurched forward, clutching at Phanes' tunic. 'Madness! This is madness! You cannot renounce your promise to the Great King! His wrath will lay waste to the land! Think of the suffering!'

'What of it?' Phanes knocked the governor's hand away. 'Have you lost your nerve, Petenemheb? Perhaps you should fortify yourself with more wine and leave the business of war to me!'

'You would kill every man, woman, and child in Memphis? You can't . . .'

Phanes' arm snaked out, catching Petenemheb by the throat. He hauled the Egyptian close, his temper flaring brighter than the morning sun. 'Oh, but I can, Petenemheb! I can! Shall I prove it to you? I will kill every living thing in Memphis, starting with you!' Cords of muscle writhed beneath Phanes' hide as he lifted the governor off his feet. With a desperation born of futility, Petenemheb clawed and fought. He may as well have grappled with a living statue for all the good that came of it. Phanes hurled him through an embrasure.

The governor's croaks turned to a wail of pure terror, ending abruptly with a sickening crunch some ninety feet below. Phanes and his captains peered over the battlement. Petenemheb's body lay broken at the foot of Pharaoh's statue. 'Foolish is the man who doesn't realize when his use is at an end,' Phanes muttered.

'Bloody Ares!' Hyperides said. 'Look there!'

Phanes and Nicias followed his gesture, looking south toward Deshur. A plume of smoke mingled with the morning haze. Even from this distance they could see knots of Egyptians milling about, their fists held aloft, sunlight flashing from slivers of metal.

'A riot,' Nicias spat.

'Menkaura's decided to show himself,' Phanes said. He fixed his captains with a chilling stare. 'Call out the phalanx. This has gone on long enough!'

Sunlight angled through a square-cut opening in the roof of the cell. Barca lay in the patch of warmth, staring up at the sliver of bright blue sky, his face a clotted mass of bruised and lacerated flesh. Ropes of woven hemp, saturated with blood, abraded his wrists and ankles. The gash in his side throbbed, and he imagined infection had already taken hold. It pained him to draw breath.

How long had he lain here? Three days? Four? He tried to count the times he had fallen unconscious, the healing touch of sleep broken by bouts of torture. A week? He could not focus, could not remember.

I will die here. Not his choice of deaths, true, but Barca had decided long ago that he would welcome Death however he came. Welcome him like a long-lost brother. They had come so close before, he and Death, brushing shoulders like strangers on a crowded street. Many nights – nights when the ghosts of the past became unbearable – Barca thought of inviting Death to his door, of putting an end to their game. Suicide, though, went against his grain. No, he wouldn't make Death's task any easier.

That task was nearly done.

Thirst raged through him like an unchecked fire. Deprived of nourishment, a man could last for a week, perhaps more. Deprived of water, however, his mortality became measurable in days. Even a man acclimatized to the heat and dehydration of the desert could not survive long without water. Barca recalled a fellow his Medjay had tracked through the desert east of Sile, a Bedouin slave taken in a raid on the villages of Sinai who slipped his shackles and escaped to the high sands. By the time the Medjay caught up to him, the wretch had gnawed open the veins in his wrists in hopes blood would quench his thirst. Barca reckoned that to be Ujahorresnet's plan. The old bastard wanted him mad with pain and thirst, insane enough to beg and plead and whimper.

'I will be damned,' Barca clenched his teeth, 'if I give him the satisfaction!' Groaning, the Phoenician rolled over and struggled to his knees. He lurched to his feet, his back against the wall. His head swam. Bile seared the back of his throat. Barca shook his head to clear it, and gritted his teeth against the waves of nausea. Time to see about getting clear of this cell. He had seen no other guards save that son of a bitch, Esna. Him Barca could dispose of easily, if only his hands were free.

From outside the door, he heard the scuff of a sandal on stone.

'I am surprised to see you upright,' Ujahorresnet said, peering through the grate in the door. 'Indeed, I half-expected to find you bled dry.'

'How's the throat?' Barca smiled, ghastly in the pale morning light.

The priest's nostrils flared. 'Do be considerate and try not to die too soon. That would cheat me of my hard-earned vengeance.'

Barca shuffled to the door. 'Explain something to me, old man. I thought you were a firm believer in the superiority of the Egyptian people. How is it that you're in bed with the Greeks? A traitor, no less?'

The priest's eyes were troubled. 'Grief drives a man down paths never contemplated.'

'Anger does the same,' Barca said. 'Believe it or not, I loved Neferu. You think I have no remorse . . .'

'Remorse? You?' Ujahorresnet laughed. 'Please! I am not a half-wit, Barca. I've peered into your soul and taken measure of your true self. You live to kill, to feel death rise up around you like a warm blanket. You're only truly alive when another man's blood spills at your feet. Remorse? That's as alien an emotion to you as love!'

Barca snarled. 'It's good you know me so well,

priest! And since you do, you know what I'll do to you when I'm free.'

'Cling to your false hopes,' Ujahorresnet said. 'You will die in that cell, and soon. However, since you are so full of venom, I will see about having Esna continue where he left off last night.'

'Send him quickly,' Barca said, a sneer twisting his lips. 'I would talk further with your lapdog!'

'We will see how light your mood is when you're broken and bleeding. I look forward to hearing your pleas for mercy.' Ujahorresnet stalked away.

Barca hobbled to the door and watched him cross the sunlit sward, vanishing inside the temple proper. Time was growing short. He had to quit these ropes and this cell. He glanced around, his eyes falling on the door frame beside him. The passage of time knapped the corners of the mud brick, making it as jagged and sharp as a flint spearhead. It just might work . . .

Blood trickled from his wrists as he worked the ropes against the serrated edge of brick, sawing despite the pain. He stopped for a moment, listening. Yes, he did hear a sound; a panted breath, a scuff of a foot. He pressed himself against the door and peered through the grate.

A fat man slipped through the morning shadows, his bald head gleaming with sweat. His eyes were painted Egyptian-fashion, and he was clad in a pleated linen robe. He could have been a priest or a merchant, but his attitude was one of stealth, of fear. Quivering, glancing each way, the man reached the door. 'Barca!' he hissed.

'You don't seem like an assassin,' Barca said. The fat man jumped, not expecting a reply from such close proximity.

'I'm no assassin. I'm a friend. Callisthenes, I am called.'

'I have no friends named Callisthenes and no friends who are Greek. What do you want? Have you come to taunt me?' Barca said.

Callisthenes shook his head. 'I bring you aid.' He held the haft of a knife to the grate. Barca's eyes narrowed. He sensed a trap. A cruel jest on Ujahorresnet's part to tease him with a small glimmer of freedom.

'Why?' Barca replied, slowly reaching for the weapon. 'Why would you risk your life to aid me, a man you've never met?'

'Honestly,' Callisthenes said, 'I look at it as not so much aiding you as thwarting Phanes. The land of Egypt should be ruled by Egyptians, not . . .'

'You're from Naucratis,' Barca said. He took the knife. It was a fine weapon, its blade the length of a man's forearm, both edges capable of splitting hairs. The carved ebony grip, capped with a bronze pommel, sent a sensual thrill through the Phoenician's body.

'How could you tell?'

'You men of Naucratis are more Egyptian than Greek,' Barca said. He slashed the ropes holding his wrists; knelt and freed his legs. Despite the pain, despite the dizziness, Barca felt a new strength surge through his limbs. He flexed his arms till his joints cracked. 'I never thought I would tell a Greek I am in his debt.'

Callisthenes smiled. 'Don't let it pain you overmuch.' He kept glancing around, fearing he would be detected. 'I must go. You can escape without further aid?'

Barca's eyes darkened. 'I think so. Tell me something, and quickly. Did Phanes lie when he said my Medjay were dead?'

'I am sorry,' Callisthenes said, nodding. 'They were slain in an ambush in the Square of Deshur. Not that it's any consolation, but that ambush galvanized the Egyptians against Phanes.'

Barca ground his teeth in anger. 'My score with him mounts by the second. Soon, I'll have to summon his shade from beyond the river and kill him twice just to break even!'

'I hope I am there to . . .' the Greek's breath hissed between his teeth. 'Someone's coming!'

👁 ⚱ 🏛 👤 𓏤

Smoke darkened the morning sky. Armed Egyptians choked the Square of Deshur, pressing close to watch the impromptu trial of a half dozen Greek soldiers. Menkaura had drawn them out by firing a barley wagon; his kinsmen subdued them with spear-butts and clubs as they sought to smother the blaze. Their officer had put up a fight, but Menkaura, clad in antique armour, proved unstoppable. The Desert Hawk strode like a conqueror up and down the line of kneeling captives.

'You stand accused!' Menkaura roared. 'Accused of crimes against the people of Egypt, against the Son of Ra himself!' He held his curved sword aloft; blood rained from the blade, showering the upturned faces with scarlet drops. 'We, who were once your victims, stand in judgement of you! And our judgement is death! Death to the traitors!'

A hundred throats caught up his cry. 'Death to the traitors!'

Their officer spat in defiance. 'Loose us! You wretched jackal! Loose us, I say! By all the gods! I will make sure each and every one of you pay for this!'

Menkaura laughed recklessly.

Near him, Amenmose, Ibebi, and Hekaib stood in a knot.

'I don't like this,' Amenmose hissed. 'We reveal ourselves too early.'

Ibebi shrugged. 'Menkaura came to me this morning, said we make our first move within the hour. He said our kinsmen would be enough for this strike and our bravery would turn our hundred into thousands by dusk.'

'Men are drawn to bravery, yes,' Amenmose said, 'but not to foolishness.'

Hekaib sidled close. 'What of the garrison? Will this commotion not draw their eye?'

Amenmose's face darkened. 'It will draw more than their eye! I guarantee they are mustering as we speak. If we're not careful, Deshur will see a second massacre. This reeks like week-old fish, my friends! Menkaura's thirst for Greek blood will kill us all!'

'Death to the traitors!' Menkaura wrenched back a Greek head and slashed his blade across the exposed throat. Blood fountained. Down the line he went, ripping through soft trachial tissues, severing engorged arteries. The bodies flopped and contorted, drowning in their own blood. The Greeks next in line muttered prayers to Zeus, to the archer Apollo, and to chaste Athena, making their peace before Menkaura's blade laid their throats open as well.

Last in line, the officer glared at the crowd, his eyes wild.

'Death to the traitors!' the crowd roared in approval.

Esna emerged from the temple proper, shading his eyes against the glaring sun. He scowled at the figure outside the cell door. 'What are you doing? Get away from that door!' His hand wrapped around the hilt of his knife.

Callisthenes did not miss a beat. He turned, smiling. 'Peace, good fellow. I am here at Phanes' request. The general was curious as to how your master's vengeance was faring. I thought I'd get in a few taunts of my own, since he is helpless.'

Esna looked Callisthenes over, his eyes narrowing with suspicion. 'One of Phanes' Greeks, eh? Well, tell your master lord Ujahorresnet's vengeance fares well. Indeed, you may stay if you like and witness it firsthand.'

Inside the cell, Barca listened as he crouched and looped the severed rope about his feet, then did the same with his wrists. He kept hold of the knife, angling it down his forearm. It would be all but invisible. He moved away from the door and leaned his body against the wall. He could still hear them.

'Delightful!' Callisthenes said. 'Then I can take the tale back to Phanes. That should warm his heart.'

Barca heard Esna chuckle, followed by a key rattling; wood scraped wood as the bolt slid back. The door swung open. Esna grunted.

'On your feet so soon? Well, we will have to remedy that.' He took the gauntlet from his belt and slipped it on. He glanced back at Callisthenes. 'My task is to weaken him. Lord Ujahorresnet wants him to be . . .'

'Esna,' Barca whispered.

The Egyptian turned and saw a severed length of rope drop to the ground. Where . . . ? Then, he saw the knife. Terror filled Esna's dark eyes. He backpedalled, his hand clawing at the hilt of his own blade. Behind him, Callisthenes slammed the cell door closed. 'No . . . !'

Barca sprang. His knife darted out with surgical precision, its keen edge slicing through the muscle and tendon of Esna's elbow. The Egyptian hissed in pain, tucking the wounded limb to his body. His half-drawn knife clattered to the floor.

Barca's other hand caught Esna by the throat. The Phoenician hurled his tormentor bodily across the cell, slamming him into the far wall with bone-crunching force. Esna breathed a strangled cry as he slid to the ground.

'Callisthenes,' Barca said, as the Greek eased the door open. 'My thanks to you, again.'

The merchant stared in awed silence. In the back of his mind, he wished, beyond all other wishes, that his corpulent frame possessed a fraction of Barca's speed and strength. To be a tautly muscled warrior, not a flabby merchant, had been his dream since youth.

'Leave now.' The Phoenician hammered his knife into the wooden door-jamb. 'If you have a weak stomach, you're not going to want to see this.' Barca smiled viciously, cracking the knuckles of his left hand as he stalked toward his former jailer.

'P-Please . . . !' Esna whimpered.

Callisthenes turned away as the first of many blows fell. Barca was right. He didn't want to see this.

'Death to the traitors!'

Menkaura stood like a conqueror of old above the bound form of the Greek officer. Gore from his upraised sword trickled down his arm. He could feel the emotions of the crowd rising to a fever pitch. They had seen blood. Now, they wanted more.

Hunting spears and old swords thrust at the sky. Faces, twisted with hate, swelled and ebbed before him, their voices mingling with his, their anger mounting.

'Kill them!'

Menkaura wrenched the officer's head back. 'Tell it in the streets and the courtyards, the alleys and bazaars,' he yelled, 'that all traitors, all sympathizers, will meet a similar fate!'

The soldier screamed as the Egyptian's blade descended, shearing through his neck. Menkaura kicked the twitching corpse aside. 'Death to the Greeks!'

'Death to the Greeks!' the crowd echoed.

Ibebi rushed to Menkaura's side. 'They've come!' he growled, jabbing his sword toward the edge of the bazaar. Hoplites flowed into the square, forming an armoured wing, shields locked, spears held upright. Their front stretched twenty men long, at a depth of three men. In the fore stood Phanes, his cuirass buffed to a mirror-like sheen; his shield bore the symbol of the garrison of Memphis, the snaky locks of Medusa delineated in black. He shunned a helmet, preferring to let his enemies see his face. And at that moment, his face was a mask of raw fury.

'Disperse!' he roared. 'Before . . .'

186

The Egyptians raised a clamour, yelling, screaming, pounding swords and spears against shields, anything to drown out the Greek's voice. They outnumbered the Hellenes. Menkaura snarled as he stepped out in front of the crowd. 'We will not disperse!'

'Then you will die!' Phanes raised his shield. As one, the hoplites advanced on the massed Egyptians, their spears snapping with chilling precision into attack posture, an iron hedge of death. A hymn rose from their throats:

Mighty Ares, shield-carrying Lord of the Spear, Father of fair Victory!

The voices of the men of Egypt faltered under this display of training and discipline. Menkaura sensed their anger turning to fear. The Egyptians gave ground.

'Stand!' Menkaura cried. 'Stand together!'

'They're behind us!' a terrified shout. Menkaura turned. True enough, a second wing of hoplites entered the square at their backs. A quick glance showed a third and fourth wing closing in from each side. They were outnumbered, now, and surrounded.

'You arrogant fool!' Amenmose spat. 'I told you your grief would kill us all!'

Menkaura's eyes flared with a desperate fire. He whirled to face Phanes. 'Coward! You would order a man's death without looking him in the eye! You are a coward!'

At a gesture the hoplites stopped, their spears less than a foot from Menkaura's breast. The

Egyptians huddled together, and fear crackled through their masses.

Phanes stepped out, raking the crowd with a withering glare. 'Disperse now, and I will hold none of you to blame for these murders! You've fallen under the spell of a man consumed with hatred! Do you hear me? I hold Menkaura to blame for this! The rest of you may go free!' Phanes' voice rose in volume, carrying to all corners of the square.

'Liar!' Menkaura said. 'You are the only murderer here! You and those who follow you!'

Phanes' smile was dagger-sharp. 'There's no blood on my hands, Menkaura. Can you say the same? You were beaten by Greeks years ago, and since then my people have been the bane of your existence. The Medjay kill your poor son, Idu, and who do you blame? Hasdrabal Barca? No, you blame me! I could have tolerated your hatred . . . indeed, I understand it . . . but when you murdered these men you crossed the line. Surrender yourself to me now, Menkaura. I'll not ask again.'

'Let's allow the gods to decide who is the murderer here! I challenge you to single combat!'

An awed silence fell over Egyptian and Greek.

'I do not fight old men,' Phanes said, dismissing him with a wave.

'Why? Afraid I might teach you a lesson or two about swordplay?' Menkaura said. 'As I said, a coward!'

Phanes laughed, drawing his sword. 'So be it!

Zeus! You are either the bravest man I know, or the stupidest!'

'Greek arrogance!' Menkaura shouted. He turned to stare at his kinsmen, his friends. They looked pitifully small and mean against the gleaming host around them. 'They believe themselves to be the only people schooled in war! Our ancestors were mighty warriors when theirs were but ignorant swineherds! Do you fear swineherds?'

'Have you come to preach, old man, or to fight?' said Phanes.

Menkaura faced him. At a gesture, Thothmes brought him a shield, hippopotamus hide stretched over a wooden frame and rimmed in tarnished bronze.

'Don't do this, cousin,' Thothmes whispered. Their eyes met, and a faint smile touched Menkaura's lips. He looked at Phanes.

'Time for your lesson, boy!'

Menkaura circled Phanes, his sword ready, evoking images of the ageing Nestor beneath Illium's walls. The Greek feinted in, the tip of his sword weaving like the head of a striking serpent. His shield gleamed in the morning sun. Menkaura gave ground, wary, calling on years of experience to counter the younger man's speed. He shuffled back, circled, and lunged without warning, thrusting the point of his blade at Phanes' face. Bronze struck iron with a deafening clang.

Phanes sneered and launched a whirlwind of blows. Menkaura parried and ducked, catching blow after blow on the edge of his shield. Sweat beaded his forehead, streamed down his face. An icy premonition clutched at Menkaura's heart, the hand of Osiris.

The Desert Hawk swung wildly.

With a dancer's grace Phanes slid beneath the Egyptian's sword, his own blade sweeping up and out in a glittering arc. Menkaura heard its chilling whistle; he felt its razored edge bite into the taut muscles of his neck. An unimaginable pain tore into him, then Menkaura heard and felt no more.

Pregnant silence gripped the square as Menkaura's headless body toppled, landing with a crash at the feet of the Egyptian mob. Phanes stooped, caught up the severed head, and held it aloft.

'The gods have decided! I have fought for Egypt, bled for Egypt, nearly died for Egypt! Now, I will conquer Egypt! If any man here would challenge my claim, then do it now! Do it now!'

Thothmes moved to take up Phanes' challenge, but a stealthy hand on his arm stopped him. He glanced back, saw Amenmose behind him. The merchant shook his head. Beside him, Hekaib's pale face gleamed beneath his helmet.

Phanes' eyes raked the crowd; few could meet his gaze. 'Just as I thought! I know you all, every man here, and I extend amnesty to you. This man who led you was a fool, and I hold you blameless for his folly! But, I swear . . . by the gods of Hellas! . . . if the slightest rumour of unrest reaches my ears, I will kill every male member of

190

your families and sell your wives and daughters to the Nubians! Now kneel and recognize your new king!'

For a long moment none moved. Then, Amenmose stepped forward, his fingers locked on the forearms of Ibebi and Hekaib. 'Live to fight another day, brothers,' he whispered as he knelt. In twos and threes, the other Egyptians followed suit. Last came Thothmes. He glared at Phanes as he dropped to his knees.

'I am your king!' Phanes roared, his arms spread wide. Their hatred coursed through him, driving him to the brink of ecstasy. With it, he felt waves of fear radiating out from the Egyptians. To them he had become Amemait, the Devourer, waiting to consume their souls at the Scales of Judgement. Their weapons were nothing against the Devourer.

'I am your god!' Phanes' smile grew ever wider.

9

EVE OF BATTLE

Outside the cell, Callisthenes tried to ignore the sounds of a fist striking flesh, and the flesh giving way. Colour drained from his face; he winced at the crunch of bones. Esna's strangled wheezes – cries of pain, he supposed – became less frequent, then ceased altogether. A moment later, Barca staggered from the cell, his eyes blazing with yet unquenched fury. Fresh blood covered his arm to the elbow.

'Is he . . . ?'

'Esna was too soft to play his own game,' Barca said, wrenching his knife from the door-jamb. He turned and stared at the squat bulk of the temple proper. 'Now, it's his master's turn.'

'And when you finish your . . . *business*, what then?'

Barca's frank stare sent a shudder through the Greek. 'It's best not to know too much, Callisthenes. If Phanes learns what you've done and decides to put the hot irons to you . . .' He trailed off. 'Besides, there's not much left that I can do. Find an out of the way place, perhaps, get some rest, and discover a way to deprive Phanes of that head he holds so dear. Maybe see what progress Menkaura's made. Even twenty men with fire in their bellies could be useful when battle is joined.'

'My home is yours,' Callisthenes said. 'If you desire a safe haven.'

Barca's lips peeled back in a snarl as he remembered Matthias' wrecked corpse. 'No, thank you, friend. I have enough blood on my hands. I don't need to add yours to it. I will find shelter my own way, and without anyone risking their necks over it.'

'I understand. I must go, before Phanes grows suspicious. Peace to you, Hasdrabal Barca,' Callisthenes said, then scuttled to the tiny postern door. He opened it, glanced about like a frightened hare, and was gone.

Barca turned back to the temple, his face hardening.

The precinct of Neith was comparatively small for such a prolific goddess. The granary-turned-cell where they had thrown Barca lay at the rear of the temple, among the outbuildings dedicated to the more mundane matters of temple life. Here, too, were storehouses and supply sheds, crude mud brick buildings needing repair ranked against the low outer wall. The whole precinct gave Barca the impression of shabbiness, of neglect. Still, despite its size the temple itself was an impressive structure. He could see, even from here, the pylons flanking the temple entrance.

Banners hung limp, a lull in the light winds sucking the life from them.

Barca had visited the temple once before, years ago, when he brought the body of his old captain, Potasimto, an adherent of Neith, to Memphis so the priests could entomb him at Saqqara with his ancestors. The brightly painted entrance, he recalled, led to a hypostyle hall, a forest of stone columns capped by chiselled granite images of the goddess herself, in all her myriad forms. From there, the temple widened, becoming a colonnaded courtyard that housed the sacred pool. The shrine itself lay in the shadow of the colonnade.

The temple had few lesser priests, as far as Barca could remember. Those it did employ spent their days on errands in the markets and bazaars, or on loan to the larger temples. With luck, he would conclude his business with Ujahorresnet and be gone before any clamour was raised.

The sun reached its zenith in the azure and white sky as Barca slipped around to the temple entrance. Inside, the shadows were cool, inviting. Shafts and windows high in the walls kept the air circulating. In the pervasive silence he could hear a soft voice. He crossed the hypostyle hall, cones of brilliant sunlight lancing down from apertures in the roof. Barca skirted these, keeping to the shadows. The voice grew louder as he crossed into the courtyard.

At the far end, beyond the glittering sacred pool, he spied his prey.

Ujahorresnet knelt before a statue of his goddess, his mind focused on the complex liturgies and rituals required of him, as First Servant of the Goddess. Offerings lay on the cool stone before him; fresh loaves of bread, a ewer of water, sweet-smelling incense on a bed of hot coals. They were gifts for the goddess, exhortations for her favour, her guidance.

Barca padded to the edge of the sacred pool, watching the priest's back as he crouched and dipped out several handfuls of water to slake his thirst. Ujahorresnet was oblivious, so intent was he on his ritual. The very image of pious supplication.

'O Opener of the Ways!' the priest said, his arms raised, his shaven head tilted toward the heavens. 'O Wise Mother! Deliver unto thy children the milk of thy breast, so that we might live fulfilled in the light of thy divine *ka*.'

'Why should she? You've strayed from her path,' Barca said.

Ujahorresnet lunged forward, still on his knees, a look of shock on his face. He scattered the offerings as he put his back to the statue. His eyes bulged as he stared at the knife in Barca's bloody fist.

'Esna!'

'Call louder,' Barca said. 'He cannot hear you in hell.'

'Damn you!' said the priest, sagging in defeat against the statue's base. 'What will you do now? Kill me? Then do it and have done with it! It's what you have dreamed of. What you have lived for. I am at your mercy. Send me to join my daughter in the next world.'

'What happened to your compassion, priest?' Barca said, stalking toward Ujahorresnet. 'What happened to your kindness, your quietude, your honour? Are these not the virtues of your goddess? You've exchanged all you hold dear for base revenge. Is it any wonder your goddess has deserted you?'

'Do not talk to me about honour!' Ujahorresnet spat. 'You have no conception of it! Or of compassion. You broke the most sacred of bonds, the bond between husband and wife, and for what? To soothe your pride? To assuage your anger? I may have strayed from the path of my goddess, but your *ka* is blacker than mine, you bastard!'

Barca snatched the priest up by the neck and pinned him against the wall of the alcove. 'I loved your daughter!' he whispered through clenched teeth. 'Loved her more than I have loved another living soul, and I have had to live with what I did for the last twenty years. She betrayed *me*! She dishonoured *me*! If I could return to that night, I would stay my hand, I would leave Egypt with never a backward glance. But I cannot undo what happened. Neferu is dead, and her death is on my conscience. I do not weep for her . . . she made her own choice, just as I made mine.'

'I weep for her!' Ujahorresnet said, his voice thick, strangled with emotion. 'Every day I weep for her! You killed my little girl!'

Barca's grip loosened; his knife sank. He looked at Ujahorresnet again and saw an old man consumed with grief, wracked with the guilt of a father who could not protect his only child. The black rage seething in Barca's soul drained away. He let go of Ujahorresnet; the priest slid to the floor, gnarled hands cradling his head.

'You killed my little girl,' he sobbed.

Barca turned away, the pain in his limbs, his face, his side crushing down on him like an impossible weight. 'I should kill you, too, old man, but it will serve no good. If you leave Memphis, Pharaoh will never learn of your betrayal from me.'

'Leniency? From you?' Ujahorresnet barked. 'How droll.'

Barca stopped, inclined his head. 'It's called compassion, priest. You should become reacquainted with it. One warning: forget I exist. Trust in your gods to punish me when my time comes and let me be. Because if you so much as cross my path on a crowded street, they won't find enough of your body to give a proper burial.'

With that, Barca quit the precinct of Neith, leaving a broken old man in his wake.

Broken, but alive.

The afternoon sun shimmered on the surface of the Nile, reflecting the light a thousand times over. A stiff northerly wind belled the sails of

Pharaoh's barge, the *Khepri*, sending her prow slicing through the water like a wedge through sand. Sailors, naked save for leather loin cloths, scurried about the deck of the ship, moving with a rhythm that suggested brachiating monkeys rather than men.

The *Khepri* was a massive vessel, well over two hundred feet long, a monument to the extraordinary skill of Pharaoh's Phoenician shipwrights. Its cedar mast and railings were elaborately carved with images of Pharaoh receiving the blessings of falcon-headed Horus as a cavalcade of gods looked on. Hieroglyphs wove spells of protection around the ship. Statues of the goddesses Neith and Nekhebet, made of precious woods and inlaid with ivory and gold, stood watch over Pharaoh's path, warning all and sundry that a son of heaven sailed the life-giving waters of the Nile. At the stern of the *Khepri*, under a white linen awning upheld by slender columns of gilded cedar, rested a replica of the Saite throne. Here, Ahmose held court, agitated, surrounded by ministers and advisors.

'I will not sit in the baggage train like a doddering old fool!' Pharaoh said. The awning covering the throne snapped in the wind. 'Am I a coward to hide my face from Phanes?'

'No, Great One,' Pasenkhonsu, his senior admiral, wheedled. 'But neither can you place your royal life in the van, in the thickest of the fighting. We could be sailing into an ambush, O Pharaoh. You must . . .'

'You would presume to order me about like a common serf?'

Pasenkhonsu wrung his hands. 'No, Great One, a thousand times, no! But, your divine blood is too precious to spill in battle with mere rebels. Please, listen to reason!' The other ministers agreed, adding their assents with the perfect timing of a trained chorus. 'Please!'

Ahmose dismissed them with a curt gesture. He turned and watched the landscape pass by, the villages of mud brick, the green fields, the temples and monuments. Men, women, and children flocked to the Nile's edge, awestruck at the glimmering splendour of the god-king's procession. A deep melancholy gripped his soul, as if he stood witness to the ending of an age. His allies were gone, swallowed up by the Persians. Croesus of Lydia. The Chaldean, Nabonidus. Even Polycrates of Samos, once his staunchest ally, had given in to the lure of Cambyses' gold. Ahmose was alone. Adrift on a sea of foes, all of whom wanted what he had devoted his life to rebuilding. And now, Phanes.

The hero of Sardis. Ahmose remembered that day well, when the combined armies of Egypt, Lydia, Babylon, and Sparta stood strong against the swarming hordes of Cyrus the Mede. The Plain of Thymbra, before the walls of Sardis, ran red with blood; the slain circled the living like a ring of mountains. His forces alone fought the Persians to a standstill, fought with such fury that Cyrus granted them a separate treaty. His generals awarded the gold of valour to a young mercenary, a hoplite from Halicarnassus, who had waded into the thickest fighting to prevent the Egyptian standard from falling to the Persians.

That young mercenary was Phanes, and Sardis was just the beginning. Year piled upon year; battle upon battle. Phanes' rise through the ranks had all the hallmarks of a Homeric saga, and his genius at warfare was beyond compare. He was a Hellenic ideal, a living Odysseus. A shame, Ahmose reckoned, that such an auspicious career had to end like this.

Pharaoh looked up, saw Nebmaatra approaching. The Calasirian commander maintained the perfect blend of nonchalance and watchfulness, his frame relaxed, his eyes never still. His hands did not stray far from knife and sword hilts. He stopped at the proscribed distance and bowed. Ahmose motioned him closer.

'I envy you your iron nerves, my friend,' Pharaoh said, smiling. 'Nothing gets under your hide, does it?'

'Just the opposite, Golden One. Everything gets under my hide. I just disguise it better,' Nebmaatra said. 'I've heard you plan on fighting in the vanguard.'

Pharaoh's eyes flickered to Pasenkhonsu, who stood among a knot of his underlings, talking in hushed voices. Ahmose sighed. 'Will you counsel me otherwise, too? I am an old man, Nebmaatra. Old and sick. If you live to carry the weight of my

200

years on your back, you will understand why I need one last taste of battle.'

'To die in battle, you mean,' Nebmaatra said.

'If I fall it is Amon's will. Who am I to declare otherwise?'

Nebmaatra bowed. 'And who am I to deny the will of Pharaoh? My Calasirians will fight at your side, Golden One.'

Ahmose pursed his lips. 'On another matter, has any word reached you of Petenemheb? His father and I served together in Nubia. Surely, he is not part of this?'

'If Phanes has not disposed of him already, then my guess is he is in collusion with the Greeks. Even if he is not, his silence is suspect, to say the least.'

Ahmose grimaced, looking his age in the afternoon light. He stared off to the west. Nebmaatra felt Pharaoh withdraw into himself, bringing the audience to a close. He bowed and took his leave.

Nebmaatra left the stern of the *Khepri*, descending into the waist of the ship. He closed his eyes for a moment, listening to the thrum of wind in the cordage, to the snap of sails, to the creak of the hull, to the slap of water. Harsh sunlight seared his face. He opened his eyes and stared at the endless buff-coloured cliffs and rich green marshlands. He, too, looked to the west.

Squadrons of chariots, the regiment of Amon,

kept pace with the ships, raising a pall of dust that could be seen for miles. Behind them, marching at a punishing pace, came columns of infantry – spearmen and archers. The native militia, the *machimoi*, had mustered with uncommon speed, answering Pharaoh's call to arms. In a few days' time, Pharaoh's displeasure with Phanes manifested itself as an army five thousand strong, including five hundred chariots, the Calasirian Guard, and Pasenkhonsu's river fleet.

Nebmaatra caught sight of Tjemu leaning against the railing, staring at the western bank of the Nile – no, beyond it. Nebmaatra walked to his side.

'Your thoughts are far from here,' he said.

Tjemu started, then ducked his head to spit into the water. 'Funny how you sometimes remember things at the most inopportune times.' He nodded off to the southwest. 'My home is a week's ride in that direction, the oasis of Siwa. I have . . . had . . . a wife, two sons. I still can recall the smell of her bread as she baked it, the sounds of my boys playing in the dust, the cool taste of freshly drawn water.' He laughed sadly. 'Hell, I doubt the lot of them would remember me.'

'Why haven't you returned?'

'I have, as my wife put it, a restless soul.'

Nebmaatra leaned on the rail beside him. 'Why do we do this to ourselves? Why do we have this urge to see what lies over the next hill, as if it might be better than the valley we are in? I blame it on Fate.'

202

Tjemu looked askance at him. 'Fate?'

'Yes. Look at how Fate makes one man a farmer, one man a carpenter, and one man a soldier. I envy those men who can take a wife and settle down to till the land, or turn lumps of clay into elegant vases. But, such is not for us, my friend. By some whim of Fate, we are destined to tread the battlefields of the world, in search of that one thing that we each long for.'

'Which is?' Tjemu said.

'Immortality.'

Tjemu laughed. 'You sound like a fucking philosopher!'

'But you don't deny it, do you?'

'No,' Tjemu said. 'No, what you say is true. I may die tomorrow, if that's the gods' will. It does not concern me greatly if I do. I've made my peace with them. What saddens me is knowing that, in a thousand years, no man will remember Tjemu of Siwa. Who will speak my name so I might taste eternity if no one knows I ever drew breath?'

Nebmaatra straightened. 'I can offer you no solace, brother, save this: the gods will know what kind of men we were. They will know which man cheated, which man lied; they know which man showed the enemy his back, and they will know which man stood firm and faced his death with courage. So long as the gods remember, I am content.'

They stood in silence as the sun dropped behind the western cliffs, bathing the sky in fiery shades of orange, red, and violet. Purple shadows crept across the Nile. It was the eve of battle; the last sunset many of them would ever see.

It stretched like a long drawn-out sigh into twilight.

The throne room at Memphis was cavernous, a wonderland of granite and gold that could have been hewn from living rock by the hand of a god. Glorious scenes incised and painted on the walls told the tale of Egypt's antiquity . . . the peoples conquered, the cities razed, the offerings made to Ptah, Osiris, and Horus. The wavering light of a handful of oil lamps imbued the carvings with life. They danced and flickered in the gloom, re-enacting the pageantry of the past in endless cycles: birth to death to rebirth.

There was nothing like this in Halicarnassus, Phanes thought, nothing like this in all of Hellas. My son would . . .

My son.

Phanes frowned. He had not thought of his boy in years. Nor would he be a boy any longer. Menander would be over twenty, by now. Probably with a wife and a clutch of brats all his own. He wondered what kind of man his son had turned into. A merchant like his grandsire? Perhaps a politician of Halicarnassus? Whatever he was, Phanes wished him health and long life.

For all his prowess, his genius at slaughter, all

Phanes ever truly wanted was to rear his son. But when the Daughters of Themis, the Fates, wove the cloth of his life, the thread that came off the spindle was not earthy as a farmer, or gilded as a merchant. The threads of his life were as red as the blood spattering his arms.

Movement caught Phanes' eye. He looked up as one of his men escorted Ujahorresnet through a side door. The Greek noticed fading bruises decorating the old priest's throat.

'I would have thought your sport kept you too busy for social visits,' Phanes said.

'And I thought yours would have left you little time to entertain delusions of grandeur,' the priest replied, indicating the throne Phanes occupied. 'Barca has escaped.'

'Leaving you alive? Perhaps your gods *are* greater than mine.' Phanes leaned back in the golden throne, his fingers caressing the armrests. His eyes were glassy, feverish.

'Not without conditions. I must leave Memphis.'

'Must you, now.'

'I felt the need to warn you. The Phoenician will doubtless seek to cause you trouble. Do with Barca what you will. It is no longer my concern.' Ujahorresnet's shoulders slumped in defeat.

Phanes smiled. 'I see. You've gleaned a valuable insight, priest. You've learned that pride is often the first victim of ambition. Good for you. Unfortunately, you can't leave the city.'

'You do not understand . . .' Ujahorresnet began.

205

'No!' Phanes said. 'It's you who doesn't understand! Tomorrow, when I remove the double crown from Amasis' bleeding corpse, I will be king, and it is your king's will that you remain.'

'You forget yourself, Greek,' Ujahorresnet said, indignation raising his voice a level. 'And you forget our bargain.'

'Ah, our bargain . . . would it not be interesting to see the reaction of the people of Memphis to news of your dealings with the hated Greeks? I imagine they would drag you out in the streets and tear you limb from limb! And what would your fellow priests say?'

'You wouldn't dare!'

'Would I not?' Phanes motioned to his door wardens, who opened the doors to the throne room to admit a cortege of shaven-headed, robed men. A squad of his soldiers flanked them, seeming less like a guard of honour than herdsmen. The reaction of the priests was one of almost comical diversity. Some goggled in abject terror at the hoplites. Others maintained a mask of politesse, adopting the air of honoured guests. Still others were livid at the Greek's sacrilege.

'What is the meaning of this?' the eldest of them, Inyotef, high priest of Ptah, snapped.

Ujahorresnet stood rooted to the spot, his face a mask of anger tinged with dread. He glared at the smiling Greek reclining on the throne. 'Gentlemen,' Phanes said. 'Calm yourselves. I've brought you here for a reason . . .'

Inyotef bristled. 'If you expect to cow us like

206

that rabble in the street, to get on bended knee and proclaim you king, then I'd say you've buggered one too many prissy boys and caught a brain fever!' Several of the priests begged him to be silent. He brushed them off, defiant.

'Age makes your lips looser than an Athenian whore!' Phanes said, rising. He descended the dais to tower over Inyotef. 'I will be your king, whether you acknowledge it or not.'

'Fool!' Inyotef said. 'Controlling a city does not make you king, even a city as great as Memphis! Are you so ignorant that you believe Thebes and Sais will capitulate to you simply because you hold a crown in your hands?'

Phanes' hand flickered out, brushing the side of Inyotef's neck. The old man's eyes widened in shock; age-spotted hands flew to his throat as the first geyser of blood spewed from the paper-thin incision. Inyotef clutched at Ujahorresnet's shoulder as he fell.

'No,' Phanes said, holding up the narrow blade which none of the priests had seen him draw, 'I expect them to do it out of sheer terror.'

Ujahorresnet crouched and held his hands to Inyotef's throat, striving through will alone to stop the inexorable tide of blood. Inyotef clawed at his forearms, his yellowed eyes pleading. Slowly, the spurts turned to trickles, then ceased altogether. Inyotef's glazing stare rammed through Ujahorresnet's heart like a lance of ice.

'What have you done?'

Phanes turned and bounded lightly up the dais,

reclaiming his throne. 'I've made a point. You're all familiar with the tale of the golden footbath? No? Then listen, and I will educate you. In the early years of his reign, Amasis got little respect from his nobles. How dare he, a mere soldier, defile the throne of the god-kings? They were indignant, rebellious, but they needed a sign from the gods before they'd move against him. So, Amasis steals a golden footbath, one that these selfsame nobles had used to lave their feet, to piss in, to vomit in. He takes this footbath and has it melted and recast as a statue of Osiris, giving it to these nobles as a gesture of reconciliation. Such a glorious thing went far toward assuaging their anger. They sacrificed to it, worshipped it, showered it with gifts and offerings. Then, Amasis tells them what it was they were venerating.

'Gentlemen, I am a mercenary, but I have been recast, albeit temporarily, as your king. I do not ask your love, but I will have your respect! Otherwise, you will be joining your colleague in the next world!'

Phanes leaned back, his legs thrust out before him. He looked every inch a mercenary usurper: sweat-stained corselet of quilted linen, kilt speckled with blood, bronze greaves, sandals of ox-hide. The Greek stared at each man in turn, daring them to voice their opposition; he was pleasantly surprised to see only resignation. They had the shocked look of refugees, of men who had forgotten the face of violence. All save the priest of Neith. Something lurked in Ujahorresnet's eyes, something obscure, something evolving from passive to deadly. Phanes noted the look with a sardonic grin. 'Good. Please, accept my hospitality for the evening. Tomorrow, I will decide your fate.' He nodded to his soldiers, who ushered the priests out at spear-point.

Silence returned to the throne room, and the shadows continued their dance.

Phanes' eyes were drawn to the corpse prostrate on the floor. Egypt lay dead and defeated at his feet. Egypt's antiquity danced for his amusement. And, tomorrow, Egypt's blood would spill like a rich red rain. It would be the birth of a new age.

Barca woke to the sound of water. For a moment he was disoriented, unsure of his bearings. Was he in Tyre, again? Of course he was. The water could only be the sound of waves slapping the pilings near his home. A cooling breeze made him restless. He should rise and go check on that shipment of lapis bound for Egypt. No use lying here . . .

Barca tried to move but a hand on his chest calmed him.

'Be still,' said a woman's voice. 'I have to see to your wounds.'

The fog of sleep evaporated and the events of the last few hours calcified in his mind. Night had fallen, and stars dusted the sky from horizon to horizon, a milky river of light. Barca lay on a divan atop Idu's villa, under a loggia whose columns were crafted to resemble towering papyrus stalks. Jauharah knelt at his side. Near her were two pottery bowls and a bundle of linen strips.

Her hands moved over his gashed side, sponging away the fresh blood that welled from the wound. She probed the torn flesh with her fingertips.

Like loose threads on a loom, Barca gathered his thoughts. The Phoenician had left the temple of Neith at midday, making his way across a city strangely quiet. He could feel something writhing below the surface. Anger. Fear. He overheard snatches of conversation, a whispered name. By the time he crossed Memphis, Barca had pieced together the details of Menkaura's death, and the death of his fledgling uprising.

He cursed Menkaura for a fool. The word was his grief had caused him to move too soon; his anger had goaded him into challenging Phanes to single combat. Afterward, Menkaura's 'army' had melted away like fat left too long in the sun. So much for his plan of an Egyptian insurrection . . .

A sharp pain tugged him back to the present. 'Just stitch it and have done!' Barca snapped.

'It must be cleansed,' Jauharah said. 'If it festers, the corruption will seep into your internal organs and kill you one piece at a time. I've seen men die in this manner. It's not pleasant.' Jauharah nodded to herself, confident that there were no fragments or debris in the wound. She reached for the second bowl containing equal parts vinegar and water. 'This will sting,' she warned, and poured the mixture over the wound. A sharp intake of breath from her patient gave Jauharah a measure of comfort. She was beginning to think Barca wasn't human.

'Did you do as I instructed?' Barca said through clenched teeth.

Jauharah nodded. She took up a bronze needle and a length of gut. 'I carried your message to each of master Idu's friends. If their courage holds, they should arrive soon.'

Barca watched her prepare for the delicate task of stitching flesh. 'Where did you learn that?'

'The House of Life, from a physician's slave. Master Idu thought it a good skill to have.'

The Phoenician's brows arched. 'Have you ever put that skill in to practice?'

'No.'

'Wait,' Barca said. He motioned for the needle and gut. 'Best let me do that.'

Jauharah frowned. 'You cannot possibly see what you're doing. Now be still and let me do my work. For the love of the gods, will you trust no one?'

Barca stared at her for a long moment, weighing his options. She was right. He could not see well enough to stitch the jagged gash in his side. Loss of blood left him weak; his hands quivered and twitched. Slowly, Barca nodded. 'I'm trusting you.'

'Lie back.' Jauharah acknowledged his trust with a slight smile as she began the slow process of stitching. 'The Egyptians are true masters of healing,' she said, her voice soft, measured. 'I have seen papyri concerning the treatment of wounds that date back to the time of the god-kings.' Jauharah fell silent and did not speak for a long time, then: 'You are lucky to be alive. The knife nearly severed the wall of muscle protecting your abdomen. A little deeper, and it would have gutted you.' She finished stitching, then wrapped Barca's abdomen in clean linen bandages.

The Phoenician grunted. 'Death never seems to finish what He starts.' He flexed his arm and back, feeling the sutures tighten. 'You have a gift for this sort of thing. You should be in the House of Life, not serving in a merchant's household.'

Jauharah sat back on her heels, wiping her bloody hands on a scrap of linen. 'The gods make us what . . .'

The clatter of a gate hinge echoed up from the courtyard at the back of the house. Barca rose and stepped out from beneath the loggia to peer over the roof's edge.

Jauharah followed. The Phoenician could see down into a partially-enclosed kitchen with its own secluded garden. Strings of dried fish and bundles of herbs hung from the exposed ceiling beams, while a trio of conical brick ovens stood like great beehives against the courtyard wall. From the small garden, with its Persea tree and immaculate flower beds, the light of a shielded lamp illuminated four figures, their features cast in shadow.

'Phoenician! Are you h-here?' one of them hissed.

'Up here,' Barca replied. At the sound of his voice, the newcomers stiffened, looking like thieves caught in the act. He motioned them toward a flight of stairs built into the kitchen wall, then turned to Jauharah. 'Their names?'

'The short one in front is Hekaib. Behind him, Ibebi. The man with the close-cropped grey hair is Amenmose. The last one is Thothmes, Menkaura's cousin.' She frowned, touching his sweat-slick brow. 'You should sit. Here, let me help you.' She led him back to the divan as the four men gained the roof and joined him under the loggia.

'Phoenician!' Amenmose said. 'We-We thought you were dead!'

Barca chuckled. 'Far from it, though I think Phanes will regret not killing me when he had the chance.'

'Why have you called us here?' Hekaib said, fear giving his voice a high, almost feminine, pitch. He clutched one of the loggia's columns for support. 'If the Hellenes find us like this . . .'

'Hekaib's right,' Thothmes said. 'After the fiasco in the square, Phanes will have his eyes and ears everywhere.'

'But not here. Here, you are safe.'

'Why *have* you summoned us, Phoenician?' This from Ibebi.

'Because it falls on you to carry on what Idu and Menkaura started. I've heard the whispers. Your younger kinsmen are undaunted. They . . .'

213

'They are fools,' Amenmose said softly. 'Noble intentions and fiery passions will not stand against Greek armour. I am not without courage, but I am in no hurry to throw my life away for a lost cause.'

'Then master Idu died for nothing!' Jauharah said. The men glanced at her, taken aback at her outburst.

'She's right,' Barca said. 'If you choose to hide from the truth, then your friends wasted their lives. You can live out your days in shame and defeat. But, if you choose to believe they died to give the rest of you strength, then no amount of armour or training can stand before your rage.'

'We're not cowards!' Ibebi growled.

'I did not say you were. A coward will not look at Death; he will sprint like a hare in the opposite direction. But men like you, men caught in the grip of fear, will stand their ground and let Death inch ever closer, never raising a hand to stop it.'

'We do not fear Death, Phoenician!' Hekaib said. He drew himself to his full, unimposing height. 'Death is but the doorway to the afterlife.'

'Then why did you not leap to Menkaura's defence?' Barca studied each man, feeling their shame as they stared at their feet in self-recrimination, unable to meet his gaze. 'There is no wrong in fearing Death; all men do. Every hoplite in Phanes' command fears Death, but they master their fear, they step across that line separating soldiers from common men, and they fight, regardless of what happens to them, regardless of the outcome. You must emulate them.'

'We have no weapons,' Thothmes said.

'Give me that indomitable Egyptian spirit that made your people masters of the ancient world, and I'll get you weapons!' Barca replied.

'It seems so . . . futile,' Amenmose whispered.

'It is futile, my friend. Egypt is in peril. Foreigners stand on the threshold, intent on destroying the land of your ancestors. I am not of your race, but I love Egypt as if she had given me life. My men died for your freedom. My friend Matthias ben Iesu endured hideous torture and death in defence of your sons and daughters. Idu was murdered for his beliefs, and Menkaura sacrificed himself to show you what true resolve really is. Do these acts truly mean nothing to you?'

The men glanced at one another, each seeking strength in the other's eyes. Barca could sense the good in them. Here were men thrust into an uncompromising situation, men with families, men whose lives did not include a penchant for violence. They earned the Phoenician's respect simply by heeding his summons.

Thothmes shuffled forward. 'I will stand with you.'

'I, too,' Ibebi said. The other two could only nod.

Barca's face grew grim. 'I'm not looking for men who will stand beside me. I need men who will fight, who will die. Men willing to throw their lives away for the love of their home-land.'

'You don't want men, you want martyrs,' Amenmose said, uneasy.

Barca smiled. 'Now, you're beginning to under-stand.'

10

LINES IN THE SAND

Callisthenes tossed a clay tablet aside and leaned forward, resting his head in his hands. He had risen early – far earlier than normal – in an effort to bring some semblance of order to his life. Since returning from Delphi, he had done little actual work. The chaotic ruin around him bore mute witness to that fact. He had a mercantile empire to run. Rolls of papyrus lay in a wicker basket, contracts that could not be processed until he affixed his seal to them. Letters, both papyrus and clay, awaited his perusal, his reply. A ship's captain from Cyprus had a hold full of Iberian tin to sell, and his man in Byblos needed more capital to make the purchase. Bankers on Delos wanted payment for a lost shipment of wine. A consortium of Athenian artists sought his aid to purchase marble from Tura . . .

Callisthenes tried to concentrate, but found his gaze drawn to the flickering flame of his candle. His imagination swirled with scenes of glory, with triumphs earned in close combat. What was it like to stand shoulder to shoulder with Death, to feel the press of bodies and hear the whistle and crunch of blades? What was it like to feel hot blood spraying from a dying man? How *alive* it must feel, this dealing of death. Callisthenes returned to himself with a start and shuffled through the rolls of papyrus, the tablets of dried clay, looking for something he knew he would not find among them.

Freedom.

He had lived a life of safety, shackled by the chains of caution and cushioned by the blanket of wealth. He had never placed his life on the line for a cause; never risked his neck for an ideal. Grounded by the reality of invoices and bills of lading, Callisthenes did not realize, until now, how much he longed to be free, a footloose wanderer. He sighed. A fine dream, but his life was something altogether different, his father had made sure of that. His life was *respectable*.

'Master!' A voice echoed through the silent villa.

Callisthenes heard the slap of bare feet on stone. The Greek frowned as a slave rushed into his office. 'What is it, Nebamun?'

'Soldiers, master!'

'Bring their officer to me, and see that the others are comfortable.' This was how it happened before, how he became Phanes' envoy to Delphi. What did that madman want now? Suddenly, an icy sense of dread clutched the merchant's heart. Could Phanes know his true feelings? Could someone, somewhere have fingered him? Despite his dreams to the contrary, Callisthenes was a soft man, and images of torture too hideous to comprehend ran through his mind. He had to stay calm.

Callisthenes glanced up as Nebamun ushered a Greek officer into his presence. The soldier wore a cuirass of burnished bronze, and his shield bore the head of Medusa, Phanes' emblem. He stood straight and tall, his manner deferential.

'How may I help you, captain?' Callisthenes said, his voice far steadier than he could have hoped for.

'We have orders to escort you to the temple of Egyptian Hephaestus.'

Callisthenes nodded. He placed his hands palms down on his desk, surveying the papyri, tablets, and ostraka representing a lifetime of hard work and respect, tangible evidence of a huge empire. An empire he was about to destroy. 'Fine. Await me out front.'

The soldier nodded and left the room.

The summons could only be a ploy, a precursor to murdering him for his betrayal. Callisthenes wasted no time speculating on how Phanes found out. It was purely academic. It was enough for him that he did know, and desired revenge. Sweat poured down the Greek's face. Callisthenes opened an ornate trunk and took out a small bag of gold and a thin-bladed knife. He secreted these in his robe, then glanced about his office. This must be what freedom felt like: a dull ache in the pit of his stomach, a tightness in his chest.

Callisthenes was not so sure freedom agreed with him.

The Greek opened the rear door of his office and scurried down the shallow stone steps that led to his garden. All around, Memphis shivered and came alive, rising like the sacred baboons of Thoth to greet the sun with howls of adoration. Soon, the oppressive heat would return; the sky would glow white-hot and the stones underfoot would burn like slag from an ironmonger's forge. For now, the air was crisp and cool, spiced with the smell of baking bread and the light fragrance of water lilies arising from his garden pool. Gathering his robes about him, Callisthenes darted through the garden and paused to unlatch the back gate.

Once he crossed this threshold, there was no turning back. In a literal sense he had reached a crossroads. Perhaps he could manipulate Phanes into believing . . . ? No. Phanes was beyond being used. If he did not act now, he would not see the end of this day. He knew it in his marrow.

'Winged Hermes, give me strength!' he whispered, and then he was gone.

The merchant dwelt in a section of the city reserved for wealthy Egyptians, lesser aristocrats and scribes of modest rank. Three streets over, the White Citadel rose on its man-made acropolis. He hurried south, hoping to lose himself in the tight warrens of the Foreign Quarter. He would have to skirt the bloody Square of Deshur, where the Greek companies would be mustering, but he couldn't envision any problems. The growing dread of battle had fairly well cleared the streets.

'Merchant!' a voice bawled. 'Why do you run?' Callisthenes glanced over his shoulder and saw three soldiers pounding after him. They played their parts well; their surprise looked genuine. Callisthenes cursed his fat, his years of indolence. He had little chance of escaping three men in their prime. Perhaps, though, he could outwit them.

'What's wrong with you, merchant?'

Callisthenes took a side street, remembering the story of the labyrinth at Knossos, on Crete. He would confuse the soldiers by taking side streets and alleys, lose them by guile rather than force. White linen awnings fluttered in the light dawn breeze; a haze of cooking smoke wafted through the air. He whirled and plunged down an alley that stank of urine and rotting vegetables. Here, all was midnight and shadow. He hurried past an open doorway and . . .

Hands clutched at Callisthenes. The Greek had time for a single bleat of terror before a spade-like palm clamped over his mouth. He felt himself dragged into a darkened building. Behind him, something crashed into his pursuers. The sounds of butchery, of flesh giving way beneath a keen edge, sent a wave of nausea through the Greek. A single terrible wail rose in pitch, only to be abruptly cut off.

The hands holding the merchant steadied him until he found his legs. Dark faces pressed close. Egyptians. Men Callisthenes knew. Thothmes was there, as was Ibebi, the haughty merchant Amenmose, squat little Hekaib, and a woman he was unfamiliar with. The men were weaponless, though their eyes burned with a righteous fury. A larger shadow loomed in the doorway.

'We're even now, Greek,' a voice hissed. Barca.

'I had thought you'd be gone from here, off to join Pharaoh's army,' Callisthenes said, breathing heavily.

'I'll be joining that fight soon enough,' Barca replied. 'What was that about?' He nodded back out the door, indicating the dead soldiers. To Hekaib he said: 'Strip them. Divide the weapons and armour. Bring me the largest cuirass.'

Callisthenes shrugged. 'Phanes. Somehow he must have learned about my change of heart toward his cause. He sent his thugs to kill me.'

'You have nothing to lose, then?' Barca extended his knife to Callisthenes. 'Take this, fight with us.'

'He's Greek!' Thothmes hissed. The others echoed his indignation. A single sweep of Barca's eyes silenced them.

'And I am Phoenician. It matters little. What matters is his life will be worth even less than yours should Phanes win. Is it not his right to defend himself?'

Thothmes and the others said nothing, unable to find fault with Barca's logic. Grudgingly, they nodded. Barca turned to Callisthenes, proffering the hilt again. 'You are a man of Naucratis. If you won't fight for your Pharaoh, then fight for the land that has adopted you. And if that does not stir your blood, then fight for your life.'

Callisthenes stared at the weapon. 'I-I have never . . .' He took the blade gingerly, as if Barca handed him a scorpion, then looked around at his newfound allies. 'I know where we can find weapons.'

At cockcrow, the Greek army marshalled in the Square of Deshur. Under Hyperides' watchful eye, three companies of peltasts – archers from Crete in their felt caps, tunics of supple leather covering their torsos – marched past, forming around the hardened bronze centre of the hoplites. Guidons snapped and fluttered in the morning's breeze. The skirl of pipes punctuated every move the companies made. The Ithacan gestured, and in response a horn sounded above the din. By column, the Greeks took the first step onto the road of conquest. Egyptians lined that road, silent, hoping beyond hope that dusk would find the Greeks dead and bleeding in the sand beyond the city. No maidens rushed out to kiss the departing soldiers; no old men bid farewell with a knowing salute. Only dark impassive faces and eyes brimming with hate.

Above the Square, Phanes trod the paving stones of the western pylon of the temple of Ptah. His armour gleamed in the sun; a white cloak billowed out behind him. The look on his face was one of barely controlled rage. Nicias stood to one side, out of the path of his commander's anger.

'What the hell happened? Why did he bolt?'

Nicias shrugged. 'I have no answer for you, *strategos*, though privately I've always felt Callisthenes to be more Egyptian than Greek.'

That idea struck Phanes crossly, something he had not envisaged. *Could* Callisthenes, jolly Callisthenes, betray him? Lysistratis had thought so. If his sympathies did lie with the Egyptian people, then he could have leaked details of Phanes' plans to Pharaoh's agents at any time. Suddenly everything the merchant touched grew suspect; every delay, every word, every question became the work of a traitor. Phanes gave Nicias a look that would curdle milk. 'You think he's double-crossed me?'

'Why else would he run?'

'If he has betrayed me, he'll not live long enough to savour it. It's too late to alter our plans. Send word to the men inside the temple walls to remain vigilant, as a precaution.' He would deal with Callisthenes later. Phanes took a deep breath as he turned to face the rising sun. 'Can you feel it? The air itself is alive.'

The cloudless sky faded from light blue in the west to white and orange in the east. The Nile glittered like liquid silver. Phanes peered down on the temple grounds. His men were moving into position; sunlight angling through decorative pylons and colonnades struck fire from breastplates, helmets, and spear tips. A short avenue of human-headed sphinxes led from the quay to the temple proper. Phanes chose that spot as the site of Pharaoh's death.

'It's a fine day to die, should the gods decree it,' Nicias said.

'Not for us, my friend,' Phanes said. 'This is our day for triumph.' Below them, his men ushered the gaggle of captive priests through the temple gates. He spotted Ujahorresnet among them. 'Bring me the high priest of Neith.'

Soldiers relayed the order. Ujahorresnet was cut from the herd and escorted up the long interior stairs of the pylon. He marched like a man going to meet his doom. Would Petenemheb's fate be his, a sacrifice to the crude gods of Hellas? Whatever Phanes' designs, the priest resolved to meet it with head held high.

Ujahorresnet blinked as he emerged into the bright morning sunlight. He paused at the head of the stairs. The view from atop the pylon was staggering. Off to the west, cloaked in haze, he could make out the pyramids of Saqqara; the smaller bench-like mastaba tombs were dark smudges against the lighter sands. Even the plumes of dust rising from the wheels of Pharaoh's chariotry could be plainly seen.

'Impressive, is it not?' Phanes said.

Ujahorresnet tore his gaze away from the distant panorama. 'Very. Should I thank you for not betraying me to my colleagues, or should I brace myself for a long fall?'

'I like your mettle, Ujahorresnet. If things were different, I think you and I might have become friends. Have you, in your newfound piety, decided to put aside the terms of our agreement?'

Ujahorresnet sighed. He had wrestled with that same question for much of the night. The thirst for vengeance had sent him astray, to be sure, but the idea of an Egypt reinvigorated by foreign rulers, by men who would give his countrymen a new sense of themselves, remained unchanged. 'No, general. I will honour our agreement. Egypt still suffers the rot of corruption. A symptom of that rot was my misguided attempt to use you as a tool of my vengeance. The Goddess has shown me the error of my ways.' Ujahorresnet gripped the Greek's arm. 'Make sure your plan is sound, general. If you die . . .'

'All men die,' Phanes said. 'But not all men stand on the threshold of greatness. If I die today, if the Fates forsake me, then so be it. I will enter Elysium secure in the knowledge that I stood where so few men ever had.'

'And where is that?'

'On the brink of immortality!'

A messenger rushed up the stairs to the pylon's roof. 'A sail, *strategos*!' he said, out of breath. He pointed off to the north. Phanes followed his gesture, grinned. True enough, a sail glimmered through the morning haze.

'What is it?' Ujahorresnet said, shading his eyes.

'Pharaoh's barge, the *Khepri*, and she'll dock

within the hour.' Phanes turned to his men. 'Get to your stations!'

Ujahorresnet hastened to stay abreast of the fighting men as they made their way down from the pylon and through the temple. He followed Phanes through the Temple of the Hearing Ear, built by great Ramses, and through a succession of decorative pylons dedicated to a smattering of different pharaohs. Their footfalls echoed about the great hypostyle hall. The noise and movement, the flash of sunlight on bronze, the cool shadows, all gave the priest a disjointed sensation, as if he stood outside his body and watched.

Word of the *Khepri's* approach had circulated through the ranks. All around the temple enclosure, soldiers hurried to take up their positions. A squire hustled to Phanes' side bearing his helmet and shield. The general caught up his helmet by its white horsehair crest.

'Any word from the scouts?'

The squire shook his head. 'No word, sire.'

Silence fell over the temple precinct.

Phanes stopped and glanced around. Save for a single squad, a guard of honour, his men had faded into the shadows of the first pylon, called the Gate of the Dawn; they were ready to charge the quay at Phanes' command. Nicias, he could barely discern, along with scores of hoplites, crouched down behind the row of sphinxes leading to the quay. All was in readiness.

'You are fond of tales and stories,' Ujahorresnet said. 'My own misfortune reminds me of the Tale of the Doomed Prince. Perhaps you could apply its lesson to your own situation.'

'Enlighten me, priest.'

'The prince was a son of a Pharaoh from antiquity, an ambitious man who lusted after his father's throne. This prince tried everything he could to remove his sire, from assassins in the night to fomenting uprisings among client-kings, all to no avail. At his wit's end, the prince begged and pleaded with the demonic Apophis. The Great Serpent heard the young man's cries and sent a cobra to do what had to be done. His father dead, the prince gained his throne.'

'An encouraging tale,' Phanes said, accepting his shield from the squire. The silvered Medusa's head flashed in the sun.

'There is more to it. You see, even though he had attained his dream, this prince-turned-Pharaoh could not enjoy his triumph. He could not sleep without seeing his father's poison-wracked face. He could not eat for fear of assassination. He could not trust for fear of betrayal. Be careful what you wish for, general. The reality of power is never as sweet as the dream of it.'

In the red haze of dawn, a horseman thundered through the northern suburbs of Memphis. He was a scout, dusty and haggard, his leather corselet streaked with blood. The narrow road he travelled widened into a tiled court with carefully manicured trees and a stone-kerbed pool of water lilies. To the right lay a sheltered colonnade that led to a complex of buildings attached to the temple of Thoth; to the left, an avenue of hard-packed dirt wound down to the Nile's edge; straight ahead, obelisks rose above the trees, marking the northern entrance to the temple of Sokar. The air smelled faintly of hyacinth.

The horseman reined in, unsure of his bearings. A solitary soldier, lounging near the pool, looked up, frowning.

'What word do you bring, brother?' the soldier said. He looked foreign, though he wore the bronze cuirass of a hoplite ranker, an infantry-man; the bruises on his face bore silent witness to the brutality of their training.

The scout leapt from his horse. 'T-The army!' he huffed. 'Has it marched out yet? Quick, man!'

The soldier bolted upright. 'Scarcely a half-hour gone, why?'

The scout cursed. 'Their infantry landed a few miles north, a heavily reinforced regiment shored up by elements of the Calasirian Guard! Their vanguard engaged us north of Saqqara. I fought clear and hurried back with word.'

'They'll be cut to ribbons!' the soldier said, fingering the hilt of his knife.

'That'll be the right of it,' the scout nodded, kneeling at the pool's edge and scooping up handfuls of water. 'That's why I have to warn them! See to my horse, friend,' the scout said. He looked askance at the powerfully built soldier. 'I must . . .'

Fingers like iron clamped around the back of the scout's neck. 'You should have stayed and died with your mates, boy-fucker!' the soldier, Barca, hissed. The scout had time for a sharp intake of breath before Barca's knife smashed through his heart.

The Phoenician eased the corpse to the ground.

Callisthenes and a handful of men crept out of hiding. 'That was close,' the Greek whispered. Barca nodded, lost in thought.

Their numbers had swelled since acquiring Callisthenes' aid. Another ten men had joined their cause. Ten farmers and one frightened Greek merchant. This smacked of suicide. Still, for the folk of Memphis to have any chance of aiding their Pharaoh, they had to have weapons beyond crude spears and hunting knives. Phanes had emptied the White Citadel of troops, sending half out to engage the chariots while the rest remained inside Ptah's temple, supported by two companies of peltasts along the perimeter. These peltasts were the Phoenician's target. They were mercenaries, archers and slingers, provincials from the Aegean who were only lightly armoured and marginally trained. Barca knew if his Egyptians hit them hard enough, they would crack like sun-dried plaster.

And, the key to hitting them hard enough lay in weaponry. Javelins, swords, perhaps bows and arrows would do the trick. As for armour, Barca doubted they would find anything useful except for bucklers of hippopotamus hide. Body armour was out of the question. Each Greek cared for his own breastplate and helmet, or had a squire look after it for him.

With weapons, more Egyptians would follow. He had sent Amenmose, Hekaib, and Ibebi to spread the word, albeit quietly, and Jauharah to gather what medical supplies she could. Once the fight was joined, Egyptian casualties would be catastrophic. Still, it was the best he could hope for.

'The weapons are kept in there,' Callisthenes hissed, pointing through the colonnade. Barca spotted a squat building sitting off by itself, across a grassy square littered with stone blocks. High windows pierced the sides of the supposed armoury, and the door looked ancient, its bronze bindings green with verdigris. 'My father's hired man was a scribe here. Before he died, he told me how the old Pharaohs had kept a spare weapons dump near the northern entrance of Sokar's temple.'

Barca led his raiders through the colonnade. The precinct was a scriptorium, a scribal college where young men trained to serve the god Thoth and, by extension, Pharaoh. Here, the builders of Memphis chose function over ornamentation; mud brick walls plastered and whitewashed, decorated with simple scenes of scribes and officials. The dominant symbol was that of Thoth, baboon-god of wisdom. Painted hieroglyphs related the saga of man's quest for knowledge and offered prayers for Thoth's renewed patronage.

'Get in there quickly,' Barca told his companions. 'But quietly. Phanes has Egyptian allies, too. No need to draw undue attention to ourselves. Stick to the shadows and keep your wits about you and we'll get out of this with our hides intact. Any questions?' The Egyptians stared at him, their eyes glassy with fear. 'Good. Let's go.'

Thothmes led the way, keeping low to the ground, running with a long, loping stride that reminded Barca of a jackal; next came Callisthenes, the merchant sweating like a man going to his execution. One by one, the others followed, with Barca bringing up the rear.

The thick door stymied them.

'Locked,' Callisthenes whispered. The merchant rolled his eyes in terror.

'I can pick it,' Thothmes said. The others disagreed.

Barca snatched a sledge from a stonecutter named Khety and smashed the door open with a single explosive blow. 'Grab everything you can and get out,' he said as the echo of splintering wood faded away.

Inside, dust swirled through the thin morning light seeping down from the high windows. Bronze swords stood ready for battle; rank after rank of spears stretched back into darkness. Bow staves and sheaves of arrows flanked a heap of round wood and leather shields bearing the *shenu,* the name-rings, of Wahibre Psammetichus, first of the Saite kings. The Egyptians laughed among themselves as they scattered and looted the armoury.

The place was a gift from the gods. The desiccated air of Egypt kept the wood unwarped, the bronze free of tarnish, the leather safe from rot. From a rack along the wall Barca selected a sword, long and straight with two edges of finely-honed iron. Ivory and lapis lazuli adorned the hilt. It was a princely weapon, easily worth a year's wages. The Phoenician looked around in wonder. How had all this material gone unclaimed through the years?

Callisthenes, following in his wake, picked up on Barca's unspoken question. 'It's said that before the first Psammetichus became Pharaoh, he was but a prince of Sais and Memphis. During that time he built dozens of these armouries and hid them from the prying eyes of his Assyrian overlord, Ashurbanipal. Most were looted through the years for this war or that, but this cache was forgotten, hidden by the priests of Thoth.' Callisthenes selected a sword not unlike Barca's. 'You think he knew?'

'Who?'

'The old Pharaoh. You think he knew that, in time, Egypt would again be beset by foreigners?'

'If he did, I doubt he would have welcomed the Greeks with such open arms.' The words came before Barca could think about it, a knee-jerk response to a long-cherished hatred. He regretted every last syllable.

Barca's scorn struck Callisthenes like the blow of a mace. He turned away, his face downcast. 'My people are a scourge! All my kinsmen ever did for Egypt was abuse her people and lust after her wealth. Every man, woman, and child of Hellas should be put to the sword before our blight spreads any farther!'

'Not all of you.' Barca clapped the smaller man on the shoulder. 'You are not like those others, Callisthenes. You, I would call a friend.'

Callisthenes nodded, not trusting words for fear they would be rendered incoherent with emotion. He was spared answering by a commotion outside the armoury.

'Barca!' Thothmes called, his voice quivering with trepidation. 'Come, quick!'

The Phoenician scowled and darted past Callisthenes. Outside, the sun had risen above the surrounding buildings, flooding the scriptorium with bright yellow light. Barca shaded his eyes.

'Well, I'll be damned,' he grunted.

They were surrounded by dozens of Egyptians. More waited beyond the colonnade; tradesmen, merchants, field workers, scribes, priests. Every strata of Memphite culture was represented: rich and poor, learned and ignorant, pious and profane.

Barca drove his sword point-first into the ground.

One of the men stepped forward, a captain in the temple guard by his crisp white kilt and gold-scaled corselet. 'I am Pentu, and my brothers and I have come to aid you, Phoenician. Last eve the Greek seized the leaders of our temples as his hostages and slew the First Servant of Ptah to drive home his point. We could do nothing to thwart Inyotef's murder, but we can avenge him.'

A ripple of consternation went through Barca's raiders. Inyotef? Murdered?

Another voice raised in anger. This from a man whose stained clothing marked him as a brick maker. 'My sister died in the Greek's ambush of your Medjay. Me and mine are with you, too!' The same tale echoed from every throat, from men fed up with Greek atrocities. Whole families stood ready: fathers and sons, nephews and brothers; from fresh-faced boys to gnarled grandfathers.

It was the rebellion Barca had hoped for.

'This will not be like the travesty in the Square,' Barca said. 'This will be true battle. It will be savage and ugly; you will hear things and see things that will stay with you till your dying day, provided you live through this one.'

'We understand,' Pentu said. 'This is our home. We will fight to defend it.'

'Make no mistake, most of you will die.'

Pentu smiled mirthlessly. 'We are Egyptian, my friend. We die better than most men live.'

꞉ ꞉ ꞉ ꞉ ꞉

The creak of oars presaged the *Khepri's* approach. Seconds passed. Tense. Expectant. Thousands of eyes watched the quay. The structure was ancient, its foundations perhaps as old as Memphis itself. A canal led from the Nile, and the resulting lake provided a more stable surface for the loading and unloading of ships. Paved in brilliant white limestone and flanked by twin obelisks dedicated to Ptah, the quay formed a U-shaped niche where barques and barges could be docked even during the Nile's yearly flood.

The *Khepri* entered the canal, sails furled as her oarsmen propelled her slowly through the blue-green water. Sunlight gleamed on the gilded statues decorating her decks. Thin poles rising from the bow and stern displayed floating banners of deep Tyrian purple, embroidered with symbols of gods and pharaoh. Phanes trembled in anticipation.

'Will you translate for me, priest?' he said to Ujahorresnet, his voice calm, measured.

Ujahorresnet nodded. 'Should the need arise. Frankly, that barge looks deserted.' Indeed, save for sailors and oarsmen there was little movement on deck. Where were the glittering ranks of Pharaoh's guard? The bureaucrats and functionaries who shadowed the Son of Ra like jackals shadow a lion? Phanes found their absence disturbing.

The barge thumped against the quay, its hull protected from damage by fenders of woven reeds. Sailors dropped down on either side, securing the *Khepri* with strong ropes lashed to bronze-ringed mooring posts; others lowered an elegant boarding plank of gold-chased ebony into place. The oarsmen rose from their benches, sweating from far more than the exertion of guiding their master's ship home. Many of them muttered prayers. The small hairs on Phanes' neck stirred. Something was amiss.

The crew of the *Khepri* glanced at one another as they edged toward the railings. The soldiers facing them radiated menace. Phanes could feel his men's impatience; it mirrored his own. They could barely contain their lusts for blood, gold, and glory.

'This feels wrong.' Phanes signalled Nicias to advance. Howling like pirates, the Greeks mobbed the barge. Egyptian sailors shrieked in terror at the sight of a horde of bronze armoured hoplites storming the quay. They had no fight in them. As one, they hurled themselves over the railings and into the water. Phanes sprinted down the sphinx-lined avenue and mounted the steps leading to the quay. Ujahorresnet followed, his lips a tight line. Soldiers rushed to either end of the quay to secure their flanks. It occurred to them that the *Khepri's* hold could be packed with fighting men.

'Something's not right,' Nicias said. 'There were maybe two dozen men aboard. We . . .'

Phanes shouldered past him and ascended the gangplank. Nicias and a squad of soldiers followed on his heels. No opposition greeted Phanes; he stalked to the stern of the ship, to where linen curtains hid the royal throne from view. Fabric ripped as he tore the curtains down.

The throne stood empty, save for a roll of papyrus pinned to the seat with a knife.

Nicias reached down and pulled the papyrus free. He unrolled it. It contained a single sentence, written in the priestly script. 'Hieratic,' Ujahorresnet said. He glanced at Phanes. The Greek commander nodded. Nicias handed the papyrus to the old priest.

'It says: "Enjoy this, the least of my thrones, for it is as close as you will get, you ungrateful son of a whore!".' Ujahorresnet braced himself for a tirade.

But Phanes remained cool, calculating, even as the last piece of the puzzle clicked in his mind. 'Zeus! That old bastard is craftier than I thought! He's landed his infantry elsewhere! Redeploy to the square!'

As one organism possessed of a single mind, the Greeks wheeled and made for the western gate of the temple precinct. Squads peeled off in unison, with common rankers cleaving to their file leaders, file leaders dogging the officers. They streamed through the close confines of the temple proper, the columns like tree trunks in a forest of stone.

Dodging Greeks, Ujahorresnet found his brother priests huddled about the feet of a colossal statue of Pharaoh. Like a shepherd, the First Servant of Neith gathered them together and led them back through the temple maze. Soldiers cursed as they jogged past them; the jangle of bronze on bronze, of wood striking metal, created a deafening clamour that dislocated their senses. Above the din, though, Ujahorresnet discerned a different sound, a chilling sound.

The thunder of hooves.

Phanes skidded to a halt, a curse forming on his lips. Ahead, through the gated pylon of the western entrance to Ptah's temple, the Greek saw a dust cloud rolling toward the Square of Deshur. For an instant the dust cleared, and Phanes beheld the shattered remnant of Hyperides' men, the sky above them black with arrows and javelins. Beyond, a wall of chariots loomed. Phanes' face hardened. There were more of them than he had realized. Far more.

And, he realized something else . . . he had been outfoxed.

'Dress the lines!' he roared, setting his helmet into place and drawing his sword. Outfoxed by an old man!

11

BATTLE

The Egyptians struck the Greek vanguard less than a mile from Memphis, crushing their centre and driving them back toward the Nile as a shepherd drives sheep. The mercenary infantry, still in column formation, could not withstand the deadly effects of an arrow storm coupled with the impact of a bronze and iron wedge of chariots. A man on foot stood little chance against the harnessed strength of two stallions, whose hooves crushed hastily-locked shields and the bodies they strived to protect. The Greek formation splintered; some sought refuge in the necropolis of Saqqara. The larger number of them fell back to the Square of Deshur.

Ahmose rode in the forefront, Nebmaatra at his side, forming the tip of the wedge. The Calasirian Guard followed in their wake. Pharaoh, resplendent in his corselet of golden scales and blue war helm, leaned out and brained a soldier with his axe. Their ruse had worked. The Greeks had been so focused on the *Khepri*, on the men who had volunteered to play into Phanes' hands, that they discounted the chariots as a tangible threat. Now, they were being shown their folly.

A choking curtain of dust and soil churned up from the horses' hooves obscured the battlefield. Ahmose knew Phanes and the bulk of his hoplites would form ranks in the Square. Once his chariots had penetrated as far as the Way of the Truth of Ptah, Ahmose would order them to wheel. Then, they would drive the Greeks north into the arms of the waiting infantry, crushing them in a vice. Pharaoh grinned as his axe sheared through a Greek helmet.

Pharaoh's chariot reached the western edge of the Square of Deshur. He drew up; his squadrons flanked him. In front of the Egyptians, the Greek vanguard stood in disarray. Beyond their struggling forms, through the dust, Ahmose could see a shining phalanx of hoplites.

'They'll be a tough nut to crack,' Nebmaatra shouted. Pharaoh glanced around, seeing his Calasirians around him. In one chariot he glimpsed Tjemu. The Libyan had shaken off his melancholy when the first blows had fallen on the road from Saqqara. He laughed, slinging droplets of blood from his sword.

'But crack they will!' Ahmose said, his breathing heavy through the congestion in his lungs. His charioteer, a man with legs like knotted tree trunks, hauled on the reins, waiting for the order to charge. 'I want Phanes alive, if it is possible.'

'If it's possible, it will be done, Pharaoh,' Nebmaatra nodded.

Ahmose touched the charioteer on the shoulder. With an earth-shaking roar, the Egyptian chariots charged.

☥ 𓂀 𓏏 𓀀 𓊹

Hyperides watched his vanguard crack and slough away like old plaster. Dust and grit choked him, caking on his sweat-dampened cheeks and forehead. Pharaoh's chariots were invincible. Oh, his troops had done some damage, gutted a few horses, slain a few men, but nothing like the carnage wrought by the Egyptians. A lull gave Hyperides a moment's respite. Greek soldiers milled about, confused, walking like dead men through the mist of war. Hyperides had expected better of them. Gods be damned! He had trained them better than this! Still, he wasn't a sorcerer. He couldn't forge gold from dung.

His men cowered as the Egyptians charged. The ground underfoot shook, and the sun glimmered through the haze, striking fire from the tidal wave of bronze that hurtled down on them.

Hyperides cursed as his mercenaries stumbled back. He flailed about with the flat of his blood-stained sword, striding out in front so his men could see him.

'Stand, you sons of whores!' Hyperides roared. 'Stand and fight!'

He looked back in time to see the sun reflect from a spear head. For a split second Hyperides froze, mesmerized by the scintillant play of light on bronze, and that instant was enough. The spear punched through his breastplate, his chest, and erupted from his back in a welter of blood. The impact lifted him off his feet and flung him back into the roiling curtain of dust.

With him, the Greek vanguard died.

Phanes saw his light troops dissolve beneath the wheels of Pharaoh's chariots. He motioned to Nicias. 'Go forward and rally where you can.' The squat captain saluted and hustled to the fore. Phanes felt a chill, and a familiar presence at his side. A sense of loss and longing washed over him.

'Say it, Spartan.'

The disembodied voice of a slain Lysistratis echoed through Phanes' skull. *'Not as infallible as you once thought, are you?'*

Phanes turned. 'The battle isn't won. Our soldiers will give Amasis the fight of his life.'

The soldiers nearest Phanes glanced around, wondering who it was their commander addressed. Had he lost his sanity? Merciful Zeus! Let that not be true.

'I am sure. But, our victory is no longer a foregone conclusion. What if you lose?'

Phanes laughed mordantly. 'If I lose here, then I will return with a larger force. Egypt is mine, Spartan! She just doesn't realize it yet.'

At the northern entrance of Ptah's temple, a skeleton force of peltasts listened to the distant fighting with an awe bordering on the supernatural. They could imagine what went on outside the zone of safety afforded by the temple walls. Hoplites, ranked out in a phalanx with their shields interleaved, would present a hedge of spears to the Egyptians. The chariots would harry them; arrows and javelins would seek out chinks in the Greek armour. Yet, for every Greek who fell, another would take his place, replenishing the phalanx with machine-like efficiency.

The officer in charge at the northern gate, a dispossessed nobleman from Rhodes, wiped at the sweat pouring down his face. He stared at the statues flanking the huge twin-towered gateway, at the images depicting Pharaoh crushing his enemies in the presence of a solemn-faced Ptah, at the hieroglyphs carved deep into the rock on either side of the silver and cedar flagpoles. To get from this entrance to the interior of the temple proper, an intruder had to pass through four such gateways, each named for a king of antiquity. 'These sons of whores know how to build a defensive wall,' he said, patting the cyclopean stonework. From their summit, his peltasts could hold off a superior force of Egyptians. 'Sit tight, lads. It might fall upon us to save the day, after all. Dion, bring me that water skin. This cursed country is like an oven.'

The young man called Dion caught up the skin of water and ambled over. He had only gone a few feet when he stumbled and fell. Amid the laughter and the jeers, the officer sprang to his feet, clawing for his spear. An arrow stood out from the juncture of Dion's neck and shoulder. The peltasts' laughter died as a howling mob of Egyptian peasants stormed through a door in the side of the gate.

𓂀 𓏤 𓆓 𓀀 𓊪

Sweat dripped down Callisthenes' nose. His slick hands clutched the hilt of his sword. This was battle. The real thing. He felt no sense of power, no thirst for glory. All Callisthenes felt was the cold hand of fear. He hugged the wall as Ibebi and the others surged past, slamming into the unprepared Greeks. One of the Egyptians, the stonecutter Khety, took the blade of a spear to his chest. It rammed through his body, exploding out his back. Khety died on his feet. Callisthenes felt his gorge rise.

Another peltast leapt Khety's body and barrelled straight for Callisthenes, levelling his javelin. To his credit, Callisthenes did not allow his fear to master him. He darted aside in the last possible second, his foot dragging out behind him, and swung wildly. The peltast skidded on the stones, then tripped over Callisthenes' foot.

The man hit the ground hard, on his stomach, air exploding from his lungs. Before he could rise, Callisthenes spun and drove the point of his sword between the peltast's shoulder blades, into the gristle and bone of his spine. The man spasmed and died.

I killed a man. Callisthenes' hands trembled. He looked down at the dead Greek and felt colder still. *I killed a man of Hellas.* There was no glory in this. The cacophony of battle drew him from his reverie. All around him knots of Egyptians engaged the demoralized peltasts. He saw Hekaib gut a soldier nearly twice his size. Thothmes wielded a sword like a man possessed, hacking limbs and skulls. Ibebi, he noticed, fought with the cool precision of a veteran. Even stately Amenmose howled and flung himself into the fray. Barca, Pentu, and a handful of others mounted the steps to the parapet.

'Back! Force them back!' he heard Barca yell.

𓂀 𓏏 𓋴 𓀀 𓏤

'Force them back!' Barca roared, dashing along the parapet. A Cretan archer gaped at him, his mind not registering what his eyes beheld. The back of Barca's hand sent the man spinning from the parapet. The sound and smell of bloodshed reached into Barca's soul. He felt the Beast fighting against its chains, longing to be free.

Another Cretan spun, notching an arrow. His eyes widened as the Phoenician bore down upon him. Barca loosed a hideous scream, his face screwed up in a rictus of hate. The archer's trembling hands released the arrow too soon. It splintered on the stones of the parapet. As he groped for another shaft, Barca's sword sheared through his collarbone and lodged in his chest. The Cretan gurgled as Barca kicked him free of his blade.

A second peltast charged him, thrusting a javelin at Barca's midsection. The Phoenician weaved, allowing the javelin to pass between himself and the wall, as he drove his shoulder into the peltast's body. The soldier catapulted from the parapet, his screams lost to the thronging mass of fighters below. Barca scooped up the fallen Cretan's bow and a pair of arrows.

Pentu and the others swept the Greeks from the wall. Barca left it to the guard captain to station archers at key points while he rushed to the juncture of the north and west walls to get a handle on the battle taking place in the Square. He found himself looking down on the right flank of the Greek phalanx. He looked for Phanes as he nocked an arrow. Instead, the Greeks were rallying to a squat man in blood-splashed armour. Not Phanes, but an important fellow, nonetheless. Was it one of his regiment commanders?

Barca shrugged and took careful aim. He could see the squat man reinforcing the phalanx, bawling orders that Barca could not hear. The Phoenician exhaled . . .

Nicias staggered, clawing at the arrow that sprouted from between his shoulder blades, lodging in his armour. He turned. A second arrow threaded through the eye socket of his helmet.

Nicias toppled; leaderless, his men fell into disarray.

Above the battle, Barca threw the bow aside and caught up his sword.

The fight for the gate was brutal. Callisthenes saw men he had known as peaceful farmers take on the guise of feral beasts – kicking, spitting, biting. They fought for their homes, their wives, their children. The Greeks fought for their lives. It was a bitter struggle, without quarter or mercy.

Caught up in the press of bodies, Callisthenes found himself near the forefront. Ahead of him, partially engulfed in the shadow of the second pylon, a gateway named for warrior-queen Hatshepsut, he saw Amenmose stumble backward. A Greek surged forward, driving his spear toward the old man's belly.

Callisthenes acted from instinct. He batted aside the spear and kicked the peltast in the groin. With the adrenalin coursing through his system, though, Callisthenes might as well have struck the man with a feather. The soldier tried to bring his spear back into play, its head skittering on the stones. Sickened, Callisthenes had no other choice.

His sword struck the man where neck and shoulder joined. It sheared through leather, flesh, and bone, driving the peltast to his knees. A second blow ended his suffering.

'Help me up!' Amenmose ordered. Callisthenes pried his gaze away from the second Greek he had killed and moved to the old Egyptian's side. He was weak, exhausted, and bleeding from a score of gashes. Ibebi materialized at his side.

'Get him back!' he yelled, pointing the way they had come.

'What about you?' Callisthenes draped Amenmose's arm over his shoulder.

'Our infantry is coming! Only have to hold for a few more minutes!' And with that Ibebi plunged into the fighting. He and the others stood firm in the gateway, slowly forcing the Greeks back. Swords and spears licked out. One of Ibebi's flankers went down, his entrails spilling across the stones. Three arrows avenged the fallen youth, slashing into the charging peltast. His corpse snarled the feet of his mates as they pressed forward, intent on securing the gate and, with it, their freedom.

'They only need to hold a moment longer!' Callisthenes muttered. Already, elements of the Egyptian regular infantry streamed through the northern entrance.

Ibebi hurled the young man at his side back and was turning to make room for the Egyptian soldiers when a Greek spear took him low, in the spine. He fell, clawing at the dust as a half a dozen more spears ended his life.

'Where is he? I cannot see him,' Amenmose said.

'He is with Osiris, now.' Callisthenes slumped

against the wall of the gate and looked out over the roiling sea of bodies, his eyes moist. This madness owned nothing of glory. Nothing!

𓂀 𓋹 𓆓 𓇋 𓏏

Barca descended the stairs inside the gate, shaking drops of blood from his sword blade. The Greeks had not fought well, but they died well. It was enough for their gods. He wished their shades the best as they crossed the river. The Phoenician's skin burned with fever and he could feel warmth oozing from his gashed side, but he felt no pain. Perhaps it was true about the thrill of battle negating the effects of wounds. Matthias had told him that, once. A pang of guilt stabbed Barca's heart. He had caused the deaths of too many of those closest to him. Matthias. Ithobaal. His men. Neferu.

Guilt turned to rage.

He emerged from the gate and found Jauharah aiding the priests who were tending to the wounded. Her arms were covered in blood up to the elbow; blood streaked her forehead where she had pushed her hair out of her eyes. Those eyes glanced up, catching sight of Barca. She disengaged herself from a young man whose screams of agony intermingled with pleas for his mother. She drifted across to the Phoenician, moving like a woman caught in the grip of a nightmare.

'I-I never imagined . . .' she trailed off, her eyes roving over the carnage.

'Most never do. This is how peace is kept.'

She glanced down. 'You're bleeding.' Barca followed her gaze. Blood seeped out from under his cuirass, soaking the hem and side of his kilt. She reached for the buckles holding the heavy breastplate in place, but Barca brushed her hands away.

'Later.'

'What will you do now?' she said.

Others had clustered around him, their lips framing the same question. He saw Thothmes and Hekaib, Pentu and his temple guardsmen, and beyond the circle of Egyptians, he spotted Callisthenes and Amenmose sitting with their backs against the foot of a pharaonic statue, passing a wineskin back and forth. The merchant of Naucratis had an odd look in his eyes, a look Barca had seen a thousand times over. The look of innocence shattered.

Barca glanced out over the battlefield. 'I have my men to avenge.'

'I'm with you,' Thothmes said. Hekaib nodded. 'And me.' Several other Egyptians expressed an interest in joining their Pharaoh.

'Fine,' Barca said. 'But know this. Once we leave these walls, you men are on your own. If you fall behind, I'll not drop back and guide you by the hand.'

'So be it!' Thothmes bristled. Barca nodded. He stooped and grabbed a fallen shield. The Egyptians followed his lead. Men with no armour stripped the dead, taking their greaves, their helmets. In a twinkling, the farmers and masons and artisans were gone, and in their place stood a score of Egyptian soldiers, faces grim and bloody.

Without a word, Barca led them out through the northern entrance.

𓂀 𓏤 𓋴 𓀎 𓊽

The men alongside Phanes fought like the sons of Achilles. They used their spears, their shields, even their bodies to repulse the first wave of chariots. Horses screamed and died. Men leapt from their chariots as their mounts ran amok. Chassis of wood and bronze split apart, tumbling end over end to crush friend and foe without prejudice. Peltasts ranged along the borders of the fray, using javelins, arrows, and sling bullets where they could, to dubious effect.

Phanes perched his blood-blasted helmet on his forehead, inhaling great lungfuls of dusty air as he surveyed the battlefield. He could read it like a scroll, and its didactic text told a tale of defeat. Pharaoh's infantry chipped away at his right flank; his centre bore the inverse bulge of an imminent break. Already, his Greeks were falling back, giving ground as the chariots broke over their ranks in endless waves, eroding their numbers with each successive crash. Once their centre broke, once the formation split in two, the battle would be over. Phanes tasted gall; the bitter sting of ambitions lost. He cursed himself for falling for the Pharaoh's ruse, his scouts for not

252

properly assaying the Egyptians, his captains for not stoking the fire in his men's bellies. Most of all, though, he cursed the oracle at Delphi for promulgating lies. By his own hand? Bah! With each passing moment, his reign as king of Egypt became more and more a thing of smoke and fog. A fever dream.

Phanes reseated his helmet and waded back into the thickest of the fighting, where men, horses, and chariots tangled in a morass of thrashing limbs and murderous bronze. Egyptians fought on foot, hurling themselves against a wall of Greek armour. Here, with their commander at their side, the phalanx held firm, their shields locked and their spears ripping through man and beast with equal ease.

A weight struck Phanes' shield; from instinct he braced his legs and thrust back, sending an Egyptian sprawling. As the soldier struggled to his feet, Phanes lashed out, cleaving the man's head to the teeth. Another Egyptian charged, spear levelled at Phanes' belly. The Greek commander sidestepped and drove the edge of his shield into the hollow of the man's throat, all but decapitated him.

Beyond the sea of helmets and faces, Phanes spotted Pharaoh's banners. He could see the blue war crown, the axe that rose and fell amid a scarlet rain. Phanes longed to get closer, within sword's reach, but a cordon of Calasirian guardsmen made that impossible. His line could not hold, not for much longer. The cost of Greek lives in stopping the chariots had been too high; too many men died repulsing their infantry charges. With each successive wave, his lines crumbled like a sandbank. It was time to think of cutting free.

'Fall back!' Phanes ordered those men nearest him. 'Fall back to the quay!' He could yet save himself, and perhaps a handful of his men.

👁 ⚱ ⚚ 👤 🏺

Corpses littered the Square of Deshur. The Egyptians in Barca's wake drew a collective breath as they rounded the northwestern corner of the temple of Ptah, awed by the carnage that cut a broad arc from the Saqqaran Road to the Western Gate. Most had never seen a battle up close, never smelled the stench of death or heard the plaintive cries of a man dying from a sword-cut to the belly. This was uncomfortably new to them; to a man of Barca's experience, it was commonplace, almost banal. He felt nothing as his eyes scanned the field, fixing on an empty chariot.

Skittish, the horses danced and gambolled, their eyes rolling in fear. Barca leapt onto the platform of the chariot, ignoring the blood left behind by its previous occupant. True to his word, he did not wait for the Egyptians. The Phoenician seized the reins. Thothmes and Hekaib had barely scrambled on, grasping the side rails, before the horses found their rhythm and shot forward. The Egyptians stared at each other as Barca, his

254

face a mask of grim determination, snapped the reins, lashing more speed from the team. He angled them toward the thickest of the fighting, to where Pharaoh's battle standard floated above the wrack.

As they drew closer, the sound of armoured men in close contact, fighting for their lives, was nothing less than chilling. Even to Barca, who had heard the sound for most of his adult life, the crash of armies sent a thrill down his spine. It was the sound of a vast engine of destruction, its grinding blades lubricated with slick, hot gore.

It was music to the Beast.

The Phoenician gritted his teeth. His chariot crossed the intervening ground. A forest of clashing spears rose before them, swaying like saplings in a squall. The wounded crawled among the dead, some begging for succour, others for death. Barca hauled on the reins, his muscles knotting as he slewed the chariot sideways. The wheels skipped and clattered on the pavement.

Ahead, Greek and Egyptian were locked in death's embrace. Those not dancing with the reaper surged forward in search of a partner. Peltasts targeted the chariot. Javelins flew. One thudded into the wood of the chassis, near Thothmes. Another found a different mark.

The inside horse collapsed, the javelin cleaving its heart. Unbalanced, the other fell, flipping the chariot on its side and spilling its passengers. Barca, his body a compact ball of muscle and sinew, rolled to his feet with the grace of a gymnast. His companions fared worse. Both Egyptians struck the ground hard, leaving patches of skin across the abrasive stones. Thothmes regained his senses first. He clambered to his feet, casting about for his sword.

A peltast broke ranks and charged Hekaib. The Egyptian presented a tempting target: a man on his hands and knees, fighting for breath. An easy kill. He took two steps forward, his arm cocked back over his ear. Barca intercepted him. His shield knocked the javelin aside as he rammed his sword through the soldier's body. Behind him, Thothmes rushed over and helped Hekaib to his feet.

'Merciful gods of the desert!' a voice roared to Barca's left. 'You know the value of a good entrance!' Tjemu hobbled up, his weight supported by a broken spear. The Libyan bled from countless small wounds, though Barca judged most of the gore spattering him to be Greek.

'And you know you're supposed to leave me someone to kill, Libyan,' Barca said, clapping the smaller man on the back. Tjemu grinned ruthlessly.

'These Egyptians got their hackles up.' He glanced around, seeking a familiar face among Barca's men. 'Where's that old maiden, Ithobaal?'

Barca's jaw grew tight. He shook his head. Tjemu's shoulders slumped. 'Did he die well?'

'He died as a Medjay should,' Barca replied. 'But he died in vain unless we stop Phanes.'

'Then why are we standing here yammering like old women while that bastard makes good his escape?'

Ujahorresnet and the other priests stood together in the thick shadow of the hypostyle hall. They were unguarded, but with battles raging inside and out, where could they run? No, best to stay put and pray. Ujahorresnet prayed for a different outcome.

The First Servant of Neith knew his prayers had gone unanswered when he saw a blood-splashed apparition crossing the columned hall. Phanes ripped his helmet off and threw it aside. Sweat and blood matted his dark hair. His lips curled in barely contained rage.

'You have failed,' Ujahorresnet said.

'Not failure!' Phanes snarled. 'Merely a set-back.' Men withdrew around them, sprinting to the quay to make the *Khepri* ready for departure. A rear guard of hoplites fought a delaying action against the Egyptians. The sound of fighting echoed through the hall.

'You are tenacious, Greek. I'll give you that. Have you not the wisdom and the humility to know when you have been bested?'

'Bested? Not by any length, priest. All that has changed is my focus. If I cannot give Egypt to Cambyses, then I will engineer its destruction. Your confederates have become a liability.'

Phanes pointed to the cowering knot of priests. 'Kill them.'

Ujahorresnet interposed himself between his countrymen and the Greeks. 'Let them go,' he said. 'Don't force me to sacrifice myself to save their lives.'

Phanes and the old priest stood toe to toe. They stared at one another without flinching. Neither man gave back an inch. The tableau could have held for an eternity, but Phanes' time was limited. 'I would have liked to have been your friend, Ujahorresnet,' the Greek said. 'When I return, perhaps we can meet under different circumstances and share a glass. I give you your life, and theirs, though I will doubtless live to regret it.' Phanes motioned his men away, then stopped. A slow smile spread across his features. 'This place, it's full of oils and unguents?'

Ujahorresnet nodded.

'Good.' He turned back to face his soldiers. 'Burn it!'

Smoke guttered from within the hypostyle hall. Flames gnawed at the stones, searing away ancient layers of paint and plaster. A thick black haze drifted across the battlefield. Through it Barca stalked like Death personified. Egyptians formed at his back, creating a fighting wedge with the indomitable Phoenician at its tip. The remnants of the hoplites, cut off by the flames, locked shields and braced for the final thrust, their palisade of spears all that remained between Barca and his prey.

'Phanes!'

With that ear-splitting roar, Barca loosed the Beast from the prison of his soul. He moved through the Greeks like a farmer threshing grain, reaping a bloody harvest among them. Spears thrusting at him he turned aside, swords whistling toward him he deflected, and men seeking to stand against him he struck down with impunity.

In his wake Hekaib and Thothmes fought to emulate him. The Egyptians were madmen, but to the Greeks they were the lesser of the two evils. Men who stood no chance against Barca threw themselves against his comrades with zealous fervour.

Their ends came quickly.

Hekaib fell first. He could not maintain the brutal pace Barca had set. His lungs burned; his arms and legs felt like leaden weights. Each step, each thrust, became agony. His mind wandered back over the years, seeing again his wife and children, the laughing face of Ibebi, dour Menkaura. *Homage to thee, Osiris.*

Hekaib stumbled, his shield falling. A shadow loomed out of the smoke; a hoplite surged in and drove his eight-footer into the little man's belly. The Egyptian screamed once, then fell silent as a sword hacked through his neck. Thothmes turned in time to see the head and body fall in different directions. Spears and swords licked out, driving him back. Blood sheeted from a cut on Thothmes' scalp, blinding him. He tripped over a corpse. Thothmes rolled over on his stomach and clawed at the gory stones, fingers seeking the hilt of his sword. His will, his spirit, did not falter, but in his mind he knew it was time. He knew . . .

A hoplite spear, driven through his back, freed his *ka* to travel to the next world.

Through the haze of *katalepsis* Barca did not see the two Egyptians die. His eyes were fixed on the far side of the hypostyle hall. He hacked his way through the last of the Greeks and rushed alone into the inferno.

'Phanes!'

Precious oils and fine linens fed the flames equally as well as common lamp fuel and resin-soaked rags, creating only a sweeter-smelling miasma to burn the lungs and sear the eyes. The Phoenician emerged from the temple complex in time to see the *Khepri* backing water. With a bellow of rage, Barca flung his shield away and rushed down the avenue of sphinxes to the quay, too late to stop their exodus. Though smoke and exhaustion blurred his vision, he could see Phanes standing in the bow of the retreating barge. The Greek smiled despite his defeat.

'You son of a bitch!' Barca roared. 'I will hunt you to the ends of the earth!' The Phoenician swayed, sword falling from his loosening grip. 'To the e-ends . . .' The world spun. Cold, leaden limbs weighed him down. No. Too much left to do. He needed a ship. A ship. Pharaoh would grant him one.

Figures staggered through the smoke, their bodies pierced by spear and sword, wracked with exhaustion. Tjemu sat in the shadow of a sphinx, a rag pressed to his thigh, his curses lost amid the general clamour.

Nearby, ringed by Calasirians, Ahmose leaned against a stone obelisk. Pharaoh's breath came in wracking gasps and his armour bore witness to the fury of the battle; several scales were missing, others were dented, and the whole was dulled by a patina of fresh gore. His arms were criss-crossed with cuts and gouges. Dishevelled priests prepared bandages and poultices for their king. Ahmose removed the blue war crown and passed it to an aide. Nebmaatra crouched at his feet. The Calasirian commander knotted a scrap of linen around his lacerated forearm.

'So much for Phanes' loyalty, eh?' Pharaoh said. A shout went up from the surrounding soldiers, cries of 'Medjay! Medjay!' as Barca staggered through their ranks. Swords were thrust heavenward; spears clashed on shields. Oblivious to the din, Barca shouldered his way past the Calasirians.

'G-Grant me a ship, sire,' he said. 'A s-ship . . .'

'Hasdrabal Barca!' Ahmose smiled. 'We owe you your heart's desire. If it's a ship you want, you will have it. But not today. Rest, Hasdrabal. The gods know you have earned it.'

'C-Can't . . .' Barca collapsed to his knees, his

face pale. Nebmaatra caught his shoulder before he could topple, easing him to the ground. Frowning, he unbuckled Barca's cuirass and tore away the sodden linen bandages. The slash in his side had widened. Through the weakened sutures, Nebmaatra saw the moist red-blue of viscera.

'Fetch a physician!' Nebmaatra motioned to one of his Calasirians.

'How bad is it?' Ahmose said.

'He's lost much blood.'

The Phoenician stirred. His words, when he spoke, came out slurred. 'S-Ship . . . y-you . . . must . . .'

'Whatever the physicians need will be put at their disposal. I owe this man too much to allow him to die,' Pharaoh said. He reached out, patting Barca's arm. 'You hear me, son? You don't have my leave to die. Not while Phanes yet lives.'

Hasdrabal Barca groaned as the darkness rose up about him.

PART TWO

Year One of the reign of Ankhkaenre Psammetichus
(525 BC)

12

INTERLUDE

Time passed. The Nile rose and fell; the Inundation gave way to the Sowing. By the month of Pharmuthi, on the cusp of *Shemu,* the Harvest, news had trickled out of the East and into the great cities of Palestine. Merchants from the desert oasis of Palmyra carried ominous tidings through the Lebanon Mountains and down into the Phoenician littoral. Rumours blazed through the bazaars of Byblos, the streets of Sidon; priests of Ba'al in Tyre sought to divine the truth using the livers of sacred bulls.

Merchants from Jerusalem brought word to the *shaykhs* of Sinai, who traded turquoise and copper for worked metals and weapons. Over fires of dried acacia and camel dung, the Bedouin consulted their oracles, the stars and rocks of their desert land; their oracles spoke of a day of great slaughter just over the horizon. This news spread from Sinai to Egypt, from Bedouin to villager, from merchant to soldier, from priest to nobleman. At every turn, the news was met with a terrible sense of foreboding. The Persians were coming.

An army had set out from Babylon, an army whose ultimate goal was the Nile valley. Envoys of King Cambyses had been sent to the lands along the Persian road to Egypt demanding tokens of earth and water, the age-old symbols of capitulation.

An emissary reached Sais on the first of Pakhons, half a year since the battle at Memphis, and found the city in chaos. Ahmose lay on his deathbed, attended on all sides by grim-faced priests. Shovels of incense were offered on braziers of glowing coals. Through the sweltering days, the temples swarmed with those begging intercession from the gods. Through the cool nights, the music of sistrum and tambourine prepared all of Egypt for Pharaoh's imminent passing.

The emissary, Gobartes, was not without friends in Sais, friends who had survived the purges that followed the Greek uprising at Memphis. One such was Iufaa, a priest and aristocrat. Gobartes could not remember what god Iufaa served; truly, these Egyptians had more gods than Scythia had horses. Whatever his religious leanings, Iufaa's political affiliations left little to doubt. He would welcome Persian interference to end the illegitimate reign of Ahmose and his brood. Gobartes gave Iufaa the name of a man he had a pressing need to speak with.

Ujahorresnet.

Since Memphis, the old priest's fortunes had risen. Tales of his bravery in the face of violence grew, taking on a mythic quality. Oh, there were rumours – bred, no doubt, by jealous rivals. The most persistent had the kind old man acting as an ally of Phanes in the capture of Hasdrabal Barca and the deaths of his Medjay. It was hard for such a rumour to grow and thrive when Barca himself discounted it. Regardless of his detractors, Ujahorresnet found himself in the presence of Pharaoh, who gave him a host of honours, not the least of which was the office of First Servant of Neith in Sais.

Iufaa, ever cautious, arranged a dinner on Ujahorresnet's behalf. If his guests thought it an extreme display of arrogance that he should invite Gobartes, they wisely said nothing. The evening went well. After being greeted by their host, the guests repaired to the roof to take their meal in the coolness of night. The echo of music rose from the distant palace. Small talk, gossip, idle chatter flowed as they worked their way through a brace of succulent geese, breads, cheeses, wine and beer. Slaves cleared away the last of the platters and crocks, and Iufaa escorted his other guests down into the garden, leaving the Persian envoy alone with the guest of honour. Gobartes wasted no time.

'We have a common interest,' Gobartes said, 'and . . . dare I say it . . . a common ally. You see, my good priest, I, too, subscribe to your theory of foreign invasion as a way to reinvigorate a flagging culture. In my own land, the Medes conquered their neighbours to create a stronger people. It could be the same with Egypt.'

Ujahorresnet glanced sidelong at the Persian. 'You have me at a disadvantage. I am but a priest, albeit of some importance, not a politician or a courtier. I . . .'

Gobartes laughed. 'Phanes did not lie when he praised your cunning.'

'Phanes!' Ujahorresnet glanced around, expecting to see soldiers pour from the darkness at the merest mention of the Greek's name. 'He is no more my ally than he is yours! Phanes serves no man but Phanes.'

'True,' Gobartes said, 'but does he not embody the very theory you expound? He is the epitome of the foreign invader, and his presence, his existence, could serve as a catalyst for the change you have so fervently prayed for. Aid me, and I swear to you that tomorrow's Egypt will eclipse the glory of your forefathers like the sun eclipses the moon!' He went on, describing what the King intended to do with Egypt once it was part of the empire. Ujahorresnet found himself drawn into the Persian's argument. He found himself imagining the glories of yesteryear returning; a flowering of culture and civilization unheard of since the days of the Amenhotep the Golden. Temples arose from the squalor of his imagination, cities of the living and the dead, fields of boundless plenty. 'Your master,' he began, his voice quivering, 'will he rule as Pharaoh? Will he honour the gods of Egypt over the gods of his own people?'

'Yes!' Gobartes said. 'The gods, the titular, the

ceremony, he will adhere to every custom of Egypt, but he will require guidance. A mentor. Someone familiar with the old ways. He will require your aid, Ujahorresnet.'

The priest turned away, his head bowed in thought, his hands wrung together in an unconscious display of nerves. His last foray into intrigue and deception had nearly killed him.

'I assume you desire something in return?'

'Only a trifling thing, I assure you,' Gobartes said. 'As First Servant of the Goddess, you advise Pharaoh on spiritual matters?'

Ujahorresnet nodded, frowning.

'Can you make yourself indispensable to him?'

Ujahorresnet turned away, staring at the distant palace. The music reached a shuddering crescendo . . .

Ladice heard that mournful music as she knelt by Pharaoh's side, keeping him quiet and still as disease ravaged his body. She watched his every movement with a passionate intensity, seeing to his every comfort. On nights when sleep was denied him, Ladice would sing of the gods and heroes of Hellas, her voice a balm. This night, though, Ahmose could not be placated. The dying Pharaoh thrashed and moaned.

Psammetichus stood near, his attention wavering as Nebmaatra briefed him on current events.

'The regiments of Osiris, Khonsu, Bast, Sekhmet

and Ptah have been called up and ordered to Pelusium to reinforce Amon, Anubis, Neith, and Horus. Also, a vanguard has been dispatched to Palestine to harry the Persians. The Mede, Gobartes, yet awaits an audience.'

'Let him wait. What of the funerary arrangements?'

'Pharaoh's chapel in the precinct of Neith is complete,' Nebmaatra whispered. 'Artisans and priests are working in shifts on the sarcophagus.'

Psammetichus held up his hand, signalling an end to the briefing. Nebmaatra bowed and padded from the room, gesturing for the guards to close the huge cedar doors.

Soft golden lamplight danced, giving artificial life to the ducks, fish, and marsh grasses painted on the plastered walls. Ahmose lay on a low bed strewn with cushions, sweat gleaming on his livid skin, his veins standing out like blue cords on his temples as his lungs sought breath. The old Pharaoh could scarcely rise, but he had enough strength left in his withered body to clamp Ladice's hand in a vice-like grip.

'W-Wife!' he wheezed.

'Zeus take them!' Ladice exclaimed. 'Those vultures and their damned music! They would entomb him while there is life yet in his veins!'

'We cannot ignore the inevitable,' Psammetichus said quietly. 'Ritual must be adhered to, and the music is our way of telling lord Osiris that a Son of Ra stands at the edge of his realm.'

Sobs wracked Ladice's shoulders. 'Then there is

no h-hope, is there?' Her fingers smoothed the creases on Pharaoh's damp brow.

'There is always hope,' Psammetichus said. 'Though not always for this life.'

Ahmose writhed, fighting against Ladice's soothing touch. His eyes were glazing with the nearness of death. 'I s-see them! Swords! Glittering and cold, t-thirsting for the flesh of the Nile! Wait!' he cried, his body knotted with spasms. 'Stand firm! Hold the line against them! Psammetichus!'

'I'm here, father,' the Prince said, grasping the old man's other hand.

'C-Cambyses is coming,' Ahmose gasped. Psammetichus leaned close, striving to hear his father's faint words. 'D-Deny him even an inch of Egyptian s-soil! Promise me! Promise me you w-will not fail!'

'I promise you, father,' Psammetichus said, his face solemn. Across from him Ladice bowed her head. Tears spilled down her cheeks.

Ahmose stiffened. His eyes rolled back into his skull. Psammetichus and Ladice each holding one of his hands, felt his strength return for a brief instant before it ebbed away. Pharaoh's dying breath rattled in his chest, and then he was still.

Somewhere a jackal howled, the summoner of Anubis . . .

13

GAZA

'There,' said the captain of the *Atum*, a heavy, sun-blackened Egyptian. Barca followed the captain's gesture. The galley heeled drunkenly on the swells of the Mediterranean, rising and falling with each white-crested wave. Ahead, couched beneath mountainous sand dunes, the harbour city of Gaza smouldered in the late afternoon heat.

'We'll put in ere the sun sets.' The captain turned and bellowed orders. Sailors scampered over the tarred lines as they furled the sails and took up positions on the padded benches. A thick-bellied Nubian drummed a swift cadence; the rowers fell easily into rhythm. Their voices rose above the clack of oarlocks:

Pilot who knows the water;
Helmsman of the weak,
Guard us from the devils of the Uadj-ur:
Brothers who share my bread,
Brothers of my soul,
Pull, for the love of Amon!'

Barca leaned against the rail, watching the

growing coastline. He had visited Gaza often enough in his youth. It had been a regular port of call for his father's ships. A three-mile stretch of desert divided the city into two districts: Maiumas, the harbour in the sand dunes, and Gaza proper, situated on an inland plateau. The ancient coast road, the Way of Horus, ran between the two and gave Gaza a strategic importance that its size belied.

A strategic importance that had mushroomed in the past few months.

Barca stroked the ridge of scar tissue creasing his side, frowning. The Phoenician could not remember those last hours at Memphis. He had no recollection of leading the final assault against the shattered dregs of the Greek garrison, no recollection of Phanes' narrow escape. Only a scarlet haze of half-seen shapes and the roaring of dream voices. Barca recalled waking once, he recalled bright sunlight and starched linen and incense-laden smoke. Pottery clattered against stone. He struggled, and the pressure of a hand on his chest stilled him. A voice, soothing and feminine, whispered, 'It's not your time yet, Hasdrabal. Do you hear me? Go back to sleep. It's not your time.'

He doubted he could ever forget that voice. Later, he learned Jauharah had presented herself at the palace as his slave, and that the lie went unquestioned. She refused to leave his side the whole time he hovered at Death's threshold, tending night and day to his fever, his infection; she sent lesser slaves to scour the archives of the House of Life for every scrap of knowledge on wounds and their treatment, seeking some sort of weapon against the demons ravaging his soul. Under her care, his strength returned gradually, and with it came impatience.

Phanes had slipped Egypt's grasp at Memphis and, later, Pharaoh's spies lost track of him after he crossed the Orontes, in the foothills of the Amanus Mountains of northern Syria. With vengeance for his men unslaked, Barca's rage worsened.

He recalled an afternoon spent in the shade of the palace gardens, a sweet, warm breeze ruffling the leaves of a grape arbour. None too carefully Barca had stretched his bandaged torso through a series of sword drills meant to restore flexion to his damaged muscles, exercises that left him trembling and bathed in sweat. He began again, then cursed as his sword slipped from his weakening grasp.

'You push yourself too hard,' said a voice from beneath the arbour. Ahmose hobbled out into the dappled sunlight. Pharaoh looked pale, drawn, the dark circles under his eyes giving him a singularly ghoulish cast. 'That's what happened in Memphis, isn't it? You pushed yourself to the brink of death?'

'Majesty,' Barca said, bowing stiffly. Pharaoh dispelled such pleasantries with a wave of his hand and indicated a bench near the lotus pool. 'A soldier's duty is to push himself unto death.'

'Sit with me, my friend.' For the first time Barca saw the tales of Pharaoh's ill health were more than mere palace gossip. 'The physicians tell me you will recover. Myself, I am not so lucky.'

Barca struggled into a more comfortable position. His fingers rubbed the blood-spotted bandages and the itching wound beneath. 'They are wrong, Majesty. You are the Son of Ra, and you will live for ever.'

Ahmose sighed. 'The spirit is willing, but the flesh . . .' he trailed off. Pharaoh suffered from a wasting sickness, aggravated by the daily exertion of retaining his throne and accelerated by the lingering effects of the clash at Memphis. 'Did you know,' he began, 'Sethnakhte entered my service the same season as you, virtually the same month? He spoke against you often, counselling that I should have you put down as if you were a feral dog. I should have recognized the weakness in his character from his penchant for spreading lies, but instead I fostered his career over yours because the gods, in their inscrutable wisdom, deigned to place him in the womb of a fine Egyptian noble-woman. Yet, never did he risk his life for me with such frequency and savagery as you, a child of foreign merchants.' Pharaoh smiled. 'With Sethnakhte banished, it becomes my inclination to foster your career . . . until I remember that I am not the reason you risk your life, am I, Hasdrabal?'

The Phoenician bristled. 'My life has always been yours to command! I—'

Ahmose held up his hand. 'Stay your indignation, my friend. These eyes are old and rheumy, but they yet possess the faculty of sight. You serve me because I am a means to an end. Your end. I cannot fathom what it must be like for you, existing with a rage so expansive and all-consuming that it drives you to seek entrance to the Halls of Judgement. It has blinded you to the simplest of truths: Death comes for us all. It requires nothing of you, save patience.' Pharaoh stood, his hand on Barca's shoulder. 'I am dying, Hasdrabal, and I have a last command for you: I order you to live. Banish your rage and be patient. Let Anubis seek you on his own terms.'

Barca's mind returned to the present. He straightened, frowning. *I order you to live.* Did Pharaoh understand what this entailed? To live without rage, he would have to descend into the darkest part of himself to do battle with that grim phantom he called the Beast; he would have to defeat the very thing that gave him strength. Could he survive without it? What's more, would he want to?

The *Atum* was a troop transport, wide of belly and long of keel, packed to the railings with soldiers of the elite regiment of Amon. They, along with the garrison at Gaza, would, under Barca's command, harry the Persian advance. Barca suspected, even before the rumours started, that Phanes had drifted down the Euphrates to Babylon and attached himself to the court of Cambyses of Persia. A solid move on the Greek's part. Cambyses longed to accomplish what his father, Cyrus, had been unable to do, extend his dominion over the lands of Egypt. Like his sire, Cambyses would soon learn a hard lesson: the Negev Desert was too formidable a barrier for an army to cross. Barca had little doubt that a soldier of Phanes' calibre could find a way to ferry an army across the inhospitable wastes of Negev to within striking distance of the eastern Nile. Could a soldier of *his* calibre stop him?

Barca put his back to the rail and folded his arms across his chest, watching. In the waist of the *Atum*, the Nubian boatswain kept a brisk cadence; the oarsmen bellowed their songs in time with his staccato drumbeats. Further aft, the captain harangued a sailor at the tiller, his words drowned out by the rising song, the clack of oar locks, and the hiss of water sliding past the hull.

With Ahmose ill and Psammetichus an untried ruler, Barca had no illusions about the coming months. It would be a hard fight; Egypt's fate rested in the hands of the self-styled kings of Arabia, Bedouin bandits who controlled the scant water resources of the Negev Desert. If they could be convinced to side with Egypt, then Cambyses – and Phanes – could be dealt with before ever reaching the eastern frontier. If not, if Arabia fell under Persia's spell . . . well, if that happened, he prayed Psammetichus had the stomach for a prolonged war.

Barca spotted Callisthenes moving toward him.

The months since Memphis had wrought serious changes in the Greek. The fat merchant was gone, dead, slain in the fighting at the Northern Gate only to be reborn as the lean figure who cat-footed across the *Atum*'s deck. Callisthenes still bore some resemblance to his former self: a shadow of a paunch; a fold of loose skin under his chin; the ever-present scarab amulet thonged about his neck. But everything else about the man had changed, including his temperament. Barca could tell as he approached that the Greek was in one of his now-frequent sour moods.

'You could have handled this without me, you know,' Callisthenes said by way of greeting. He leaned over the rail. Below, several sinister grey fins paced them.

'How many times must I defend my decision with you? You are politic, my friend,' Barca said. 'I have neither the stomach nor the inclination to play games with the Arabians. I will have my hands full assaying the Persian approach. I need you to act as my liaison to the governor.'

'And the woman?'

For all his Egyptian sensibilities, Callisthenes yet retained a Greek's contempt of women. To the Hellenes, women served a twofold purpose: to bear sons and manage the affairs of the home. They had no legal rights beyond those enjoyed by slaves. Of course, there were exceptions. Spartan women were free to own property, to participate in the gymnasium; older Athenian women were accorded more leeway in their public dealings. On the whole, though, a Greek woman's life was one of bitterness and pain.

'What about her?' Barca said. 'Jauharah's people are Arabian. She knows their tongue, and we'll have need of our own interpreter. I'm evidence enough of her skills as a healer. She will be useful.'

Callisthenes spat. 'There's no use for a woman in the vanguard of war, Phoenician. You know that better than any man here. Why is she really with us? Are you taken with this woman, or are you seeking to atone for the past?'

The look in Barca's eyes as he stared at Callisthenes turned the Greek's blood to ice. Rage piled upon fury, like clouds in a thunderstorm, waiting to unleash elemental ruin at the slightest provocation. Callisthenes realized with a shudder that the only thing keeping him alive at that moment was the Phoenician's iron will.

'I spoke out of turn. Forgive me,' Callisthenes said glumly. 'I am so far out of my element that death would be a godsend right now. You just don't understand, Barca. If I help you, men will die. If I do not, if I bury myself beneath invoices and bills of lading, those men will still die but their blood will not be on my hands.'

'I understand guilt, Callisthenes. Better than most men, I understand it, but there comes a time when we must rise above guilt and do what is expected of us. We must prove ourselves worthy.'

Callisthenes frowned. 'How can we say we are worthy of survival and the Persians are not? Is that not the purview of the gods? When I killed those soldiers in Memphis, I also widowed wives and orphaned children. I ended the bloodline of their fathers and inflicted soul-searing grief on their mothers. Where is the glory in that?'

Barca said nothing for a long time. When he finally spoke the words came quietly, without bravado or embroidery. 'It is not a question of worth or glory. The fabric of your life is woven at birth, Callisthenes. Those soldiers wished you dead, they wished your wife to be widowed and your children to be orphaned. Why? Because you stood in the way of their survival. Did you live because the gods thought you more worthy? I don't think so. I think you lived because it was not yet your time. When it does come, all of the worth and glory in the world will not spare you from that killing blow.'

'Then why are we here? Why do we fight? Every oracle from Siwa to Delphi has foreseen Egypt's fall. What difference will it make if we meet them in Gaza or await them in Pelusium?' The Greek's shoulders slumped. An air of defeat hung about him like a well-worn cloak.

Barca smiled. 'Because the gods hate a quitter. Look, my friend, I agree with you, in spirit at least. But going belly-up and awaiting death has a foul stench to it, does it not? By nature, men are violent; we are fighters. We fight our way from the womb, and we fight against going to the grave. I don't know why the gods made Fate our master then gave us a fighting spirit, perhaps only for their own amusement, perhaps to give us a thirst for life. All I know is I have a duty to perform, and in the course of that duty, men will die. To perform my task to the best of my ability, I need you. That's why *you* are here. We won't stop Cambyses at Gaza, Callisthenes. We are here to slow their advance, to scout out their numbers. We are here to be a thorn in the bastard's side.' Barca chuckled at that thought. He straightened and clapped the Greek on the shoulder. 'A nugget of advice, my friend: don't dwell too long on the word of priests and oracles. They have been known to spread falsehoods. Ready yourself. We'll make landfall soon.'

Jauharah watched the exchange between Phoenician and Greek from her perch in the stern of the *Atum*. An awning and partition of linen kept the glare off – both from the sun and the lecherous sailors. Since boarding she had overheard snatches of jokes and rude comments as she went about the daily chores she set for herself of fetching water and cooking Barca's meals – though he ordered her to stop serving him as a slave would a master. Most of the crew thought the Phoenician had brought his concubine with him. Others simply stared at her with a possessive hunger that made her skin crawl.

Barca kept telling her she was free. Pharaoh's gift. Free to choose where to go, where to stay.

She had been a slave for so long, though, that the idea of freedom terrified her. Every night, she prayed she would wake in Memphis, in the villa of master Idu, rested and ready for a day of baking bread, making beer, and serving the needs of the family. Every morning, she woke to find her prayers unanswered.

Barca twitched the partition aside. 'We'll make landfall soon,' he said, moving to where Jauharah had laid out his *panoplia*. He glanced sidewise at her. She sat cross-legged on the deck polishing his bronze breastplate. With a soft cloth she applied a thin coating of oil to the ridges of sculpted muscle, to the lapis, ivory and gold *uadjet* inlaid in the chest. The oil would stave off the caustic effects of the salt air. Barca exhaled. 'You are the most stubborn woman I have ever known. A thousand times have I told you to stop that, and I'll hazard a guess that it will take a thousand times more before it penetrates that thick skull of yours.'

'If that's your way of thanking me for making sure you don't leave this ship looking like a tousle-headed rube in corroded armour, you're welcome.'

'The gods have mercy on the man who takes you to wife,' Barca said, grinning.

'Your Greek friend does not care for me, I think.'

'Callisthenes? Oh, he's a good man, for a Greek.' Barca knelt and fitted bronze greaves over his ox-hide sandals. The natural flex of the metal kept the greaves snug about his calf. Next he drew on a linen corselet, padded to absorb the weight of his cuirass. Barca stopped in mid-gesture and laughed. Jauharah stared at him, questioning.

'I used to hate his people,' he said, 'hate them with a passion known only to madmen. If someone had told me then that I would come to call a Hellene friend, to defend him to another, I would have cursed him as a lying wretch and split his skull to the teeth. Strange, these little ironies of life.'

'Not all Greeks are like Polydices,' Jauharah said, her voice barely above a whisper.

Barca's head snapped up, a frown knitting his brow. An unreasoning wave of anger washed over him, a need to strike out and destroy something. Pharaoh's command rushed back into his mind: *Banish your rage.* He said nothing, but forced his trembling hands to tie the leather thongs holding his corselet in place. Finally, he spoke. 'I had almost forgotten his name. How did you . . . ?'

'I heard you speak it in Memphis. Later, while you were on the mend, I asked around among Pharaoh's slaves. The tale is out there, if you know who to ask,' she said. 'I was curious, though, why the Greek's commander never pursued you, and why Pharaoh never charged you with murder.'

'What does it matter?' The Phoenician's jaw tightened. Jauharah sensed his discomfort. It was like probing a raw, unhealed wound. She knew she should drop the matter, but her intuition told her to press forward.

'It matters a great deal, Hasdrabal. It matters because it is the difference between guilt and innocence. The law—'

'I know the law!'

'Then you know you're innocent,' Jauharah said.

Barca turned to the railing, his back to Jauharah as he stared out over the choppy sea, his shoulders quivering in barely suppressed fury. The similarities the Phoenician bore to the mythical Herakles struck Jauharah, then. Both hounded unto death for the misfortunes of their youth, both prone to fits of black rage and blacker melancholy.

'Innocent under the law?' Barca said. 'Yes. But the law does not judge a man, only the gods are granted that right. In the eyes of God, my God, I am guilty and nothing I do can ever change that. In a way, Ujahorresnet spoke true. Neferu was a woman of passions and appetites. What choice did she have when her husband ignored her?'

'You can't blame yourself for her indiscretions,' Jauharah said.

Barca spun, bristling. 'Who should I blame? Polydices for doing what any hot-blooded man would do? Her father for raising her improperly? I am to blame. Myself, and none other.'

'What about Neferu?' Jauharah said. 'Does she not deserve a lion's share of this blame you cherish so? Life is organic, Hasdrabal, ever growing, ever evolving. A person's actions are like vines on the arbour, free to take whatever path they choose, but influenced by the paths of others. Neferu did not have to fall prey to the lure of the flesh. Polydices could have refused her advances—'

'And I could have stayed my hand,' Barca snarled.

'Yes,' she said. 'You could have stayed your hand. But you did not, Hasdrabal. In a rage you killed your wife and her lover. You reacted the only way you knew how. It was wrong. But, in its own way, it was necessary. If the events of your youth had not unfolded as they did, you would not be the man you are today.'

'Do not mock me,' Barca said, turning away.

Jauharah caught his arm. 'On that night, years ago, you became a man obsessed with honour and fairness. Your anger at yourself drove you to become a better man, a man who neither minces words nor hides behind them. My past has taught me that most men are dull-witted animals whose only concerns are their loins and their bellies. You have taught me otherwise. You are a man I respect.'

A long silence passed between them. For a brief moment the façade cracked and Jauharah saw the grief and anguish that had haunted him for twenty years. Slowly, he forced the mask back into place. 'We make landfall soon,' he said through clenched teeth.

'You have not yet explained what my duties

will be. Truly, I cannot understand of what use I will be to you on the field.'

'You will be my ears in places I can't go. In camp, I want you to maintain the house of life. I will make sure you have whatever you need.' He took his cuirass from her and stared at his reflection in the polished metal.

'They'll be loath to take orders from a slave woman.'

'They will take their orders from whomever I tell them to! And you are no slave, Jauharah. Do you understand that?'

Jauharah sighed. She rose to her feet and helped Barca don his breastplate, buckling it into place as he held it. 'All I have ever known is how to serve. How master Idu took his morning meal; how his children . . .' her voice caught in her throat. 'How Meryt and Tuya liked to make clay animals for their mother; how mistress Tetisheri enjoyed accompanying me to the markets. The life of a slave is all I've ever known, Hasdrabal. And it was a good life. A g-good life . . .' Jauharah turned away and sat, hiding her tears.

Barca heard a discreet cough coming from beyond the linen awning. 'General? We are near.'

'Thank you, captain,' Barca said. He crouched next to Jauharah and clasped her hands in his. Her eyes were red and moist; she looked away, but he gently lifted her chin and made her look at him. She saw *something* flickering in his eyes. 'You are free now, Jauharah,' he said, his voice barely above a whisper, 'and you have an

opportunity most people will never understand –
the opportunity to remake your life. You can right
the wrongs done to you as a child, decide your
own fate. That is freedom. We are all slaves in
some way or another: to destiny, to class, to
blood, to gods, to fear. For this brief moment in
time, you are a slave to nothing, to no one. I envy
you your freedom, your future, for you have been
given something I will never have . . . a second
chance. Use it to make the life you want.' Barca
stood and, with a ghost of a smile, caught up his
sword.

Jauharah watched him go. For the first time in
what seemed an eternity, the tears spilling down
her cheeks were not born of grief.

Feluccas crested the waves, their triangular sails
tacking in the breeze. Inquisitive faces studied the
carved prow of the *Atum*, with its hieroglyphic
symbols and mysterious figures, as the galley
slipped past the mole and into the calmer waters
of the harbour. They approached the wharfs with
a slow sweep of the oars, angling for an empty
slip where a crowd had gathered. Barca stood
alone at the bow.

Jauharah had stirred an emotion deep within
him, something he had thought long since dead.
Twenty years dead. Many times in those long
years, he had been moved to pity; moved by some
dark deed, some painful secret. At Habu last year

he had felt an overwhelming sadness for the children slain by Ghazi's wolves. Sadness and pity he knew well, but this . . . this emotion toward Jauharah was something wholly alien to him. He wanted to sweep her up in a crushing embrace and keep the world at bay. He wanted to fight her battles and allay her fears. He . . . Barca shook his head, thrusting those emotions aside. This was not the time. Not now. With titanic effort Hasdrabal Barca brought his mind to bear on the task at hand.

For all its cosmetic differences, the port of Maiumas evoked powerful memories for Barca, memories of his home in Tyre. Whitewashed buildings of stone and brick ascended the dune ridges, rising from the beaches and quays that were the heart of the harbour. Mercantile houses, like armed camps, occupied the waterfront. Here, bales and bundles of goods awaited the caravans that would carry them to the corners of the known world. Incense bound for the new temple at Jerusalem sat beside tusks of ivory destined for the markets of Byblos; ingots of gold, favoured by the kings of distant Scythia, were shrouded by bolts of silk soon to grace the shoulders of a Babylonian noblewoman. The wealth of the world poured into Gaza's coffers and, like Tyre, only a select few profited from it.

Wood scraped wood as the ship sidled close to the dock. Ropes were passed from sailor to longshoreman, and a gangplank levered into place. Quayside taverns and stalls emptied at the spectacle of the *Atum* docking. A festival atmosphere gripped the crowd, replete with street hawkers and food vendors, their voices mingling with the cacophony of tongues rising from the bystanders. Barca gazed out over a sea of turbaned heads and curious brown faces. His eyes locked on a small, self-important man standing apart from the crowd, surrounded by a cadre of soldiers in spired bronze helmets and studded jerkins. The welcoming party.

'Soldiers to the fore,' Barca ordered. Squads of spear-bearing Egyptians in golden-scaled corselets and plumed helmets hustled down the gangplank and took up defensive positions around the *Atum*. Barca followed them down, pausing at the base of the plank. The onlookers pointed, chattering amongst themselves.

The small man pushed past the soldiers and inclined his head in greeting. 'I am Merodach, chancellor to His Highness, King Qainu of Arabia, overlord of Kedar and protector of the peoples of Edom. Who commands here?' He looked past Barca, expecting to see a high-born Egyptian materialize at the head of the gangplank.

Merodach moved in a manner that reminded Barca of the sandpipers he had seen on the beaches of Pelusium; small, brown birds forever flitting between waves, fearful of the water but knowing their next meal would come from the silvery surf. Merodach's features added to the avian caricature: he was small and dark, his wiry muscle hidden by a smooth layer of fat; he had no chin or forehead to speak of, only a long, hooked nose, like a bird's beak, and small darting eyes the colour of wet mud. He kept his head shaved, and above his left eye he displayed the faded bull tattoo of a former Babylonian slave. Barca ignored him, addressing an old soldier who stood at the head of the Arabian troops.

'We require an encampment, a defensible position, preferably to the south of Maiumas and of close proximity to the Way of Horus,' said Barca. 'All native troops of the garrison will be placed at our disposal.'

'Nothing shall be done,' Merodach fixed the Phoenician with a cool, unyielding stare, the look of a man confident in his position, 'until I speak with your commander.'

Barca matched the smaller man's stare with one that would curdle milk. 'Who are you?'

'Fool! Are you deaf? I am Merodach, chancellor to His Highness, King—'

'Fool, is it?' Barca towered over the chancellor. 'Deaf? I am neither. I am Hasdrabal Barca, overseer of the Eastern Frontier, general in the armies of the Lord of the Two Lands, servant of the Great King, the Beloved of Amun, Khnemibre Ahmose, Pharaoh of Upper and Lower Egypt. As of now this garrison and all its troops and resources are under my command!'

Merodach bowed low, partly out of deference and partly to hide his discomfiture. 'I beg your forgiveness, General. I did not expect Pharaoh to send a . . . a mercenary to handle affairs of state.

I trust your voyage was without incident? Good. My master bid me bring you into his presence with all due haste. He is eager to meet you and hear the tidings you bring from the Lord of the Two Lands. We've brought a palanquin for your comfort.'

'Who commands the garrison troops?' Barca snapped. Merodach blinked, caught off guard.

The grizzled old soldier Barca addressed earlier stepped forward. 'I do.' His face was like leather, his short beard the colour of snow. 'I am Ahmad.' Amusement twinkled in his eyes.

Merodach tried to interpose himself between the two. 'General, my Master awaits you—'

Barca swept him aside. 'How many men do you have?'

'Two hundred,' Ahmad replied. Barca found nothing remiss in the man's lack of honorifics. Ahmad was a professional soldier, no different from the men Barca had led as captain of the Medjay, with well-mended armour and weapons worn from use.

'Divide them into four squads. Two squads will remain on station in Gaza on rotating shifts. The other two will serve as forward scouts and guides. Pick those who know the terrain best as scouts.'

Ahmad nodded. 'They all know the terrain, but I understand what you want.'

'I must insist!' Merodach howled, unused to being so patently ignored. 'King Qainu demands—'

'Callisthenes!' Barca jabbed a thumb at the diminutive Babylonian.

The Greek threaded through the ranks of Egyptian soldiery, a scribe bearing papyrus scrolls in his wake. Callisthenes wore the regalia of an envoy. Crisp white kilt; wide belt of gold-scaled leather; a pectoral of gold, carnelian, and lapis lazuli; a short black wig held in place by a golden band. This display of wealth and splendour had the desired effect on the flustered chancellor. Merodach bowed and scraped as if Pharaoh himself had arrived.

'At last! I am pleased there is at least one among you of noble blood and breeding who will not run roughshod over the protocols of state.'

The Greek smiled warmly at Merodach. 'Greetings, Merodach. I am Callisthenes, aide to General Barca. While I am not overburdened by blood or breeding, I assure you I am capable of serving as a liaison between my general and your noble king.'

'It would be wise to remind your General that if Egypt wishes dealings with Gaza, then the servants of Egypt must bow to the desires of their host.' Merodach glanced at Barca.

'Does not Gaza crave Egypt's friendship? Egypt's patronage?'

'Egypt's friendship?' Merodach said. 'You speak like it's a precious commodity. Gaza, and by extension Arabia, has survived for many long years without Egyptian patronage, but how long will Egypt survive without Arabian? Your dilemma is not unknown to us. We . . .'

Callisthenes' smile was genuine. 'Ah, my friend,

perhaps this is not the place for such discussions. I think both our causes would be better served if we continue this in your lord's presence.'

After a moment's thought Merodach grinned, gesturing to the palanquin. 'You are right, of course. Let us repair to more palatable surroundings.'

'I avail myself of your lord's graciousness,' Callisthenes said, boarding the proffered palanquin and making room for the Babylonian. Barca watched as six massive eunuch slaves hefted the sedan chair onto their shoulders and moved off in unison. Curtly, Barca detailed a squad of Egyptians to accompany them. The Greek's scribe scurried after the cortege. Barca turned back to Ahmad.

'I'll never understand their kind,' the Arabian said, shaking his head.

'Their kind?'

'Bureaucrats.' The word sounded like a curse.

Barca grinned. 'Some men are gifted with the skills of a healer, others with the craft of a killer. But those two are a rare breed. They can spin cloth-of-gold from camel dung.'

Ahmad cackled and ordered his men to disperse the crowd. Observing the old soldier in action gave Barca a degree of insight into his personality. Ahmad was not the bark and bluster type. He issued his orders in an even voice, forceful, like a father leading a company of his sons. In return, the Arabs respected their captain. They shared that sense of brotherhood, that bond, which only men who have stood together in battle could understand.

Barca glanced back at the *Atum*. Longshoremen, sailors, and soldiers worked in unison to unload the bales of equipment and jars of supplies. Scribes ticked each parcel off their manifests, then gave completed manifests to the quartermaster, Bay, a priest of Thoth and possibly the most meticulous man the Phoenician had ever met. Barca's eyes were drawn to the stern of the ship.

Jauharah stood at the rail, her hair flowing around her, her body in sharp silhouette against the golden sky. Barca felt her eyes on him. A fresh wave of emotion swelled in his breast. There was something unsaid between them, words and deeds yet to be consummated. Was there anything more? Barca frowned and motioned for Ahmad.

'Send scouts out tonight. I want news of the Persians.'

14

ALLIES

Evening sunlight slanted through windows high in the western wall of the palace at Gaza. Motes of dust swirled and eddied through the air, their drifting disturbed by the approach of a man. Columns lined the way to the throne, casting alternating bands of light and shadow over the newcomer. A white cloak billowed out behind him like diaphanous wings.

King Qainu of Gaza knew the approach of the cloaked figure would not be a cause for joy. When word had come of a solitary rider entering Gaza from the north, Qainu had an idea of who it was. He ordered his courtiers and nobles away. Whatever message the newcomer bore would be for the ears of the king, alone. Qainu sat on a dais, on a throne of ivory-inlaid ebony wood, feeding gobbets of raw meat to a tiger crouched at his side, a gift from a king of distant Sind. The Arabian was a repellent man, fat and soft from years of debauchery. His long hair and beard were plaited and, in accordance with his gods, dyed blue-black. Qainu wore no crown but rather a five-thonged leather skullcap held in place by bands of gold and silver, indicative of the vast wealth of the incense trade.

Qainu had never been a man of war. He gained his throne in the time-honoured traditions of treachery and guile. Poison in the cup and a knife in the back, those were methods he understood. Not armies. Not conquest. Those were the instruments of an Assyrian, of an Egyptian, of a Persian. Organized violence was the playground of the man who stalked toward him.

'You play a dangerous game, friend,' Qainu said as the man drew near. 'Your enemies are at my gate, and yet you stroll into my palace as if it were the agora at Athens. The Egyptians would pay well for your head, or so I've heard. Perhaps I should present it to them as a symbol of my loyalty?'

Phanes of Halicarnassus laughed, offering the Arabian king nothing in the way of homage. 'Don't try to bluff me, Qainu. We both know you don't have the balls to take my head. Were I in your place, I would worry more about what my Egyptian masters would think when they saw me ensconced not as a governor, but as a tyrant.' The Greek indicated the throne room.

Phanes presented the perfect blend of insouciance and arrogance tempered with the wariness of a stalking lion. He had changed little since the Fates frowned on him at Memphis. Leaner perhaps, his muscles sharpened by deprivation; a vengeful light in his eyes gave him the aspect of a homicidal Adonis. Beneath his cloak the Greek wore a bronze cuirass inlaid with figures of silver and obsidian, Charon leading a slain Achilles across the river Styx.

The tiger at Qainu's side stretched, growling, its yellow eyes fixed on the Greek, a predator sensing its own. Perturbed, Qainu said, 'Why have you come? Is Cambyses displeased with my preparations? Have I not met the letter of our agreement? Camel trains of water are stationed along the desert route with trustworthy men from the tribes guarding them. What more . . . ?'

'No, you've done well, Qainu. Cambyses appreciates your cooperation. The vanguard approaches. As we speak, Lord Darius is exacting tokens of submission from the cities of Phoenicia. I'm here because I heard a troop of Egyptians left Pelusium bound for Gaza. I came to observe.'

Qainu's throne creaked as he shifted his weight. The king scowled. 'You are welcome in my court whenever it suits you, my friend, but you could not have chosen a worse time. Your very presence is enough to wreck my plans. The Egyptians have not forgotten Phanes of Halicarnassus.'

'I will be the soul of discretion, Qainu.'

The king leaned forward, his fingers gripping the arm rests of the throne so tightly his whitened knuckles cracked. 'Please, return to Lord Darius! As a show of good faith, I'll not send you away empty handed.'

Phanes waved him off. 'Keep your gold. I have no need for it.'

'I would not insult you by offering something of little interest to you. Where other men crave wealth, you crave information. Something has come to me that is of paramount importance to our Persian masters!'

'So important that you did not at once relay it to Cambyses?' Phanes said, his manner one of open scepticism. 'Tell me, and I will decide as to its worth.'

'The Son of Ra has rejoined his Father,' Qainu said.

Phanes blinked. 'You lie!'

'A messenger arrived two days ago from Sais instructing me to relay the information to the Egyptian commander, along with the blessings of Ankhkaenre Psammetichus.'

'Amasis is dead, and Psammetichus wears the crown?' Phanes said, his voice like the low hiss of a serpent. His teeth ground in silent anger as he paced back and forth, cursing under his breath. Soon, the spasm passed. 'How long were you planning to keep this close to your heart? Did you not think what it might mean to Cambyses' strategy? Without an experienced leader, Egypt's armies will flounder. Psammetichus may have sprung from his father's loins, but he is no Amasis. The native generals will tear him apart. Zeus Saviour, you fool! You'll be fortunate to escape the King's wrath!'

'So, you will take this back to Lord Darius.' Though the thought of Cambyses' anger chilled him, Qainu had more pressing concerns at the moment. He was wedged between the two greatest powers of his generation – not a safe place to be for someone harbouring ambitions of his own. For his plans to achieve fruition, he had to present the façade of a loyal subject. For *that* to happen, he needed Phanes as far from Gaza as possible.

'You leave me little choice,' the Greek said.

'Good. I'll have my grooms prepare a fresh horse. You—' But, the Arabian king did not have a chance to finish. Guards thrust the polished cedar doors open and filed in, escorting Merodach and the envoy of the Egyptians. Qainu turned to hiss a warning to Phanes, but the Greek was gone, vanished into the shadows as if he had never been there at all. The Arabian felt as though he walked along the edge of a razor.

Merodach scuttled up to the throne and prostrated himself.

'My lord King,' he said. 'I present to you Callisthenes of Naucratis, aide to General Barca and liaison to the Egyptians.'

Callisthenes approached, bowing. 'King Qainu of Arabia, overlord of Kedar and protector of the peoples of Edom, for your household, your wives, your sons, your nobles, your horses, your troops, Pharaoh sends his blessings of prosperity and health.' Callisthenes drew breath to continue, but an inarticulate howl of rage cut him off. He looked around, scowling.

A figure hurtled from the shadows. Callisthenes had the impression of burnished bronze and white

299

cloth as a whirlwind of fists hammered him to his knees. A voice he had not heard since Memphis screamed in his ear: 'You traitorous bastard!'

No longer the soft merchant of Naucratis, Callisthenes ducked a blow that would have snapped his neck, snagged Phanes' sword belt, and shot a series of quick punches into his groin. Phanes staggered, off balance, as Callisthenes clawed at the hilt of his sword. On the dais, Qainu's tiger roared.

A split second later, Merodach and the Arab guards separated the Greeks. Dazed, Callisthenes sat back on his haunches, blood starting from his nose and lip. Soldiers in studded corselets and spired, turban-wrapped helmets held Phanes at spear point.

'I must protest!' Merodach shrieked. 'This is a grave breach of protocol! Are we dogs to cast aside the sanctity of our pledge? The Egyptians have come to us under a banner of truce, a banner of good will! I—'

'Be silent, Merodach,' Qainu said. His eyes were slits. 'You know this one, Phanes?'

'Know him? He's the one who betrayed me to Pharaoh at Memphis!' Phanes said, his features hard, vengeful. 'Your father was one of my dearest friends, like a brother to me! I trusted you!'

'And you're more the fool for it!' Callisthenes hissed, rising to his feet. 'My father curried your friendship because it was expedient. You were a tool, and he warned me your ambition far outstripped your ability. Egypt does not need Persian rule, much less Greek!'

'Spoken like a true native!' Phanes said. He looked at Qainu. 'Kill him! He is a snake, a serpent in the garden who would strike at our heels when our backs are turned. Further, if our positions were reversed, I would order my men to excise this Egyptian cancer from my shores. Kill them all!'

The tiger at Qainu's side twitched its tail, growling, agitated by the scents of blood, adrenalin, and fear. The king stroked the nape of its neck. 'And were I you,' Qainu said, 'I would return to my masters with all due haste. Remember what I have told you!'

'I will go, but he comes with me!' Phanes said, jabbing his thumb at Callisthenes. Qainu shook his head. 'He is not for you, Phanes. Not today. Perhaps I will give him to you when you return, perhaps not. As of now, I need this one as insurance should my plans fail.'

For a moment fury blazed in Phanes' eyes. His hand twisted into a claw, itching to feel the hilt of his sword. He might have thrown himself on the Arabian king were it not assured he would die on a hedge of spears before ever touching the hem of Qainu's robe. An eternity passed in the span of a heartbeat. Hands shifted their grips on spear shafts. Sweat rolled down Merodach's nose. The tiger coughed in anticipation . . .

Suddenly, Phanes laughed and offered a deep bow, ending it with a dramatic flourish. 'I stand corrected, Qainu. You have balls the size of melons. I will inform Lord Darius that the road to Egypt's border is clear, thanks to our Arabian friends. But, remember this, and remember it well, when I return, if you try to withhold him from me, I'll pull this palace down stone by stone!' He turned and glared at Callisthenes. 'Keep yourself safe, merchant. We have business yet to finish!'

To Phanes' surprise Callisthenes did not quail or grovel. He drew himself up and spat, his face flushed with defiance. 'I'll be here waiting, boy-fucker!'

Phanes spun, his cloak billowing out behind him. His laughter redoubled as he retraced his steps from the throne room.

Silence ruled. Men stared at one another, and at the Greek. At a word from their King, the soldiers would impale the Egyptian envoy on their spears. They waited expectantly. Merodach wrung his hands and finally spoke.

'I cannot be a party to this! By all the laws of hospitality, of protocol, held sacred by the goddess Alilat and thrice-blessed Orotalt, by Ishtar and Marduk, I beg of you, O King! Reconsider this course of action. These seeds of deceit will bear bitter fruit!'

'Listen to your chancellor, Qainu!' Callisthenes said. 'You're making a grave mistake! Barca will—'

'Your general will be dead by sunrise. My mercenaries will see to it. For the moment, though, I require your silence. Guard.' Qainu stroked his beard, his brows furrowed in thought. Before Callisthenes could react, the soldier behind him reversed his spear and rammed the weighted butt against the base of his skull. Callisthenes staggered and fell and did not move.

Merodach stood aghast.

'Did an honour guard accompany him?'

'Y-Yes, O King,' the chancellor stammered.

'Send them away. If they resist, tell them the noble Callisthenes is under the protection of the King of Gaza, and he will call for them upon the morrow.' The king motioned to the unconscious Greek. 'Take him away. Lock him in the Dolphin Chamber, above the West Hall. Feed him well and see to his every need.' Qainu chortled at the goggle-eyed expression on his chancellor's face. 'I'm not daft, Merodach, and I yet possess a shred of common sense. It's not often I get to flaunt a man like Phanes. We will hold this Callisthenes safe until his return.'

Merodach could only stare as soldiers carried out their master's orders. What manner of madman did he serve?

The encampment site lay scarcely half a mile from the harbour, on the southern edge of Gaza. Barca stopped on the shoulder of the winding road. Egyptian soldiers tramped along, happy to be ashore after two weeks at sea. Torches cast circles of lurid orange light over the heavily rutted track.

The Phoenician glanced back the way they had come. Maiumas at dusk was a chaotic sprawl with no identifiable plan, no meticulously plotted grid of streets and cross-streets. Instead, squat, flat-roofed buildings grew like a fungus from the beaches and quays, rising to a precarious height along the ridge of sand-scoured rock. In the sky above, crimson fingers of sunlight pierced the velvet as stars flared into existence, constellations forming beacons, landmarks for navigator and oracle alike.

The mood in Maiumas spoke of quiet desperation. Men and women laboured as they had for centuries, their lives inexorably tied to the sea. They wove their nets by hand; scrounged through refuse heaps for cast-off bits of copper or bronze to forge into hooks; lived from day to day on a broth of fish guts and brine, their eyes rarely leaving the far horizon. In many ways their reliance on the currents and rhythms of the Mediterranean mirrored Egyptian dependence on the Nile. To survive, the folk of Maiumas became intimate with the mercurial waters; they knew the patterns of the winds, where the reefs and shoals were, what time of year the harshest storms arose. They sacrificed to Marna, to Anat, to Resheph: gods of wind and rain, squall and typhoon. In times of dire need, when the gods demanded immediate appeasement, their children were delivered to the priests of Ba'al to be immolated in the sacred fire. The men and women of Maiumas lived with hardship and deprivation, eking what life they could from their pitiless world while the wealthy of Gaza, three miles inland, reaped the rewards of their blood and tears.

Barca scanned the ships moored along the quays. Could any of them have belonged to his family? The house of Barca had wielded powerful influence along this coast at one time, before the disastrous thirteen-year siege of Tyre by the armies of Nebuchadnezzar. That debacle had broken Tyrian supremacy and scattered her more influential citizens to the four winds. His grandfather fled to Carthage; his father, Gisco, settled in Egypt. Barca himself had only the slenderest recollection of those days, images and emotions rather than true memories.

He turned and found Jauharah waiting for him. She smiled. 'You look deep in thought.'

'Remembering,' Barca replied. She fell in beside him as he followed in the wake of a rumbling ox-cart. Soldiers and sailors bantered, and their laughter seemed out of place along the lonely road. 'I was a child the last time I saw the harbours of Tyre, but I remember enough. This place . . .'

A stone shifted under Jauharah's foot. Barca made to catch her, but their hands stopped short of actually touching. Jauharah steadied herself with an outstretched arm. 'My body still rolls with the sea swells.'

Barca smiled. 'Your balance will return soon enough.' He lapsed into silence, his brow furrowed in thought. Soon, he glanced sidelong at her. 'Your people, they are from this region?'

'Not quite,' Jauharah said. 'My family lived in the Shara Mountains, perhaps a week's ride to the southeast, on the borders of Edom. My father was Bedouin, an exile from the tents of the Rualla, who found refuge with my mother's family. Beyond that, I remember very little about them.'

'Do you miss them?'

Jauharah sighed. 'Not particularly. I have forgotten so much. My only clear memory is of the narrow chasm leading to the heart of Sela, the rock-cut fortress where my family dwelt. The air in that crevice was always cool and moist, no matter how hot the surrounding desert got, and in the evening it smelled of garlic and searing meat. I can recall kneeling on a ledge beneath the sentry posts praying my father would never return from trading in Elath.'

'You disliked your father?'

Jauharah hugged herself, shivering despite the warmth of the evening. 'He was barbaric, even by Asiatic standards.' Jauharah employed the Egyptian term used to describe the inhabitants of Palestine: *Asiatic*. Usually preceded by 'wretched' or 'cursed', the name encompassed Syrians, Phoenicians, Ammonites, Israelites, Moabites, Edomites, and Arabs. To Egyptians, all Asiatics were one and the same. 'I had six brothers and four sisters. A fifth sister was born, and in a rage my father bashed the infant's head against a rock. Later, my mother defended what he had done, saying sons were a sign of strength and daughters

306

a reminder of weakness. My father did not need another reminder.'

As she spoke a sheet of white-hot anger blurred the Phoenician's vision. He clenched his fists, digging his nails into his palms until they bled. He could tolerate many things, but violence against children went against his grain. Slowly, he brought his rage under control. His voice, when he at last found it, was tight. 'I have never been a father, but I know in the depths of my soul that I would love my daughters as much as my sons, and none of them would have anything to fear from me.'

'That's one of the differences between you and my father, Hasdrabal. Where you are noble and kind beneath a hard exterior, he was loathsome and weak. I hope—' Jauharah stopped. Barca turned to see what was wrong, and she waved him on. He could see she was flushed, her eyes glistening with unshed tears. Respecting her wishes, Barca continued on. Jauharah melted into the baggage train.

Ahmad approached. He and his men led the Egyptians, and already the two cadres were mingling, trading knives, belts, and trinkets. 'Trouble with your woman?'

Barca glared at him. Wisely, the Arabian let it drop.

'How long since you left Egypt?'

'Two weeks. We left Sais and sailed for Pelusium, thence to Gaza. Why?'

Ahmad leaned close to Barca. 'A messenger

arrived two days past, from Egypt I'm told. Heard from my men in the palace that he bore ill tidings. Thought you might know what it was about. The old Pharaoh has been ill, has he not?'

Barca's face betrayed no emotion. So, word of Pharaoh's poor health had spread to the frontiers. Did the Persians know? Most likely. 'He is an old man,' Barca said. 'Old men are frequently down with this ailment, or that. If Psammetichus leads the army rather than Ahmose, it changes nothing. Tell me, you said you have two hundred men. At full strength Gaza is supposed to field a thousand. Where are the others?'

The Arabian captain shrugged. 'The King is not as quick to replenish our numbers. Instead, he hires mercenaries from among the Bedouin of Sinai as guards for his caravans and his person. If you ask me, it's like letting the lions shepherd the flock.'

'You and your men are not his personal guard?'

'That honour belongs to a sand-rat named Zayid. The King calls him his general, but he's nothing more than a desert brigand. Bah! We used to stake his kind out over anthills before Qainu stole his father's throne.'

'What of the Persians?' Barca asked. 'Does Qainu not fear them?'

'Why would he?'

'Should Cambyses win, he will depose Qainu and install a satrap, a puppet he can easily rule. Your king does not seem the type, from what I have heard, to sit idly by while his throne, and his source of income, is handed off to another.'

'He is already a puppet.' Ahmad looked pointedly at Barca, and the Phoenician read the revelation in the Arab's dark eyes. 'I like you, Phoenician, and I will do what I can to aid you against the Persians. But only against the Persians, if you understand my meaning.'

Barca nodded, his eyes like a winter storm – icy and wrathful. 'Perfectly.'

Callisthenes awoke in the arms of a woman. He gave a start, wondering who the Arabs had thrown him in with. The back of his skull felt tender, and his head throbbed. Slowly, the haze lifted from his vision, and he was able to make out his surroundings.

The woman under him was Amphitrite, daughter of Oceanus, and she was part of the exquisite painting decorating the floor of his make-shift cell. The chamber was spacious and colourful, done in every imaginable shade of blue and green. Frescoes reached to the ceiling, depicting sea life both real and imagined, dolphins, octopi, fish, serpents, nereids. Callisthenes felt as if he were drowning in a watery prison.

A divan and a low table were the only furnishings, and a pair of bronze lamps provided ample light. Callisthenes groaned, rising to his feet. He shuffled over and sat on the divan, putting his face in his hands. He was weary beyond anything he had ever known. As a counterpoint, his whole body vibrated with pent-up rage, a ferocity that he could feel as if it were a source of heat. 'Zeus Saviour and Ares!'

Callisthenes exhaled slowly and tried to slow his pulse. His head drummed in time with the beating of his heart; a dull ache spread behind his eyes. He had learned from Barca that it was best to conserve your strength, to practise quietude in such situations. It did no one any good to pace around and rail at the gods. As bleak as his prospects looked, at least that Arabian bastard hadn't given him over to Phanes or simply killed him out of hand. Now, every day spent in captivity was a day he could use to make good his escape.

Escape to where? Qainu said Barca would be dead by sunrise. Callisthenes did not believe it, but whatever the King had planned could not be in Egypt's best interest. And Phanes! His being in Gaza could only mean Qainu was in bed with the Persians.

The sound of a key scraping in the lock of his door brought Callisthenes to his feet. It swung open, allowing him a brief glimpse of the lamplit corridor and a hawkish Bedouin guard leaning on his spear. A cortege of women bustled into the room, bearing platters of food, beakers of wine and water, fresh clothing, and stone pots of Egyptian cosmetics. In their wake came Merodach.

310

The chancellor waited as the women deposited their burdens on the table and the divan, then with a curt gesture he motioned them from the room. He closed the door behind them, giving him and the Greek a bit of privacy.

When he turned to Callisthenes, the Babylonian's face was screwed up in a look of supreme distaste. 'Forgive me! Had I known what my King intended . . . he told me he would listen to both sides, Egyptian and Persian! I had no idea his loyalty was already decided,' he said, his teeth grinding. 'King Qainu says the Egyptian star is on the wane. He has no desire to attach his fortunes, and the fortunes of his kingdom, to a hopeless cause. He claims it would have been madness to refuse the Great King of Persia! Sheer madness!'

Callisthenes fixed the little chancellor with a baleful stare. 'And is that what you believe?' He could read displeasure in the Babylonian's body language. The jut of his jaw, his rigid posture, spoke volumes about his character. Merodach had been suckled on deceit, weaned on deception; he had forgotten more about palace intrigue than Callisthenes would ever know. Yet, whatever he might say, the Greek knew he was furious with his lord.

'I believe he is a fool! A fat, greedy fool!' Merodach hissed. 'But what I believe changes nothing. He plans on giving you over to lord Phanes when the Persian vanguard arrives.'

Callisthenes grabbed the chancellor's arm. 'Can you get word to Barca?'

Merodach shook his head. 'It is too late to warn him. Your general is in Marduk's hands now. All I can do is try and secure your freedom before the Persians arrive.'

'Why is it too late to warn Barca?' Callisthenes said. 'What treachery has your master planned? He mentioned mercenaries . . . ?'

Merodach rubbed the bridge of his nose. 'All I can tell you is that tomorrow it will be as if the Egyptians never existed. It would be best if we looked to your safety.'

'Damn you, Merodach! Get a message to Barca, and I will make sure he knows what part you played in all this!' said Callisthenes.

The chancellor sighed, opening the door. 'There are things I cannot be a party to, and betraying the trust of my master is one of them. I wish I could do more for you, Callisthenes.' He turned to leave then stopped, indicating the tray of covered dishes. 'Try the lamb. You'll find it particularly delicious.' He spun and left, locking the door behind him.

The sound stung Callisthenes like a whip. His body stiffened. His lips peeled back from his teeth in a bestial snarl. 'Try the lamb?' he hissed. And the part of him that sought to master his anger shrank, then vanished altogether. Rage boiled in his chest – rage at Qainu, at Phanes, at Merodach – a blood-red inferno that seared away logic and reason and left him with only the insatiable desire to destroy.

Callisthenes cursed every god, demi-god, hero,

man, woman, and child he could think of; he spewed blasphemies in Greek and Egyptian that would have shocked the court of Dionysus. Still, his rage grew unchecked. He smashed beakers of wine, hurled a stone bowl of dates against the far wall. His fists shattered pottery bowls and plates. Callisthenes battered aside the lid covering Merodach's precious lamb . . .

. . . and stopped cold. He blinked, unsure of what he saw. In place of a succulent rack of lamb Callisthenes found a curved Bedouin knife, long as a man's forearm. He picked it up and stared at his reflection in the polished bronze blade. Beneath it, in charcoal, someone had drawn a crude map of the palace. Callisthenes blinked again. His anger fizzled and died, like a torch thrust into water.

'Merodach,' he whispered, 'the gods love a hypocrite.'

Jauharah stood beside one of the wagons and watched the Egyptian camp rise from the darkness around her. Torches blazed, turning the flat, sandy plain into a surreal landscape of light and shadow. She spotted Barca. He moved among the troops, Ahmad at his side, his every gesture curt, professional, with never a wasted movement, never a misstep. Like his own soldiers, the Arabs would not doubt any command he gave them, no matter how fruitless or absurd. He was their ideal, what they aspired to be. Where they had slain dozens, he had slain hundreds. Where they were wolves, Barca was a lion.

Of the men she had known, Hasdrabal Barca was perhaps the most singular. Violent when provoked, otherwise he was quiet, even gentle. He endured the terrible burden of being born a killer. Oh, her father was a violent man, as well. But, where he used violence to subjugate his family, to bend the helpless to his will, to make a point, Barca used it to protect and to punish.

Jauharah felt a pang of guilt. Almost without thinking she had lied about her recollections of family. Such memories lived in the darkest recesses of her mind, rarely recalled and never discussed. He did not need to know how her father had used his daughters as his own private harem, or how her mother had bled to death after piercing her womb with a knife to avoid the curse of another daughter, or how her father had sold her off to pay a debt. These were wounds to her soul that were scabbed over, crusted by time and distance. But they would never heal.

Probing them earlier loosened the scabs. Sharp tendrils of pain wormed their way through her heart. She sifted through her feelings, through the morass of emotions that had arisen since Memphis. Anger, longing, fear, shame, confusion, grief – crippling, soul-searing grief. Not her manumission by Pharaoh or even the growing intimacy between her and the Phoenician could assuage that grief.

Amidst the turmoil Jauharah felt useless. She stood out of the way, watching as sailors from the *Atum* erected a haphazard tangle of tents. Egyptian soldiers established a perimeter for the sentries to walk and gathered wood for watch fires, while shaven-headed priests supervised the unloading of a shrine to Neith. Everyone had a task to perform, save her. She glanced around.

The level spit of land Ahmad led them to was good ground, well ventilated by the constant breezes flowing off the Mediterranean. Behind her, to the north, lay Maiumas, its lights glittering like jewels on velvet; south, the dark gulf of the open desert. To the east, she had been told, beyond the low hills, lay the worn and dusty track of the coastal road, the Way of Horus; west, she could hear the sough and sigh of the ocean. A sand-scoured jumble of stones stood on a promontory overlooking the beach. In its heyday the place had been opulent, its colonnades and gardens the scene of countless trysts, assignations, and rendezvous. But its day was long past. Untold years ago the pleasure palace fell victim to the internecine wars plaguing Palestine. Torch and sword shattered columns, toppled walls, and laid waste to gardens. Now, the only good the ruin served was as a nesting place for gulls.

The *Atum*'s captain ambled past. He was an apish man, squat and broad-shouldered, with a face seamed by countless squalls. She caught his arm. 'Just get 'em up, dogs!' he bellowed, then turned and glared at the woman who had dared lay her hands on him. She met him eye to eye.

'What is your name?' Jauharah asked.

'Senmut,' he said. His eyes slid up and down her body. She felt her confidence waver. She was a slave, subservient to his every whim. Her eyes should be downcast. Her—

No! I am a free woman. 'Senmut, order your men to erect the tents around this ruin.' Her voice quavered slightly, then grew stern and commanding, becoming the voice mistress Tetisheri used when her will was not to be questioned. 'This will serve as the general's command post. The tents of the house of life should go on the desert side of this ruin, unobstructed, so they can receive the benefits of the sea air. The mess tent should go on the side of the ruin facing the harbour, so resupply will not be too difficult. Above all, make the tent rows orderly and neat, like columns in a temple.'

To Jauharah's surprise Senmut inclined his head, saying, 'As you wish.' He turned back to his men and barked orders. 'Not like that, you ignorant wretches! Make 'em neat . . .'

Jauharah moved on to the tents that would house any casualties they might receive. Old soldiers, men who had fought in battles since before she was born, deferred to her wishes, realigning the tents to take advantage of the freshening breeze. She consulted with Bay about sending a deputation into the city to replace some herbs and medicines that had spoiled during the sea voyage. The quartermaster agreed, promising to seek her out tomorrow for a list of what was needed. She hid her elation at their nascent acceptance by throwing herself into her work.

It was after midnight before Jauharah's elation faded into exhaustion. She asked after her belongings and learned they had been tucked away in Barca's tent. To the rank and file, she was his woman; they expected her sleeping arrangements to reflect that. Jauharah shrugged. She would sleep on the floor so long as no one disturbed her.

The Phoenician's tent was larger than the others, though beyond that there was nothing ostentatious or gaudy about it. It surely did not reflect the rank of the man who would dwell within. The interior maintained that air of Spartan simplicity. An Egyptian-style bed with a mattress of cord matting lay inside a frame draped with sheer linen panels. That bed, a table, and a soot-stained bronze brazier were the extent of the furnishings. Someone had left a loaf of bread and a jug of beer on the table, alongside an urn of fresh water. Jauharah blessed whoever it was. At least she could sponge off the sweat and grit.

Jauharah found her chest under the table. Beside it sat Barca's battered leather rucksack. His was an unremarkable piece of baggage, worn and scarred from countless campaigns. Jauharah had seen similar rucksacks decorated in the time-honoured style of the foot soldier: amulets and charms and reminders of various postings tacked to the leather. Barca's had only one, a yellowed ivory *uadjet*.

Her chest was an admirable companion to the Phoenician's kit. She had salvaged it from a nobleman's refuse heap and tried to restore it to its former glory. Crafted of aged cedar, polished from years of handling, and stripped of its gold leaf and precious stones, the side panels of the chest depicted scenes of home and family, along with hieroglyphic prayers to Isis and Hathor. It served a twofold purpose as both coffer and shrine.

Jauharah raised the lid and looked at her meagre possessions: a blue-glazed pot holding smaller stone tubes of eye paint and fragrant oils, a sewing kit, a leather pouch of frankincense, a mirror of polished copper, combs and cosmetic tools of wood and bone, items of clothing. She removed a fresh linen shift, dyed blue, a tube of fragrant oil, and an old length of cloth suitable to wash with.

She stripped off her soiled shift and used water from the ewer to give herself a brisk sponge bath, then rubbed the oil into her skin. She took the last bit of water and rinsed the grit and stiffness from her hair. Times like these, Jauharah wished she had adopted the Egyptian custom of shaving her scalp and wearing a heavy wig. She preferred natural tresses to those woven from fibre, but a bare scalp would be so much easier to clean.

Jauharah dressed and put away her things. She settled into the corner nearest the bed and would have fallen right off to sleep had the tent flap not rustled open. Barca stepped inside. He held a pottery flask of wine, still stoppered and sealed. Jauharah noticed a tightness about his jaw, a smouldering fire in his eyes. His brow furrowed when he saw her.

'You did not wish to have your own quarters?'

Jauharah shrugged. 'They assumed we would be . . . that I'm . . .'

'Merciful Ba'al! Do they think this is some kind of leisurely outing?' Barca said. 'That I would bring a woman along for pleasure?'

His voice held such a vehemence that Jauharah was taken aback. His tone stung. She stood, her back straight and stiff. 'Do not be troubled, Hasdrabal. I can sleep in the ruin, if need be.'

Jauharah made to leave, but Barca caught her before she could go. The Phoenician sighed, shaking his head. 'I'm sorry. Stay, if it pleases you. The gods know I could use the company.'

'What's wrong?'

Barca tore aside the linen panels and sat on the edge of the bed. He pried his greaves off and tossed them in the corner, followed by his cuirass. He drew a small knife from his belt and pared away the seal on the flask. With his teeth, he removed the stopper, then drank deeply.

Jauharah frowned. 'Hasdrabal? Has something happened?' She crouched at his feet.

'A messenger arrived from Sais bearing ill news. Ahmad did not know exactly what, but I think I know. I think Pharaoh has gone on to the realm of Osiris.'

Jauharah's hand flew to her mouth. 'What? Great Isis! No! That cannot be!'

Barca tapped the wine flask against the bed frame. 'I can't think of any other reason why Sais would risk sending messengers to the frontier. Our placement here has nothing to do with their strategic plans, so they would not change our orders via messenger. Pharaoh has been ill for quite some time. There is no other explanation.'

'Then,' Jauharah scowled, 'where is the messenger? Why didn't he await your arrival? Say he had pressing business elsewhere. Why, then, didn't Qainu's man deliver the message to you himself?'

'Because,' Barca said, a dangerous light in his eye, 'Qainu's loyalty is suspect. Something else I had from Ahmad . . . his king does not fear the Persians. That means he is either a fool or he has already paid homage to Cambyses. From what I know of Qainu, he is no fool.'

'Do you think Callisthenes is in danger?' Jauharah asked, voicing Barca's own concern.

The Phoenician thought about it for some time. He took another pull from his wine bottle. 'No. That wretched chancellor had orders to escort me into his king's presence. They did not expect I would send a deputy. So, harming Callisthenes would do them no good. Qainu will try something else, that or he'll present the illusion of loyalty and stall until the Persians arrive. Either way, I've doubled the sentries.' Barca's fists clenched and unclenched. 'I'm not accustomed to standing idle. It's not my nature.'

Jauharah sat beside him, taking his hands in hers. Barca shifted nervously. He glanced at her, then looked away.

'You seemed upset earlier this evening,' he said.

Jauharah lowered her head, her hair spilling over her face. 'It . . . saddens me to talk of my family. I'm one of those rare souls to whom happiness is denied. I was abandoned by one family and lost another to violence. What else could the gods do to me?'

'You're too hard on yourself,' Barca said. 'True, the Fates have made sure your path is strewn with obstacles, but the gods themselves have gifted you with the wits and the wherewithal to overcome anything. You told me the events of my youth made me who I am today. The same can be said of you. And, despite the pain and the hardship you've had to endure, I am glad you're the woman you are.'

Jauharah nodded. Tears sparkled on her cheeks. She laughed, nervous, wiping her eyes. 'Look at me. An hour ago I was ordering men about like a general on the field. I suppose I should thank you for that, too. Whatever you told them about me must have struck a nerve. Even the captain, Senmut, did as I asked.'

Barca smiled. 'So, you're the spirit of Ma'at who appeared and turned chaos to order. I heard about you. But, I had nothing to do with it. Truth be told, it slipped my mind. Whatever respect you earned was from your own actions, not from fear of me. You showed them confidence.'

'Confidence. I must have learned it from you,' she said. Jauharah opened his hands, staring at the thick sword callouses, the frieze of thin scars etching his flesh. Beneath that veneer she saw the hands of an artist. Long fingers, nimble and quick, driven from the gods' original purpose by chance. She traced each finger, each line, seeing in her mind's eye this selfsame hand wrapped around a sword hilt, drenched in blood. 'Do you . . . enjoy killing?'

'No,' Barca sighed. He tried to clench his fist but her hands kept it open. 'No. It's a skill, like any other. Some people build great monuments or fashion exquisite jewellery. My skill is at killing. I'm not proud of it, but it is something that must be done. And I'm good at it.'

'You told me earlier that I had an opportunity you would never have. What if you were in my place? What would you do?'

'I don't follow,' Barca said.

'If you could remake your life . . .'

Barca took another sip of wine, then set the bottle aside. 'When I was a boy, in Tyre, I would go down to the quays and sit on my father's ships. Just sit there, listening. Sailors are a garrulous bunch. Always a ready tale to spin for appreciative ears. Some days, this old man would hobble on board and every man there would fall silent. Even my father would step aside out of deference. I thought him some kind of merchant king or a priest. Later, I learned the truth.

'He was a navigator. As a boy, he had sailed

with Hanno around the tip of Africa. He knew the position of every star in the heavens, every shoal, every reef. What this man had forgotten about sailing most men would never know. If I could go back and make my life over, I would take a ship and sail through the Pillars of Herakles, just like that old man.'

Jauharah smiled. She said nothing for a moment, then, 'I wish I could give you your dream.'

'Don't squander your gift on me. Make a dream of your own come true,' Barca replied. Gently, he touched her cheek; caressed the line of her jaw. His fingers felt unaccustomed to such delicate gestures. She saw trepidation in his eyes. Apprehension. Even fear, if such an emotion were possible from him. She saw something else in his eyes, too. Something he had kept locked away for years uncounted, imprisoned in a cage of ice. His eyes glittered with passion. Hot, bright, intimate, a fire stoked from embers never wholly smothered.

Jauharah turned her head slightly, kissing his scarred knuckles. His hands trembled. Could these be the same hands that had dealt such death? 'You're shaking,' she whispered.

Barca made to pull away, his eyes clouding as he realized what he was doing. 'I shouldn't . . .'

She laced her arms around the Phoenician's neck and pulled him closer, covering his lips with her own. Barca returned her kiss awkwardly, almost chaste. His body vibrated, tremors coursing down his spine, his legs. His arms quaked. His body fought a war against itself. Primal desire against iron discipline. He disengaged Jauharah's arms. 'I cannot.'

She hugged herself; her cheeks crimsoned. 'I'm sorry. I . . . I assumed you had the same feelings for me.'

'That's not it.' He looked away.

'Is it my age? The fact I was a slave?'

'No!' Barca said sharply. 'No. It's nothing like that. You're one of the few women I have admired. You're strong. Strong enough to hold your own against any man. It's . . . I . . . I don't want to hurt you should something go wrong.'

The image of a young wife and her Greek lover flashed in Jauharah's mind. He was terrified the past would happen all over again. Slowly, she cupped his face in her hands, feeling the muscles of his jaw twitch. Jauharah smiled as she spoke. 'You're not the same man you were then, Hasdrabal. If you were, I wouldn't be here. You trusted me once. I trust you now. I trust you . . .'

Jauharah's words, her touch, melted the hardness in his dark eyes; she felt his body relax. Their lips met again, this time sharing an exquisite, languid kiss that remained unbroken as they sank down on the bed.

For some time, the only sounds that escaped their throats were the sighs and moans of passion unleashed.

15

A SERPENT UNDERFOOT

Sais sweltered under a sickle moon. Nebmaatra
tossed in his bed, exhausted yet unable to find
comfort in the arms of sleep. Outside, heat
radiated from the stone of the palace walls. Inside,
humidity made the darkness unbearable. Forges
and foundries added their din to the sultry night
as smiths worked in shifts to turn out the para-
phernalia of war: whole forests of spears; arrows
enough to blacken the sky; swords, helmets, and
corselets of burnished bronze; shields of thick
hippopotamus hides. More weapons than
Nebmaatra had seen in his lifetime, enough to
outfit a vast host, and all of it bound for the
eastern Delta, for Pelusium.

Nebmaatra sat upright in bed, sleep an impos-
sibility. He rose and padded over to a small table,
pouring a basin of water from a bronze ewer.
Gently, he laved his face, scalp, and neck. A dull
ache spread from his eyes and threaded down to
the muscles of his shoulders. Nebmaatra felt a
subtle charge in the air, akin to that moment
of calm before lightning struck. Since Pharaoh's

passing, chaos ruled the streets of Sais. The city's famed linen weavers abandoned their looms; the stone-cutters and artisans cast aside their half-realized statues. Men's thoughts should have turned to the defence of their land, to preserving their culture from barbaric invaders. Instead, neighbour accused neighbour of harbouring Persian sympathies. Mobs hunted phantom spies through the marketplaces and questioned loyalties at spear-point. Even the gods voiced their displeasure, through portent and prophecy. At Shedet, in the Faiyum, the priests of Sobek found the sacred crocodile dead in a lotus pool. At Thebes, rain fell on the temple of Amon. At Yeb, near the first cataract, ram-headed statues of Khnum cried tears of blood. Fear burrowed into the dyke of Egypt and weakened an already decaying bulwark.

A timid knock at Nebmaatra's door presaged its opening. He turned as a young soldier crept across the threshold then stopped, startled to see his commander awake. He stammered his apologies. 'What is it, boy?'

'It . . . It's Pharaoh, lord,' the young Calasirian said, shaking, his scaled cuirass clashing like a dancer's cymbals. 'He's vanished from his rooms again.'

Nebmaatra swore, an expansive, all-encompassing wrath that gave sacrilege new meaning. The young soldier paled as gods were invoked and blasphemies spoken, things best not said by the dark of night. Pharaoh's rooms lay at the heart of the palace, relentlessly guarded by his Calasirians and attended by an army of servants. Psammetichus, like his father, preferred to sleep alone, visited on occasion by wives and concubines who always departed after they took their pleasure. This night, he had given orders not to be disturbed. Now Nebmaatra knew why. 'Rouse the Guard,' he ordered. 'Fetch my armour. He can't have been gone too long.'

The palace came alive as the Calasirian Guard turned out in full panoply. Slaves and nobles peered out, wondering at the sudden commotion. Torches flared. Nebmaatra's voice roared orders, detailing squads to search every nook and cranny of the palace and its grounds. 'Detain anyone who seems suspicious. Find Gobartes and keep him under guard until ordered otherwise.' Scribes, servants, and soldiers scattered like frightened birds before the commander's fury.

Neith's temple lay atop a rounded knoll, surrounded by dykes and canals that shunted the Nile's flood waters into the fields. The lands around the temple formed a bureaucratic hub, an age-old infrastructure that grew and hardened around the throne as calcium around stone. Offices and archives; granaries and storehouses, it was a microcosm of the city itself where priest and scribe worked in tandem to turn Pharaoh's will into reality.

Tonight, Pharaoh's will was to be left alone to ponder the past, present, and future in relative solitude. Clad in a short kilt, a linen cloak thrown over his shoulders, Psammetichus walked barefoot beneath huge ornamental pylons, his eyes drawn to the mammoth figures of the goddess etched into the stone. Neith, patron goddess of Sais and protector of the royal house, was the Primeval Woman: hard and merciless to Egypt's foes, yet nurturing in her guise as mother of Sobek. Warriors prayed to her for strength in battle as women did for strength in motherhood. Who needed her more?

Psammetichus passed through the gate and into the temple courtyard. Here, ancient sycamores and willows lined a long reflection pool. The scent of lilies hung in the heavy air. Chapels flanked the pool, some small and austere, others like miniature temples with colonnades and galleries and monumental statues. They were his ancestors, the kings of his line: Wahibre Psammetichus, who threw off the yoke of Assyrian rule and reunified Egypt; Wehemibre Nekau, the canal-builder; Neferibre Psammetichus, who brought Nubia back under Egypt's thumb; Haaibre Apries, the hated. The tomb closest to him he knew well – it belonged to his father.

Compared with the tombs of the ancient kings, the burial chapel of Khnemibre Ahmose was little more than a stone hall set above a burial vault. His father's mummy would not be in residence, not until the customary seventy days of mourning were over. Psammetichus mounted the steps and crossed the threshold, waiting for his eyes to adjust. Ambient moonlight trickled through the door, giving a haunting semblance of life to the statues and hieroglyphs. He wandered along and studied the carved walls, the painted columns, reading again the exploits of his father. Here, against the north wall, was his favourite depiction of his sire. He called it Ahmose Triumphant, upraised axe menacing a horde of fleeing Asiatics, a romanticized retelling of Egypt's bloody legacy in Palestine. Psammetichus knew no such event happened during his father's reign. Ahmose ruled through diplomacy rather than violence. 'Do not plunder the house of your neighbours,' he was fond of saying, 'when they will gladly give all they have to aid a friend.'

Psammetichus traced a finger across his father's stone visage. 'What would you do, Father, now that diplomacy has failed? Would you mass an army at Pelusium to entrench and wait, or would you attempt something more daring?'

A sound roused Psammetichus from his introspection, a scuff of a foot on stone. He glanced up, expecting to see Nebmaatra's glowering visage, and beheld the concerned face of the priest, Ujahorresnet.

'Your honoured father would have done very little differently, I think,' Ujahorresnet said. The older man bowed. 'I am sorry if I intrude, Pharaoh. I saw you in the courtyard and decided to follow in case you had need of anything.'

'You didn't like my father, did you?'

Ujahorresnet pursed his lips. 'I will not lie to you, Pharaoh. No. Your father and I disagreed on many things. Bitterly disagreed. A loose tongue earned me banishment to the temple in Memphis. Now, I fear my tongue wags too freely again. If you will excuse me, majesty, I will leave you to your introspections.'

Psammetichus sighed, touching the walls, running his fingers along the *shenu* of his father. 'It's all right, Ujahorresnet. I would talk with you. You said my father would do very little differently. What would he have done that I have not?'

'Far be it from me to criticize, Majesty, but I believe your father would have placed his trust in those men around him who have made waging war their life's work.'

'Are the generals I have not adequate?'

Ujahorresnet clasped his hands and bowed. 'I am sorry. I presume too much.'

'No, please. I would appreciate hearing your counsel on this matter,' Psammetichus said.

'As you wish,' Ujahorresnet said. 'Your generals at Pelusium are politicians, not soldiers. They achieved their rank through fortuitous birth rather than martial skill. They are fine men, of that I am sure, else you would not have placed your trust in them, but they have no conception of the art of strategy. Would it not be better if one man alone acted as your regent on the field? A born soldier who is not mired in the politics and backbiting of court?'

The thought intrigued Psammetichus. 'Who would you suggest I trust with this command?'

Ujahorresnet had a man in mind, a man Gobartes assured him would falter if given such responsibility, but he did not say it at once. Instead, he gave the impression of great soul searching, deep thought. Finally, he said, 'The man who has proven himself most worthy of that honour is Nebmaatra.'

'Are you mad?'

'No, majesty,' Ujahorresnet said. 'I am quite sane. Nebmaatra has skills your generals could not match if they were to pool them. He is a decisive leader, of a good family, and highly regarded by the nobles. In raw martial skill, he is the finest. Only Barca,' the priest's voice cracked, 'can eclipse him.'

'I agree with you that he's capable, but placing him in command of all my forces? I cannot see the wisdom in that.'

'If nothing else,' Ujahorresnet said, 'it's what your father would have done.'

Psammetichus said nothing for quite a while, his brows furrowed in concentration. He paced back and forth, pausing once to stare at the image of his father. 'I don't know about this.'

Ujahorresnet tried to regulate his breathing, to appear nonchalant. In truth, he did not feel like a traitor. Despite Gobartes' thoughts to the contrary, Nebmaatra *was* the best candidate for such a position. Pharaoh only needed a bit of nudging to see it. This whole enterprise might lead to

Persia's defeat at Pelusium. If that happened, Egypt would have lost nothing by his meddling.

'In truth,' Ujahorresnet said, 'have you anything to lose?'

Pharaoh sighed. 'No. No, I have nothing to lose. Preparing for war is difficult in its own right, and all the more so when I must devote my waking hours to many things, my father's funeral not the least of them. If I could trust someone with this, it would be a tremendous weight off my shoulders. The generals I have now are capable men, as you said, but you are also correct in your assessment of their political aspirations. They fight each other when they should be united to fight the Persians. I don't trust them to do what's best for Egypt.'

'Nebmaatra will do just that, Majesty. As for trust . . . do you not trust him with your life and the lives of your wives and children? Would the trust of Egypt mean any less to him?'

'Yes. I begin to see your wisdom, Ujahorresnet. I believe I will take your counsel to heart,' Psammetichus said. 'Nor will I dawdle. Come. Accompany me back to the palace.'

Ujahorresnet bowed and flashed his best self-deprecating smile. A sense of triumph welled up from deep inside him, a sense of still having the wherewithal to play the game of kings. It was a heady feeling. 'I am honoured I could aid you, Majesty, but my place is here, in the temple. I could not—'

'You cannot refuse me.' Psammetichus laughed.

'Come, my friend. I have need of a man like you, more so now that I am sending my right hand away. You are a man who speaks true and has no ambition beyond service. Follow me. I will show you a little known way into the palace.'

Ujahorresnet, smiling to himself, could do nothing but agree.

'Anything?' Nebmaatra barked.

'No, sir,' the lieutenant said, sweat running down his face. 'We searched the river quarter and among the quays. No sign of Pharaoh.'

'Redeploy!' Nebmaatra's anger rose by the second. 'Search the whorehouses and wine shops of the foreign quarter.'

'Surely Pharaoh would not—'

'Do it!' Nebmaatra's voice cracked, his jaws set and locked. The lieutenant, knowing his commander rarely lost his temper, wisely saluted and rounded up his foot-sore troopers.

Hours had passed since the Calasirians had mustered in the palace courtyard. Hours since he dispersed them into every conceivable nook, cranny, street, alley, rooftop, and cellar. They returned bearing a steady stream of reports, all negative, that wore Nebmaatra's nerves to breaking. It was as if Pharaoh had vanished from this world.

Nebmaatra looked up, his brows beetling, as an escort of soldiers brought the Persian envoy to him.

'What is the meaning of this?' Gobartes said, his beard bristling. He spoke fluent Egyptian, but his Persian accent slaughtered the syllables mercilessly. 'You think me some kind of sneak-thief or base murderer?'

'Yes,' Nebmaatra said flatly. 'And if I discover you had any hand in this, I'll gut you myself!'

'Hand in what? Perhaps I could help you if I knew what happened,' said the Persian.

'Do not play me for a fool, envoy!'

'I cannot play you for what you are!' The Persian did not quail as Nebmaatra's hand went to his sword hilt. 'Will you kill me now for speaking what I know in my heart is true? Perhaps whatever happened tonight is your doing, eh?'

Metal hissed against leather. 'Release him,' Nebmaatra ordered the guards on each side of the envoy. 'Give him a weapon. I am not Persian, Gobartes. I do not kill unarmed men!'

'Enough, commander!'

The voice came from above, from the Window of Appearances. All eyes glanced up, seeing the cloaked figure of the Pharaoh with the priest Ujahorresnet at his side. Nebmaatra's blood boiled, but he maintained his composure and even forced a brief chuckle through gritted teeth. Psammetichus seemed less solemn, as if a weight had been removed from his shoulders.

'Pharaoh,' Nebmaatra said, 'your safety is not a trifling thing. We—'

'I am sorry, commander,' Pharaoh said. 'Consider my nocturnal roaming as an exercise in

334

preparedness and leave it at that.' He gazed at the men clustered in the plaza below, then nodded to himself. 'Attend me, all of you.'

Nebmaatra sheathed his sword. 'We will finish this soon, Persian,' he whispered to Gobartes as he passed.

The audience chamber lay off the main throne room. By design it was smaller, more intimate, meant to be a place where Pharaoh could greet special guests, foreign ambassadors, even members of the royal family. The friezes and paintings on the walls placed less emphasis on the military aspects of rulership and more on the promotion of the hearth. There were scenes of Pharaoh honouring the goddesses Isis and Hathor, of a husband and wife fowling in the marshes, of children frolicking among lotus blooms and papyrus stalks.

Pharaoh sat on a low dais, smiling, as Nebmaatra led the way into the chamber. His Calasirians took up positions along the walls, their glittering armour incongruous against the pastoral decor. Courtiers, priests, and servants filed in after, roused from their slumber by the commotion. Gobartes, flanked by guards, entered last.

Psammetichus motioned to his servants. 'Fetch the Overseer of Scribes.'

Nebmaatra looked at him curiously. Pharaoh sat still, his nervous twitter gone. His eyes glittered with resolve. For a moment Nebmaatra wondered if Pharaoh had been poisoned. The commander let his eyes slide around the audience chamber, noting the cryptic smile on the face of the old priest, Ujahorresnet. It occurred to him that there were many forms of poison, the most insidious being the poison of words. Words spoken to promote an agenda, to undermine, to cast shadows of doubt on the sound judgement of others. It was a poison with no easy antidote.

Psammetichus had been gone long enough to ingest a lethal dose.

'Majesty,' Nebmaatra said, moving close so as not to be overheard by the milling throng which grew by the second. 'You are tired. Are you sure you wish to conduct affairs of state by the light of the moon?'

'Nonsense, commander. I am fine,' Pharaoh replied. He smiled. 'Indeed, my course of action has never been clearer.' Murmurs swept the crowd as the Overseer of Scribes, hastily clad in a rumpled linen robe, came huffing into the audience chamber. Pharaoh gestured to his side. 'Khasekhem, my friend, assume your position at my right hand.'

Psammetichus waited patiently as the heavy-set chief of the royal scribes readied his palette and papyrus. When he continued, his voice reverberated about the small chamber. 'Regnal year One under the majesty of Horus: Strong of mind, appearing in truth; He of the Two Ladies: Who establishes laws and brings plenty to the Two Lands; Golden Horus: Great of mind and body; the King of Upper and Lower Egypt, Lord of the Two Lands: Ankhkaenre Psammetichus, chosen one of Ra, Son of Ra, may he live,' Pharaoh recited the royal titular, pausing for effect as his courtiers held their breaths. Their eagerness for Pharaoh's next words crackled, palpable. Even Nebmaatra found himself leaning forward in anticipation. 'To My generals on the eastern frontier, I say this: You have served Me well, now attend My wishes. I send one to you who shall oversee in My stead. His voice shall be My voice. His will shall be My will. He is Nebmaatra, the Sword of Ra, General of the armies of Egypt, Right Hand to the King. Obey him as you obey Me.'

Nebmaatra was silent, stunned, as the chamber erupted in shouts of approval. General? The flush of pride that should have accompanied the moment was stillborn as he realized its implications.

Psammetichus motioned for silence. 'Do you accept this honour, my friend?'

Nebmaatra bowed, an almost perfunctory gesture. 'If it is truly your will, I have no choice but to accept.'

Psammetichus looked askance at Nebmaatra. 'It is a great honour, is it not?'

Nebmaatra's mind raced as he tried to assimilate every factor, every nuance of what this promotion meant. 'Yes, a great honour,' he replied. He could not have been caught any more off guard if Pharaoh had risen and brained him with an axe. The smiles and congratulatory nods of those about him assumed a sinister aspect; the whispered prayers of victory grew thick with imagined mockery.

'Take what officers and men of the Calasirians as you feel you need and make ready to depart. I will be along as soon as my father's funerary rites are concluded. Remember, Nebmaatra, it is not enough to defeat the Persians at Pelusium.' He jabbed a finger at the envoy, Gobartes. 'We must make them rue the very thought of invading Egypt.'

'I understand, Pharaoh,' Nebmaatra said. 'But, in my absence, who will ensure your safety?'

Psammetichus smiled, glancing at Ujahorresnet. 'I place my safety in the hands of the gods. Their priests will be my spiritual advisers, my counsellors, and my bodyguards if need be. Too long have I listened to the advice of men who seek to gain through deception and poor counsel. This is a new beginning, the dawning of a new era. Go, my friend, and pave the way for victory!'

Nebmaatra bowed, spun, and strode from the audience hall, so deep in thought that he failed to acknowledge the raucous applause following in his wake. He glanced up once, his eye catching the envoy, Gobartes.

The Persian smiled ruthlessly.

∩ ☥ 𐦀 𐦀 ﻻ

The ship was called the *Glory of Amon*, and its quay had become the focal point of a flurry of activity in the predawn gloom. Sailors and long-shoremen worked furiously to get her ready to sail, loading supplies as quickly as the porters arrived with them, scampering up and down the lines and guide ropes. Rowers worked the kinks out of their thick shoulders as they adjusted the sheepskins padding their benches. The *Glory of Amon* was a bireme, stripped down, its low lethal prow glazed for speed. At full sail she could cut the green water of the Mediterranean like a knife through fat.

By all rights, Nebmaatra should have been beside himself, elated beyond words. He had reached the pinnacle of his dreams. Why, then, did he feel uneasy? He stood to one side, watching the preparations without seeing them, his arms folded across his chest. Was it the timing of this triumph, or perhaps his ultimate destination? He could not imagine a decisive battle fought at Pelusium, not against a Persian army thick with cavalry and archers. They would be in their element on that flat grassy plain. A better solution would be to lure them into the swamps and sloughs of the Eastern Delta and await the coming inundation, let the Nile purge itself of this Persian infection.

No, strategy wasn't the source of his concern. He reckoned that, with enough time and enough men, he could make even Pelusium defensible. Nebmaatra stroked his chin. As he understood it, the idea to send him from Sais did not originate with Pharaoh. It came from the mind of the priest,

Ujahorresnet. Why? What possible benefit could the priest gain by promoting him? He had heard cryptic rumours that the old man's behaviour at Memphis during the Greek uprising had been something less than beneficial. Yet, since his installation as First Servant of Neith in Sais, Ujahorresnet had been the model of Egyptian piety. Why, then? Did he harbour aspirations after all? Nebmaatra shook his head. 'Politics,' he said.

'I heard the news, general,' said a voice at his side. He turned and saw Ladice approaching. She seemed pale, withdrawn. Alone. 'I would have thought you would be more . . . jubilant.'

'Why celebrate what may be just a hollow victory?' he said.

'Hollow?' Ladice smiled, a wan gesture that lacked even a shred of her old fire. 'Ahmose told me once he could see in you the ability to inspire men, to lead them to their deaths and make them proud to die. In Egypt's darkest hour, I can think of no better place for you than in command of Pharaoh's armies. My—' Ladice's voice caught in her throat. 'My husband would have agreed with his son's decision.'

Nebmaatra felt a wrench of sadness for Ladice. She was a foreigner, a Greek, adrift on a hostile sea. After the required time of mourning, Psammetichus planned to return her to her family in Cyrene, but even that did nothing to assuage her grief. 'Thank you, lady, but Psammetichus is not his father. He has a simplicity about him; he wants to believe the best in all men, and that makes him a liability in this, as you put it, our darkest hour. Whoever may have engineered this is exploiting Pharaoh's weakness to good effect.'

'Who's behind this conspiracy, general?' Ladice said. 'The nobles? The priests? Does Sais harbour Persian sympathizers?'

Nebmaatra started to reply, then stopped, his eyes narrowing. His mind registered the subtle hint of sarcasm. 'You think I'm foolish?'

'Not foolish, just narrow minded. I do not mean that as an insult. Set your paranoia aside and think, Nebmaatra. What will happen if the Fates smile on you and grant you victory at Pelusium? Egypt will be spared from oblivion, and you will have the power and prestige to exact vengeance on those who crossed you. You have the opportunity to transform this "hollow victory" into a triumph for you as well as Egypt.'

Nebmaatra said nothing for a long moment, his mind navigating the labyrinth of politics. When he finally spoke, his voice held a note of new-found respect. 'You paint a persuasive picture, lady. Maybe this is a matter of perspective, after all. I thank you for your counsel. Your grasp of intrigue is surely worthy of Ahmose, himself.'

Ladice smiled. 'It is hard to be the wife of a Pharaoh and not learn something of politics and intrigue. Truly, though, I sought you out to ask a favour of you.'

'You have only to ask, lady, and perhaps you

can do Egypt a favour in return by availing yourself on Psammetichus. He needs your wisdom.'

Ladice bowed her head. 'You ask the one thing I cannot grant.'

'Why, lady?'

'Because,' Ladice looked up, tears sparkling in her eyes, 'I wished to ask your permission for my maids and I to accompany you to Pelusium.'

Nebmaatra frowned. 'But, I leave within the hour. There are many days of funerary preparations yet to complete for your husband. I do not see . . . ?'

'Ahmose has crossed the River, Nebmaatra,' she said. 'The rites are an Egyptian formality. I have said my farewells after the fashion of my people. After a dozen years of living among Egyptians, I am not one step closer to understanding your liturgies or beliefs, but I do understand your people. We, my maids and I, desire to provide succour to the wounded at Pelusium as a way of repaying the kindness they have shown us.'

Nebmaatra had a thousand arguments for why she should stay and counsel Pharaoh, but as he looked at the tears wetting her cheeks, he could not bring himself to deny her.

'Now, it's you who think I'm foolish,' Ladice said.

Nebmaatra placed a comforting hand on her shoulder. 'No, lady. I understand very well. You should understand, too, that this will be dangerous. Should the battle go against us, I cannot guarantee your safety. If you fall into Persian hands . . .' He trailed off.

'I only wish for a chance to serve,' she said.

Nebmaatra stared at the lightening sky, at the ruddy glow spreading across the eastern horizon. It was going to be a beautiful morning. He sighed. 'To Pelusium, then.'

16

KNIVES IN THE DARK

Her legs wrap around his waist, urging him deeper. Their bodies undulate with a sinuous grace. The sweat of lovemaking rolls down her breasts and pools in the hollow of her throat. He grunts, his hips thrusting against her buttocks; she moans, purring in feline contentment. The room is dark save for a cone of brilliance illuminating their sweat-slick forms. A figure approaches from the shadows. The light strikes fire from a blade held in his hand. He sees the interloper, but he cannot move. Her legs and arms bind him to her. She laughs, her teeth cruel yellow points that rip his flesh. She laughs, caressing him with hands rotted to bone . . .

Barca jerked awake, eyes flaring open, hands fending off something only his mind's eye could see. He bit back a scream before it could escape his throat. Slowly, he sank back down on the bed. The Phoenician shifted his frame and tried to relax, listening to the sounds in the night. Beside him, Jauharah whimpered in her sleep. The tent soughed in the breeze. The flame in the lamp crackled, flickering, its oil almost exhausted. A horse whinnied in the distance, followed by the faint cry of a sentry's challenge.

You are a fool, Barca! He should have been angry with himself for what he had done, for breaking a twenty-year-old promise to the gods to never let a woman close to him again, yet he had no anger in him. Not at this moment. Only a strange feeling even the after-effects of his nightmare could not taint. He looked down at Jauharah's sleeping form.

Her body was balled up tight against his side; her hands twitched, and the muscles in her legs quivered. A veil of hair hid her face from view, though Barca heard a faint moan escape her lips. He kissed her gently, stroking her scalp. Jauharah was an exceptional woman: strong yet compassionate, brave yet vulnerable. She could have been a queen had Fate not made her a slave. But then, in Barca's experience, Fate had a way of punishing the innocent and rewarding the wicked.

Quietly, he rose from the bed and slipped on his kilt. There was no way he could sleep, not with so many concerns running through his mind. How to handle Qainu, how to extract Callisthenes from the Arabian's grasp, how to defend Gaza from within and without, even how to treat Jauharah. What did he feel for her, and would it interfere with his judgement? He . . .

'Hasdrabal?' Jauharah said, her voice thick and drowsy. She stretched and rolled toward him. 'Is something wrong? Come back to bed.'

'No, everything's fine. I have never been able to sleep for any length,' Barca said. He picked up his breastplate and set it on the small table, trying to ignore the lush invitation of her body.

'Nightmares?' Jauharah asked. She reached down and snagged her shift off the floor, draping it across her naked breasts and thighs.

Barca shrugged. 'Sometimes. You have them too, I noticed.'

Jauharah sat up and swung her legs over the edge of the bed. 'I only have one,' she said. 'Every time I close my eyes, I see Meryt and Tuya's tiny bodies drowning in a lake of blood. They're screaming my name, begging me to help them, but I can do nothing. I'm afraid, and that fear keeps me rooted to the spot as they slip under the surface . . .' Tears clung to her lashes, spilling down her cheeks as she squeezed her eyes shut.

Barca moved back to the bed and sat. His hand stroked her back. 'I'm sorry I wasn't there to save them.'

'You can't save everyone, Hasdrabal,' she said, leaning her head against his shoulder. 'You had your hands full that night, as I recall. No, I should never have left them. I try not to imagine what their last minutes were like. Their father lay dead in front of them. Their mother, too. I try not to think about how terrified they were.' She sighed and slipped her shift over her head, running her fingers through her hair. 'I failed them, and it will haunt me for the rest of my life.'

'There's nothing I can say that would ease your

346

mind. The pain is something time will lessen, if you allow it. I'm proof that rage and guilt aren't simple things to live with.'

'I could never forget them,' she said.

'No. You'll never forget them, or what happened. Just try – try as though your soul depends on it – not to let it control you.'

'How—' she began, then stopped. A scream drifted in, a cry of alarm that ended abruptly. Barca shot to his feet. His nostrils flared; he caught the acrid smell of smoke. The Phoenician swore as he grabbed his sword and raced from the tent. Jauharah snatched a knife off the table as she followed in his wake.

Outside, lurid flames leapt from the supply wagons and from tents on the outskirts of camp. In the ghoulish light, Jauharah saw the silhouettes of horsemen thundering through camp, men wearing the tell-tale robes and turbans of Bedouin. On the ground, a handful of Egyptians struggled to rise, to extricate themselves from the clinging folds of their shelters, only to be cut down by the flashing swords of their attackers. Men screamed in pain and rage.

'Awake, dogs!' Barca roared. 'Awake!'

⌒　⚚　⌂　♀　�

They rode in from the northeast, a wedge of half-wild horsemen who trampled tents and slaughtered men as they bore down on the ruins forming the geographic centre of the Egyptian

347

camp. Chaos ruled as men, torn from the arms of slumber by Barca's cry, stumbled out of their tents only to be set upon by Bedouin wolves. Arab and Egyptian strained breast to breast, fighting with a primal fury that erased all vestiges of humanity. Men reverted to their animal nature, slashing with knife and sword, tooth and nail. Barca saw a naked Egyptian, his standard-bearer, drag a Bedouin from his horse and kill him even as another rode him down from behind.

Snarling, Barca slung his sword over his shoulder, snatched a bow from a weapons rack, and strung it in one fluid motion. The Bedouin were overwhelming his men, forcing them back to the ruins. With machine-like efficiency, Barca drew and loosed, sending arrow after arrow into the fray. He saw horses rear, pitching their riders into the dust. Men screamed as bronze-heads slashed into their bellies, their chests, their faces. So tightly were they compacted that the Phoenician's arrows could not miss.

The timbre of the battle changed as Barca's archery provided a toehold. The Egyptians shook off the effects of surprise and rallied together. A hedge of spears arose, skewering horse and rider alike. Bedouin flung to the ground by their terrified mounts were set upon and slaughtered.

The stench of spilled blood, the clash and clamour of battle – these things stirred the anger in the pit of Barca's soul. Bare-chested, clad in only a brief kilt, he waded into the fray. Furious cries of 'al-Saffah' rose from the throats of the

Bedouin, mingling with curses and prayers. The Bloodshedder had come. As a mob, the desert men charged the Phoenician, robes flapping, beards bristling.

A horseman screamed wordlessly and leapt from the saddle. Barca dropped his bow and caught him in mid-air, slamming him into the ground with bone-crunching force. A savage kick from the Phoenician ended the fallen man's struggles. In an instant the other Bedouin were on him. Barca ducked a sword-cut, his left fist stretching the man out senseless, and batted aside a knife-wielding arm that streaked toward his face. His own sword sang from its sheath. Bearded faces rose and fell; swords and knives lashed out only to be knocked aside as Barca scythed through their turbaned ranks.

The Bedouin fell back in dismay. In that instant, the Egyptians seized the advantage, pouring into the breach Barca had wrought like air in the wake of lightning. They surged past him, sinewy bodies naked, brown hands grasping axe, spear, and sword. Though slow to anger, the men of the Nile did not lack for courage; they fought like men who had little to fear from death.

Dripping blood, very little of it his own, Barca dropped back and surveyed the dead. With his foot, he flipped a Bedouin corpse over. An arrow had pierced his throat and broken off; the shaft forced his chin up in an almost comical pose. Barca rifled the body, found nothing. His weapons and clothing were of a better quality than what could be expected of a desert raider. Someone had paid this man, and paid him well.

'Phoenician!'

Barca glanced up. In the orange glow of the fires, he saw Ahmad and his men approaching. The old Arab gasped for breath. 'We came as soon as—'

Barca did not let him finish. 'Son of a bitch!' the Phoenician snarled, back-handing the garrison captain. Ahmad staggered and would have fallen had Barca not snatched him up by the front of his tunic. 'Decide who you're loyal to, and decide it now! I want answers! Are these Qainu's Bedouin?'

Barca's fury took Ahmad's men unawares. By the time they recovered their wits enough to draw blades, their captain's upraised hand stilled them. Ahmad tore himself free of Barca's grip. He dabbed at the blood oozing from his split lip as he knelt and studied the dead men at his feet. 'Aye, these are Zayid's men,' he said at length. 'I recognize this one by the scar above his eye. Could be they were just after plunder.'

'Don't be a fool, Ahmad! It was plain for all to see that we were heavily armed, yet they attacked regardless. Why? If it's plunder they were after, why not loot one of the outlying caravan camps? No, this is Qainu's doing!'

Ahmad stood. His shoulders slumped. 'What do you want from us?'

'Loyalty,' Barca said. 'Tell me what Qainu has planned. We need—'

Barca's head snapped up. Above the shriek and din of battle, he heard a scream of a different sort. His lips peeled back over his teeth in an expression of bestial rage.

It was a woman's scream.

⌒ ⚓ ⌂ ⚱ ⚲

Callisthenes paced the perimeter of his prison, the knife in his hands like an impossible weight. The fury and bravado he had felt upon discovering the weapon had petered out. Despite all he learned from Barca, the thought of having to kill again left a cold knot of apprehension in his belly. What was he afraid of? Death?

After Memphis, Callisthenes had sought to approach the dynamics of killing from a philosopher's point of view. Violence, he decided, was a necessary evil; indeed, the gods of Hellas held those capable of dealing death in high regard. Even the afterlife was segregated; warriors and those who excelled at violence were offered eternal bliss in Elysium, while the common man faced the grim reality of Tartarus.

He thought back to the countless afternoons spent in Barca's company learning the intricacies of swordplay. The Phoenician instructed him in the best ways to kill a man, where the arterial points were, how to incapacitate the enemy by targeting his torso and belly. What struck Callisthenes was not the feel of a hilt in his sweat-slick palm, or even the sound of metal grating on metal. No, the thing Callisthenes remembered most was the nonchalance in Barca's voice. He could have been a farmer describing the most economical ways of harvesting grain.

'I don't kill out of joy or capriciousness,' Barca had told him later, as they prepared for Gaza, 'but to preserve what I hold dear . . . my life; the lives of my friends; Egypt. And those I kill are generally deserving of it.'

Slaughter bred arrogance, Callisthenes reckoned. Killers justified it to themselves by painting their foe in the worst possible light; by telling themselves they helped rid the world of another vile soul. It was a skewed sense of justice that Callisthenes just did not possess. Men like Barca saw the world in stark primary colours – black and white, right and wrong – defined by their experiences. They were confident in their own perceptions and as unflinching as granite. For Callisthenes, right and wrong, like the truth, were mutable. Ask a hundred men to describe the same struggle, and you would get a hundred different answers. Which one was the truth?

There was no easy solution to his situation. He would have to kill again, damn the consequences. His fate and the fate of his friends hung in the balance. Resigned, Callisthenes stopped pacing.

'Guard!' the Greek roared, battering on the thick cedar door. 'Damn you, you impertinent fool!' He hoped Qainu had told them to see to his every desire.

'What do you want?' a voice grated from the

hall beyond. Callisthenes mumbled something. 'What?' A key rattled in the lock. The bolt was thrown back. The door opened enough to admit the guard's head and shoulders. A hawkish Bedouin face peered within. 'What is it you—'

Callisthenes moved quicker than he thought possible. He hurled his weight against the door, pinning the guard's shoulders as his hand clamped down on the Bedouin's skull. His knife ripped across the man's throat. Blood gushed over the Greek's fist. He hauled the still-thrashing guard into the room and threw him headlong over the divan. The Bedouin's helmet clashed and clattered; his spear skittered across the tiled floor. Callisthenes risked a glance into the empty hallway, then closed the door and turned back to finish off his victim.

The Bedouin clutched at the wound in his throat, his fingers trying to stem the tide of blood spurting from his severed arteries. He gurgled like a man drowning, and his voice weakened with every pulse of his racing heart. Callisthenes could only stare as the Bedouin guard – a man he did not know; a man he had no quarrel with save for his choice of loyalties – died. His blood washed over Amphitrite's feet.

'I'm sorry,' he whispered, snatching up the Bedouin's spear. It was a sturdy weapon, a six-foot-long shaft capped with a bronze blade the length of the Greek's forearm. It would do. He thrust the knife into his gold-scaled belt and moved to the door, inching it open. The hallway was deserted. A few well-spaced lamps provided succour from the oppressive darkness. Callisthenes exhaled. With a prayer to fleet-footed Hermes, he stepped out into the hallway, pulled the door closed behind him and shot the bolt.

He crept along quickly, following the path Merodach had sketched on the platter. He descended a flight of stairs and darted into a broad hallway. Callisthenes had no clue how he would deal with Qainu's guards, but he prayed the Arab had gone to slumber and his retinue with him. If that were the case, it would be a small matter to slip out into the courtyard and steal over the wall. If not . . . well, if not, Callisthenes would do his utmost to earn entrance to the endless feasts of Elysium.

Tension and fear exaggerated his senses, causing him to notice little details about the palace that he had not had the luxury to study earlier. Flaking plaster, crude reliefs imitating the Egyptian style, lamps and fixtures of hammered copper. It seemed to Callisthenes that the Arabs sought to emulate the art and architecture of the Nile, but with far less aplomb. Even the aromatic cedar he could smell seemed less than clean, barely masking an underlying stench of decay.

He was nearing the end of the hallway, and the side door leading to the throne room, when a sound made him pause. Voices. His heart leapt into his throat. Callisthenes cast about for a hiding place, then stopped. The voices were not growing closer, only rising in intensity. He was hearing an argument emanating from the throne room, itself.

He glided closer, listening . . .

Jauharah left Barca's side and sprinted across the sand. She could serve no one by cleaving to the Phoenician's shadow; her knife would not sway the fight's outcome in the tiniest degree. At the hospital tents she would be in her element. She darted through the ruins, dodging fallen columns and leaping a low wall, clutching her knife close to her body.

The sounds of fighting – the screams of rage and agony, the crash and slither of iron on bronze, the moist impact of iron on flesh – echoed beyond the wall of the ruin. She tried not to think of the Egyptian soldiers out there as young men, tried not to recall their laughter, their voices. Soon, they would come broken and bleeding into her care. Some would die; others would pray for death.

Jauharah rounded the corner and skidded to a halt. Flames erupted from the hospital tents. Men were locked together, heaving this way and that in an obscene dance that would end with a life extinguished. As she watched, Bay, kindly, meticulous Bay, hurled himself on a Bedouin's back, a surgeon's knife flashing in the firelight. The raider fell, his throat slit. Another stepped in and rammed his spear into Bay's chest. Jauharah screamed as the quartermaster was lifted off his feet and slammed to the ground, gurgling through the blood filling his lungs as the Bedouin cruelly twisted the spear.

At the sound of her voice, a woman's voice, the Bedouin turned. Malice glittered in their dark eyes. Malice, and lust. Dread clutched Jauharah's heart with talons of ice.

Suddenly, she doubted the wisdom of leaving Barca's shadow. Jauharah backed away, then turned and disappeared into the ruins. Like hounds, the Bedouin bayed and gave chase. They had taken only a handful of steps when a squad of Egyptians fell on their flank. The woman was forgotten as spear, knife and sword licked out, driving them back into the crackling flames.

Jauharah slowed, her breath coming in ragged gasps. She pulled herself over the low wall and stopped. No one followed her. Tears blurred her vision. She turned . . .

. . . and screamed as a raider blind-sided her, lunging from the darkness like a desert spirit. He caught her like a man does a child, his arms wrapping around her, pinning her to his chest. 'Come, my sweet lotus flower!' he whispered in her ear, his breath foul.

Jauharah's shrieks had an altogether different quality as she struggled against the Bedouin, her lithe strength brought to nothing by bands of iron muscle. He chuckled darkly and hurled her to the ground. Jauharah hit hard, her breath whistling from her lungs. Somehow, she kept hold of her knife.

Light from the distant fires seeped in through chinks in the crumbling walls, striping the darkness with slashes of orange. 'Qainu said kill you all,' the raider said, grinning. 'But he said nothing against taking our sport first!' He drove his sword point-first into the ground and hiked up his robe, tucking the hem into his sword belt. Leering, the Bedouin stalked her, his ugly, goatish body naked from the waist down. Jauharah smelled the reek of smoke and sweat, the stench of horses permeating the Bedouin's frame. She pulled herself to her knees and staggered to her feet.

'Q-Qainu?' she said.

But the Bedouin offered her nothing more, save a cruel bark of laughter as he threw himself at her. Grimy hands pawed at her breasts, tearing her shift from her shoulders. In that instant, Jauharah remembered the knife in her fist. Snarling, she drove it forward with all the strength in her arm.

Flesh parted under the keen blade. The Bedouin's howls changed pitch and timbre as her knife slashed up through his groin, emasculating him before continuing deep into the juncture of his inner thigh. He sank to the ground, clutching himself, gobbling at the blood spurting from his lacerated femoral artery. He pushed himself away from her and crawled to where his sword lay.

Jauharah's world shrank to a pinpoint, a speck dominated by the writhing body at her feet. Her mind's eye no longer saw a Bedouin, but a Greek, an assassin, covered in the blood of children. He tried to rise. 'No!' she snarled, throwing herself on his back. Her knife flashed again and again. She had to save them! She . . .

When Jauharah looked down the Greek was gone. Instead, she straddled the Bedouin's twisted corpse. The blood-slick hilt of her knife protruded from the shredded flesh of his shoulders. She held her trembling hands up. They were covered in blood, as well. Jauharah spun away, vomiting.

'Egyptian women are soft!' A figure sat atop the low wall. He dropped to the ground. His silhouette gave Jauharah the impression of a bird of prey; his ripped robes and blood-blasted turban left no doubt that he was Bedouin. He walked closer and levelled a gory scimitar at her breast.

'Salim was a fool,' he said, 'but I'll not make the same mistake. Touch that knife and I'll split you in two, girl!'

Fear hammered through her brain as she sought a way out, some kind of edge over the lean desert fighter. The other Bedouin, Salim, had been blinded by lust; this one was different. This one had lusts no woman could slake. She pushed herself away from him, passing through a shaft of light.

'You are an Arab!' he said, grunting in surprise. 'Are you Barca's whore?'

Jauharah spat. 'I'm no whore, you cursed Asiatic swineherd!'

The Bedouin chuckled. 'You have learned impertinence in the cities of Egypt. That is good. Taming you will provide me with a challenge. Remember my name, woman, for you will be

Zayid's whore after I have killed the Phoenician dog.'

'You're not man enough to kill Barca!' Jauharah said, with far more bravado than she felt. 'If you were a man, you'd be out there dying with your kin instead of cowering in the darkness with a woman!'

Zayid's jaw clenched and there was a dangerous glitter to his dark eyes. 'Do I have to show you how much of a man I am?'

'Don't show her. Show me.' Barca stepped from the shadows and leaned against a shattered column, his sword held loosely at his side. Zayid spun and backed away as Barca stood erect and walked toward him.

'Gods! How I have waited for this moment!' Zayid said. 'The great al-Saffah! Did you think you could spill the blood of my brothers and escape unscathed?'

'You've overestimated your ability. It seems to be a common failing among you Bedouin. Make your peace with the gods, sand-fucker!'

'I may die, but I'll send you to Hell before me!' Zayid surged forward, his blade whistling in a tight arc about his head. A blood lust gripped him that made him ignore any thought of defence. He loosed an eerie undulating howl.

Jauharah saw them crash together. She caught the flash of blades, heard the slaughterhouse sound of iron cleaving flesh. She blinked, and in that brief span, Barca's sword slammed into Zayid's chest, left of the sternum, shattering

bone and splitting the muscles of his heart. The
Phoenician held Zayid on the end of his sword as
the Bedouin clawed feebly at the blade.

'Not a man, after all!' Barca growled, and
kicked him away. Zayid was dead and forgotten
before he hit the ground.

Barca rushed to Jauharah's side. 'Are you hurt?'
He tried helping her stand, but she threw her arms
around his neck, instead. Her body trembled; he
did not trust her legs to hold her. 'Are you hurt?'

She shook her head. For a long time Jauharah
held him tight, her head buried in his shoulder as
sobs wracked her already weakened form. He
stroked her hair. 'H-He was g-going to rape
m-me. I—'

'You did what you had to.'

She looked up, the anguish in her eyes like a
knife to his soul. 'I'm going mad! B-Before I killed
him I thought he w-was one of the Greeks w-
who . . .'

Barca held her close and said nothing. He could
have told her a similar tale, about the face he saw
when in the grips of *katalepsis;* he could have told
her that every man he had slain bore an uncanny
resemblance to himself. But, she needed to believe
it would pass, that Time would lessen the pain.
Only then would her heart start down the slow
path of healing.

A path she shouldn't travel alone.

Outside the ruin, the sounds of fighting died
away. Jauharah stirred. 'I heard him say Qainu
ordered them to kill us.'

'I know.'

'What do we do?' Jauharah asked. She did not know what was more disconcerting: Barca's silence or the look in his eye as he stared at Zayid's corpse.

Callisthenes crept to the door of the throne room, listening.

'Why are you badgering me about this Greek?' Qainu was saying. 'What matter is it of yours what I plan to do with him?'

'It is wrong, what you plan!' a voice answered. Merodach. 'He came to us in good faith and we repay his candour by clapping him in chains! Have we become like the wretched Bedouin? Men who possess not a shred of honour?'

'Guard your tongue, Merodach,' Qainu said, his voice a dangerous hiss. 'The future of Arabia lay with the Bedouin. Had you sense, you'd see it too.'

'All I see is a weak fool dancing on the end of a string . . . a string held by the Persians!' Merodach said.

Callisthenes inched forward. Silently, on well-kept hinges, the door opened on a small alcove that widened out into the throne room proper, with its forest of columns. The place was dark, the only source of light a trio of bronze lamps burning about the throne. The Greek saw no evidence of guards, for which he breathed a prayer of thanks, as he crept along the wall.

Suddenly, Callisthenes stopped. Qainu's tiger, chained to the king's throne, glared at him and coughed. The big cat's eyes glowed a sorcerous green in the dim light.

'What has happened to you, Merodach? You were once my staunchest ally. Now, you sound like your predecessor, a snivelling toad who lacked a spine. Have these Egyptians cast some sort of spell over you? Do you hunger for my throne?' The Arabian king looked thunderstruck. 'That's it! You've made some unholy alliance with the Egyptians!'

'Don't be absurd!' Merodach said. The chancellor paced back and forth, the movement catching the tiger's eye. 'It pains me to see these Persians using you as a pawn in their political games. Cambyses doubtless has never heard of you, Majesty. Not with a glory-hound like Phanes at his side. You are nothing to this man whose attention you crave. A puppet!'

'Rather a puppet than a corpse!' Qainu said. He leaned down and loosed the tiger's collar. With an ear-splitting roar the beast launched itself off the dais, clearing the intervening space in a single lithe bound to crash full onto Merodach's chest. The pair fell in a welter of thrashing limbs. A chilling shriek echoed about the throne room as the tiger's powerful claws disembowelled the chancellor.

Qainu's laughter amid the cracking of bone roused the Greek from his shocked silence. An unfathomable rage clutched him. A rage that could only be sated with blood.

'No!' Callisthenes screamed. He sprinted out into the open.

The sight of the blood-splashed Greek hefting a spear sent a paroxysm of fear through Qainu. The Arabian king recoiled, curling up into a ball on his throne as he awaited the cold hand of death.

The tiger glared at the Greek from above the gory mess that was Merodach, ears flattening against its skull. The spear cocked behind Callisthenes' ear flew straight and true, a cast worthy of Hector. The long bronze blade flashed through the dim light of the throne room and smashed into the tiger's side. The god of war must have blessed that cast, for the spear knocked the beast sidewise off Merodach, splitting its heart in two. Without breaking stride, the Greek ripped his knife from his girdle and leapt at the king.

'Guards!' Qainu hurled himself off the throne and tried to run. Years of sloth, of debauchery, had taken their toll on the fleshy Arabian. Callisthenes caught him easily by the scruff of the neck and hurled him back against the dais. 'Guards!' the king squealed. In a rage, the Greek struck Qainu across the mouth, his fist stiffened by the hilt of his knife. The Arab fell back, stunned. Callisthenes gave him not a moment's respite. Again and again he pommel-whipped the king, his face a mask of fury. Barely did he hear his name being called.

'C-Callis . . . C-Callisthenes!'

The Greek looked up. Amazingly, Merodach yet clung to life. With great effort the chancellor

extended a hand toward Callisthenes. The Greek
let go of the king and rushed to Merodach's side.

'I am sorry, my friend. I brought this on
you.' He stroked the Babylonian's forehead. The
tiger's claws had shredded his abdomen, exposing
intestine and bone. A lake of crimson formed
around the fallen man. 'I am so sorry.'

'P-Please . . .' Merodach whispered, bubbles of
blood breaking on his trembling lips. 'Do n-not
kill h-him . . .' His eyes rolled toward the dais,
toward the bruised and bleeding form of his king.
'P-Promise . . . m-me . . .'

'I promise, Merodach,' Callisthenes said quietly.
'I will not kill him.' Merodach gripped the Greek's
arm, then gave a last, wet, shuddering sigh. Tears
rolled down Callisthenes' cheeks. This man, a
stranger to him, had shown more grace and honour
in dying than any man the Greek had ever known.
Far more grace than the wretched dog he served.

Callisthenes glanced up, hatred in his eyes. His
hand gripped the hilt of his knife.

Qainu's scream echoed about the throne room.

⌒　⚓　🔔　⚲　☥

Dawn striped the eastern sky with bands of coral
and ivory, fading overhead to diamond-studded
lapis. Bedouin guards crouched at the gates of
Qainu's palace, passing a skin of fermented goat's
milk back and forth. They were supposed to be on
station inside the walls, as sentries and door-
wards, but the desert men felt uneasy surrounded

by so much stone, constricted. A man needed open sky in order to breathe.

They had passed the night cursing and grumbling in their beards at being left behind to watch over the fat king while their brothers gained gold and glory in the Egyptian camp. Zayid had promised each of them an equal share of the booty. In that, at least, they did not feel cheated.

'How much do you think we will get?' the youngest of them said, his beard a mere wisp on his chin. The others laughed.

'More than you've ever seen, boy,' one said. 'Enough to buy every whore from here to Damascus!'

'You lie!' the boy said, walking away from the others. He stopped at the stone kerb of a well occupying the centre of the plaza. In a few hours time, women would bring their jars here to be filled, the first of many chores.

'He speaks true, Khatib,' another said, rising from a crouch and stretching. 'Gold in Egypt is like sand in Arabia. You have only to stoop and pick it up. What *shaykh* Zayid takes from their camp, even divided, will make all of us rich beyond our dreams.'

The boy, Khatib, grinned. 'I will buy herds, not whores,' he said. 'And wives! I will have a hundred wives! I . . .' Khatib paused as something came arching out of the gloom. It struck the ground with a meaty squelch and rolled to the well's edge. Khatib frowned as he walked around to the thing and squatted. The others laughed, shouting to their young cousin.

'What have you found, boy?'

Khatib rose and turned toward them, eyes wide, face pale. He cradled a severed head in his hands. Its features, frozen in the act of dying, were all too familiar to the Bedouin.

Zayid.

The guards surged to their feet, cursing and howling in rage. 'Watch yourself, boy!' They gestured behind the young Bedouin.

'What is it . . . What . . . ?' Khatib spun as Barca stepped from the shadows, his sword splitting the boy's skull like a ripe melon. The Phoenician kicked the corpse aside and fell on the remaining half-dozen guards. Egyptians poured into the plaza at his back.

The Bedouin did not stand a chance.

'Take the gate!' Barca roared, droplets of crimson falling from his blade. Qainu's palace, a temple in a previous incarnation, was designed to be easily defended. The crenellated walls had murder-holes and sally-ports carved into the ancient brick. Besieged archers and soldiers could easily rain death down on an attacker. Even the simple gate was a heavy, ponderous affair of corroded bronze and cedar; it looked to Barca like it had not been closed in a generation or more.

A handful of Bedouin, along with a sprinkling of slaves and servants, rushed to the gate and threw their backs into closing it. It moved an inch. Two. Four. Grins of triumph on their faces were short lived as the huge portal ground to a halt. They panicked as a wave of Egyptians in glittering armour crashed against the gate, forcing it open. After a flurry of blades left Bedouin corpses across the threshold, the rest turned and fled into the courtyard.

Barca expected some kind of organized defence. Arrows and rocks from on high.

A rush of swordsmen. Something. Even a mutiny among Ahmad's men who were secretly loyal to Qainu. But, this last stand of the grooms-men and the kitchen help had taken him unawares. Surely Qainu was not so foolish as to commit his entire household guard to the fight in the camp?

'Are any of your men within?' the Phoenician asked Ahmad. The Arabian captain shook his head.

'No. We're billeted in the city. Qainu fancies himself more of a *shaykh* than a king. The only soldiers within are Zayid's mercenaries.'

'He's neither,' Barca growled. 'He's governor of a city under Egyptian rule. His folly is thinking beyond his station.'

'Whatever his folly,' Ahmad said, 'he is my king. I swore allegiance to Qainu and his fore-bears, not to Egypt. I cannot help with what you intend.'

'Then do not hinder me, either!' Barca said, turning and leading his Egyptians through the gates.

The courtyard was a blending of worlds; an

Egyptian lotus pool surrounded by Arabian date palms and Hellenic sculpture. The servants faced them with cleavers and kitchen knives, fear shining in their eyes. Barca stalked toward them. The look on his face promised murder should his will not be done. He raked them with a withering stare. 'You've proven your valour,' he said. 'Stand down and you'll not be harmed.' There were murmurs among them; then, one by one, their weapons clattered to the ground. To his Egyptians he said, 'Keep them here.'

Barca ascended the steps to the throne room doors, his wrath cold and righteous.

With a snarl, he shouldered them open . . .

. . . and stopped in amazement. Instead of a horde of Bedouin warriors, he saw a sight that brought a deep, throaty laugh from him. Callisthenes. The Greek sat upon the ebony throne of Gaza, a bloody knife driven point first into the inlaid armrest. A tiger lay dead, a spear sprouting from its body like a grisly vine, and near it a corpse Barca recognized as that of Merodach, the chancellor. Something else crouched at Callisthenes' feet, something barely discernible as a naked man, his face streaked with blood. An indelicate hand had taken a knife to the fellow's hair and beard, shearing both away without thought for the skin beneath, and a leash trailed down to a collar around the man's neck. With a start, Barca realized it must be Qainu.

Barca chuckled. 'I'll be damned, Callisthenes. Here I thought you might be in need of my help.

What happened to the squeamish Greek who abhorred violence?'

'Someone tried to kill him,' Callisthenes said. He rose and tossed Qainu's leash to Barca. 'I promised Merodach I would not kill him, but you're under no such constraints. I only ask you do it elsewhere. I've had my fill of murder for the day.'

Barca passed the leash to Ahmad. The Arab captain crouched, his fierce face inches from the deposed king's, his blood-spattered beard bristling. 'You wretched bastard! I served you, and your father before you, with faith and honour and this is how you repay me? Damn your black soul! You will share in Zayid's fate, you son of a bitch!'

Qainu whimpered and pleaded as Ahmad and his soldiers dragged him into the bowels of the palace.

Barca followed Callisthenes out into the courtyard. Overhead, the sky faded from the coral-ivory of dawn to a bright and vibrant azure. Sunlight filtered through a pall of dust raised by the battle as the last of the servants were bound together in an uneven line.

'I bear ill news,' Callisthenes said, sitting on the stone curb of a lotus pool. The adrenalin rush left his body cold and shaking. 'Phanes. That bastard was here; he travels with the Persian vanguard. They have crossed the wastes and already sit on our doorstep. The cities of Phoenicia must have given in to Cambyses' demands.'

Callisthenes tensed for a sulphuric tirade, but Barca did not waste breath cursing his countrymen. He stood in silence, studying the tracery of shadows cast by the date palms lining the pool. His people were merchants; they dealt in profit and loss, leaving the vagaries of morality to those who could afford it. All of the treaties signed with Egypt, all of the pledges of friendship and offerings of fealty were nothing compared to what the Persians offered: capitulation or annihilation. To a Phoenician, it was not that difficult a choice.

'What do we do now?' Callisthenes asked.

'We'll have to pull back, choose better ground,' Barca said. 'If the Persians use ships to get troops behind us, our delaying action will become our last stand. No, we must abandon Gaza. It's too open to properly defend ourselves. We . . .'

A clamour at the gate drowned Barca out. He heard a flurry of incredulous shouts, cries to the gods for mercy. Frowning, he went to investigate. Callisthenes followed in his wake.

A crowd gathered in the plaza outside the palace. Arabs, for the most part, leavened with a sprinkling of Judaeans; dark-skinned Nubians, even a pair of scarred horse-traders out of Thrace. Egyptian soldiers rested in the morning shade. Barca could not make out what was being said, though he divined the gist of it. Peering northeast, shading his eyes with a blood-grimed hand, he could see what had inspired their sudden panic. Behind him, Callisthenes mumbled a prayer in his native Greek. Barca remained quiet, his jaw muscles knotted.

In the distance, a pillar of dust marred the blue perfection of the sky.

The Persians.

17

RETREAT TO RAPHIA

The hills ringing Raphia were slashed with gullies
and arroyos; bleak cliffs stood sentinel over the
Way of Horus. The road curved serpentine before
plunging into a deep cleft surmounted by ridges
of loose rock and scree. The natural bottleneck
was the perfect site for an ambush, and Otanes,
who commanded the Persian outriders, knew it
too. He and his men were part of a probe, the
tentative thrust of a hand well-versed in strategy
and tactics. This was the third time they had
tested this section of road in as many days; Otanes
had lost count of how many such sorties they had
attempted in the week since leaving Gaza.

Otanes reined in his horse, peering through
the swirling dust kicked up by the column of
soldiers at his back. His throat was raw and dry;
sweat poured down his ribs, soaking the linen
corselet he wore under his scale armour. By the
blessed Ahuramazda! This place was a furnace.
The cooling winds of the Mediterranean did not
reach this far inland. Here, nothing moved the
humid air.

He scanned the ridges above, wary. Otanes' heritage gave him the right to command – he was of undiluted Persian blood from Anshan, at the heart of the empire – and his wits gave him the wherewithal to command well. A soldier born, as the old adage says, to bend the bow and speak the truth, Otanes did not consider it a slight that his name was never offered as a candidate to lead the regiment left behind to secure Gaza in preparation for His Majesty's arrival. He knew his instincts made him more useful in the field. These same instincts warned him: the cursed Phoenician and his soldiers were waiting ahead.

'Sir?' his lieutenant, a young Mede called Bagoas, leaned forward in the saddle. 'Do we proceed?'

'So quick to find glory and death, Bagoas?' Otanes murmured, not looking at the man. His gaze was riveted on a spot where the jumbled boulders clung precariously to the cliff-side. 'Tiribazos rushed in, and look what happened to him. An Egyptian arrow in the gullet. Myself, I'd like to die in a different kind of saddle, if you get my meaning.'

Bagoas chuckled.

After a moment Otanes nodded to himself. He saw no sign of an ambush, despite the tightly-clenched ball of foreboding in his gut. Perhaps it was farther up the road this time, or perhaps the Egyptians had withdrawn. Either way, he would proceed with caution. He held his hand up and motioned his column forward.

Harness jingled as the Persians entered the defile. Dozens of eyes rolled skyward, staring at the silent cliffs. With every step breathing became more difficult as the noose of apprehension tightened about their throats. Each soldier made a promise to himself to sacrifice to the blessed Ahuramazda should they live to see the far end of the ravine.

Otanes' neck muscles creaked as he glanced over his shoulder. Behind him, Bagoas shifted uneasily and looked up. His breath caught in his throat as he spotted the reflection of sunlight on metal. He opened his mouth to shout a warning . . .

'Loose!' a voice roared from above, echoing through the narrow defile.

Arrows slashed down through the bright morning sunlight, a bronze-barbed rain that found chinks in armour, punched through hastily raised shields, and clattered on scorched rock. Otanes shouted as he toppled from his saddle; horses bucked and reared as arrows raked their dusty flanks. In an instant, the well-ordered Persian ranks were thrown into disarray.

Young Bagoas, so far unscathed, controlled his mount with his knees, spinning the horse about. For the rest of his life, Bagoas would remember only one thing about that ambush, a single vision sharpened by adrenalin and fear: Otanes slumped against the rocks, his eyes fixed and staring, with an arrow jutting from his cervical spine.

Bagoas signalled a withdrawal.

Barca nocked his final arrow and sighted down the shaft. Clouds of dust rising from the terrified horses obscured his vision. Regardless, he let loose into the heart of the chaos. No thrill arose from the act. No exultation flowed through his veins, roaring up from that dark wellspring of his soul to inflame his limbs with renewed vigour. During the fight at Gaza, his anger had been reticent, difficult to provoke. Now, the source of his anger felt cold and dead.

A horn brayed, and the horsemen below withdrew, their shields held high against the dwindling barrage of arrows. From Barca's vantage the Persians were patient, unperturbed. Not even the lack of potable water disturbed them. Barca had sent men all around with orders to poison every well and water hole they could find, while others burned granaries and slew livestock. Most of the people of this district had fled from the coming destruction, disappearing into the trackless wastes with all they could carry. In spite of his efforts, the Persians would be well-supplied by Phoenician ships.

Barca gave the signal and his Egyptians, barely two score, broke off their attack and faded down the hillsides toward Raphia. Gaza and the strategic withdrawal down the Way of Horus had taken a fearsome toll on his men. Of the three hundred who had followed him from Sais, scarcely one third could move under their own power. All bore tell-tale signs of fighting: blood-smeared bandages, notched swords, dented corselets. Each quiver in their possession had enough arrows for one last ambush. This was fast becoming a hopeless fight.

The Egyptians drifted down a narrow gorge, moving quickly but silently away from the ambush site. These jagged hills were full of switchbacks and box canyons, arid flats and dunes; the eroded sandstone cliffs were dotted with withered grass and sedge.

They crossed a bare valley scarred by a cruelly twisting dry streambed. Beyond the next ridge the hills opened up, and a goat trail led down to Raphia.

From the heights the village was unlovely, a collection of stone huts clinging to an indentation in the coastline, and its beauty grew less with proximity. Rutted streets, flaking plaster walls, and the smell of rotting fish gave it all the allure of an open sewer. The folk of Raphia were rustics, by Egyptian standards; a dull and unimaginative people who divided their time between fishing and herding sheep. The Way of Horus brought caravans through Raphia, and the ancillary profits earned from serving the whims of the drovers and guards should have made the village wealthy. From what Barca saw, they more than likely drank their profits away. Beyond the village, the Way of Horus entered a stretch of harsh sand-scoured waste, a desert buffer that ran to the very threshold of Egypt. Barca did not relish the thought of fighting a running battle through that inferno.

Callisthenes stumbled toward him through the scrub. In his corselet and helmet, scavenged from the dead at Gaza, Callisthenes looked the part of a soldier: grimy, bloodied, his eyes possessing that unfocused stare of a man who had seen too much of death.

'Tenacious bastards,' the Greek grunted, jacking his helmet back and wiping sweat from his eyes. 'How many days now have they tried the same tactic? What the hell are they waiting for? I heard the scouts say the Persians are five thousand strong, the cream of the Hyrkanian steppe. Why don't they just wash us aside like a sand wall before a storm?'

'Are you always so full of questions?' Barca snapped.

The Greek shrugged, metal scales clashing. 'It is a gift. Some men are blessed with fair features, others with gilded tongues, still more are granted martial superiority. The gods saw fit to grant me boundless curiosity.'

'Gods, indeed. You remind me of Tjemu,' Barca said. A part of him regretted leaving his Medjay behind at Pelusium; they, too, had scores to settle with Phanes. 'In answer to your questions: I do not know. If I could read other men's minds, I'm sure the waging of war would have lost its lustre long ago.'

'Would you care to speculate?'

Barca said nothing. Exhaustion left him silent

and brooding, bereft of the will to explain. Despite his accolades and triumphs, Barca knew it was no great thing to wage war. Any fool with sense and speed could take up the sword and do as much or better than he. True courage came not in facing death, but in facing life. In that, the Phoenician branded himself a coward. For twenty years he had hidden from life, burying himself in battle and blood in hopes that life would pass by, or at worst it would see him and know fear. Where other men raised families and grew crops, Barca razed crops and slew families. He had murdered the woman he professed to love. What was left, then, but to follow her down that self-same road to hell?

No, he did not believe that. Not any more. Just as a patch of burnt earth would become green with time, a soul could mend itself and become whole again. The anger and self-recrimination that had sustained him for these long years had burned itself out, as a fire left unattended in the hearth, leaving him open to feel . . . not happiness, no, that was the fodder of poets and romantics. Peace, then? He could live with peace.

Callisthenes continued, sullen. 'I'm not like you, Barca. I'm scared shitless. What if they try another assault later today, or tomorrow? What will we do? What plan . . .'

'Like me?' Barca frowned. 'Am I so different from you? Am I some kind of monster who lives only for the smell, taste, and feel of strife? Truth be told, Callisthenes, I'm just a man, with every weakness and flaw embodied by that small word. If you're scared, then imagine the terror that must be upon me, for I have not only your life and mine, but the lives of every man among us to be concerned about.'

'But, you seem so . . . unaffected.'

'Would you follow a man who wore his fears on his sleeve? For as long as I can remember, I did not allow it to affect me. I thought it a sign of weakness to fret over the lives of men pledged to war. I had a healthy hatred for death and that, coupled with bravado, would take the field in every battle. I was only partially correct.'

'I don't follow,' Callisthenes said. Barca stopped and faced the smaller man.

'I did not have a hatred of death, after all, rather a fear of life. Callisthenes, you're not going to die here, not today. I have an idea of what our options are, but I need time to breathe and think. Give me a few hours, and I'll have the answers you seek.'

The Greek nodded as Barca descended into the village. In the back of his mind, he wondered if the Phoenician would have the answer to what was fast becoming his most pressing question: *What has happened to you?*

⌒　⚱　🌴　☥　☩

Jauharah lifted the iron from the fire, eyeing its white-hot tip. The man on the table writhed against the two soldiers holding him down, muscular men in blood-spattered kilts. Pain and madness glinted in his eyes. She had removed an arrow from his shoulder, a gift from the Persians, and now she moved to cauterize the puncture.

'Hold him steady,' she said. Her orderlies nodded, bracing themselves against the wounded man's thrashings. Jauharah exhaled and brought the tip of the iron down into the raw, bleeding puncture.

Blood hissed, and the stench of seared flesh filled the small hut. The man screamed. The soldiers held his upper body immobile while his lower body twisted this way and that, like a serpent in its death throes. Pain unclenched his bowels and bladder; a new stink clogged the already foul air. Jauharah stepped away, allowing her aides room to bathe the wound in a solution of vinegar and water and bandage it in fresh linen.

Dropping the iron in the fire, she shuffled to the door. Her eyes were red, her hair plastered to her back with sweat. The man on the table would live, unlike so many she had treated since that night at Gaza. How many lives had fled to the netherworld under her hands? A score? Two? She had lost count. Not even their faces could be dredged from the abyss of her memory.

Jauharah stepped into the bright sunlight, feeling its heat on her shoulders and back. Though only two hours since dawn, already the day had a merciless edge. The only respite came from the breeze, heavy with the tang of salt, that blew constantly off the sea. It stirred her lank, sweat-heavy hair and tugged at the hem of her shift. She plucked at the fabric. It was stiff with dried blood and crusted with fluids whose origins she did not care to ponder, and it stank. The smell of Death clung to her.

A bath was in order. She went to the hut she shared with Barca and gathered up a few things: a clean linen shift, a towel, her bronze razor, what cosmetics that remained to her, and a flask of aromatic oil. There were pools down the beach from the village, screened by rocks and scrub trees, where she could bathe in relative peace. She placed the items in a reed basket and bent her steps toward the sea.

What few villagers remained eyed her as she passed with a mixture of curiosity and mistrust. They sat in doorways, on benches, their hands busy with such make-work as they could find; mending nets and sharpening copper hooks. Most were aged and infirm; their reluctant kin had left them behind, taking everything else of value and vanishing into the waste. To Jauharah, these elders were the true riches of Raphia: men and women with a lifetime of experience to draw upon; a lifetime of tales and stories. Barca called them dull, but their simple wisdom comforted her.

She crossed the bare patch of packed and rutted earth that served as Raphia's bazaar, pausing by the tent where the soldiers took their meals. They sat together in twos and threes, hollow-eyed, shattered from heat and exhaustion, eating bread and dried figs and drinking water.

'Are there any wounded among you?' she asked.

They shook their heads. 'We were posted off to the north,' one of them offered, scratching at a scab forming on his grimy forearm. 'Near the boulders called the Tits . . . begging your pardon. The attack came on the main road. Arrow storm. I thank Horus I am not a Persian.' A dozen heads bobbed in assent.

Jauharah set her basket down and checked a bandaged forehead. The soldier winced as her fingers lifted the edge of the linen. 'Have the orderlies clean that,' she told him softly. 'And the rest of you keep water handy. This heat is as deadly as a spear or a sword.' They nodded, smiling, as she caught up her basket and continued down to the sea.

At the verge of the beach Jauharah shaded her eyes. The *Atum* lay down the strand beside a palisade of upright oars, canted to expose her hull. Under Senmut's guidance, half the sailors scraped and cleaned the planking, the surf washing at their ankles. The rest worked at patching sail and mending rope. Jauharah could hear snatches of song that faded into coarse laughter. A few noticed her, glancing up from their work. That sense of menace she had felt so strongly after boarding the ship was gone, replaced with an almost sisterly affection. She had saved the lives of several of their comrades along the road from Gaza; that gave her worth in their eyes.

She moved up the beach, away from the sailors,

sand crunching underfoot. She passed several inviting spots before choosing one screened by a spur of worn rock. The pool, a depression high up on the beach, away from the crash and hiss of the breakers, was fed by a brackish spring; it had a natural sandstone edge, and its bottom was easily visible through the crystalline water.

She stripped off her filthy shift and tossed it aside, enjoying the feel of the sun and wind on her naked flesh. Carefully, she slipped into the pool. The water, waist-deep and warm, had a whole-some feel that drove away the darkness of the past few days. She washed her hair, scrubbed her body, and shaved herself as best she could with her small razor. Afterward, wrapped in a feeling of cleanliness, she floated in the pool, her eyes closed.

'You're almost purring,' a voice said, soft from exhaustion.

Far from being surprised, Jauharah opened an eye, smiling. Barca sat near the pool's edge. 'Every time I turn around,' she said, 'I catch you watching me. Why?'

'Better I keep an eye on you than someone else.'

'That's not an answer,' she said, playfully splashing water over his foot. 'At least, not an answer that would set a woman's heart to fluttering.'

Barca rested his elbows on his knees, cradled his head in his hands. He tried to knuckle away an ache behind his eyes. 'How soon can you move the wounded to the ship?' he asked, his voice little more than a whisper.

Jauharah pursed her lips. 'Some of them should not be moved, but if needs must, it can be done in two hours at most. Why?'

Barca exhaled. 'We can do no more here. It's time we see to getting ourselves to safety before our escape can be blocked. I fear I've cut it too close. The Persians' probes are becoming too uniform, as if they have found a way around the hills and are trying to divert our attention. If we stay longer, Raphia will become our tomb.'

'What of the Phoenicians?'

'I'm too exhausted to worry about them.' He closed his eyes. Jauharah could see lines of concern etching his face. He had not slept more than two hours at a stretch since leaving Gaza; he led every ambush, sometimes two or three a day. From what she could tell he ate sparingly. He was eroding before her eyes, wearing away like a boulder in a raging river.

'Come, let me bathe you,' she said. Her tone left no room for argument.

Barca stood, stripped off his armour and kilt, and drove his sheathed sword point-first into the sand. With a groan, he sank into the pool. Jauharah floated up behind him and laved water onto his shoulders and back. He closed his eyes, going limp in her care. Once his body was clean, Jauharah wet his hair and washed it with aromatic oil, massaging his scalp with gentle fingers. After she rinsed his hair, Jauharah urged him to lie back, his head resting on her breasts, as she deftly trimmed the wild edges of his beard. She finished, intertwining her body with his in the sun-warmed water.

'It's been years since a woman . . .' Barca trailed off. Jauharah said nothing, her fingers brushing a loose strand of hair off his forehead. His brow furrowed. 'This morning, as we ambushed the Persians, I had no rage, no fury. I felt,' Barca chose his words carefully, 'sorrow. For their loss, for what I had to do to them to ensure your safety, and mine. What you do to me . . . what I feel is dangerous for a man in my position.'

'What do you feel?'

Barca remained silent for a long while. Jauharah could tell he was engaged in something he rarely did. He was searching deep inside himself. Finally, he spoke. 'There is a small voice inside my head that curses me for a fool, that chides me for trading my edge in battle for a few hours of pleasure. Before that night in Gaza, I lived on hatred, on rage, on a dark deed I thought unforgivable. Now . . .' Barca lapsed into silence, his brows knotted, his eyes turned inward.

'Do you regret that night in Gaza?' Jauharah said, the bitterness in her voice surprising even her. 'I do not wish to be a burden to you, physically or mentally.'

Barca silenced her with a kiss. 'It is not you or our time together that I regret. It is my life *before* Gaza. Understand, I lived as a dead man. I breathed, and my heart beat and blood pumped.

But I was only passing time until violence separated my body from my *ka*. I've wasted the last twenty years on regret. I don't plan to waste what time I have left.'

Barca kissed her again with a tender passion; a long kiss accompanied by stroking fingers and caresses. Jauharah moaned and held him tight. It was not a furious ardour that drove their love-making, but a gentle, insistent ache inflamed by touch and the nearness of their bodies. For a time, both succeeded in forgetting the world around them.

After a while the Phoenician stirred. 'We'd better be getting back,' he said, glancing at the sun. It had passed its zenith, morning giving way to afternoon.

'If only all of this could pass us by,' she sighed. 'Just one day and night together without the pall of violence hanging over us is all I ask.'

'Perhaps that day will come,' Barca said. 'But not today. Not now.' He rose from the water and helped her out. Droplets of moisture shimmered against her brown skin as she towelled off and slipped into her shift. She ran a comb through her hair. The sun would do the rest.

Meanwhile, Barca went about rearming. Jauharah watched in fascination as a metamorphosis occurred; a transformation. Kilt, sandals, greaves, corselet, each element of armour donned in its turn, as a mason sets individual stones in a wall. Finally, the carapace of bronze, so like the shell of a crab, that protected more than the flesh within – it camouflaged the vulnerability of the man who wore it. Barca glanced up, and Jauharah saw his transformation as more than physical. His eyes reflected the cold, unyielding strength of the bronze. In its embrace he would have no doubts, no concerns. His actions would be beneficial to his allies; swift and deadly to his foes. In that, Jauharah found a measure of comfort.

'Jauharah,' Barca repeated. 'Are you ready?'

She blinked, smiling. She had been so lost in thought that she did not realize he was speaking. 'Yes.' He nodded, and they set off together.

Gulls wheeled overhead, their mournful cries lost amid the crash and hiss of breakers. In the distance, Senmut and his sailors knocked the canting beams aside, floating the *Atum* in the surf. Their hurrahs were faint.

'Who is that?' Jauharah said, pointing at a figure sprinting toward them.

'Huy,' Barca murmured.

The young soldier, his corselet dulled even in the brilliant afternoon sun, crunched through the damp sand, waves tugging at his ankles. He ran up the strand as if the Children of Anubis nipped at his heels. He slowed as he approached Barca. Huy was a tall lad, still in his teens, with a shock of black hair that defied any attempt at control. A gash across his jaw had scabbed over; one hand was bandaged, several fingers missing.

'What is it, Huy?' Barca said.

The lad was out of breath. He gasped, clutching at his sore ribs. 'It . . . It's . . . the Persians, lord!'

The Persian herald sat his horse like a man born there. Despite the heat, he wore trousers of wine-coloured cloth tucked into calf-length boots. Over a sleeved tunic, the herald's armour gleamed in the sun, a jacket of triangular bronze scales, resembling the skin of a fish. A small shield of leather and wood hung from his saddle-bow, and – save for the long lance in his right hand – he appeared unarmed. Beneath the bronze lance head a white scarf fluttered in the breeze.

'Huy found you. Good,' Callisthenes said as Barca and Jauharah walked up. 'I think they wish to surrender. He keeps saying the same thing over and over.'

'I bear a message for your commander,' the herald repeated, his voice deep and rolling. He spoke Egyptian with a heavy accent.

Barca pushed through the crowd of Egyptians. 'I am he.'

'My master would speak with you, under the flag of truce. He awaits you on yonder road.' With that, the horseman wheeled and rode off.

'Surrender,' Barca grunted, shaking his head at Callisthenes.

'A man can dream, can he not?' the Greek said. 'Anyway, what do you intend to do?'

'We're done here,' Barca said, looking at the remnants of his men. 'It's time to cut our losses and get out while we can. The Persians are toying with us.'

'What do you suggest?' Callisthenes said.

'The *Atum*,' Barca replied. 'We can escape so long as the Phoenician triremes haven't marshalled and put to sea. Still, any withdrawal has to have cover. I will buy you and Jauharah enough time to get the wounded on board.'

'Me?' Callisthenes said. 'I'm no general, Barca. I—'

'This is not a task for a general, damn you! It's a task for a merchant! Use the skills you have at organization and make it so! Now, move!' He raised his voice so the Egyptians could hear. 'We must make ready to be away within the hour. Take only those supplies we will need to make it to Pelusium; burn the rest.' He thrust a hand at Callisthenes. 'The Greek will command in my stead. Should I not return by sunset, set sail and make for Pelusium. Report all you have seen and done to whoever commands there. Understood?'

Muffled assent as the men scattered to make their preparations. Callisthenes glared at him, then turned and hustled down to the beach to warn Senmut. Jauharah lingered.

'Be careful,' she whispered. Barca winked at her, nodding.

'I'll be the picture of care,' he said. She touched his hand, then turned and followed Callisthenes. Barca watched her go. His face became expressionless, hard. For the time being, he put her out of his mind. The Phoenician turned and struck off in the direction the herald had indicated.

The afternoon heat was oppressive. Once beyond the ridge line, the air grew still; not even the gulls ventured inland. Barca stewed in his armour, basting in his own sweat. Cautiously, he followed the trail of the horseman. By instinct he marked the places where archers could hide; once, he imagined he saw the flash of sunlight on metal. He knew how the Persians in the gorge had felt this morning. There were men behind the rocks, he was sure of it. Barca approached the track leading down to the road as if an ambush lay behind the next overhang.

In the valley below, straddling the Way of Horus, the Persians had erected a pavilion. It was nothing fancy, Barca noticed, a campaign tent fly-rigged, its sides open in an effort to catch some hint of a breeze. The Phoenician rode an avalanche of loose gravel to the valley floor. The herald waited nearby, off his horse now, stroking the beast's withers.

'My master awaits you within,' he said. 'Do you speak Aramaic?'

'Yes.'

Barca walked to the edge of the pavilion. A man sat inside on a jumble of plush rugs, a tray with dates and wine at his elbow. The fellow was young, far younger than Barca imagined a Persian commander should be, and dark eyed, with features sharpened on the whetstone of curiosity. He wore a simple soldier's corselet of sweat-stained linen and scarlet trousers, embroidered with gold thread, tucked into leather boots. A tangled skein of black hair hung nearly to his shoulders.

'Your fame precedes you, Hasdrabal Barca,' he said. 'I am Darius, son of Hystapes, *arshtibara* of King Cambyses and commander of the vanguard. Please, sit and join me for some refreshment.'

Barca sat cross-legged opposite Darius, his sword across his knees. He helped himself to a handful of dates and a goblet of wine. 'I know you haven't called me here just to exchange pleasantries. What do you want?'

Darius ran his fingers through his well-groomed beard, an unconscious gesture. 'Phanes did not lie when he called you blunt, Phoenician. You are right, this is more than a chance to share a cup and a jest. You and those who follow you are men of honour and courage. I hate to see such as yourselves wasted in this fool's errand. Please, I beg of you, stand down and let us pass.'

'I am surprised a man who values honour as you do would consort with the likes of Phanes,' Barca said.

Darius grimaced. 'It was not by choice, I assure you. My king finds him to be a useful asset. Personally, I find the Greek repellent.'

'At least in that we agree. If I concede the road to you, Darius, what will you give to me in return?'

'Your life, and the lives of those who follow you,' the Persian said.

Barca laughed, draining his goblet and pouring himself another. 'You say that like a man who believes he has control over my fate. Do not make the same mistake so many have before you.'

Darius frowned. 'What do you want, then?'

Barca did not get the sense that Darius played a game with him. The young man was passionate in his plea, his concern genuine. 'I have a ship in Raphia. Give me one day to get my people on board.'

'And where will you go? Pelusium?'

'Does it matter? The road will be open to you.'

Darius sighed. 'Unfortunately, it does matter. I would be remiss in my obligations to my king if I allowed you to rejoin the fight at Pelusium. You are too valuable—'

'You realize,' Barca cut him off, his voice dangerous, 'I could kill you where you sit?'

Darius met his stare openly, unflinching. 'I believe you could,' he said. 'But my archers would cut you down like a stag in flight before you took two steps. Afterwards, my successor would fall upon Raphia like the wrath of God, and if any of your men lived to see Egypt again, it would be as slaves chained to the oars of a Persian galley.'

'We've reached an impasse, then,' Barca said. 'You want the road, which I'm willing to concede, but you're unwilling to suffer my price for it. If you Persians are so sure of your superiority, what difference will it make if I fall at Raphia or at Pelusium?'

'Your death is not the bone of contention, it's your life,' Darius said. 'You have the uncanny ability to inspire men to their utmost; to make them desire to emulate you. You will fight like a demon, here or at Pelusium, and those men with you will be inspired to the same level of savagery. Can you understand my position? I would rather face a few hundred men emboldened by you than a few thousand.

'But, I am not without a sense of fair play,' Darius continued. 'We outnumber you so many times over that it fades into the realm of the absurd. That said, I am willing to give you a fighting chance. A head start, if you will.'

'I'm listening,' Barca said, tentatively.

'I give you one hour,' Darius said.

'One hour?'

'Yes. From the time you leave my camp you have one hour to get as many of your men aboard as you can. After one hour, my horsemen attack. Is this acceptable?'

Barca snarled. 'This is your sense of fair play? It took nearly an hour to arrive at this spot!'

'We're not haggling in the markets of Tyre, Phoenician. This is a battlefield, and mine is the upper hand. How many men will you rescue if I order an immediate attack? My guess, not many. At least this way you have some kind of chance.'

The Phoenician's brow furrowed, calculating. 'How do I know you'll remain true to your word?'

'I swear it on my honour,' Darius replied.

Jauharah pushed her hair out of her eyes and peered over the railing of the *Atum*. Over the crash of breakers she could hear Callisthenes ordering the soldiers carrying the wounded to make haste. Behind her, Senmut's men scampered over the rigging, preparing the sail to be unfurled once the oars carried them into the bay. The captain shouted vulgarities at those sailors who moved too slowly in their tasks. It had been a chaotic hour, but the pieces of the plan were starting to fit together. Callisthenes and the soldiers carried the wounded up a makeshift gang-plank while she, with her orderlies, got them situated and saw to their comfort. They had made better time than she thought. Once Barca arrived, all that remained would be for the soldiers to force the ship off the strand, strike the oars, and make for open sea. It sounded simple enough.

'How many more?' she yelled down to Callisthenes.

The Greek glanced around, mentally counting men as a merchant tallies wine jars. 'A dozen, perhaps,' he said. 'But they are those with the worst wounds, the unconscious. They are expendable, if need be.' Callisthenes frowned as something caught his eye. Jauharah followed his gaze. From the hills ringing Raphia a dust cloud rose into the blue sky.

'Persians.' The word rattled through the Egyptians like an icy breath. Stolid and courageous as they were, every man among the raiding force harboured a deep-seated fear of dying in this barbarous land, unburied, cut off from their families, their *ka* forced to wander aimlessly through eternity. It was a thought that loosed the bowels of the strongest among them. Its implications flogged them like an overseer's whip, driving new life and purpose into their limbs. As Jauharah watched, they redoubled their efforts.

'Callisthenes!' She ran to the gangplank. 'What did you mean by expendable? None of the men can be left behind!'

Callisthenes ignored her.

Men clogged her path, the wounded and their handlers. Frustrated, her anxiety rising by the second, Jauharah snagged a rope tied to the rail and slithered down the side of the ship. Once her feet touched the sand, she was off and running up the beach toward the village.

The Greek spotted her. 'Jauharah! Damn you, woman!' He nodded to a trio of men. 'Don't just stand there! Follow her and bring her back!' The Egyptians followed in her wake.

Raphia was deserted. Eerie. She could faintly hear the rattle of stones, the jingle of harness, the voices raised in command as the Persians moved unseen through the hills above them. The air was pregnant with tension. As sure as a woman heavy with child would give birth, Jauharah knew something would happen here to shatter the tomb-like stillness. Something violent and bloody.

Quickly, she set about getting the rest of the wounded. The last hut, larger than the rest, contained those soldiers no longer able to move; head and spinal injuries. These were patients that were beyond her skill. The papyri Jauharah had studied while in Memphis had been noticeably silent about such trauma, prescribing treatments that mixed magic, prayer, and luck. All she had been able to do was keep them comfortable.

The Egyptians following her stopped, fear and exertion making them short of breath. 'Lady! Please! The Greek wants us back at the ship!'

'You go! I have to get these men to safety!'

'We can't leave you here, lady!'

'Then help me!'

The Egyptians looked at one another. 'How?'

'We need litters!' she said to her newfound helpers. They nodded and looked around for something suitable. One of them stopped, a burly Egyptian with a strawberry birthmark on his shaven head. Jauharah followed his gaze.

'Barca!' she said. The Phoenician pelted down the goat trail, heedless of the loose rock and scree.

'All of you! Get to the ship!' he roared.

'We need more time!' Jauharah said. 'There are a dozen or more left in there!'

Barca's breath came in gasps, his chest racking like a forge's bellows. 'The Persians are coming! We have no more time to spare! Grab those men you can help. The rest—' he trailed off, touching the hilt of his sword.

Jauharah caught the gesture. 'No,' she said, her voice cracking. Tears welled in the corners of her eyes. 'There has to be another way.'

'Go!' Barca hissed through clenched teeth.

'Get to the ship!' He turned and made to enter the hut.

'Wait!' Jauharah sobbed, clutching at his arm. He caught her hand in his. Barca knew well the look in her eye, the helpless despair tinged with failure.

'They cannot be left behind,' he said softly. 'Not alive, at any rate. The Persians could use them to undermine morale at Pelusium. Go. Please. Get to the ship. I'll be along.' A sick feeling crept over him as he pushed into the hut.

Sunlight trickled in through a hole in the ceiling, giving the faces of the wounded a greyish pallor. The air was cool, thick with the reek of sweat and the stench of men unable to control their own bodies. Of the fourteen wounded, only two were conscious, and they just barely. One, a grizzled old sergeant, winced as he sat up. His name was Intef; an unlucky arrow had threaded through the rocks of his hiding place several days past, catching him in the lower spine.

'Time to strike camp, sir?' he said. 'Thank the gods—' he stopped mid-sentence, noticing the grim look on Barca's face, how his hand never strayed far from his sword hilt. The old soldier glanced down at his useless legs and nodded. 'I understand, sir.'

'What is it, Intef?' asked the other conscious soldier, his eyes wrapped and his crushed legs splinted. 'Are we going home?'

'Lie back, boy,' Intef said. 'When next we open our eyes, we'll behold the beauty of the gardens of

Amenti.' The young man knew what was coming. He, like Intef, was a soldier to the core. Neither of them begged or pleaded for their lives.

Barca's sword whispered from its sheath. He knelt beside the closest soldier – a boy of eighteen years, blood oozing from beneath the linen strips bandaging his skull. Though he did not know his name, Barca had watched this lad take a blow intended for another man, then kill the bastard who struck him before falling himself. His face was hollow, lifeless; though his chest rose and fell, Barca knew his *ka* had already departed for the West. Barca glanced up and stared into Intef's hard eyes.

'Quick and clean, sir,' the sergeant said. 'He won't feel a thing.'

The longer he looked at this boy, this soldier, the more his hands shook. He was already dead, Barca told himself. All of them would likely die on the way to Pelusium if they did not die here in the next few moments. Why prolong their suffering? He adjusted his grip on his sword, the hilt growing slick with sweat. *What's wrong with me? They're soldiers; soldiers die.*

'Do it, sir!' Intef hissed. 'Do it quick and get clear!'

Soldiers die, he repeated to himself, seeking solace in that mantra. Soldiers die.

Soldiers die. Soldiers die . . .

'Mother of bitches!' Barca roared, rising. 'Not today, Intef! You're not going to die today!' He sheathed his sword and scooped the lad up, whirling. Outside, a pair of Egyptians had cobbled together a makeshift litter as Jauharah bound a wounded man's broken legs together with lengths of rawhide. All of them stopped, staring. 'Get some help and get these men to the ship! Damn it! We'll not leave them behind!' He passed the unconscious lad to one of the soldiers, then glared at the looming dust cloud.

'What are you going to do?' Jauharah leapt up and ran to his side, the relief and pride in her voice tempered with fear for his safety.

Barca snarled. 'Buy us more time!'

⌒ ⚚ ✳ ◈ ◉

'He's planning some deviltry. I can smell it,' Phanes said. The Greek stood alongside Darius, a step behind and to the right out of deference, as they surveyed Raphia from the safety of the ridge line. The beach swarmed with activity as sailors and soldiers made the *Atum* ready to sail. 'You should have killed him while you had the chance. Now, you'll have no choice but to fight him.'

Darius made a subtle spitting gesture, not deigning to look at the Greek. 'I am no dog. When I offer the flag of truce, I offer it genuinely and without guile.'

Phanes chuckled. 'War is a game of guile, lord Darius. Sleight of hand and deception are weapons as useful as swords and spears. I am not criticizing you,' the Greek said, heading off Darius' angered reply, 'but the goal of any commander is to slay as many of the enemy as he can, by whatever means, while preserving as many lives among his own men as possible. Killing Barca when you had him would have saved many Persian lives.'

'You speak from experience, I understand.' Darius glanced sidelong at the Greek. 'You could have slain him in Memphis, yet you baulked. Why?'

'Arrogance,' Phanes said, his eyes narrowing to slits. Though a year had passed, his failures at Memphis yet festered like a septic wound. 'Cursed arrogance. The gods often build a man up only to tear him down again. They find perverse pleasure in the suffering of the gifted. Perhaps that is why His Majesty paired us together, lord Darius. So you might learn something of arrogance.'

'Or so you might learn something of humility.' Darius walked back to where a groom held the reins of his horse, a magnificent black Nesaean stallion caparisoned in purple and gold. The young Persian sprang lightly into the saddle. 'I have learned much from you, Phanes, but learn this from me: if you acquit yourself with honour, it matters not if the battle goes against you. A man in possession of his honour will always triumph, even in defeat.' Darius motioned to his aides. 'I have given Barca an hour, and more. Sound the advance.'

Phanes turned back to face the village as Darius clattered off to join his troops. Honour? Faugh! Honour, no matter how keen, would not stop a sword blade or a spear thrust. Was a dead man in possession of his honour any less dead? 'What are you planning, Phoenician?' he whispered. 'What are you planning?'

⌒　⚚　✳　�　☥

Trumpets blared through the hills, ringing off cliffs and echoing through valleys. Barca's mind raced. How do you stop five thousand determined horsemen? By stopping their horses. How, then? The only answer that came to mind was fire. He needed to set the upper reaches of Raphia ablaze.

The Phoenician snatched up the brazier Jauharah had used to heat her cauterizing irons and hurried to the edge of the village. The huts along the goat trail were older than most of the others, their stone foundations reinforced with old ship's timbers – timbers soaked with pitch and encaustic. Barca fanned the coals to life. Working swiftly, he set several of the huts afire.

Sun-dried wood blazed like torches; clouds of black smoke roiled across Raphia, a choking veil that effectively hid him from view. Fire alone, though, would not stop the Persians for long. He needed to snarl their advance. Barca cursed himself for not thinking ahead and ordering his men to rig rockslides along the goat trail. A wall of stone would have slowed them. His eyes lit on a bow one of his soldiers had cast aside, a near empty quiver beside it. He needed a wall . . .

Above the village, horsemen pounded down the goat trail, heedless of the incline, of the loose stone. They were Hyrkanians, half-wild tribesmen from the shores of the Caspian Sea, reckless and mad with the anticipation of slaughter. They had taken a drubbing since Gaza; they were eager to settle the score. Thanks to the narrow approach, no more than a few could enter the village at a time. The rest, though, could dismount and take up positions along the ridge line where they could ply their bows with deadly effect.

Smoke drifted across the Hyrkanians' path, sending ripples of fear through their horses. One among them sprang from the baulking pack. The horse, a fine chestnut mare, floated over the gravel and scree, guided by the gentle pressure of his rider's knees. Hugging the animal's neck, the Hyrkanian plunged into the drifting veil. For an instant the world was black, acrid, a void without light or air, and then he was through.

A single enemy waited on the other side.

Barca sighted down the arrow, his target perfectly aligned. He felt a pang of regret as he loosed. The arrow flew straight and true, slashing through the chest of the mare. The horse reared and buckled, pitching its rider to the ground. Barca heard the snap of bone as the Hyrkanian struck face first and did not move. A second horseman exploded from the smoke; a third. Barca drew and loosed as quickly as he could, his arrows creating a thrashing wall of horseflesh. His last shaft spent, Barca tossed his bow aside and sprinted for the beach. He prayed Jauharah had got everyone on board.

From the ridge line, Persian archers loosed a hail of death on Raphia. As the first arrows thudded around him, Barca braced himself for an impact, for the feel of a razored tip slicing through flesh to shatter the bone beneath. The Phoenician scrambled for cover. He flattened himself against the seaward wall of a small fishing shack, listening to the crack of bronzeheads on wood. He thrust aside a veil of netting and peered through the door, through the round window cut into the back wall. Soldiers had cleared the trail and moved into the upper reaches of the village as their brothers lobbed fusillades over their heads. Barca turned back to face the sea.

Beyond the strand the *Atum* backed water, its prow rising and falling on the swells. Senmut's voice could be heard as he howled orders and curses. On the stern, he could see a wall of helpless faces, Jauharah and Callisthenes among them. Suddenly, the drumming of arrows slowed. Barca risked a glance around the corner of the shack. On the ridge line, the bowmen tossed their empty quivers aside and were clawing for another.

The lull was the opening Barca needed.

The Phoenician pushed away from the shack and hurtled for the ship. Without pause, he unbuckled his cuirass and shrugged out of the heavy carapace, hurling it aside as he flung himself into the sea. With powerful strokes he swam through the breaking surf, vanishing under water then reappearing. He gasped for breath. His chest ached; his limbs felt leaden as he forced muscle and sinew into action. Salt spray burned his eyes and reminded him of every scratch and cut he had accumulated over the last week. He glanced up. A rope snaked down from the stern of the *Atum*. The frayed end lay just out of reach. Barca drew on his dwindling reserves of stamina, propelling himself forward with one last burst of speed. His fingers brushed the rope.

'He's got it!' He heard Jauharah's voice as she yelled to the Egyptians. 'Pull!'

Soldiers and sailors hauled the rope inboard. Barca clambered up the side of the ship. Shouts of triumph erupted around him as he grabbed the rail and pulled himself over.

'Thank the gods!' Jauharah said, helping him to his feet. Barca stood on shaky legs. He turned to face the dwindling shoreline. Phanes waded into the surf, striking the water with his sword.

'How does it feel? You son of a bitch, how does it feel?' Barca clutched the railing white-knuckle tight.

'I want to finish this, Barca!'

The Phoenician laughed recklessly. 'Then hurry to Pelusium! I'll meet you there!'

18

PELUSIUM

Pelusium guarded the door to Egypt.

In ancient times, Egypt's boundaries extended into the heart of Palestine, to the very banks of the Euphrates River itself. Inside this sphere every king, prince, or potentate owed his position to the whim of Pharaoh; to maintain this goodwill, yearly tributes were sent to Memphis, to Thebes. Failure to tithe properly, or not at all, met with swift reprisal. Inevitably, Egypt entered periods of decline where these foreign rulers could reassert their independence. Wars flared up, trade ceased, and common men suffered for the ambitions of their liege. With the return of vigorous pharaohs, the violence would subside; order would rise from the ashes of chaos. It was a cycle as perennial as the rise and fall of the Nile.

Barca sat on the crest of a hill, one of three anchoring the Egyptian position, and watched the sun rise. He ate a light breakfast of day-old bread and grilled fish, washing it down with a crock of beer. Earlier, scouts had reported that the main body of the Persian army had crossed the desert and were approaching. Finally, three weeks of waiting, of counting the hours until battle, were at an end.

On the morning the *Atum* put in to Pelusium, three weeks past, Barca was made aware of Nebmaatra's promotion. He saw nothing amiss in it. The Egyptian was a capable man, unaffected by the in-fighting that was the hallmark of the nobility. There were worse men he could serve. Barca sought him out and briefed him on everything that had happened; their arrival in Gaza, Qainu's duplicity, the Bedouin attack, the retreat to Raphia, his encounter with Darius, their escape.

'This Darius is a different sort of Persian,' Barca told him. 'Straight as an arrow and as concerned with truth as a servant of lady Ma'at.'

'Sounds as though you admire him,' Nebmaatra said.

Barca frowned. 'I do, and that is what bothers me.'

'How is that?'

'It doesn't sit well with me to admire a man I may have to kill.'

Around him, on the hill Barca occupied, the ruins of a watchtower thrust like dead fingers from the thin soil. Scrub brush grew along the crumbling wall of stone; a gnarled tamarisk served as home to a family of sparrows who darted and whirled in the morning air, cursing Barca in their shrill tongue. Studying the land, he could see why Nebmaatra chose this particular spot to meet the Persians. The landscape formed a natural hourglass. To the north, on Barca's left hand, the rocky coastline looked as though a titan had taken a deep bite out of it. The indentation came within a mile of Barca's position. South, the land became a tangled, impassable marsh. Between the two extremes lay a gently sloping plain of orchards and fields, a vision of pastoral bliss.

The Way of Horus came straight out of the east, a whitish scar skirting the arms of Mt Casius and the foul waters of Lake Serbonis. This narrow spit of dry, passable land would funnel the Persians down into the fortified Egyptian position. Its closeness would negate their superior numbers, and the natural obstacles of marsh and sea would seal the field against flanking manoeuvres.

Nebmaatra wasted no time in preparing for the Persians. Under his firm hand, soldiers were organized into work-gangs and ordered to dig shallow trenches across the plain – trenches deep enough to snap the delicate leg of a horse. Others were instructed to make obstacles. The general gave his overseers latitude and encouraged creativity. He wanted anything they could think of, any obstacle that would disrupt a charge of cavalry. Barca grinned. Nebmaatra's overseers proved a cunning lot. There were palm trunks lashed together upright in groups of three; mounds of discarded stone and mud brick; huge sycamore roots grubbed from the marshes; fields of sharpened stakes.

'Won't this defeat our own chariot corps?'

Callisthenes had asked him the day before as they took their turn among the workers. Sweat poured down the Greek's face. He leaned on his mattock, accepting a skin of water from a young boy. Barca had seen little of Callisthenes since their return, their duties keeping them separate and exhausted.

Still, he looked even thinner since Gaza.

'Yes. Nebmaatra's dismantling the chariots and using their crews as irregular infantry.'

'You know what worries me? Those Persians in Raphia were rather fond of their bows. What if they decide just to stand beyond our reach and pepper us with shafts? Are we prepared for that?'

Barca paused in his digging and glanced at the thin clouds scudding across the blue vaulted sky. 'As prepared as we can be. It wasn't chance alone that drove us to choose Pelusium,' he said cryptically.

Barca finished off his breakfast as a troop of workmen ascended the path to the crest of the hill, chattering among themselves. They were sent to scour the ruins for useable stone. Make-work, since the field below was already choked with debris. Still, Nebmaatra wanted the men to stay active. It gave them less time to brood over the coming battle.

'General Barca,' one of them said, spotting him. He was a short, dark-skinned young man with a round face. 'Are we to fight soon, or should we give up building obstacles and build homes instead? This waiting . . .'

'Look there, boy,' Barca said, rising and pointing east.

The workers shaded their eyes. 'I don't see anything, sir. I—' The young man's voice caught in his throat. 'Lord Amon have mercy!'

Columns of dust rose from the Way of Horus, cloaking the horizon like clouds of an immense storm. From its heart, they could discern the lightning flash of armour. The men glanced down at the ground, shock and disbelief on their faces. Barca could feel it too, faint but unmistakable, a vibration rising up through the soles of his sandals.

The measured tread of eighty thousand men.

'What do we do, sir?' The young man took a step back, fear driving his voice up an octave.

'Stay sharp and keep your wits about you,' Barca said. 'Treat this day as any other. Eat when you normally eat; drink when you normally drink. Keep yourself busy, as inaction quickly turns to fear. It will take them time to prepare, just as it has taken us time. We'll see nothing of them today.'

Barca turned and descended the western face of the hill, following the well-worn trail down to the sprawling Egyptian camp. The waiting was nearly over . . .

The camp buzzed with activity. Rumours of the Persian advance rustled from regiment to regiment, company to company. A hundred thousand men, some said. Maybe more. Someone heard that the Son of Ra, in his infinite wisdom, had ordered the mercenaries to strike before the Persians could entrench. Wrong, another countered, the army would pull back. Phoenician sails had been spotted moving up the coast, intent on landing an invasion force on their flank. Men shivered in fear despite the morning sun.

Jauharah stood in the doorway of the House of Life, that vast complex of scribes, priests, and physicians forming the bureaucratic spine of the Egyptian war machine. From here, every asset and liability was accounted for and noted on endless scrolls of papyrus, on pottery shards, on waxed boards. Shrines to the gods were maintained, and offerings made by priest and layman, alike. For the moment, Jauharah was attached to the Overseer of the Horse for the regiment of Amon. Her task was keeping track of the regiment's arrows.

Behind her, Jauharah could hear Ladice addressing her charges.

'Maintain your composure at all times,' she said. 'Most of our soldiers are children of peace. They have never fought in battle. Some will look to their leaders for guidance; others will look to us. If we panic, they panic.'

The Lady of Cyrene was an enigma. She had used her influence to usurp control of the house of life from the high priests, knowing those men would lose their focus and resume their petty bickering. It was a breach of protocol that worked out to the army's advantage as she proved herself a relentless organizer.

'Any questions?' Ladice said. After a moment's pause, she dismissed the lesser priests, the scribes, and their apprentices. These last would serve as runners between the individual commanders, relaying messages and orders.

Jauharah snagged a young apprentice by the arm. The boy stared at her, his eyes glassy with excitement and fear. She pressed a folded square of papyrus into his hand. 'See that General Barca gets this.' The boy nodded and rushed off.

'Jauharah.' Ladice approached. 'I wanted to talk to you for a moment.'

Jauharah bowed. 'I am at your service, lady.'

Ladice smiled. 'I heard your tale from Nebmaatra. I find it extraordinary that you learned the healer's art simply from reading ancient texts. You have a gift for it, I think.' Ladice had a sadness about her, a heartache she wore like a badge of honour. 'It would seem Memphis was unlucky for the both of us. You served the family of Idu?'

'Yes,' Jauharah replied. 'As their slave.' A shadow of anguish passed over the Lady of Cyrene's face. Before she could speak, Jauharah set her at ease with a smile. 'Do not pity me, lady. My life then wasn't the terror of whips and chains you imagine it to be. I didn't row a galley or work in the fields. I helped raise a family, aided in the birth of two daughters, taught my native tongue, and learned the secret of writing. I lived easier than most freeborn women.'

'And it was all taken from you by my countrymen,' Ladice said, quietly. She closed her eyes. 'We have caused more grief in Egypt than joy, I fear.'

'For every Greek whose wickedness is trumpeted to the heavens, there are a dozen more who live lives of noble obscurity. It would be foolish, I think, to judge a whole people by the actions of a few vile souls. Foolish as well as misguiding.'

'How do you forgive so easily?'

'I don't, lady. I only place the blame where it belongs. I don't forgive the men who shattered my life, and neither do I hold you accountable for their actions because you happen to be Greek.'

Ladice sighed. 'Your soul is older and wiser than mine, Jauharah. I want you here tomorrow, in the surgeon's tent. I think your skills would be better utilized removing arrows instead of inventorying them.' Jauharah started to reply, but Ladice put a hand on her arm and leaned close. 'When men decide to make war, it is the women who are left to pick up the pieces.'

'I understand,' Jauharah said. Ladice nodded and rushed off to attend to her duties. Jauharah watched her go. The Lady of Cyrene gave voice to something she had felt during the battle at Memphis and, later, while stitching the wounded in Raphia. In the aftermath of fighting, a woman's touch was invaluable.

By their very nature women were nurturers. In times of peace it meant they were hearth-warmers, child-rearers, possessed of a practical magic men found inscrutable. In times of war, that selfsame magic could be used to soothe the sick and heal the wounded; it flowed through a woman's finger-tips to strengthen hearts and souls; it carried in their voices, in the soft-spoken reassurances that everything would be better. Ladice was right. Men would fight and men would die, but it was the women who would make their riven bodies whole again.

Lost in thought, Jauharah wandered out through a flap in the back of the pavilion. A copse of sycamores and tamarisks grew at the rear of the house of life, casting welcome shade over the sun-browned grass. A shallow ditch scarred the ground, its sides heaped with freshly turned earth. The light breeze carried the smell of wild mint. It was hard to believe that, in a matter of hours, a river of blood would flow through that ditch while mounds of severed limbs would cover the grass, a grim monument to the lords of violence.

A sob brought Jauharah up short. She glanced around. There, hidden in the shadow of an ancient sycamore, a figure sat alone. She moved closer.

It was Callisthenes.

He sat with his legs drawn up before him, his arms on his knees, oblivious to the world around him. He stared at his hands. They were shaking. 'I can't do it,' the Greek said, his voice hoarse. 'I can't do it.'

Jauharah edged closer. Callisthenes glanced up. His eyes were red-rimmed and swollen, and the look in them was one of unreasoning terror.

'I can't do it,' he repeated.

'What?' Jauharah frowned. 'What can't you do?'

'I can't kill again. It's not in me, I think,' Callisthenes said. He clenched his hands to stop the tremors. 'As a child, I dreamed of fighting at the left hand of Ajax, beneath the walls of Illium. Odysseus was my mentor; Achilles, my god. Patroclus. Paris. Agamemnon. These were the names of my personal pantheon. I worshipped glory and battle.' Callisthenes grunted, rubbing his hands together. 'Look at me now. Every time battle is offered, my knees go weak and my blood turns to ice . . . a man in name only.'

Jauharah sat beside him. 'You want to know a secret, Callisthenes? Something only women understand? A man is not measured by the lives he has taken, rather by the lives he has preserved. Your actions at Memphis, Gaza, and Raphia speak louder than any words. You are, barring none, one of the bravest men I have ever known – and it's precisely because of your concern for life. You have to do what *you* think is right, Callisthenes, not what others believe is right for you. If fighting is not for you, then you can still help us here, in the House of Life.'

'With the women!' the Greek said bitterly.

'There are men here, too. Men equally as brave as the soldiers in the field,' Jauharah said. 'Some men are put on this earth to preserve life; others to take it. You are one of the rare few whose sense of compassion overrides their desire to kill. Yours is a rare heart, Callisthenes. Trust it. It will not lead you astray.'

Callisthenes looked at her, a newfound respect in his eyes. 'It's little wonder Barca has changed. For a time I dismissed you as nothing more than his way of atoning for the past. I can see I was mistaken.' He grasped her hand. Jauharah could feel him shaking. He looked down, cleared his throat. 'My people do not hold women in high regard, save as a way to propagate the future. We do not accord them the independence they deserve. I swear to you, Jauharah, should I live through this, I will devote my remaining days to righting this wrong.'

Jauharah smiled. 'I know you will, Callisthenes. I know you will. For now, though, let's deal with today. Would you like to aid us here?'

Callisthenes sat for a long time, perfectly still, his eyes closed as he searched the deepest recesses of his heart. Finally, he stood. He helped Jauharah to her feet. 'Lady,' the Greek said. 'I am honoured by your invitation, but my heart tells me my place is with the men of Naucratis.'

Barca caught Nebmaatra coming out of his tent, a roll of papyrus tucked under one arm. The Egyptian's face creased in a mirthless smile. 'News travels swiftly,' he said. 'I've sent word to each regimental commander. I want campaign discipline maintained. If the men go off to empty their bowels, they had best keep their weapons handy.'

Barca nodded. 'It would be wise to send patrols around the marshes, just in case they think to flank us from that direction.'

'We'll see to that after we brief Pharaoh. Come.' The Phoenician fell in beside Nebmaatra.

Barca had not seen Psammetichus since the latter's arrival a few days past. As Tjemu would say, Pharaoh knew the value of a good entrance; he made his with all the pomp and glitter of a conquering king. Preceded by the gods of Egypt and a swarm of shaven-headed priests, Psammetichus reviewed the troops from the back of his chariot. In his golden-scaled corselet and blue war crown, the young monarch looked every inch his father's son. But looks could deceive.

'Have you talked with Pharaoh?'

'Once,' Nebmaatra replied. 'When he informed me of his desire to command the centre, behind his Calasirians and the regiment of Amon.'

'You explained to him that he must stand firm, that Cambyses will doubtless hurl the Immortals against the centre in an effort to split the line?'

Nebmaatra nodded. 'He assured me he would hold the line together.'

'You trust him?' Barca knew the young Pharaoh had never commanded so much as a raiding party, much less the core of a professional army. The Phoenician had seen his share of recruits freeze when the sounds and smells hit them for the first time. He expected no less from Psammetichus.

Nebmaatra glanced sidelong at the Phoenician. 'He is Pharaoh. What choice do I have? I must admit, though, it warmed my heart to see him go against Ujahorresnet's advice.'

Barca's head snapped around, his eyes narrowing to slits. 'Mother of whores!' He had seen the old man in the entourage and assumed he was there in his capacity as lady Neith's high priest. '*He's* Pharaoh's new adviser?'

Nebmaatra nodded. 'Not just adviser. Pharaoh named him Overseer of the High Sea Fleet, Fan-bearer on the King's Right Hand, a whole host of titles. Apparently, they have quite a rapport. I suggested Pharaoh award you the Gold of Valour for your deeds at Gaza, but Ujahorresnet convinced him not to. He said it would not look proper to bestow Egypt's highest military honour for a mere skirmish.'

'I should have killed that meddlesome bastard in Memphis!' Barca said, his teeth grinding in anger. 'Do not trust him, Nebmaatra! If an order springs from his lips, question it, if not openly then in your own mind. He does not have Egypt's best interests at heart.'

Nebmaatra's brow furrowed. 'How do you know? Thus far, he has—'

'I know!' Barca snarled, and would say no more.

A subaltern of the Calasirians ushered them into Pharaoh's presence. He occupied a temporary throne room, an understatement in simplicity walled in pure white linen that diffused the morning sunlight. The golden throne itself rested on a dais of ebony wood inlaid with scenes of Pharaoh smiting his enemies. Beside the throne, Khasekhem, Overseer of Scribes, sat cross-legged on the ground, his palette and pens prepared. Ujahorresnet, resplendent in his robes of office, stood at Pharaoh's right hand. Barca stared at the old man with undisguised contempt.

'I have heard the Persians have been sighted moving into position. When do you expect an attack?' Psammetichus said.

'Not before midmorning tomorrow, at the earliest.'

'Are we prepared, Nebmaatra? Tell me I have not misplaced my trust in you?'

Nebmaatra unrolled his papyrus, revealing a hastily sketched map. He spread it on the dais at Pharaoh's feet. 'The regiment of Amon and the Calasirians will hold the centre along this height. To their left will be the regiments of Ptah and Sekhmet, to their right, Osiris and Bast. Barca will command the left flank from the seaward hill. The mercenary units will form on him: the Medjay, the Greek regiment, the Libyans and the Nubians. I will command the right. With me will be the regiments of Khonsu, Anubis, Horus,

418

and Neith. That's twenty-five thousand men massed in the centre flanked by roughly twenty thousand apiece. Sixty-five thousand men against eighty thousand. We are as prepared as we can be, Pharaoh.'

'Outnumbered as we are, do we stand even the slightest chance?' Pharaoh asked, despair thick in his voice. He looked from Nebmaatra to Barca. The Phoenician could barely recognize him as the laughing young lion of Sais. His once vigorous face seemed dissipated; the skin stretched too tight over the bone. Dark circles ringed his eyes.

Barca nodded, glancing down at the map. 'We have the advantage of position and, by the will of the gods, weather. If our courage holds, victory will be well within our grasp.'

'Still,' Ujahorresnet spoke up for the first time, 'would it not be wise to prepare a contingency plan for retreat should we be overwhelmed?'

'You speak what is in my mind, good Ujahorresnet. What about it? How will we fall back should the occasion arise?'

Nebmaatra cleared his throat. 'I have not given it much thought, Majesty.'

Barca's anger exploded. 'Let the first blows fall before you plan our surrender! Merciful Ba'al! Why not order us to fall on our swords and get it over with?'

Psammetichus' eyes flashed dangerously. 'Guard your tongue, Phoenician! You may have spoken freely around my father, but I am not Ahmose!'

'Retreat is not an option!' Barca hissed through clenched teeth. 'Do either of you have the slightest idea what it is we fight for here? Well, by the gods, I'll tell you! Egypt's survival! This is the boundary stone, the line the Persians must not cross! No contingency plans! No retreats! If we dwell on those, we give our courage an option to fail, and that we cannot do! If we . . . *we!* . . . do not stop Cambyses here . . .' Barca trailed off.

'I understand,' Pharaoh said, his frame deflating, his anger leached away by the grim realization of Barca's words. 'I swore to my father on his deathbed that I would not fail Egypt, and I swear it to you now. If I desert Egypt in her hour of need, may I be stricken dead and my body left unburied and unmourned.' Psammetichus dismissed them with a wave. 'Go, both of you. Go and see to my army.'

Barca and Nebmaatra bowed and retraced their steps. Outside, in the golden sunlight, Barca shook his head. 'He's right. He's not his father.'

'He may be untried, but Psammetichus has heart, and heart has won many a battle on its own,' Nebmaatra said. 'See to your men.' The Egyptian turned and headed for his command tents, where already the regimental leaders were mustered.

Barca was unconvinced. Oath or no oath, once the fighting got thick and the blood spattered Pharaoh like rain, his lack of experience would show. The Phoenician would feel better if Psammetichus bowed out of the fray and watched it

420

from the safety of camp. At least there if his courage flagged, it would not infect the men like a plague.

A scribe's apprentice, a boy of perhaps twelve, rushed up to the Phoenician and handed him a square of papyrus. Barca eyed the boy as he ran off again, then opened the note. It was written in Jauharah's firm hand:

I must see you. Come when you can.

Below that were directions leading south and west of the Egyptian camp. Barca frowned.

The spot the Persians chose for their encampment lay three-quarters of a mile from the base of the Egyptian hillocks. Priestly Magi made the proper sacrifices and libations; reconnaissance units scouted between the marshes and the sea; servants and slaves set about erecting the royal pavilion along the banks of a creek, in the shade of a palm grove. The son of Cyrus did not travel as another man would, with the bare essentials only. All the luxuries of court accompanied him, from the ladies of the *apadana* to the children of his noble families to an entourage of eunuchs, governesses, cooks, bakers, weavers, orderlies, an army to service an army, and all of it centred upon the person of the King.

As morning eased into midday, individual marshalling salients were staked out and an order of battle decided. Soon after, a summons came from the King's pavilion, and his generals rushed to heed his call.

A forest of carved cedar poles turned the interior of the King's pavilion into a fragrant orchard. Around the ivory and gilded wood campaign throne, a legion of slaves and servants waited on the King, seeing to his every whim as if it were the will of blessed Ahuramazda. Indeed, perhaps it was. At the very least, Cambyses of Persia considered himself a demigod. His father had rejected the idea. 'In Egypt, the King may be divine, but in Persia, we are but tools of the divine,' Cyrus was wont to say. Cambyses scoffed at that. He was the pinnacle of justice, the fountainhead of law, with the power of life and death over every living thing under his rule. Could a mere mortal make such a claim?

Heavy-lidded eyes gave the King an indolent look that matched his appetite for pleasures – both of the flesh and of the cup. His rugged frame and falcate nose may have marked him as the son of Cyrus, but there all similarity ceased. To live in the shadow of a man who had conquered much of the world had bred in Cambyses a certain depravity: if he could not match Cyrus on the field, he would match him at the banquet board and in the bedchamber.

Cambyses dismissed his servants with the slightest of gestures as his inner circle of generals and councillors filed in. Among these, Prexaspes held sway. He was a cunning old Mede with the face of a fox and eyes colder than a viper's. The

Magus Ariarathes followed, wrapped in the self-righteous fervour of a follower of the one true god, Ahuramazda. Darius came next, moving with the self-assurance of a man who wore the truth like armour. Phanes entered behind Darius, the Greek's manner at once beautiful and deadly, like the play of lightning in a summer storm. Last came Gobartes, the envoy, his face as unreadable as a wax mask.

After displaying the appropriate level of veneration to the throne, couches were brought in and wine served, a cool aromatic vintage from the King's own stores. Despite their relaxed postures, tension clouded the air. His Majesty was in a dark mood, and men had been known to vanish during his bouts of melancholy.

'Well?' the King said.

Prexaspes spoke, his voice low and controlled. 'Based on the reconnaissance, we face nine regiments of Egyptian troops and four of mercenaries. Under seventy thousand men. They have fortified the hillocks directly in front of us, and the field is strewn with all manner of debris. We cannot use cavalry, but neither can they make use of their chariot corps. If our esteemed Gobartes is correct, they are led by Nebmaatra, an able leader, but unimaginative.'

'What Nebmaatra may lack, Barca makes up for a thousand times over,' Phanes said, staring into the depths of his wine.

'Forgive me if I do not share your admiration for this Phoenician,' Prexaspes said, his lips twisted into a sneer. 'He is one man amid thousands. He will reign supreme in his little corner of the field, but beyond that . . .' The Mede made a negligent wave.

Before Phanes could voice the angry retort that formed on his lips, Darius stepped in. 'You are wise, Prexaspes, and like a father to me, but I am forced to agree with the Greek in this matter. I have talked with this Phoenician. His courage is infectious. It will spread from man to man until it engulfs the whole of their army, and in the grip of this glorious fever, they will fight with redoubled effort. He is beyond doubt Pharaoh's finest asset.'

Cambyses shifted on his throne. 'And what of Psammetichus?'

All eyes swivelled to look at Gobartes. The envoy swallowed. 'He is not cut from the same cloth as his father. Psammetichus is a weak ruler, Majesty. Easily swayed by the advice of his nobles.'

The King's eyes narrowed. 'Men say the same of me,' he said, his voice deadly calm. 'They say that perhaps my brother, Bardiya, would make a more suitable king. Do you believe that, Gobartes?'

Sweat popped out on the envoy's forehead. He walked a razor-thin line. One misstep, one wrong inflection and his life would be forfeit. 'You are the soul of Persia, Majesty. You are her fire, her conscience, her righteousness. With respect, I ask you: can the body live without the soul?'

Cambyses said nothing, his eyes riveted on the

trembling envoy. Gobartes averted his gaze out of deference and fear. Finally, the King said, 'You speak what is in my own mind, Gobartes, and you say it with a honeyed tongue.' Gobartes breathed a sigh of relief. Cambyses continued, 'Ariarathes, what do my brother gods say?'

The Magus bowed. 'I have studied the heart of the Sacred Flame and heard the blessed voice of Ahuramazda. No matter what befalls, the enemy must be engaged at dawn. The omens will not be as auspicious for many weeks to come.'

Cambyses nodded, a thin smile warping his features. 'It is my wish to behold the wonders of Memphis. So I charge you, my generals, with the task of humbling this rabble of artisans and stone-masons. Prexaspes will command the left wing; Darius the right. I personally will oversee the centre. My Immortals will form the core, with the Median and Babylonian infantry. The remainder, you may divide amongst yourselves.'

Darius and Prexaspes bowed in acknowledgement.

'What of me, Majesty?' Phanes said. He had hoped for a command; indeed, Cambyses had promised him one at the outset.

'What of you . . .' Cambyses said, stroking his chin. 'You, I charge with another task. You will command the Ionian and Carian mercenaries, and it will be your responsibility to hunt down and neutralize the Phoenician, whether he be on the left, right, or in the centre. Find him and kill him. That is your reward for serving me.'

A malign light glowed in Phanes' eyes as his lips peeled back in a bestial snarl. The Greek nodded.

'Remember,' the King said, sweeping them with a withering glance. 'When we succeed, Egypt's riches will be yours to share. But, if you fail, if my wishes are not met or exceeded by dusk tomorrow, then not even the icy chill of the Zagros Mountains will cool my wrath!'

⌒　⚶　π　ⰲ　⏻

It was late afternoon by the time Barca was able to pry himself away from the preparations for the coming battle. He had briefed his sub-commanders, the leaders of the mercenary units, on how they were to deploy; he saw to the construction of an angled hedge of wooden stakes at the base of the three hills, a loose palisade that would slow a Persian charge up those inclines. Finally, he gave orders for sentries to be posted and rotated every three hours, and went off in search of Jauharah.

The message from her had been cryptic, its brevity worrisome. The Phoenician wondered what she had discovered. What could require this level of secrecy? Fearing for her safety, Barca picked up his pace and headed for the south-western edge of camp. During the past three weeks, he had seen very little of Jauharah. Her duties in the House of Life had taken the bulk of her time, as preparing the field had taken his.

Those few moments they had spent together left him sullen, aching.

'You love her,' Tjemu pointed out one evening as they shared a meal. His tone was blunt, no-nonsense. Barca knew instantly that discussing Jauharah had been a mistake.

'Don't be ridiculous,' the Phoenician had replied. 'I said I admired her for her strength. That's a far cry from professing my love.' His response, though, lacked conviction, and Tjemu saw through it as easily as he saw the changes in his old captain. Ithobaal would have been proud. The Libyan tore a chunk of bread off the loaf and dipped it into the stew pot.

'What's so ridiculous about it?' he said, popping the bread into his mouth. 'She's a fine girl. Reminds me of the woman I left behind at Siwa. She was strong, too. Strong and stubborn.' Tjemu chuckled. 'She could do this thing with her hips . . .'

'Never mind,' Barca growled. 'Forget I said anything.'

Barca threaded his way through the camp in silence, barely acknowledging the greetings and cheers he received from soldier and servant, alike. Stories of his many battles were spreading throughout the Egyptian army, no doubt started by his Medjay, becoming more grandiose with each telling. Before long, he would have fought the Greeks at Memphis single-handedly before ascending into the heavens on the great solar barque of Ra to do battle with the serpent Apophis. The Phoenician hated such tales. They made the commonplace mythic and did a dis-service to those who fought and died at his side. They deserved the accolades, not him.

His mind returned to Jauharah. Was it love he felt for her? He tried to recall how he had felt for Neferu, so many years ago. Usually a wave of anger preceded such thoughts. Not any more. Barca remembered her with a detached clarity. Neferu had been a gorgeous young woman, her body firm and lush, her face that of a goddess carved in stone. She had known, too, the effect her body had on men. They flocked around her, desperate to capture her attention. She en-couraged their behaviour by wearing gauzy linens and jewellery designed to accentuate her flaring hips and shapely legs. Beyond the physical, Barca could not remember one thing about her personality that he might have found endear-ing. She was shrill, opinionated, spoiled. A girl masquerading as a woman. He had loved Neferu as a miser loves his gold, an object to be coveted and shuttered away.

Not so with Jauharah. Oh, there were similarities in the way her body fired his passion, but even the passion itself seemed different. Cleaner. Stronger. Were they never to touch, Barca would feel contentment in sitting at her side, talking, listening, laughing. There was an intelligence in Jauharah that he could not remember seeing in Neferu; a self-possession he found more arousing than the roundest of hips or softest of breasts. Perhaps Tjemu was right.

428

Three-quarters of an hour later, Barca found his destination. It lay a bowshot beyond the Egyptian camp, where the tough scrub grass gave way to the sand and rock of the desert. It was a squat building fronted by a quartet of columns. A leather curtain hung in the doorway. The place had the look of an old chapel, but to what god or goddess it belonged, Barca did not know; wind and sand and the passage of time had eroded any identifying symbols.

Barca ascended the stairs and twitched aside the makeshift door. Murky sunlight sifted through ruptures in the roof. The air was cool and still, scented with jasmine. Fire had gutted the chapel at some point in its past. All that remained were the soot-blackened walls and columns. Someone had brought furniture here: a small table, a bed thick with pillows, oil lamps for when darkness fell. Movement on the bed exposed a slash of brown thigh. Barca looked closer.

It was Jauharah, asleep. She lay beneath a thin linen coverlet, her chest rising and falling with every measured breath. One arm lay across her stomach; the other pillowed her head. Barca slipped out of his armour, leaving it by the door. His sword he placed on the table, the hilt in easy reach. He knelt by the side of the bed. A finger of golden light played across Jauharah's features. Her face seemed so serene; her moist lips parted slightly. Barca leaned down and kissed her.

Jauharah opened her eyes and smiled. 'You're late,' she whispered.

'I came as quickly as I could,' he replied, cupping her breast. There was a mischievous twinkle in her eyes. Her body stretched and twisted beneath the thin coverlet.

'Does that mean you'll roll over now and go to sleep?'

Barca grinned and lifted the coverlet away from her body. He ducked his head, his lips and tongue finding her hardening nipple. Jauharah's soft laughter turned to moans of pleasure as she drew him into bed.

Afternoon faded to evening. Stars flared overhead, barely visible through the gathering clouds. Night sounds trickled past the crude door; insects, the mournful howl of a jackal, the rustle of sand on stone.

Sweat cooled on their bodies. Jauharah lay on her stomach, her arms pillowing her head. Barca stretched his body alongside hers. His fingers traced meaningless designs on the moist flesh of her upper thighs, over her buttocks, up her spine. He could feel the places where her soft skin gave way to ridges of scar tissue – reminders of her more brutal masters.

'How did you find this place?' Barca asked.

'Luck, I think,' Jauharah said, her voice a low purr. 'I overheard an old woman from Pelusium talking about it. She was a priestess here when it was a temple to Hathor.'

Barca chuckled. 'Hathor? The cow goddess?'

Jauharah shifted, snuggling closer to him. 'She's more than a cow goddess. She's the patron of women, the goddess of love and joy, of song and dance. She has a darker side, too. When enraged, she can be as vicious as the lion-goddess Sekhmet.'

'The secret heart of women. We could use the blessings of Sekhmet in the coming . . .' Barca's voice died away.

'What's wrong?'

Barca could feel her eyes on him; his hand reached out and stroked her cheek. 'A day and a night without the pall of violence hanging over us,' he said. 'Isn't that what you wanted? Tonight, I'm not a warrior or a general. I'm just a man.' Barca felt a tear roll down from the corner of her eye.

'I'm scared, Hasdrabal,' Jauharah whispered, laying her head on his chest.

'I know. I am too.'

'You are?'

'Yes. Is that so hard to believe?'

'Not to me. You're not the same man you once were. The anger . . .'

Barca kissed her forehead. 'The anger is gone. That's part of what scares me. Once, I used rage as a weapon. Now, without it, I feel naked and defenceless. All I have is hope, and hope is useless in battle.' Barca cradled her close, feeling the warmth of her body. 'For the first time in my life,' he whispered, 'I don't want to die.'

19

INTO THE STORM

Dawn broke grey and wet over Pelusium. A chill north wind drove thick clouds inland from the sea. Fat droplets of rain spattered the ground from the coast to the desert's edge. Trumpets blared in the Egyptian camp, and men who had slept uneasily stirred and went about their morning ritual.

Under a makeshift awning, Callisthenes extinguished his lantern and rubbed his eyes with ink-smudged fingers. He had slept fitfully, plagued by dreams of his aging father. In the cold hours before daybreak, he rose and went in search of a scribal palette and papyrus.

. . . *Dawn is not far off. With the rising of the sun, the army will shake itself and come to life, a beast woken from slumber. Across the field, amid the Persians, I have no doubt that there is a man like me, a man roused early by the need to send one last greeting to his family.*

I ask a favour, Father. Do not weep for me, for this is the path I have chosen for myself, regardless of whether it leads to glory or ruin.

Remember the talks we used to have, in the Hellenium at Naucratis? The talks of duty and honour? The memory of those has sustained me through many a dark night. How I use to scoff at you for deriding glory! Now, though, I understand.

Glory, like Justice, is blind. In the past year I have seen scoundrels rise to great office while those of far more noble bearing have expired. You said once that Glory has no master. It's true, I've found. But beyond that, Glory seems to bestow herself like a whore on those least worthy.

The sun's rising, Father. Already I hear the polemarchs stirring. Soon the fight will be joined, and I will be in the thick of it. I pray I will be the one who delivers this letter to you. If I'm not, if I fall, then understand that freedom is oft-times purchased with blood. If my blood is the coin of your freedom, then so be it. The gods have given no man the right to live forever.

He read the letter one last time. Satisfied, Callisthenes rolled it up, placed it in a leather pouch along with his scarab amulet, and looked to his borrowed panoply.

From the doorway of Hathor's forgotten chapel, Barca stared out at the scudding veil of clouds. The rain was a welcome ally. It would neutralize the most feared weapon in the Persian arsenal, the bow. Their archers would be useless. Barca pulled his gaze away and rubbed his eyes. Already he felt tired, drained.

Behind him, he heard Jauharah moving about. She had finished dressing and was gathering up the remnants of their small meal: bread, fruit, a finely strained beer. The leftovers went into a wicker basket. Barca turned from the door and went to where his armour lay. The bronze gleamed, buffed to a mirror-bright sheen, the leather supple, oiled. She must have spent hours on it. Barca picked up his linen corselet and held it between his fists for a long moment before slipping it on.

'Will they fight?' Jauharah said. There was a tension to her voice despite her neutral tone. 'In the rain, I mean?'

Barca nodded. 'One way or another. They'll be reluctant at first, unwilling to give up their superiority with the bow. Without archers or cavalry, they will be forced to meet us hand-to-hand. That might be too close a fight for Cambyses' liking.'

And for mine. Unsaid, the words hung in the air between them. Jauharah hugged herself, shivering. Barca glanced up and saw tears rimming her eyes.

'I had a dream last night,' she said. 'We were walking down a long slope beside a rushing river. The place was lush, groves of olive and pomegranate trees and long rows of wheat. Cattle grazed in the distance, and I could hear the voices of children . . .' her voice faltered. She looked away, remembering. Her arms tightened around

434

her chest. 'But, as we walked, men rushed along the ridges. Men in armour bearing long spears. They waved and shouted at you, and your eyes flickered between them and me. You were in torment, agonizing at having to choose. The space between us grew until my hand slipped out of yours. You drifted away, toward the ridge, toward the armed men, toward the promise of battle. After that, after you had gone, the land withered. I passed skeletal trees and fields razed as if by fire. I saw rotting mounds of flesh that were once cattle. Even the rushing river grew dry and parched. Worst of all, though, was the silence. I could not hear the children any more.'

Barca's heart wrenched in his breast. He could say nothing, his throat tight, as he blinked back tears of his own. He pulled her close and wrapped his arms around her. Jauharah buried her face in his shoulder, her body wracked with sobs.

'I thought I could be strong, thought I could let you go, but I can't! Let's leave this place while there's still time!' she said, her voice barely above a whisper. 'Please! If you go out there, I'm afraid you'll never come back!'

Barca kissed her, stroking her hair as he cradled her head against his chest. He whispered to her: 'I'm sorry, Jauharah. You have asked me for so very little. A roof, a warm bed, food. The necessities have been your only desires. And this thing, this one tiny thing, that you ask of me is the one thing I cannot do. This battle began months ago, as a skirmish with Bedouin raiders.

Now, it has finally reached its culmination. I, of all people, must see it through to the end. Honour . . .'

'Honour, Hasdrabal?' she said, pushing away from him. She wiped her eyes. 'Honour means nothing if you're dead.'

'It's more than that,' he said softly. 'This has become a thing of far greater importance; greater than any here realize. It's grown beyond individual soldiers or generals or kings. It's become a question of survival. We will be fighting to preserve the Egyptian way of life; the Persians will be fighting to destroy it. This,' he gestured around them, 'could be the end of the Egypt we know.'

Jauharah's shoulders slumped as her anger drained away. 'You're right. There's more at stake here than my own selfish needs. I'm sorry.'

'Don't be.' Barca caught her hand and pulled her toward him. 'If anyone should apologize, it should be me. I'm sorry for dragging you into the middle of all this.'

'You didn't drag me, Hasdrabal. I'm here because I could not imagine being anywhere else. And, I'll be here when the battle's over.'

'Then, when the battle's over,' Barca said, 'we'll find that long slope beside the quick-flowing river and make the best parts of your dream come true.'

Jauharah hugged him tight; Barca buried his face in her hair. Beyond the doorway, the Phoenician could hear the distant sounds of armed men, muffled by the rain. He imagined they were beckoning . . .

In his tent, Nebmaatra listened to the staccato plop of rain as he tightened the last buckle on his corselet and took up his ostrich-plumed helmet. He had risen early, dismissed his grooms, and prepared himself as he had in the past, when he was a mere soldier. His mind was calm, unburdened by dread or trepidation. The general had spent part of the night going through the contents of a small cedar-wood chest he planned to deposit at the House of Life. Old letters, drawings, legal documents, his father's scarab seal, his mother's faience bracelet. All of this would pass on to his sister, at Thebes. Both his brothers had died young, one of the fever and the other from a fall. He had no wife; no children of his own.

Nebmaatra smiled, recalling the look on his sister's face when he declined to take a wife. 'Who will care for you in your old age?' she would say, in the same patient voice she used on her unruly children. Nebmaatra would only smile and pat her cheek. He did not have the heart to tell her that, as a soldier, he would likely never see old age.

Nebmaatra's life revolved around one simple premise: service to the throne. Perhaps he had done a disservice to the gods by not marrying and begetting children, but in his mind this was balanced by his commitment to protect his land and his king. If the gods allowed their favourites to prosper, then he could not have soured too many divine stomachs. He had a modest tomb at Saqqara, a set of grave goods, and professional mourners. What more did a man need?

With a last look, Nebmaatra tucked his helmet under his arm and stepped outside. It was time to attend Pharaoh.

At first glance the camp was a hotbed of activity, almost chaotic. But there was an underlying sense of order to it, a method that spoke well of Nebmaatra's abilities as an organizer. Soldiers rushed to their mustering points. Servants handled water, food, spare weapons and equipment. Priests and scribes bore baskets of correspondence for safekeeping in the House of Life. Every man knew his place. Nebmaatra's chest swelled with pride.

Through the apparent chaos, he caught sight of Barca and Jauharah. They walked arm in arm, at their own pace. Soldiers, servants, priests, and scribes flowed around them. The pair stopped at the side entrance to the House of Life.

Nebmaatra watched, knowing he witnessed something intensely personal.

There were no drawn out goodbyes, no histrionics. Their hands touched for a brief instant; their eyes locked, a strained smile. Then she was gone, vanished into the depths of the House of Life.

Barca looked at the sky, closing his eyes against the spattering rain.

Nebmaatra approached him. 'Sleep well?'

'Like the dead,' Barca said. 'You?'

'As a babe at his mother's breast,' Nebmaatra said. Each lied, and the other knew it.

'We may have to goad them,' Barca said. Nebmaatra nodded. The Phoenician continued, 'They know their preferred tactics will be useless, but we cannot let Cambyses retire from the field. He must attack today.'

'Strange,' the Egyptian said. 'I spent three weeks dreading this day, sick with the anticipation of it. This could be my last among the living, and now that it has dawned, I'm eager to see the end of it.'

'Then our places have changed, my friend,' Barca said. 'I am near paralysed with dread. It's a new sensation for me, and I feel shamed by it.'

'Are you becoming mortal, Barca?'

'I've been mortal,' Barca said, extending his hand to Nebmaatra. 'Now, it seems, I'm becoming human, again.'

Nebmaatra nodded and clasped his hand. 'Fight well, Hasdrabal son of Gisco.'

'I'll see you when this is over,' Barca said, turning. Nebmaatra watched him go, watched him vanish as Jauharah had in the swirl and eddy of humanity.

'I hope so,' the Egyptian muttered. 'I hope so.' His heart suddenly heavy, Nebmaatra turned and walked to Pharaoh's tent.

Pharaoh sat on his golden throne and listened to the rain. He had dismissed his courtiers, his advisers, even Ujahorresnet, in order to compose his thoughts in relative peace. The golden scales of his armour clashed as he shifted; of gold, too, were his arm braces, decorated in raised reliefs depicting the gods of war. Instead of the crook and the flail, the hereditary tokens of rule, his hands caressed the haft of an axe.

It was an elegant weapon. The slightly curving handle terminated in a flared bronze head, and the whole was overlaid with gold. The scene on the blade depicted Pharaoh smiting a captive with the label 'Beloved of Neith' beneath. A gift from his father.

Father.

Ahmose had been a lifelong soldier, a man born to the art of war. Psammetichus wondered where such a man's thoughts dwelt in that hour before battle. Did Ahmose second guess his strategy? Did he spend time praying to the gods for luck and success in battle? Or did he just sit quietly and think of the wives he left behind, the children?

He conjured an image from memory. An image of his father as a younger man. He imagined him sitting in this same tent, alone, an axe in his hands. What would Pharaoh do? Where would Pharaoh turn? The answer would not come. Psammetichus could only remember his father as a man, laughing, swapping jests with his generals, drinking wine.

Perhaps that was the answer.

Nebmaatra and Ujahorresnet appeared at the door of the tent. The general carried the blue war crown. They bowed to Pharaoh.

'It's time, O Son of Ra,' Nebmaatra said.

'Wait.' Ujahorresnet held a small pottery figure in his hands, decorated as a Persian with the name of Cambyses inscribed on it. He placed it at Pharaoh's feet. Psammetichus raised an eyebrow. Quickly, Ujahorresnet explained, 'In the time of the god-kings, magic was wrought this way. The ancient ones would smash the effigies of their enemies to insure their power over them would not wane.'

'I should do no less than the god-kings, eh, my friends?' Pharaoh rose and, after a moment's pause, brought his heel down on the Persian effigy. 'I wish it were as easy as this.' Pharaoh accepted the crown from Nebmaatra, and together they rushed out to take their positions.

The priest lagged behind to gather up the shards. Inside the Persian figurine was a smaller effigy, also of pottery, faceless and undecorated. A pair of *shenu*, name rings, was inscribed on the broken figure.

Ankhkaenre Psammetichus.

Barca moved among the mercenaries, not with the pomp of a general, but as a man, stopping along the way to share a joke, to give a greeting. He laughed, and the mercenaries laughed with him.

Barca was a man they could follow. Not born of noble blood, not a man who would command from the rear ranks, but a soldier like themselves. A man who would fight, bleed, and even die with them. Nubian, Libyan, Greek, Medjay; as disparate as they were, divided by culture and language, they were bound by the same awe, the same fascination, the same love for their Phoenician general.

Barca carried himself with the supreme self-assurance of a man comfortable with war. Whatever roiled in his soul did not project to his exterior. The face he presented to his soldiers was the face of a man who wore the heavy bronze cuirass as a second skin; the sword he carried was an extension of his hand, and the shield on his arm virtually weightless. He would face the enemy alone, if need be.

But there would be little need for that. Slowly, as if the sound would dispel the glorious apparition of their general, a chant rose from the ranks of the Medjay.

'Bar-ca! Bar-ca!'

It carried from man to man, from throat to throat. Four thousand. Eight thousand. Twelve thousand and growing.

'Bar-ca! Bar-ca!'

The Nubians in the front ranks bounced on the balls of their feet, chanting in their tongue, a frenzied dance of war meant to secure victory. Their muscular backs gleamed with moisture. Libyans and Greeks pumped their spears heavenward or clashed them against their shield rims. Nowhere else along the Egyptian line was this sort of display going on. The native troops heard the clamour and marvelled. Had the mercenaries gone mad?

'BAR-CA! BAR-CA!'

And amidst this furious storm, Hasdrabal Barca stood alone. His face was solemn as he drew his sword and saluted his men. 'Brothers!' he cried as the chant reached its crescendo and began to ebb. 'Brothers! It's no hard thing for men like you or I to risk our lives in battle. It's our lifeblood, our calling. But, these Egyptians, these men who have come here to defend their homes, their wives, their children – these men are the true heroes. Today, foreigner and native will stand shoulder to shoulder, and for a time, we will all share the same cause. The cause of Victory!'

'Victory!' The cry rippled through the mercenaries. Hearing it, the Egyptian regiments took up the word. 'Victory!' The cacophony grew, until finally the combined voices of sixty-five thousand men shook the foundations of heaven.

'Take your marks! For Egypt and Victory!'

The clamour redoubled as the soldiers found their marshalling salients with the ease of men accustomed to battle.

A figure threaded toward Barca from the direction of the Egyptian camp. At first, the Phoenician thought it might be a messenger sent to deliver some last minute change of plans. As he slogged closer, Barca recognized the face under the helmet.

'Callisthenes?'

The Greek smiled, adjusting the breastplate he had procured. A shield hung from his arm; an uncrested Corinthian helmet perched precariously on his forehead. 'I could not, in good conscience, sit this one out. After Memphis and Gaza, why act squeamish now? As a boy, I dreamed of fighting in a great battle, of making my mark on the papyrus of history. Now,' he thumped his bronze-sheathed chest, 'I have my wish.'

Barca smiled and gripped the Greek's forearm. 'Take your place, then.'

Callisthenes turned and made to join his kinsmen from Naucratis, then stopped. He looked at Barca. 'If I fall,' he said, 'give Jauharah a message for me. Tell her I said thank you. I found comfort in her words.'

Barca nodded. 'You can tell her yourself, after we're finished here.'

Callisthenes waved and vanished in the throng of soldiers.

Barca searched his soul, feeling for that wellspring of anger that had sustained him in battle for the last twenty years, and found nothing. The Beast was dead. A chill danced down Barca's spine. Fine. He would fight this battle without the benefit of a red rage. His mind focused on one thing: on seeing Jauharah's face at the end of the day. Whatever he had to do to make that a reality, he would. All hesitation fled from him, replaced by an iron resolve that stiffened with each passing moment.

The Phoenician walked to the crest of the hill and stared away east. Below, beyond the angled palisades, the pennons of the mercenaries hung motionless in the damp air. Through a grey haze of rain, he could barely discern the front ranks of the Persians.

He heard the dull rumble of thunder, then realized it was the sound of an army on the move. Soldiers were crossing the interval. They would fight. To his left, he could see the hill tumbling down to the sandy strand; to his right, the colourful banners of the regiment of Ptah.

Barca took up his position at the centre of the left wing. The Medjay flowed around him, a guard of honour, presenting a front two hundred shields across and five deep. Left of the Medjay, and anchoring the flank, were the men of Naucratis, five hundred shields across and ten deep, commanded by the Olympian, Oeolycos. Between the Medjay and the Egyptian regiment of Ptah were the Libyans, led by Prince Hardjedef, arrayed in the same formation as the Greeks. The soldiers of Cyrene were held in reserve, despite the protests of their commander, Andriscus. Dark-skinned Nubians ranged ahead, each man bearing a spear, a knotty club, and a shield of thick elephant hide. Otherwise, they were naked. Even their chief, Shabako.

Through the rain, a skirmish line of Persian infantry advanced at a crawl. Thousands of men in loose formation, ten deep, clambered over obstacles and slogged through mud. The moisture had ruined any chance of an arrow storm, but Cambyses was not without options. Those men marching through the grey haze were lightly armoured javelineers. Barca had expected as much.

They drew up some three hundred paces from the Egyptian lines. An order bawled in a sibilant tongue produced a flurry of activity. Each soldier had three ash and iron shafts – one cocked behind his right ear, the other two held ready in his left fist. At a cry from their commander, the soldiers raced forward, propelling their javelins high with every ounce of strength they could muster.

'Shields!' Barca roared. His trumpeter blared the order, echoed by Nebmaatra's on the extreme right. All along the Egyptian line shields sprang into the air, angled to deflect incoming missiles. 'Brace yourselves! Here it comes!' Arching out of the grey sky came a fusillade of iron-heads – a deluge thicker than anything Barca had ever seen. There was a beauty in it, a symmetry of flight as the individual darts reached their apex then gracefully descended, pulled earthward by the weight of their razored tips. Barca watched until the last minute, fascinated.

As impressive as this volley was in flight, its impact was more so. The sound deafened; the hiss of an ash shaft followed by the hammering of iron on shield wrenched prayers from more than one man's lips. Bolts smacked the thick hide bucklers of the Egyptians like the clap of metal on flesh, amplified to the extreme. Javelins caromed off the bronze of the Greek allies, or splintered on their bowl-shaped *aspides*.

One soldier, a man of Naucratis, risked a glance over the edge of his shield and died as a javelin punched through the eye socket of his Corinthian helmet. Others screamed as iron warheads ripped into every inch of exposed flesh: neck, shoulder, thigh, foot. A Nubian made the mistake of dropping his buckler to clutch at his riven calf. A heartbeat later his body flopped to the earth, pincushioned. Casualties, while not significant, mounted.

A second volley followed. A third. Darts protruded from the earth like stalks of grain. A few daring souls snatched them up and hurled them back down the slope.

Barca felt javelins glance off his shield, skitter off his breastplate. Impacts slowed to a trickle, then ceased. He glanced around the rim of his shield. The javelineers were pulling back, beating it through the muck in an effort to escape any retaliatory strike the Egyptians might mount. Barca felt anticipation flowing from his men; they looked at him, their eyes begging permission to give chase. No. That would be playing into Cambyses' hands.

'Cinch up your balls, brothers!' Barca thundered. 'Those were love-taps compared to what's next! Move the wounded to the rear! Check your interval!'

'He's there, on their left,' Phanes said.

'How can you tell?' Darius squinted, shading his eyes from the rain with a gloved hand. Despite his age, the young Persian carried himself with all the cool and aplomb of a seasoned campaigner.

Phanes smiled, and it was not a gesture of mirth. 'You could hear them chanting his name.'

'I will pull my soldiers back so your hoplites can take the point,' Darius said. His soldiers, like the whole of the army, were a heterogeneous mix cobbled together by the King's will, alone. Most of them spoke no Persian, forcing him to issue commands through an aide well-versed in a sort of pidgin Aramaic. Darius motioned for his adjutant. Phanes stopped him, his manner brusque.

'No. Let your troops soften up their position. My men will form the third wave.'

'As you wish,' Darius replied. Both men fell silent as the Persian light infantry retreated back across the jagged battlefield. They had loosed their javelins; now, they faded behind the gathering heavy infantry and went into reserve positions. All across the Persian front assault troops found their marks and massed for a charge.

They did not have long to wait. Trumpeters shrieked their orders from the centre from beneath the King's standard.

The Egyptians waited in anxious silence, not moving, not speaking. Barca wondered if all breath had fled them. A horn brayed, and through the mist he could see the flash and glitter of enemy infantry. Cambyses' army was a patchwork of levies drawn from the far-flung corners of his empire. The Immortals, so named because their ranks were always at ten thousand – never more, never less – formed the core of the invading force. Around them were arrayed the men of Persia, Media, Chaldea; turbaned Cissians from the mountainous regions east of Susa fought beside Assyrians from the upper Euphrates, while Hyrkanians from the fringes of the Caspian Sea worked in tandem with their one-time enemies, the Sacae. The Great King of Persia employed his share of mercenaries as well: hoplites from Ionia and Caria; peltasts from the eastern Aegean; savage Thracians; even remnants of the Cimmerian horde.

At this distance Barca could not tell which of Cambyses' myriad legions approached; truth be told, he didn't care. He was ready for this fight to be over.

'They're terrified,' Barca said, his voice carrying. 'Look at them! The rain hides well the stains on the front of their trousers, stains where they've pissed themselves!' The tension cracked. Men laughed, jostling one another. 'Would you not piss yourself if you were in their place? Those men are about to die, not for their homes, not for their families, not even for gold! Those men are about to die because Cambyses wishes it! He wants Egypt! He wants to prove he is a better man than his father! Cyrus was wise! Cyrus knew what Cambyses is about to learn . . . that Egypt belongs to no man but Pharaoh!' Jeers and catcalls rose from the ranks of the mercenaries.

The enemy moved in a close formation, swaying with that curious stride only noticeable when large groups of men march together. Banners and pennons sprinkled the enemy ranks, splashes of colour in the oppressive grey. Barca heard a commotion behind him. He half turned as a runner dashed up with a message from Pharaoh. Mud speckled the boy from his belly to his toes, and his round face was pale, tight-lipped. Dark eyes rolled across the broad enemy front. He ran rampant over his tongue as he tried to deliver his message.

'Slow down, lad,' Barca said. 'Take a breath and look at me.'

The runner exhaled slowly and tried to focus on Barca. 'T-The Immortals are moving against the centre. P-Pharaoh, in his wisdom, h-has pulled back from the front. His Majesty will oversee the commander of the regiment of Amon.'

Barca dismissed the boy with a wave. So, Pharaoh has tasted combat and found it too sour for his palate. What would his father think? Unlike Psammetichus, Barca did not have the luxury of time to ponder life's little nuances. He had a battle to fight. Barca thrust aside thoughts of Pharaoh and turned his attention back to the enemy.

An order cracked like a whip over their heads, and the speed of the oncoming host increased. Ruptures appeared in their formation; the line grew ragged as men edged to the right, seeking shelter in the shadow of their comrades. Faster they came. The ground shook.

Closer. At a dead run, now. Charging uphill. Screams of fury rose above the clatter of arms and harness. Barca could discern individual faces, now. Beneath sodden turbans their eyes were wide, lips peeled back in bestial snarls. Amulets to their crude gods were thonged about their necks. These were Cissians, hillmen from the Zagros Mountains, clad in leather and iron scale and armed with spears and foot-long knives.

Closer still. Each footfall sent plumes of mud and water into the air, thicker than the descending rain. Thousands of throats loosed a blood-curdling war cry, not unlike that of the Bedouin. *'Eleleleleleu!'*

Barca raised his sword heavenwards . . .

'Now!'

A horn blast skirled, its notes hanging in the air. In answer, the Nubians took two powerful steps forward and hurled their heavy bronze-and-bone tipped lances with all the power their dusky shoulders could command. Spear casts that could bring down an elephant ripped through leather and iron and flesh. Men thrashed, impaled. Screams of agony replaced those of fury. The Cissians faltered.

And Barca, flanked by his mercenaries, charged.

The two armies met, not with the thunder of hammer on anvil, but with the subtle, terrifying sound of cracking bone, amplified to a deafening cacophony. Bodies crushed together. Spears licked and darted. Swords crashed on shields. Blood rained to the ground, mixing with the mud churning underfoot to form a hellish soup that clutched at a man's ankles like quicksand.

A cold fury gripped the Phoenician. His mind was crystal, unhampered by rage, by the Beast. A Cissian lunged; Barca sidestepped and smashed him down with the flat of his shield. After that, men strained breast to breast, hand to hand, their feet clawing for purchase on the slimy ground. Barca inverted his sword and thrust it over the rim of his shield, driving it point-first into his foeman's eyes. Spear heads skittered off his armour, gouging bright furrows in the bronze. A hand clutched at his sword-blade and lost its fingers in the process. Underfoot, the dying clung to his knees.

In all his battles, Barca had never fought in so compacted a mass of men. He had nowhere to turn. Splinters of wood and metal raked his flesh, drawing blood. Frustration mounted when he could not step to the side to avoid the flying debris. Forward or back were his only options. Any step forward meant planting one foot solidly on what he hoped was a corpse and thrusting his shield out before him. Any step back meant giving the enemy a toehold in the Egyptian line. Gouged and peppered by shrapnel hacked from sword, spear, and shield, Barca opted to press forward. Behind him, the mercenaries followed suit.

Inexorably, they forced the Cissians back.

⌒　⚶　🏮　ᕯ　🍷

Battle raged as the day wore on. Beyond the grey pall of clouds, the sun reached its zenith and descended into the west. On the ground, the lines swelled and ebbed like a tide of flesh. A wall of Hyrkanians forced Nebmaatra's men back, beyond the palisade and onto the upper slopes of the hill. The centre reeled from the savage onslaught of the Immortals; the regiment of Amon drew strength from the Sekhmet and Osiris regiments on its flanks. The Egyptian ranks were thinning. On the left, Barca's mercenaries stood their ground. The Nubians shattered charge after charge of Cissian and Assyrian infantry, sloughing the remains off to the Libyans on their right and the Greek allies on their left. The Medjay stood like a stone bulwark in a storm.

Barca slung his shield down, its bronze face staved in, and snatched another from the ground. He stood in the eye of the storm, in the pocket of calm formed by the natural ebb and flow of battle, and peered out toward the Egyptian regiments. The mercenaries were well forward of the remainder of the army; so far, in fact, that they risked exposing their flank. They would have to fall back before some enterprising Persian commander drove a wedge between them and the regiment of Ptah.

Amid the pandemonium Barca located his trumpeter cowering in the mud beside the standard bearer. He grabbed the man up and ordered him to ply his instrument. 'Fall back to the hilltop!' The notes skirled, weak at first then growing stronger as the trumpeter found his wind again. At the same time, Barca signalled for the men of Cyrene to join the fray. Andriscus and his fresh troops could screen the strategic withdrawal. 'Fall back to the hilltop!'

Slowly, like a rock split by ice, the two armies disengaged.

That's when disaster struck.

Barca himself could not be certain what happened. One moment, his front lines were falling back through the palisade and the screen of Cyrenean troops, and the next chaos ruled.

Chaos in the guise of an enemy phalanx.

Phanes' soldiers, hoplites of Ionia and Caria, smashed into the withdrawing Medjay. Their exact moment of impact could not have had a more devastating effect. Barca watched, helpless, as the loose, fluid formations of his men were shattered by the interleaved shields and jabbing spears of the enemy.

The Horus-eye standard dipped and fell as the Medjay desperately sought to repel the enemy hoplites. It was like trying to stop a bronze-bladed threshing machine. Barca saw Tjemu stumble, clutching at the man beside him. His shield went awry. Barca flinched as a spear, thrust overhand, plunged down between the Libyan's helmet and cuirass. His body vanished under foot.

The hoplites scythed through the Medjay and ploughed into the Nubians and Libyans. Ahead of them, the men of Naucratis closed ranks with the Cyrenean troops, presenting a wall of shields to the onrushing foemen. A hymn to Poseidon rose from the throats of the allies.

The two Greek phalanxes, kinsmen bound by blood and separated by politics, met in a grinding crash of armour. Bronze and muscle strained against one another. Spears thrust over the tops of shields struck their targets with homicidal precision. Helmets were punctured; breastplates pierced.

Barca let Greek fight Greek while he rallied the Libyans and the Nubians. A handful of Medjay staggered to his side, loyal unto death. The Phoenician knew where the enemy would be the most vulnerable. A strike against their exposed left flank would shatter their cohesion, forcing them to wheel and defend against this new threat. If he . . .

A sound forced its way through Barca's battle-heightened perception, shattering his tactical mind set; a sound he had heard many times and in many places. The commotion arose from his right, from among the native Egyptian regiments, radiating from the centre with a convulsive force that stripped breath from lungs and left knees weak. He turned and peered through the drizzle.

'Psammetichus, you son of a bitch!'

The Immortals were relentless. Wave after wave crashed against the Egyptian centre, eroding it like a sand wall in an ocean squall. Under the eyes of Pharaoh, the regiment of Amon fought with magnificent valour, repulsing each attack despite heavy casualties. Men stumbled past Psammetichus, reeling from their wounds, their weapons hanging forgotten in fists too cramped to open. Others rushed forward to take their places. The sounds floating up from the front lines, the furious clangour of bronze and iron, the screams of the fallen, sent tendrils of fear through Pharaoh's belly.

He stood in his chariot, the horses calmed by a pair of grooms, as the battle raged a few hundred feet away. He had intended to take his place in the front line, but the javelins had changed his mind. Now, he was working up the courage to join his men.

Nebmaatra and Barca both fought amongst their troops. As Pharaoh, could he do any less than his generals? He had to do something. Order a charge, maybe? Send reserves in to fill gaps in the faltering line?

As Psammetichus watched, the Egyptian line ceased to falter and began to crumble. A wedge of Immortals drove through the regiment of Amon and split the Calasirians in two. The breach filled with Persians. He knew he had to make a choice now: charge or withdraw. Pharaoh glanced left and right. The thick, steady drizzle cloaked the flanks in a grey haze; he could see neither Nebmaatra nor Barca. Were they still alive? Terror clutched his heart in icy talons. Charge or withdraw?

A faceless Mede, howling in fury, burst through the retaining wall of Egyptian soldiers, a spear cocked above his left ear. Just as his weight shifted in anticipation of the cast, his arm extending, a mortally wounded Calasirian rose up behind the Mede and bore him to the ground. Their thrashings were lost from view. A second Persian followed on their heels, slinging his spear haphazardly seconds before a sword tore through his guts. The shaft wobbled in mid-flight and went awry, but it was enough for Psammetichus.

'Withdraw!' he screamed, hauling on the reins of his chariot and trampling his own grooms. 'Withdraw!'

Like an infection, Pharaoh's panic spread.

⌒ ⚶ ⛩ ⚷ ⚱

Against Nebmaatra, the Hyrkanians fought like madmen. The first few hours served to pare the fat from the Egyptian lines. Soldiers who were too slow, too afraid, or too reckless fell first. They were good men, all, but they lacked the killer instinct of the survivors. Those who remained were harder than granite. Again and again the Egyptians hurled the enemy down the slope, only to watch them reform and charge once more. They were relentless.

'Watch the flank! Don't let them overlap us!' Nebmaatra shouted to his captains during one of the many lulls in the fighting. Below them, a wall of snarling faces surged up the hillside. 'Here they come again!'

A scream pierced the din of combat, a sound unlike any Nebmaatra had heard this day. It wasn't fury or pain that wrenched that yell from a soldier's lips. It was defeat. Another scream, this one closer. Then another. Sensing something wrong, the Egyptians grew panicked. They rolled their eyes toward the centre, toward Pharaoh's banners, and saw the core of the army in retreat. Panic turned to fear, and despite their granite-hard exteriors, that fear sapped any vestige of honour they might have had. They threw down spear and shield and ran, following the example of the Son of Ra.

The Hyrkanians, sensing imminent victory, redoubled their efforts.

'Stand!' Nebmaatra roared as Pharaoh's army crumbled. 'Stand and fight, damn you!' A few heeded his cry, but not enough. The Hyrkanians crushed the right flank as if it were made of pottery.

Nebmaatra found himself alone. His guard lay dead about him, crowning the small hill in a ruin of flesh and bone. The Hyrkanians gave him little respite. Already they were streaming past him, a river split by a lone rock, to fall on the unprotected flank of the centre. The Egyptian swayed. He was covered in blood, much of it his own, his corselet in tatters and his helm long since lost in the wrack. Gore clotted the blade of his sword.

For a moment he stood again in his family's home, in Thebes. A breeze ruffled the thin linen curtains; sunlight striped the tiled floor. He saw a scribe delivering his chest to his sister, saw her open it. She was thin, like their mother, with large eyes the colour of a moonlit pool. Her husband, a quiet man who served the temple of Amon, stood behind her, his hands on her shoulders. 'He lived the best way he knew how,' he said. His sister bowed her head . . .

The noose of Hyrkanians tightened. They rushed forward. The foremost among them fell under Nebmaatra's blade. The Egyptian bellowed in defiance and hurled himself at a barbarous Hyrkanian, splitting his helmet open. The injured man's axe crushed his shoulder. Nebmaatra reeled. A slender lance darted past his failing guard to bury itself in his chest. The Egyptian fell to his knees; his sword dropped from his weakening grasp. He coughed blood.

Nebmaatra craned his neck and stared at the sky. Grey and white clouds drifted across the face of the sun god, Ra, sparing him from witnessing the shame wrought by his son, by Pharaoh. Many were his tears, and they spilled down from the heavens like rain . . .

'H-He is not h-his father,' Nebmaatra whispered seconds before a Hyrkanian's axe freed his *ka*.

Though chaotic and scrambled, Barca could read the battlefield as though it were an immaculately penned text. The centre had caved in, shattering like a glass bowl. Nebmaatra held a while longer, but the Hyrkanians had overwhelmed him in a series of reckless charges. He could barely see the broken standard being paraded about the crown of the distant hill. With the right swept away, the fleeing regiments of the centre were flanked and cut off. Pockets of resistance flared as the commanders of Amon attempted a rearguard action. Barca knew in his bones that Psammetichus had escaped. He hoped Pharaoh would defend Egypt from dam to dyke, but he had a sinking feeling that his flight would not stop until he reached the gates of Memphis. The battle was over. He had to get to Jauharah . . .

A hand clutched at Barca's ankle. He glanced down.

A Greek lay tangled in a heap of Cissian dead, a shivered spear protruding from his sternum. Barca crouched, helped him off with his helmet, and stopped. Callisthenes. Rain bathed his face. His eyes blinked rapidly. 'I . . . I c-could not k-keep up,' he said, coughing blood. 'They s-surrounded me . . . I t-tried . . .'

'You fought well, my friend,' Barca said. Soldiers were rushing by, elements of the Libyan regiment. Barca motioned to two of them. 'You're going to be fine, you hear me? These men will get you back to the tents. You're going to be fine!'

Callisthenes laughed, turning his head as a spasm clenched his chest. 'I'll s-see you across the river, P-Phoenician.'

Barca clutched the Greek's hand, then nodded to the two soldiers. Both bore wounds of their own. 'Get him back to the tents,' he said, rising. 'Seek out a woman called Jauharah.' Barca watched them gently carry Callisthenes away, then closed his eyes.

Barca stood at a crossroad. Fight or flight? He could quit the battle, quit Egypt, and travel with Jauharah to some forgotten corner of the world. They could raise crops and children and grow old at each other's side. Or he could exact revenge. For Matthias. For Ithobaal. For his Medjay. For Tjemu. Their howling ghosts would never afford him a moment's respite should he turn his back on them now. Fight? Flight? He recalled Phanes' words, spoken in a cell in Memphis. *This cult of honour. I'm afraid I'll never grasp it.*

This cult of honour. Honour. For all that his heart screamed of love and compassion, Barca knew he could not turn his back on honour. He could not flee. Whatever the outcome, he would stand his ground. The road of vengeance, once taken, could not be denied.

A spear of ice impaled the Phoenician. He threw his head back and howled in rage.

In response, the Beast woke from its slumber.

461

20

MEN OF BRONZE

'Hold him!' Jauharah screamed, throwing her weight across the wounded soldier's torso. 'Someone hold him!' From the chaos a priest rushed forward, his chest and kilt slimed with blood, and immobilized the thrashing Egyptian. 'He was unconscious,' Jauharah said. 'Didn't think he would move.' She tossed the cooling flatiron aside and snatched another from the fire pot. Jauharah shifted, planting the cherry-red iron against the stump of the soldier's forearm. Meat sizzled. The soldier stiffened, his eyes rolling back in their sockets, and a moment later his contortions ceased. Jauharah smelled the nauseating stench of bowel.

'Damn it,' she muttered, dropping the iron back into the smouldering coals. The priest glanced from Jauharah to the dead soldier, not comprehending. Like most in the House of Life he was a child of the long and peaceful reign of Khnemibre Ahmose. Until this day the worst he'd seen were commonplace accidents: the gashed hands of an impatient stone cutter; the crushed foot of an inattentive herdsman; perhaps a fisherman's mangled legs in the wake of a crocodile attack. This aftermath of the collision between flesh and iron was too much for him to bear. Jauharah could see it in his eyes, a cloud of madness drifting close to the surface. She placed a hand on his shoulder. 'Go help where you can. Let lord Osiris have this one.' Blinking, the priest stood and moved away. He heard another plea for help, turned, and vanished in the chaos. Jauharah closed her eyes and leaned against the dead soldier.

Around her, men flailed and screamed as spearheads were extracted, or moaned pitifully as bones were set, lacerations stitched. Priests, scribes, cooks, grooms, everyone not germane to the fighting had been pressed into service as an aide or orderly. Hollow-eyed boys spread buckets of sand underfoot to absorb the blood, bowel, and vomit that poured from the shattered wrecks of Pharaoh's soldiery. The stench was ungodly. Chest and belly wounds, crushed skulls, punctures, long gaping slashes. Most of the wounded looked as if Persian horses had dragged them naked across a field of bronze spikes. Jauharah knew in her marrow few of them would live. She caught sight of Ladice. The Lady of Cyrene, as blood-grimed and foul as the rest of them, still possessed a sense of dignity powerful enough to calm nerves and soothe fears. But, as she passed close, Jauharah could see something was not right. There was a tightness about

Ladice's eyes, a thinness to her lips. Jauharah reached out and plucked at her sleeve.

'What's wrong?' she whispered, frowning. Ladice glanced around, making sure no one was within earshot. Her relationship with Barca made them equals in this sorority of death.

'Pharaoh has withdrawn from the field,' Ladice said, her voice cracking. 'That spineless son of a whore! He promised his father! He promised . . .' She caught herself before she could say more. Ladice closed her eyes; her trembling fingers busied themselves with smoothing the neckline of her simple shift.

Jauharah hugged herself, unable to stop the thrill of fear that raced down her spine. She thought of Hasdrabal. 'What will happen?'

'Panic and flight. Cambyses will come,' Ladice said. 'Surely he will spare the wounded?' She stared at the carnage around her, overcome at last by the sheer volume of it. Tears flowed down her cheeks. 'Or would it be more merciful to let them die?'

'We must try to save them,' Jauharah said.

Ladice nodded, again in control of herself. 'Yes. We must. Do what you can, Jauharah. I'm going to throw myself on Cambyses' mercy.' She grabbed Jauharah by the shoulders, hugging her. 'Promise me you will flee should this take a turn for the worse!'

'I promise.'

Ladice gave a brief smile, a gesture meant to bolster her own flagging confidence. They hugged one last time. 'Amon bless you, lady,' Jauharah said as she watched her go. 'Amon bless you and keep you.'

The sound of a voice bellowing her name jarred Jauharah back to reality.

'Jauharah! Is there a Jauharah here? Jauharah!' A huge Libyan in blood-splashed armour, his sandy hair matted to his scalp, stood at the rear of the tent. He curled his hands into a makeshift horn and howled her name like a barbaric war cry. 'Jauharah!'

She rushed over. 'What is it? Are you injured?'

'You're Jauharah?'

'I am. What—?'

The mercenary jabbed a thumb behind him. He plunged out the rear flap of the house of life, trusting her to follow. She did. Outside, the copse of sycamores and tamarisks shielded the wounded from the gentle rain. Around them sandalled feet had churned the sun-browned grass to mud, and the stench of an abattoir rose from the open trench.

Beneath the trees, a second mercenary crouched beside a shattered body. 'General Barca said to seek you out.'

A lance of fear impaled her. 'Is Barca . . . ?' She glanced down at the wounded man and felt her heart wrench in her chest. 'Oh gods! No! Callisthenes!'

The Greek's head moved feebly. At the sound of his name his eyes fluttered. Jauharah knelt at Callisthenes' side and took his blood-grimed hand in hers, clutching it to her breast. Breath rattled in his chest. Jauharah didn't need to look too closely to see there was nothing she could do for him.

'I-I did the best I c-could,' he whispered. 'B-Barca . . . the right . . . the right wing crumbled after . . . after the Immortals routed P-Pharaoh . . . only the l-left held, and only because of him!'

'You did well, Callisthenes,' she sobbed. 'Ajax himself could not have fought better.' She leaned down, kissed his brow, and very quietly Callisthenes of Naucratis died.

Jauharah placed the Greek's lifeless hand at his side and rocked back on her heels. The world around her bulged at the seams, threatening to come apart. The battle was lost. She had heard Ladice say as much. There would be panic and flight, but Jauharah felt neither. Only the twin aches of weariness and despair. The dream she'd had last night felt as though it belonged to someone else. Her stream lay beside her, a gash bubbling with blood and piss, and the spearmen who called Barca away were minions of Death. He was alone out there . . .

Jauharah's head snapped up, her features hardening. Weariness and despair sloughed from her like a rain-soaked cloak. 'Get me a horse!' she said with such force that neither mercenary questioned her order.

She wouldn't let him die alone.

The rain slackened. Rills of water sluiced down the Phoenician's armour, through the blood speckling his face and chest. His hair hung in lank strands about his shoulders. Wordlessly, he slung his shield aside and snatched a second sword from a dead man's hand. Below him, Greek mercenaries swarmed up the incline. Charge after charge had churned the ground underfoot to the consistency of sludge, a mixture of soil, rain, blood, and bowel that seeped into every crack and crevice and made their footing treacherous.

Enemy hoplites crawled over a carpet of corpses, their hands and feet clawing for purchase and sending an avalanche of sundered flesh down upon their comrades. Winded, the Greeks gained the summit.

And died.

The Phoenician launched himself at those who crested the hill. His swords licked and darted, drawing blood with each stroke. Bodies tumbled back down the slope, some slashed and riven, others without arms and heads. Barca felt a presence at his side. From the corner of his eye he spotted an Egyptian soldier coming towards him. Then a second. A third. They were the last of the regiment of Ptah, the rear guard, and they took up positions on either side of the Phoenician. A soldier of the Medjay, mortally wounded, lurched up and hurled himself down onto the Greek spears. Into that breach Barca leapt. His two swords wrought havoc. He was too close for their spears to do any harm. Their smaller blades were useless against him. Barca moved like Ares in his element, and killed with the impunity of a god.

The end was inevitable. There was no way this handful could stem the Persian tide; the sheer press of numbers gnawed away at the defenders, killing them singly and in pairs. Finally, beneath the crest of the hill, Barca stood alone.

Blood streamed from dozens of lacerations, mixing with spatters of grime and gore. One sword had broken off near the hilt. Barca tossed the useless weapon down and faced the horde of Greeks and Persians with a single, unwavering blade. None of them moved. They stood rooted to the spot, frozen like the victims of Medusa's stony glance.

A familiar face floated over the shoulders of the men in the front ranks. Dark hair. Flawless features. A homicidal Adonis. With a low, merciless laugh, Phanes of Halicarnassus stepped out to face Barca.

'Let's finish this,' he said, tossing his shield to one side.

'You should have killed me in Memphis,' Barca snarled, 'when you had the chance!' They circled one another slowly, a predatory dance bereft of music, accompanied by the soft squelch of mud underfoot. Droplets of rain plopped into pools of diluted blood.

Phanes grinned, his face ghoulish. A wild sword cut had removed his helmet and laid open his cheek to the bone. 'And deny myself a chance of glory? I think not! The Fates engineered this, Barca! They need us to meet over the ruins of two nations! Do you not feel it? In the air? That thrill of a god's fingers moving us about like game pieces on a board?'

'You're insane!'

Phanes laughed. 'Or a genius. The line between the two is as thin as Persephone's veil. In a minute, you'll not care either way!'

Their dance came to an end. Both men crouched in the gentle rain, blades ready, condensation trickling down to soak the leather-wrapped hilts. The crowd formed a circle around them, a mixed audience of Persians, Greeks, and Cissians. Barca's eyes flickered over their ranks for an instant.

In that instant Phanes struck.

The ferocity of the Greek's assault wrenched a gasp from the onlookers. He moved like a whirlwind, a tempest of flashing iron that rasped and slithered off Barca's lightning defence. At any moment the witnesses expected to see a Phoenician corpse flop into the muck, headless, disembowelled. Had it been any other man, the fight would have lasted a heartbeat.

For Hasdrabal Barca, the fight had only begun.

Metal grated as the two men surged together, chest to chest, their blades tangled. Phanes spat in Barca's eye; the Phoenician answered with a fist across the Greek's lacerated cheek. Phanes howled.

They sprang apart. Barca loathed giving up

his momentary advantage. He pressed forward, raining blow after blow on the Greek's guard. Barca was the taller and heavier of the two, and the thick muscle of his sword arm worked tirelessly, without respite. To the onlookers, he seemed to have boundless reserves of energy.

Phanes backpedalled. His advantage lay in speed and precision. The raw elemental fury of Barca's assault stymied his every move. Thrusts were batted aside, and a hammering counter-attack met each slashing stroke. The Greek's wrist grew numb from serving as Barca's anvil.

Phanes launched himself at Barca, a new round of slash and thrust, parry and riposte, that brought them into another close embrace. Sweat poured down their faces, into their eyes. Muscle strained against muscle, sinew against sinew. Their blades locked together, grinding. Phanes threw a punch at Barca's chin with his free hand, connected, and drew back for another. Barca responded in kind.

Quick as a snake Phanes ducked Barca's punch, hooked the Phoenician's leg and shoved with all his might. It was an old wrestler's trick, and it caught Barca at unawares.

He tried to regain his balance and failed, toppling to the ground. He landed on his back; his sword jarred from his grasp.

Barca's fall gave the Greek the opening he needed. With a triumphant yell, Phanes sprang forward and drove his blade into Barca's belly. The tip of the weapon skittered down Barca's cuirass and plunged, instead, into his thigh, nailing his leg to the ground.

The Phoenician roared in pain and anger.

The onlookers knew it was over. They knew . . .

Above him, the Greek was overextended, stumbling forward. He would have fallen had the Phoenician not caught him by the neckline of his cuirass and held him erect. Snarling, Barca grabbed Phanes' sword by the blade and wrenched it from his thigh. Phanes' eyes widened. His arms flailed; his feet sought purchase.

'I'll see you in Hell!' Barca said, ramming the blade into the exposed hollow of Phanes' throat and hurling him aside with a contemptuous shove.

Phanes of Halicarnassus died writhing on his belly.

Barca clambered to his feet, swaying, his weight on the Greek's sword. The wound in his thigh was grave; blood sheeted down his leg. Around him, the onlookers were stunned to silence, staring at the Greek's corpse. They glanced from Barca to Phanes, and back again. Suddenly, one man faced hundreds.

Barca staggered forward. 'Let's end this! Come and die, you sons of whores!'

None among the Persians moved. The battle was over; they had won. They weren't eager to die. There was some jostling amid their ranks as a few soldiers stepped to the forefront, Greeks for the most part, mercenaries from the island of Samos, not as eager to avenge their fallen commander as they were to claim glory as Barca's slayer.

The Phoenician braced himself . . .

The massing Greeks faltered, shocked to see a horse crest the hill at full gallop. Its rider was fey, covered in blood. Long hair streamed out behind her as she descended on the enemy like a harpy out of myth.

They gave ground, gape-mouthed, as the rider barrelled into their ranks. Limbs were crushed and broken in that press as men were trampled by the horse and by one another. The rider hauled on the reins and the mount, its footing unsure, reared and twisted, collapsing in a tangle of thrashing limbs. The rider was thrown clear.

In the moment's respite, Barca snatched a piece of leather off the ground, a strap from a sandal, and cinched it around his thigh. Blood gushed from the severed artery, jetting in time with the beating of his heart. He made the tourniquet tight and caught up his sword. The Phoenician felt a surge of fear as Jauharah rose to her feet to stand at his side, a shattered spear in her fists.

'What are you doing here?' he hissed through clenched teeth. The enemy advanced slowly, wary. Barca could feel his strength beginning to ebb.

Jauharah kept the spear levelled at the breast of the closest Persian. 'I'll not be left behind.' She feinted at the Persian's face, giving the man pause. The ring of foemen closed on them, weighing the odds of taking them out before too many of them were killed. In their eyes Barca read fear. Fear and respect. Not just for him. They knew well the fury of a woman. Cyrus, their beloved king and Cambyses' father, had died at a woman's hands. Jauharah's appearance would not keep them at bay for long. He had to do something.

'Give her safe conduct and I will bend my neck to your blades!' Barca said. Beside him, he felt Jauharah stiffen.

'No! Barca! You can't . . .'

'I'll not see you harmed!' The Phoenician drew himself up to his full height and glared out over the sea of exhausted faces. 'My life in exchange for hers! Who will speak for you?'

'I will,' a familiar voice said. The Persians parted their ranks, allowing the speaker through.

'Darius,' Barca said, bowing slightly. 'Will you make me beg for her life?'

The Persian commander's armour was smeared with a mixture of blood and grime, and dented by the fury of the fighting. His helm was gone. Blood oozed from a cut across his forehead. He glanced down at Phanes' corpse. 'We are weary of slaughter. You will both be spared.'

'In exchange for what?' Barca said, his teeth clenched against the cold spreading through his belly. He held Jauharah's shoulder for support, and she could feel the pressure of his weight increasing. He was losing strength. 'Kill me now and let her go, for I'll be no man's slave!'

'I admire valour in any man, friend or foe,' Darius said. 'And you showed all of us today what valour truly is. I salute you, and give you both your freedom. None will touch you, I give you my word of honour!'

'You're an admirable man, Darius,' Barca said. 'I'm glad I didn't have to kill you.'

The young Persian smiled through his weariness. 'Fetch their horse.'

Jauharah's horse wandered nearby, terrified by the stench of blood and death. One of the Persians caught its rein and led it over to where they stood. Darius himself helped Barca into the saddle. Before Jauharah could mount behind him, the Persian commander drew her aside.

'That wound in his thigh . . .'

'I know.'

'Where will you go?'

Jauharah looked away; she looked to the south west. 'It doesn't matter, so long as I am with him.'

Darius sighed. 'In the coming days, should you find yourself with no one else to turn to, remember my name and use it. I will do what I can for you.'

'You've done enough.' Jauharah swung up behind Barca. Deftly, she unbuckled his cuirass and let it fall to the ground. At a gesture, two Persians stepped forward and slipped Barca's greaves off, leaving him clad in his sweat- and blood-stained linen corselet and bronze-studded leather kilt. Jauharah touched her heels to the horse's flanks, and without a backward glance cantered off down the hillside.

Darius raised a hand in farewell. 'May the gods of your people and mine have mercy upon you.'

A west wind shredded the clouds, revealing a sunset that transformed the storm-wracked sky into a canopy aflame with colour. Inside the ruined chapel sacred to Hathor the air was still; silent, save for the faint drip of water. Motes of dust swirled through golden shafts of sunlight lancing down from the cracked ceiling.

Barca lay in a pool of light. A smear of blood led from the door to that spot, marking the limits of Jauharah's ability to drag him. She crouched above his thigh and worked furiously to staunch the bleeding. Barca's face was pale, drenched in sweat.

'C-Callisthenes?'

'Don't talk,' Jauharah said.

'W-Where is Callisthenes?'

'He has gone on ahead, Hasdrabal,' she replied, stifling a sense of helplessness. There was nothing she could do. Without fire she couldn't seal the artery.

'They're all dead,' Barca whispered. 'Matthias. Ithobaal. Tjemu. Callisthenes. I killed them. I—'

'Hush. Don't talk like that.' Jauharah tried to tighten the strap about his thigh and, despairing of that, pressed her hands against the wound, willing the edges to mend and the blood to cease its life-stealing exodus.

'T-Tell me about your d-dream, again,' Barca said, his face screwed up in a rictus of pain.

Jauharah choked back tears. 'We lived on

475

a long, green slope beside a crystal river. The land gave us everything we needed. Olives. Pomegranates. Vegetables beyond number. And, there were children. Droves of children.'

Barca smiled. 'A good dream . . .' A shadow crossed his face. 'I'm sorry, Jauharah. I-I s-should have t-taken you away from here.'

'Hush, Hasdrabal,' Jauharah sobbed. 'Please. Save your strength.'

'No!' the Phoenician said, rising on his elbows. 'Listen. T-There's something I haven't told you. Something I s-should have said long ago. I have loved you since I first laid eyes on you, Jauharah. You s-saved my soul. You t-taught me what it was like to live again. For that, I-I can never r-repay you.'

Jauharah smiled gently, her hand going to his cheek to brush away the tears. 'There's nothing to repay, Hasdrabal. Nothing. I love you more than you'll ever know. I love you for your strength, your compassion, your humanity. You—' she choked.

'I m-must go s-soon,' he said, sinking back down. 'S-So cold. L-Lie beside me and t-tell me about our children.'

Jauharah stretched out beside him, their bodies woven together as she whispered to him of the laughter of dark-haired little girls, and of the shrieks of young boys with wooden swords. Outside, the sun slipped over the rim of the world, leaving a cold, starless night in its wake . . .

EXODUS

Ankhkaenre Psammetichus, last pharaoh of the Twenty-sixth Dynasty, died not long after the Persian Invasion. In his final hours, it is said he found the will to fight he so lacked at Pelusium.

Cambyses II of Persia, too, did not live long to enjoy the fruits of his conquest. In 522 BC, while returning to the Persian homeland to quell a rebellion of the priestly Magi, Cambyses died of an apparently self-inflicted wound. His short reign would be remembered by his enemies for its brutality and madness.

Prexaspes, who commanded the Persian left at Pelusium, died in the political upheaval surrounding the rebellion of the Magi.

Young Darius, son of Hystapes, *arshtibara* to the King, commander of the vanguard at Gaza and the Persian right at Pelusium, seized the throne from the rebellious Magi. He would achieve lasting fame as Darius I, called the Great, most noble and civilized of all the Persian kings of the Achaemenid dynasty. The tale of his early years, the trilingual Behistun Inscription, is noticeably silent about his doings in Egypt.

Ladice, the Lady of Cyrene, was captured by the Persians. When Cambyses learned of her identity, he returned her to her family in Cyrene as a gesture of goodwill.

The priest Ujahorresnet was rewarded for his perfidy with such diverse titles as Chief Physician, Companion to the King, and Controller of the Palace. His funerary stela, now in the Vatican Museum, provides the best source for what followed during the Persian Invasion. In AD 1980, Czech archaeologists uncovered his tomb in the sands of Abusir.

History does not say what became of the Arabian slave-woman who dared to love a Phoenician general, nor have archaeologists uncovered a ruined chapel in the desert outside Pelusium (modern Tell Farama). It is as if they never existed . . .

THE END

ON PRONUNCIATION AND SPELLING

Ancient Egyptian is a dead language, unspoken for at least two thousand years. As such, there is no consensus among scholars on how it might have been pronounced. Linguists have taken some clues from Coptic – the last stage of Egyptian, developed in the Common Era after Egypt became a Christian country – but even that is inexact. Hieroglyphs and hieratic texts are of little help in deciphering the verbal language, since they only reflect the consonants present in each word. Take, for instance, Canopic jars. In transliterated Egyptian (assigning Roman letters to the sounds represented by hieroglyphs), they are called /qby n wt/, which I have chosen to render into English as 'qabi-en-wet'. The letter 'e' is used in place of unknown vowels, a rule of thumb accepted by most Egyptologists. Unfortunately, I know of no accepted source that translates Egyptian phonetically into English for ease of pronunciation.

The Greek in *Men of Bronze* is presented using a mix of Roman and traditional spellings, with a few Anglicized versions thrown in (*Athens* in place of *hai Athenai*). As with Egyptian, no agreement exists among scholars on how Greek should best be cited to a modern audience. I have chosen a mixture accessible to most readers while still maintaining the flavour of the original languages.

GLOSSARY

Ahuramazda: Persian god who, with Anahita and Mithras, led the forces of Light against that of Darkness (called 'the Lie'). To the Persians, Ahuramazda was the Creator, responsible for the earth, the sky, and man. In his *Histories*, Herodotus notes the essentials of Persian religion, that they had no statues or temples, that they sacrificed to their trio of gods on mountain tops and high places, and that they held fire, earth, and running water sacred. The Greeks likened Ahuramazda to their own Zeus.

Alilat: A goddess of the Arabians often identified with Greek Athena. She was a divinity of the night sky.

Amemait: The Devourer. With the hindquarters of a hippopotamus, the foreparts of a lion and the head of a crocodile, this creature haunted the Egyptian underworld, ready to consume those souls whose hearts could not balance the **Scales of Justice** (q.v.). Such utter destruction of the soul was a real fear to many Egyptians.

Amon: An Egyptian god of the district of **Thebes** (q.v.) who rose to pre-eminence during the New Kingdom

(1550–1069 BCE). Amon co-opted the attributes of the sun god, Ra, and as Amon-Ra became the centre of a vast state cult whose temporal power often rivalled that of Pharaoh himself. Artists normally depicted Amon as a handsome young man wearing a headdress with two plumes, or as a horned ram (a symbol of power and fertility).

amphorae: (sing. *amphora.*) Large, two-handled pottery vessels used to store and transport liquids such as wine and olive oil, or dry goods like wheat. They were ubiquitous in the Greco-Egyptian world.

Anat: An Asiatic fertility goddess.

Anshan: A city in the province of Persis, near Shiraz in modern Iran. From Anshan, Cyrus led the Persians in the conquest of Media to the northeast, Lydia and the kingdoms of Asia Minor, and the failing juggernaut of Babylon in Mesopotamia. Though they ruled from the great cities to the east, the kings of Persia always honoured Anshan as the heart of their empire.

Anubis: (Egyptian *Anpu.*) The jackal-headed Egyptian god of mortuary rituals. It was Anubis who guided the dead through the underworld to the **Halls of Judgement** (q.v.).

apadana: A Persian audience hall, and often the focal point of court life at the palace of the King of Kings.

Apophis: A serpent of Egyptian myth, personifying the evil that lurked just outside the confines of well-ordered society. Apophis was the enemy of the sun god, Ra, who attacked the god's solar barque every night as it travelled through the underworld to the Place of the Dawn. On days bereft of sun, either through storms or eclipse, the Egyptians believed Apophis had triumphed over Ra. The serpent's victories, though, were always short-lived.

Aramaic: A Semitic language developed by the nomadic Aramaeans from the 11th to the 8th centuries BCE. Its use spread through Syria and Mesopotamia until it became the lingua franca of the Near East. So widespread was it that the Persians adopted Aramaic as the official language of their empire.

arshtibara: A title (Persian 'spear-bearer') used to denote an individual who is held in high regard, either through birth or deed, by the King. Scholars are unsure if the title meant literally that the recipient carried the King's spear. I have adopted it here as an honorific indicative of high standing.

Ba'al: Chief god of the Phoenicians.

Bitter Lakes: Series of shallow, salty lakes on the eastern border of Egypt, following the general course of the modern Suez Canal. The area of the Bitter Lakes was a favourite entry point into Egypt for the Bedouin of Sinai; Egypt's response was to build the fortress system known as the **Walls of the Ruler** (q.v.). Around 610 BCE, Pharaoh Nekau began construction of a canal that would link the Nile with the Red Sea via the Vale of **Tumilat** (q.v.) and the Bitter Lakes. The project remained unfinished. According to Herodotus, an oracle warned Pharaoh that his labour would be 'to the foreigners' advantage'. He ceased, turning his attentions to war, instead. Years later, the oracle's predictions came true. King Darius of Persia finished the canal in a fraction of the time it would normally have taken.

Book of the Dead: A collection of spells and incantations designed to aid the deceased on how best to navigate the pitfalls of the afterlife. Once available only to aristocrats, inscribed on the walls of their tombs, by the Late Period copies of the *Book of the Dead* were universally available to rich and poor alike. Scribes wrote them on papyrus, in **hieratic** (q.v.), and they included illustrations of the journey through the underworld, passwords enabling souls to avoid the guardian creatures, protestations of innocence, and magical formulae to provide comfort and security in the afterlife.

Byblos: City on the Phoenician coast, at the foot of the Lebanon Mountains.

calendar, Egyptian: The Egyptians divided their calendar into three seasons, each with four months of thirty days with five days added at the end of the year to commemorate the births of the gods. The seasons and their months were as follows: *Akhet*, the season of the **Inundation** (q.v.) of the Nile, heralded by the rising of the star the Egyptians called Sopdu (Sirius, the Dog Star), which corresponds to the middle of our July. The months of *Akhet* were Thoth (the first month of the Egyptian year), Paopi, Athyr, and Khoiak. *Peret*, the season of sowing, when the land emerged from the waters of the Inundation and crops were planted. The months of *Peret* were Tybi, Mekhir, Pnamenoth, and Pharmuthi. *Shemu*, the harvest season, corresponding to our own summer, was a time of great festivals and celebrations, provided the crops were bountiful. The months of *Shemu* were Pakhons, Paoni, Epep, and Mesore. The Egyptians numbered their years from the beginning of each Pharaoh's reign (our 526 BCE was the 44th year of Pharaoh Ahmose's reign).

Canopic jars: Called *qabi en wet* in Egyptian (loosely translated, it means 'jars of flesh'), Canopic jars are containers used in the mortuary rituals to hold the viscera of the deceased after embalming. The vessels were squat in design and made from a variety of materials: pottery, **faience** (q.v.), wood, or stone, depending on their owner's wealth. A set contained four jars, each with a carved stopper representing one of the four Sons of **Horus** (q.v.) – human-headed Imsety, who presided over the liver; baboon-headed Hapy, who protected the lungs; jackal-headed Duamutef, guardian of the stomach; and hawk-headed Qebehsenuef, who ruled the intestines. The respective organs were removed during embalming, dried in natron (a natural dehydrating agent), wrapped, and placed in their jars to be entombed alongside the mummy.

Corinthian helmet: The standard helmet of the Greek **hoplite** (q.v.) from the early 7th century BCE onwards. Beaten from a single sheet of bronze, this helmet covered the entire head, leaving only eye sockets and a narrow slit for breathing. One variation, called the Chalcidian helmet, included cutaways over the ears to facilitate better hearing on the battlefield. Both styles had a removable crest of coloured horsehair. Against non-Greeks, the Corinthian helmet gave hoplites a serious psychological advantage: it rendered its wearer faceless; the expressionless bronze mask hid any fears or anxieties that might plague the man beneath.

Croesus: (Greek Kroisos.) Last king of Lydia, Croesus reigned from c. 560–546 BCE, and allied himself with Egypt, Babylon, and Sparta against the rising might of Persia. Even in the ancient world, the name of Croesus was synonymous with vast wealth. His went toward patronage of the arts, monumental building, and influencing lesser rulers on his borders. Stories of Croesus fired the imagination of Herodotus, who included the eastern despot in his *Histories* as an example of disastrous pride. One such story tells how Croesus consulted the oracle at **Delphi** (q.v.) and was advised that if he crossed the Halys River against Persia, he would destroy a mighty empire. Wrapped in the blanket of divine revelation, Croesus marched. The prophecy proved correct – his own empire fell to the Persians in 546 BCE.

crook and flail: The two most important insignias of the Pharaohs, said to have been given to them by the god **Osiris** (q.v.). The crook represented Pharaoh's role as guardian of the people, their shepherd and protector; the flail symbolized his role as provider (flails were used to winnow grain).

Cyrus: (Persian Kurush; Greek Kuros.) Persian conqueror who ruled from 559–530 BCE. Cyrus turned the semi-nomadic people of the southwestern Iranian plateau into one of the four greatest nations of his day

(Egypt, Babylon, and Lydia being the other three). With methodical sureness, he excised his enemies until only Persia remained as a power in the East. Despite his expansionist policies, Cyrus was a benevolent ruler, praised in the Old Testament book of Isaiah and by later Greek philosophers for his wisdom and foresight. Cyrus died in 530 BCE while campaigning against the Massagetae, a Scythian tribe living around the Caspian Sea. He was succeeded by his eldest son, Cambyses.

Delphi: A famous sanctuary of Apollo in central Greece. Situated on a terraced spur of Mount Parnassus, the site was thought to be the centre of the world and served as a neutral meeting place for the surrounding Greek city-states. It derived greater renown, though, from its oracle, the Pythia. Deep inside the temple of Apollo, this priestess would sit on a bronze tripod above a chasm in the rock that spewed a 'prophetic' vapour. An attendant would whisper the petitioner's written question to her, and she would go into a trance and provide the god's answer through cryptic exclamations, which a board of priests then rendered into hexameter verse. The examples of Delphic responses that have survived to modern times are so vague and nonsensical that the whole enterprise smacks of fraud. Still, the oracle attracted a throng of pilgrims and seekers of wisdom from all over the known world. See **Croesus.**

Edom: North Arabian kingdom bordering the **Negev Desert** (q.v.) and tributary to **Kedar** (q.v.). Edom's borders, at times, reached as far north as the shores of the Dead Sea. It encompassed parts of modern Jordan and Israel.

Elath: A trading city at the head of the Gulf of Aqaba, between Sinai and Arabia. Elath was built on the site of biblical Ezion-geber, described in 1 Kings 9:26–28 as the place from whence King Solomon launched his fleets into the Red Sea.

Elysium: A place in the Greek afterlife where the gods allowed heroes to dwell. They envisioned it as a cool, well-watered garden full of pleasure and earthly delights, a sharp contrast to the grim moors of **Tartarus** (q.v.).

faience: Called *tjehenet* by the Egyptians, faience was a ceramic substance made from powdered quartz with a vitreous, alkaline glaze (similar in composition to ancient glass). It was widely used in the production of jewellery, vessels, and figurines. By far the most common colours of faience were blue, blue-green, and green, though other shades were possible.

Fates: (Greek *Moirai*, sing. *Moira*.) Three goddesses of Greek myth who preordained the course of human life and events. They were regarded as women engaged in the act of spinning. Clotho drew out the stuff of life from thread of infinite variety. She passed it, then, to Lachesis who measured it however she saw fit. Last, Atropos cut the thread, handling her shears as deftly for a slave as for a king. Not even Zeus could change the course of fate once the *Moirai* had spun it.

First Servant of the God/Goddess: The title of the highest Egyptian priest attached to a particular deity, often translated as High Priest. Though technically only Pharaoh could offer sacrifices and liturgies to the gods, the First Servants were 'deputized' to act on Pharaoh's behalf. This spiritual commission carried with it great temporal power, and offered endless opportunities for self-enrichment and corruption.

Furies: In Greek religion, the Furies (Greek *Erinyes*) were spirits of vengeance and retribution, horrible apparitions who tormented those who had broken the bonds of society, but especially those guilty of murdering a family member. The devout sought to placate the Furies by offering sacrifices to them under the euphemistic title of the *Eumenides* (Greek 'kindly ones').

Gardens of Amenti: The dwelling place of **Osiris** (q.v.), Lord of the Dead, in the far West. Once the deceased had proven himself by traversing the underworld to the **Halls of Judgement** (q.v.), and provided his heart could balance the **Scales of Justice** (q.v.), he was allowed entry into the Gardens of Amenti where he would experience eternal life, happiness, and plenty – an Egyptian's ultimate spiritual aspiration.

Gold of Valour: An honour given by Pharaoh to soldiers who display courage and fortitude in battle.

Halls of Judgement: If the spirit of a deceased Egyptian survived the treacherous journey through the underworld, he or she would enter a great hall where **Osiris** (q.v.), flanked by **Isis** (q.v.) and Nephthys, sat in judgement. In a great flurry of spiritual activity, the deceased had to address a tribunal of forty-two minor gods by name and recite a list of crimes, declaring himself innocent of each. At the same time, Anubis weighed the deceased's heart against the feather of **Ma'at** (q.v.). If the heart balanced, or was lighter than the feather, Osiris allowed the spirit entry into the afterlife. If the deceased's heart proved heavier than the feather, though, it was thrown to Amemait, the Devourer, and utterly destroyed.

Hathor: An Egyptian goddess popular throughout the nation's long history. Hathor was the protectress of women and the patron of love and joy, song and dance. When threatened, though, Hathor could be as ferocious as a lioness protecting her young. Artists depicted the goddess as a woman with cows' ears or as a cow.

hem-netjer: (Egyptian 'god's servant'.) Egyptian priests of the lower rank. The *hem-netjer* were allowed access to the inner sanctuary as part of their allotted duties.

hieratic: (Greek *hieratikos,* 'priestly'.) A cursive form of hieroglyphic Egyptian used in day-to-day writing. It was regularly employed for business documents, legal texts, letters, and records. Hieratic was written on papyrus with a reed brush.

hieroglyphs: (Greek *hieros gluphe,* 'sacred carvings'.) The pictorial writing of the ancient Egyptians that was as much an artistic medium as it was a way of imparting knowledge. Though developed some time before 3100 BCE, the hieroglyphic symbols and signs remained comparatively unchanged for three and a half millennia. Ancient Egyptian was based on a consonantal alphabet of twenty-four characters (vowels were never written), bearing more than a passing similarity to such Semitic language alphabets as Arabic.

Hieroglyphic writing combined signs that represented an object or concept (called an ideogram) with signs that represented alphabetic sounds (called a phonogram); single signs could combine as many as two, three or four consonants, and there were signs called determinatives that hinted at the meaning of a word. Still, despite their apparent chaos, hieroglyphs were concise and strictly regulated as to grammar and syntax. They could be written in rows and read from either direction, or columns and read from top to bottom. The symbols representing human or animal figures normally faced toward the beginning of an inscription. Hieroglyphs, as their name implies, were reserved for religious texts, monumental inscriptions, or as part of the decorative scheme for a tomb. See **hieratic**.

hoplites: The heavy infantrymen of the Greek world, hoplites began their history as part-time citizen-soldiers; men up to middle age who could afford the cost of arms and armour were required to serve as a condition of citizenship in many city-states. They trained in early spring for the summer campaign season, then disbanded and returned home for the harvest and winter. Hoplites derived their name from *hopla*, a Greek word for their heavy offensive and defensive equipment: a circular oak-and-bronze shield – called an *aspis* (pl. *aspides*) – weighing close to twenty pounds, a bronze breastplate, greaves, **Corinthian helmet** (q.v.), a stout eight-foot spear, and an iron sword. All told, the *hopla* weighed in at sixty to seventy pounds. Nothing quite like it existed anywhere else in the Mediterranean, and foreign rulers were quick to capitalize on that fact by hiring Greek mercenaries to fight their wars. The hoplites serving in Egypt, the Men of Bronze, were drawn mainly from the Aegean islands and the coast of Asia Minor (Ionia and Caria). See *panoplia* and **phalanx**.

Horus: The falcon-headed son of Isis and Osiris who personified the might and majesty of Pharaoh. Horus battled **Seth** (q.v.) for the right to rule the world of the living, and their ceaseless enmity epitomized the struggle between light and dark, good and evil. Despite losing an eye in combat, Horus proved ultimately victorious and became *Horu-Sema-Tawy* to the Egyptians – Horus, Uniter of the Two Lands. See *uadjet*.

House of Life: (Egyptian *Per-Ankh*.) An institution in Egyptian society that is poorly understood by modern scholars. On the surface, the House of Life served as a scriptorium, a training ground for scribes, and a depository for religious and secular texts. But it was also a place where leading priests and scholars conducted research – astronomical, medical, and magical – and a focal point for higher learning. Little is known of its organization or bureaucracy; even its associations with the temples is vague, but it is possible that one existed in every town of any size. In *Men of Bronze*, I have assigned an additional task to the House of Life by making it the administrative nerve centre of Pharaoh's army, a rallying point for the scribes, physicians, and priests of the battle train.

hypostyle hall: Greek term for a room containing numerous pillars. In Egyptian architecture, it is applied to the forest of stone columns between the open courts and the inner sanctum of a temple. In most eras, the columns were carved and painted to resemble lotus or papyrus stalks, symbolizing the vegetation that grew around the primordial Mound of Creation, which was itself represented by the inner sanctuary.

Ineb-hedj: 'The White Walls'. Egyptian name for the fortress at Memphis.

Inundation: The annual flooding of the Nile caused by rains in the highlands of tropical Africa. Upriver, at Aswan, the flood began in late June; it reached Memphis by the end of September, crested, and receded by the following April. The floods brought rich black silt to the fields, renewing their ability to produce crops. The Inundation varied from year to year; too low a flood meant famine, too high brought devastation and loss of life to the villages along the riverbank. A whole corps of priests were devoted to keeping meticulous watch on water levels, offering sacrifices to Hapi, patron god of the Nile, and praying for a perfect Inundation.

Isis: (Egyptian *Eset.*) The most beloved goddess of the ancient Egyptian pantheon, whose cult survived into Greek and Roman times. Isis was the archetypical wife and mother, a healer and nurturer who also possessed formidable powers of magic, which she used in the service of mankind. She was depicted in temple reliefs as a woman wearing either a throne on her head (the spelling of her name in Egyptian), or a sun disc set between the horns of a cow.

Iunu: (Egyptian 'Pillar') An Egyptian city northeast of Memphis, the cult centre for the worship of **Ra** (q.v.). The Greeks knew it as Heliopolis. It is located in a suburb of modern Cairo.

ka: An individual's spirit or life force that left the body at the moment of death and made the journey through the underworld to the **Halls of Judgement** (q.v.), seeking immortality. Once the *ka* achieved entry into the **Gardens of Amenti** (q.v.), it still maintained a vital link to its preserved body. It could return to the tomb and partake of the offerings of family and loved ones, the gifts of food and drink, the adornments and pleasure items; or, the *ka* could activate the *ushabti* (q.v.) figures to comply with whatever demands the gods might make on the deceased.

Kedar: The ancient name of the north Arabian desert, as far south as Yathrib (modern Medina). The rulers of Kedar grew wealthy off the incense trade with south Arabia. At the time of *Men of Bronze*, Kedar was nominally under Egyptian suzerainty, though in reality it operated as an independent principality. The story of their pact with Persia is given in Herodotus, III 7–9.

Khnum: (Egyptian 'Moulder'.) The ram-headed god of the island of **Yeb** (q.v.), near Egypt's border with Nubia. It was Khnum, according to myth, who shaped humanity from clay on his potter's wheel. Artists depicted Khnum as a ram-headed man with corkscrew horns, wearing plumes, the solar disk and *uraeus* (q.v.).

krypteia: A Spartan institution, the *krypteia* functioned as a kind of secret police, ritualistically terrorizing the vast number of slaves ('helots') that comprised the Spartan state. Their murders were condoned each year in a formal declaration of war against the helots.

Lake Serbonis: A lagoon east of the Nile Delta whose waters are foul and salty. According to Herodotus, Lake Serbonis was home to the serpent-headed giant, Typhon.

Ma'at: An Egyptian goddess who personified truth, justice, and cosmic order. In the mortuary rituals, Anubis weighed the spirit of the deceased against a feather belonging to Ma'at. Tomb and temple scenes depicted her as a winged woman wearing an ostrich-feather headdress.

ma'at: The ethical and moral cornerstone of Egyptian society. The philosophy of *ma'at* evolved from the worship of the goddess of the same name, and it embodied the idea that for an Egyptian to become part of the cosmic order after death, he or she had to take responsibility for acting with reasonable behaviour, according to the laws of the cosmos, while alive. That meant quietude, piety, cooperation, and duty to the gods, to Pharaoh, and to their fellow man. *Ma'at* gave Egyptians a sense of security in an often chaotic world.

machimoi: The Greek name for the native Egyptian warrior class. Only about ten thousand, known as the Veterans, formed the standing army; the rest were militia, men who could be called upon to meet the needs of a specific campaign. Even when not under arms, the *machimoi* were a potent political force, capable of disrupting royal authority. The mercenaries, specifically the Greek Men of Bronze, often acted on Pharaoh's behalf to counter the power of the *machimoi*.

Mansion of the Spirit of Ptah: (Egyptian *Hiku-Ptah.*) The sprawling temple of **Ptah** (q.v.), chief deity of Memphis, that the Greeks likened to their own Hephaestus. Pharaohs of all dynasties, even during times of foreign rule, added their mark to the temple by refurbishing or adding anew to an already dizzying array of monumental pylons, obelisks, minor temples, chapels, and statues. Unfortunately, very little remains of this great structure, or of the city around it. What the Nile did not erode away, the builders of Cairo's palaces and mosques scavenged. By all accounts, though, the Mansion of the Spirit of Ptah rivalled in size the temple of Amon at **Thebes** (q.v.).

Men of Bronze: A phrase used by the Egyptians to denote their mercenary soldiers, particularly the Greek heavy infantry. It originated during the reign of Wahibre Psammetichus (Greek: Psammis), first Pharaoh of the Twenty-sixth Dynasty (664–525 BCE). According to Herodotus, Wahibre Psammetichus sent to the oracle at Buto for advice on how best to unite Egypt under his aegis and was told in reply that aid would come from the sea, whence men of bronze would appear. He considered this unlikely, but not long after a contingent of raiders from Ionia and Caria landed on Egypt's coast, victims of bad weather. In their bronze armour, Wahibre Psammetichus saw the oracle fulfilled. He befriended the Greeks and took them into his service, where they proved invaluable allies in the reunification of Egypt.

Mt Casius: A promontory between **Lake Serbonis** (q.v.) and the Mediterranean; more of a hill than a mountain.

Nabonidus: (Chaldean Nabu-na'id.) The last king of Babylon, who ruled from 555–538 BCE. Nabonidus was a general in the army of the late king Nebuchadnezzar, a respected statesman and antiquarian, who assumed the throne after a year of rebellion and misrule. His own reign was anything but smooth. He forsook Babylon and, for reasons unknown, spent ten years building a new capital at the oasis of Taima, in northwest Arabia. The Dead Sea Scrolls describe Nabonidus' sojourn in the desert as an illness caused by divine wrath, but whatever the cause, its effect was disastrous. Persia's power grew unchecked, Lydia fell, and **Cyrus** (q.v.) set his sights on Babylon itself. Nabonidus, now likely well into his seventh decade, returned to Babylon in 538 BCE, in time to watch it fall uncontested into Persian hands. Cyrus' followers captured and killed the ageing Chaldean king.

Negev Desert: An inhospitable region of hills, plateaus and desert stretching from the **Shara Mountains** (q.v.) in the west to **Sinai** (q.v.) and the borders of Egypt. It was considered inaccessible by all save the nomadic Bedouin, whose *shaykhs* (q.v.) gained a sense of power and prestige from control of the caravan routes linking the Mediterranean with the incense fields of south Arabia. To pass, merchants had to pay homage to a collection of self-styled kings who operated as little more than robber-barons. By the 6th century BCE, however, much of the Negev lay under the thumb of the Arabian kings of **Kedar** (q.v.).

Neith: (Egyptian *Nit*.) The patron goddess of Sais, in the Nile Delta, and protectress of the kings of the Twenty-sixth Dynasty (664–525 BCE). Neith's cult dated to the predynastic era, and over the centuries her roles have changed to fit the times – from mother of Sobek and a goddess of nurturing to the patroness of weavers to a goddess of the hunt and of warfare. In all her guises, though, Neith's dominance in the Saite region remained unquestioned.

Nekhebet: The vulture-goddess, patroness and guardian of Upper Egypt and protector of the king. The image of a vulture's head was often worn with the *uraeus* (q.v.), signifying Pharaoh's lordship over Upper and Lower Egypt.

nemes: The striped cloth headdress of the Egyptian pharaohs; it is worn with the *uraeus* (q.v.).

Nesaean stallion: A breed of horse from Media favoured by Persian kings and noblemen. They were the consummate war horses, bred for strength and stamina as well as sheer equestrian beauty.

Nilometer: A device used to gauge the height of the Nile's flood each year. The rate of rise enabled area officials to predict periods of scarcity or of plenty, and gave them the ability to assess taxes on crops well in advance of harvest. Nilometers could take the form of a marked pillar driven into the river bed or a flight of steps cut into the bank (sometimes both).

obelisk: (From Greek *obelos*, 'spit'; Egyptian *tekhenu*.) A large four-sided pillar tapering toward its top, which was carved into a small pyramid. Obelisks were staples of temple architecture and considered sacred to the solar deities of Egypt. Their surfaces were adorned with hieroglyphs, their pyramid tips sheathed in gold.

Osiris: Perhaps the most important god of the Egyptian pantheon, Osiris ruled the underworld where he served as the chief judge of the deceased, but he also represented fertility and renewed life. Though this duality made his position in Egyptian religion complex, it highlighted the simple concept behind all of Egypt's elaborate mortuary rituals: that from death there is life. Osiris was the template for all of their notions of life, death, and rebirth, and he was the conduit through which immortality of the soul could be achieved. In tomb carvings, artists depicted Osiris as a mummified figure wearing a tall, plumed crown adorned with a *uraeus* (q.v.), and holding the twin symbols of sovereignty, the **crook and flail** (q.v.).

ostraka: (Greek 'shards'; sing. ostrakon.) Fragments of pottery or stone that functioned much like modern notepads. Ancient Egyptians used ostraka for sketches, memos, letters, and bits of writing too transitory to be committed to a more expensive medium, such as papyrus.

Palestine: (Egyptian *Retjenu*; Persian *Abarnahara*, 'Beyond the [Euphrates] River.') The ancient designation for the area between the Mediterranean coast, the desert of northern Arabia, and the Euphrates River, at times known as the Levant or Syria (not to be confused with the modern Middle Eastern nation). Palestine was a collection of fractious kingdoms, forever at war with one another unless cowed by one of the dominant superpowers of the era. The Pharaohs of Egypt's Twenty-sixth Dynasty (664–525 BCE) cultivated the region as a buffer between their borders and those of Persia and Babylon.

panoplia: (Greek 'war gear'.) One of the many terms used by the Greeks to describe a complete set of armour and weapons. The *panoplia* of the average **hoplite** (q.v.) of the 6th century BCE included: a **Corinthian helmet** (q.v.), a bronze breastplate, bronze greaves to cover the leg from the knee down, a leather kilt reinforced with bronze studs, a bowl-shaped shield some three feet in diameter, a six-to-eight-foot-long spear, and a sword. The whole ensemble weighed close to seventy pounds, and though it afforded its wearer an unheard of level of protection, a man in full *panoplia* wasn't invulnerable; he could still receive fatal wounds in the neck, groin, and thigh.

papyrus: (Egyptian *djet.*) The papyrus plant (Latin *Cyperus papyrus*) grew in abundance in the Nile valley and the marshes of the Delta, where it was used in the manufacture of rope, matting, baskets, sandals, and small boats. Its most celebrated use, though, was as a writing surface. Because papyrus was expensive to produce, it was reserved for religious texts and more important secular documents.

peltasts: Originally, the term 'peltast' applied only to Thracian tribesmen who fought in their native dress – cloak, boots, a fox skin cap, javelins, and a wicker-work shield called a *peltai* – but it became a generic catch-all term for any lightly armed infantry, including archers. Greek generals often employed peltasts to guard the vulnerable flanks of their **phalanx** (q.v.), or as skirmishers against enemy infantry and cavalry. See **hoplites**.

phalanx: A formation of heavily armed and armoured infantry, of variable length and usually a minimum of eight men deep, designed to decimate enemy soldiers through collision and shock (Greek *othismos*). **Hoplites** (q.v.) in a phalanx stood shoulder to shoulder, their shields interleaved, with the first three ranks of spears levelled to present a veritable hedge of cornel-wood and iron. They advanced to the music of flutes and horns, increasing speed as they neared their target; by the moment of impact, the phalanx was often moving at a run. This collision could obliterate a lesser armed force. Though dangerous to face, a phalanx was by no means invulnerable. The formation could withstand cavalry attacks, but it was too slow to be a threat to massed horsemen. Also, the unshielded right flank of the phalanx was particularly susceptible to attack. Phalanx battles seldom lasted more than an hour or two.

Pharaoh: (Egyptian *Per-a'a*.) The title of Egypt's king, though originally the word signified the royal residence (much as modern Americans use 'the White House' when referring to the President). Pharaoh was considered a living god, an embodiment of **Horus** (q.v.) and the literal son of **Ra** (q.v.). Like his brother and sister gods, Pharaoh was responsible for creating order from chaos. To make his will a reality, a vast bureaucracy grew around the throne, scribes and courtiers, priests and generals, all ideally working for the good of the land, for the good of Pharaoh, and for the good of the gods. This system of government worked only while the king could assert his authority. Weak pharaohs brought on the rapid dissolution of centralized power, and the inevitable civil wars as their successors sought to reestablish control.

Pillars of Herakles: The ancient name for the Straits of Gibraltar, linking the Mediterranean with the Atlantic Ocean.

polemarch: Greek term for an officer in command of an army. In *Men of Bronze*, it is used to denote the rank directly beneath that of *strategos* (q.v.).

Precepts of Ptah-hotep: A didactic (or wisdom) manuscript dating to the Fifth Dynasty (2494–2345 BCE), which remained popular throughout Egypt's history. Ptah-hotep, a vizier and sage, extolled those virtues the gods find most pleasing: modesty, humility, truthfulness, self-control, tact, and basic good manners. His *Precepts* offered advice on how best to deal with one's inferiors, peers, and superiors while remaining true to the spirit of *ma'at*.

Ptah: The patron god of craftsmen, whom the Greeks identified with their own Hephaestus, held by the people of Memphis to have created the world, bringing it into being by thought and word alone. For the Egyptians, the heart contained the source of all intellect, which the tongue then articulated to make real. Ptah, by reciting a litany of names, produced Egypt, from its gods to its smallest grains of sand. The subtlety of Ptah's cosmogony made him somewhat obscure to the average Egyptian, whose understanding of the universe was limited to what they could see around them. Statues depicting Ptah showed an enigmatic man in the wrappings of a mummy, wearing a broad collar and holding the sceptre of power.

pylons: (Egyptian *bekhnet.*) The twin-towered gateways set into the walls of Egyptian temples, often decorated with carvings and reliefs of the gods and Pharaoh. The pylons mimicked the shape of the hieroglyph representing the horizon, the *akhet*, symbolizing the removal of the temple's sacred heartland from the physical world. They also served the more mundane function of guarding access to the temple grounds. A single temple could boast numerous pylons, each named for the ruler who ordered it built. The ruins of Amon's temple at **Thebes** (q.v.), Egypt's largest existing religious structure, has twelve.

Ra: Egypt's primary solar deity, who absorbed the attributes of many lesser gods before becoming fused with **Amon** (q.v.) by a process called syncretism. Ra, and later Amon-Ra, regulated the passing of hours, days, and years; seasons were his domain, and his energy and light made all life possible. During the Old Kingdom (2686–2125 BCE) it became widely accepted that Egypt's kings were the physical sons of Ra, a concept that remained constant throughout the nation's history. The god took many forms, from a solar disc to a sacred beetle (scarab) to a man with the head of a falcon. Ra's cult centre was at **Iunu** (q.v.).

royal titular: The formal, five part name used by Pharaoh to signify his connection to the gods and his divine purpose. The parts of the titular were: the *Horus* name, linking Pharaoh as the true representative of Horus on earth; the *Nebti*, or Two Ladies, name; the *Golden Horus* name, signifying Pharaoh's divinity; the *Nisut-Bit* name, often preceded by the phrase 'King of Upper and Lower Egypt', was the first *cartouche* name (Latin *praenomen*) and it was given to the king at coronation; finally, the *Si-Ra* name, 'Beloved of Ra', the second *cartouche* name (Latin *nomen*) and often the king's own birth name. When expressed as a whole, the royal titular and its related epithets formed a kind of litany describing Pharaoh's strengths and the intended direction of his reign.

Sacred Flame: A primary component in the worship of the Persian god **Ahuramazda** (q.v.) was fire. The Sacred Flame, the light of divine Ahuramazda, was the ultimate expression of purity; nothing could be obscured in its glow, and the powers of Darkness, called 'the Lie' could not suffer to be in its presence. The Sacred Flame accompanied the king on his travels and expeditions, along with a small army of priests to tend it, ensuring a constant link with the divine heart of the god.

Sah: The 'Fleet-Footed Long-Strider'; that constellation of stars known to the Greeks as Orion, the Huntsman.

Saqqara: The sprawling desert necropolis outside Memphis that has served as final resting place for kings and commoners throughout Egypt's long history. The Step Pyramid of Djoser dominates the area, the first Egyptian pyramid and one of the earliest stone buildings of its size in the world; countless other smaller pyramid complexes and mortuary temples surround it.

Humans weren't Saqqara's only inhabitants. Animals had their place, as well, from the tombs of the Apis bulls in the **Serapeum** (q.v.), to the mummified cats entombed in the eastern cliff-face (a site known today as Abwab el-Qotat, the Doorways of the Cats).

satrap: Persian term for the governor of a region whose power often approached that of a king. Indeed, many satraps were sovereigns before their lands were swallowed up by the Persians. Because of the exalted status of his underlings, the Persian monarch was referred to as the Great King or the King of Kings.

Scales of Justice: Located in the **Halls of Judgement** (q.v.), these gigantic scales were used by the god **Anubis** (q.v.) to weigh the heart of the deceased against the feather of **Ma'at** (q.v.), goddess of truth. A light or balanced heart guaranteed the deceased entry into the **Gardens of Amenti** (q.v.) and eternal bliss; a heavy heart meant utter destruction in the maw of **Amemait** (q.v.), who waited near the Scales to devour the wicked.

Sekhmet: The lion-headed goddess of fires and plagues. Egyptians in all eras regarded Sekhmet as violent and warlike, the personification of mankind's own vengeful nature. In myth, Amun-Ra sent her to punish humanity for their transgressions, through pestilence, famine, and outright slaughter. Once invoked, even the greatest of Egypt's gods found themselves hard-pressed to placate this powerful deity.

Sela: The one-time capital of ancient **Edom** (q.v.), Sela was at the heart of a series of easily-defensible gorges in the **Shara Mountains** (q.v.). The Arabian kings of **Kedar** (q.v.) drove the Edomites from Sela, leaving it open to occupation by tribes of semi-nomadic Nabatean Arabs. The site grew over time into an important trading centre on the caravan road linking the Mediterranean with the rich incense groves of south Arabia. We know the city today as Petra, in modern Jordan.

Serapeum: A tomb complex on the desert ridge overlooking Memphis, in the shadow of the famed Step Pyramid of Djoser, built specifically for the interment of the sacred Apis bull. The Apis bull was the living theophany of the Memphite triad, Ptah-Sokar-Osiris. Kept in royal splendour in the temple of **Ptah** (q.v.), when the bull died (after an average lifespan of eighteen years) the priests gave it a suitably royal funeral and conveyed it to its final resting place in the necropolis of **Saqqara** (q.v.). The Serapeum consisted of a series of underground vaults containing monolithic sarcophagi and all the attendant grave goods, such as **Canopic jars** (q.v.) and *ushabti* (q.v.), one would expect to find in a king's burial. Above ground, the Serapeum sported a sphinx-lined causeway and a mortuary temple.

Seth: (Egyptian *Sutekh.*) The villainous Lord of Confusion, murderer of **Osiris** (q.v.), usurper of the throne of Egypt, a god who haunted the desert regions and sent storms of sand, lightning, and thunder against the well-ordered heart of Egypt. Seth was the enemy of **Horus** (q.v.), personifying chaos and misrule against which the divine light of justice could flourish. One could not exist without the other; indeed, the Egyptians realized this and venerated Seth in their own way, albeit carefully. In reliefs, Seth was pictured as a man of forceful sexuality possessing the head of the mythical Typhonean animal – reminiscent of a jackal, but with short, blunt snout and slanted eyes.

shadouf: An irrigation device consisting of a bucket at the end of a long, counter-weighted pole, allowing a single person to dip water from the Nile and transfer it to a cistern, ditch, or canal. The *shadouf* was introduced into Egypt by Asiatic invaders during the Second Intermediate Period (1650–1550 BCE). Unchanged, it has lasted to the modern era.

Shara Mountains: A range of jagged mountains dividing Arabia from Palestine, in the heart of what was once **Edom** (q.v.). Today, the area is part of southwestern Jordan. See **Sela**.

shaykh: Archaic form of the Arabic title *sheikh*. Used here to denote the chieftain of a tribe of Bedouin.

Shedet: A city in the marshlands of the Faiyum, near Lake Moeris, Shedet served as the cult centre for the worship of **Sobek** (q.v.). The Greeks knew it as Crocodilopolis, the City of Crocodiles (modern Medinet el-Faiyum).

shenu: The carved oval that encircled the royal names of Pharaoh, found on carvings, paintings, sculpture, and papyri. The *shenu* represented Ra's eternal protection of the king. In modern Egyptology, the *shenu* is known as a *cartouche*.

Sile: A fortified town on Egypt's northeastern frontier, Sile was part of the chain of fortresses known as the **Walls of the Ruler** (q.v.). Its location north of the vale of **Tumilat** (q.v.) made it the perfect base of operations for the Medjay, who could patrol the surrounding desert for signs of Bedouin raiders while guarding Tumilat's valuable springs and cisterns. Because of its Medjay garrison, Sile had a reputation for being rough-and-tumble.

Sinai: The desolate peninsula on Egypt's eastern border that served as a buffer with **Palestine** (q.v.). Mountainous inland and fading to rocky desert on its edges, the Sinai provided abundant mineral reserves – notably turquoise, copper, and tin – for the Egyptians to exploit. Clashes with the peninsula's Bedouin inhabitants were frequent, and the Egyptians often mounted punitive expeditions to re-establish control over the region's mines and quarries.

Sobek: An ancient Egyptian crocodile god considered one of the first beings to emerge from the watery chaos, called *Nun*, at the moment of creation. At **Shedet** (q.v.), in the Faiyum, the centre of the worship of Sobek, crocodiles were held to be sacred. In other regions, though, priests ritually slaughtered the animals, equating Sobek with **Seth** (q.v.), the Lord of Confusion. In art, the Egyptians depicted Sobek either as a crocodile or as a man with a crocodile's head.

Sokar: The god of the necropolis at Memphis, worshipped in conjunction with **Ptah** (q.v.) and **Osiris** (q.v.) since the Old Kingdom (2686–2125 BCE). In some reliefs, Sokar is represented as a heavy-limbed dwarf attended by hawks; in others, as a mummiform figure with a hawk's head bearing crook, flail, and staff. See **Saqqara**.

Solar Barque of Ra: The great boat used by the sun god to traverse the sky; a poetic analogy for the sun.

sphinx: A statue of a recumbent lion with a human or animal head used in temple architecture as guardians over the processional paths and entryways leading to the shrine's heart. The human-headed sphinxes symbolized Pharaoh's power as a living god.

stelae: (Greek 'standing stone'; sing. *stela*. Egyptian *wedj*.) An inscribed stone often erected to commemorate an event or to mark a boundary. Mortuary stelae often recounted the achievements of the deceased.

strategos: Greek term for the general in command of an army.

Ta-Meht: The Egyptian name for the Nile Delta; synonymous with the ancient kingdom of Lower Egypt. Upper Egypt, to the south, was known as *Ta-Resu*.

Tartarus: A cold, grey region of the Greek afterlife where the souls of men and women dwelt while awaiting their turn to drink the waters of the river Lethe ('Forgetfulness'). Chasms dotted the landscape of Tartarus, and in their depths black Hades, god of the dead, meted out punishment to the wicked. See **Elysium**.

Temple of the Hearing Ear: A niche or series of niches, some quite elaborate, in the outer court of a temple where common Egyptians could address their prayers to the gods. In our modern conception, a temple was a place where suppliants could go to converse with the gods through prayer, meditation, and sacrifice; to the Egyptians, a temple was the dwelling place of the gods, and as such, they were off limits to all but high ranking priests and Pharaoh. Only the outer courts were open to commoners, and through the temple of the Hearing Ear they had indirect access to the inner sanctuary.

Thebes: (Egyptian *Waset*, modern Karnak and Luxor) A prominent city in Upper Egypt from the New Kingdom (1550–1069 BCE) onwards, and the centre of the worship of **Amon** (q.v.). Thebes was located on the Nile's eastern shore, roughly 500 miles south of Memphis and modern Cairo. It stood across the river from a vast necropolis containing, after the pyramids at Giza, some of Egypt's most stunning mortuary complexes, including the rock-cut tombs of the Valley of the Kings. Perhaps the city's greatest adornment, though, was the massive temple complex dedicated to Amon, called *Ipet-isut* (Egyptian 'Most Select of Places'), approximately 247 acres of shrines, temples, gardens, lakes, and chapels. Taken as a whole, *Ipet-isut* represents the largest religious structure ever built by the hand of man. Though the capital shifted north to Sais during the Late Period (664–332 BCE), Thebes remained a significant force in national politics.

Thoth: (Egyptian *Djehuty*.) The Egyptian god of learning and wisdom, patron of scribes and protector of the priest-physicians. Though normally depicted as an ibis-headed man, Thoth was also associated with the baboon and often assumed this form. The Greeks identified him with their own Hermes. His cult centre was in Upper Egypt, at the town of Khemenu (Greek Hermopolis, modern el-Ashmunein).

Tumilat: A fertile valley connecting the eastern Nile delta with the **Bitter Lakes** (q.v.) and the Red Sea. Its pools and springs presented a tempting target to the water-deprived Bedouin of **Sinai** (q.v.).

Tyre: Situated a few hundred yards off the Phoenician mainland, the city of Tyre occupied the two largest of a chain of islands, joined by an embankment and a mole to create a pair of excellent harbours. The basis of Tyre's vast maritime empire was the Lebanese cedar and the *murex*, a species of mollusc that, when boiled, produced a deep purple dye. Tyrian ships ranged the Mediterranean, trading dye and lumber for other commodities – from gold and silver to papyrus and ostrich feathers. Colonists from Tyre founded the north African city of Carthage, c. 814 BCE.

Uadj-Ur: (Egyptian 'Great Green'.) The Mediterranean Sea.

uadjet: (Egyptian 'healthy eye'.) The Eye of **Horus** (q.v.). Considered the most powerful talisman in ancient Egypt, the Eye symbolized protective strength, watchfulness, and the dominance of good over evil. In mythology, **Seth** (q.v.) plucked out Horus' left eye in battle as the latter sought to avenge the murder of his father, **Osiris** (q.v.). Once Horus was victorious, his mother, **Isis** (q.v.), restored his damaged eye.

uraeus: Golden image of the cobra-goddess Wadjet, her hood extended in warning, which was attached to the brow of royal crowns and headdresses. The cobra was expected to protect Pharaoh by spitting flames at any who would harm him.

ushabti: (Egyptian 'the Answerers'.) Small **faience** (q.v.) figurines intended to accompany the deceased on their various travels through the afterlife. They were expected to fulfil whatever responsibilities the gods might ask of the deceased, such as manual labour or errand-running. Most tombs included a full complement *of ushabti* – one for every day of the year plus extras to serve as overseers and managers – roughly four hundred figurines.

vizier: (Egyptian *tjaty*.) The chief minister of Egypt, answerable only to Pharaoh. The vizier controlled the food supply, the reservoirs, kept a census on herds, and arbitrated territorial disputes and personal conflicts among the governors of Egypt's provinces. At times, the vizier also controlled access to Pharaoh's person. The office virtually demanded a man of uncommon intelligence and zeal who could be trusted with the business of court; often, the post served as a training ground for royal princes (as well as the occasional queen or princess).

Walls of the Ruler: A series of fortresses along Egypt's eastern border designed to stem the influx of foreigners into the Nile valley. They were garrisoned by elements of the regular army, as well as the Medjay, whose patrol routes took them from Pelusium on the Mediterranean coast to the Gulf of Suez. The Walls of the Ruler were first erected in the Twelfth Dynasty (1985–1773 BCE).

War Crown: (Egyptian *khepresh.*) The bulbous blue helmet, made of electrum, worn by Pharaoh on campaigns and during military processions.

Way of Horus: The road connecting Egypt with southern Palestine. It begins at Pelusium in the eastern Delta and passes through **Sinai** (q.v.) and the **Negev Desert** (q.v.) before reaching Gaza. From there, it continues on into the Phoenician littoral.

Yeb: Known today as Elephantine Island, Yeb occupies the middle of the Nile near the First Cataract (one of six white-water rapids near the Nubian border), facing the modern city of Aswan. The ancient Egyptians considered the island to be of strategic importance; its fortress gave Pharaoh's troops command of the surrounding waterways. Yeb also served as the cult centre of the god **Khnum** (q.v.) and was the site of an important **Nilometer** (q.v.).

Zagros Mountains: A snow-capped mountain range in the heart of Media, its peaks rising to heights between twelve and fifteen thousand feet as it runs southeast from Mesopotamia. The summer capital of the Persian Empire, Ecbatana, lay in the Zagros Mountains, six thousand feet below the summit of Mount Alwand.

CHRONOLOGY

Early Dynastic Period: c. 3000–2686 BCE
  1st Dynasty: c.3000–2890 (King Menes unified Upper and Lower Egypt)
  2nd Dynasty: 2890–2686

Old Kingdom: 2686–2160 BCE
  3rd Dynasty: 2686–2613
  4th Dynasty: 2613–2494 (the Pyramids at Giza constructed)
  5th Dynasty: 2494–2345
  6th Dynasty: 2345–2181
  7th and 8th Dynasties: 2181–2160

First Intermediate Period: 2160–2055 BCE
  9th and 10th Dynasties: 2160–2125
  11th Dynasty (ruled only at Thebes): 2125-2055

Middle Kingdom: 2055–1650 BCE
  11th Dynasty (all Egypt): 2055–1985
  12th Dynasty: 1985–1773
  13th Dynasty: 1773–c. 1650
  14th Dynasty (contemporary with 13th Dynasty): 1773–1650

Second Intermediate Period: 1650–1550 BCE
  15th Dynasty (Hyksos): 1650–1550
  16th Dynasty (Minor Hyksos, contemporary with 15th Dynasty): 1650–1580
  17th Dynasty (Thebans, contemporary with 15th and 16th Dynasties): c. 1580–1550

New Kingdom: 1550–1069 BCE
  18th Dynasty: 1550–1295 (Egypt's 'Golden Age'; the Amarna Period; Tutankhamun)
  19th Dynasty: 1295–1186 (the Ramessids; Rameses II, the Great)
  20th Dynasty: 1186–1069

Third Intermediate Period: 1069–664 BCE
  21st Dynasty: 1069–945
  22nd Dynasty: 945–715
  23rd Dynasty (contemporary with late 22nd, 24th, and early 25th Dynasties): 818–715
  24th Dynasty: 720–715
  25th Dynasty: 747–656 (Nubian pharaohs; the Assyrian conquest)

Late Period: 664–332 BCE
  26th Dynasty: 664–525 (*Men of Bronze*)
  27th Dynasty (1st Persian Period): 525–404
  28th Dynasty: 404–399 (revolt against Persia)
  29th Dynasty: 399–380
  30th Dynasty: 380–343 (Egypt reconquered)
  31st Dynasty (2nd Persian Period): 343–332

TIMELINE OF EGYPT'S TWENTY-SIXTH DYNASTY AND THE NEAR EAST

Dates for Egyptian pharaohs and events used in *Men of Bronze* follow those given in: *The Oxford History of Ancient Egypt*, Ian Shaw, editor (Oxford University Press, 2000) and *Monarchs of the Nile*, Aidan Dodson (American University in Cairo Press, 2000). Greek dates are derived from: *Handbook to Life in Ancient Greece*, Lesley and Roy Adkins (Oxford University Press, 1997). Near Eastern dates are from: *Babylon*, Joan Oates (Thames and Hudson, 1979). All dates are BCE (Before Common Era).

667   Ashurbanipal of Assyria conquers the Nubian pharaohs of Egypt, paving the way for the rise of the Saite kings.

664   Wahibre Psammetichus (Greek: Psammis), a prince of Sais, seizes control of Egypt from the Assyrians and the Nubians; he becomes the first Pharaoh of the Twenty-sixth Dynasty. During his reign, Greek

mercenaries, the 'Men of Bronze', begin serving in the armies of Egypt.

c. 635   Lydia, in Asia Minor, is the first nation to coin money. The invention spreads rapidly through Greece and the Aegean.

c. 630   Greek colony of Cyrene founded in North Africa.

627   Death of the Assyrian king Ashurbanipal creates a power vacuum. Babylon revolts and the Medes of central Iran begin subjugating their neighbours.

616   Assyria's domination of the Near East is ended by the rise of the Chaldeans (Babylonians) under Nabopolassar. Along with their neighbours, the Medes, the Chaldeans begin the slow conquest of the known world. Political marriage between Nabopolassar's son, Nebuchadnezzar, and a Median princess cements an alliance between the two fledgling nations.

610   Wehemibre Nekau (Greek: Necos) becomes Pharaoh. He begins work on a canal from the Nile to the Red Sea; he sponsors the Phoenician Hanno's voyage around Africa. Nekau also resurrects the Medjay, now in the guise of foreign (non-Greek) mercenaries, to guard Egypt's eastern frontier. Babylon's rising power prompts Pharaoh to begin reasserting his interests in Palestine.

609	The (second) Battle of Megiddo. Pharaoh Nekau defeats a Jewish army under Josiah.
605	Pharaoh Nekau's forces crushed at Carchemish by Crown Prince Nebuchadnezzar of Babylon. Egypt relinquishes its hold over Palestine. Death of Nabopolassar.
604	Nebuchadnezzar ascends the throne of Babylon. Besides gaining renown as a war-leader and statesman, Nebuchadnezzar would be remembered for all time as the architect of the Hanging Gardens of Babylon, one of the Seven Wonders of the World (said to have been built to assuage his Median Queen's homesickness for the Zagros Mountains).
601	Babylon invades Egypt and is repulsed with heavy losses. In Palestine, the king of Judah, Jehoiakim, vacillates between casting his lot with Egypt or Babylon. The prophet Jeremiah counsels him to continue paying tribute to Nebuchadnezzar. Jehoiakim ignores him.
595	Neferibre Psammetichus becomes Pharaoh.
594	Egypt invades Nubia to the south and Palestine to the east, campaigns designed to discourage foreign invasion. They prove inconclusive.
593	Solon begins his programme of reforms at Athens.

589   Haaibre (Greek: Apries) becomes Pharaoh.

587   Jerusalem destroyed by Nebuchadnezzar, who deported its inhabitants to Babylon. Beginning of the Babylonian Captivity of the Jews.

586-573 Nebuchadnezzar lays siege to the Phoenician city of Tyre. Libyans ask Egypt for aid against the expansionist policies of Cyrene. Pharaoh Haaibre, not trusting his Greek mercenaries to fight other Greeks, marches with an army of *machimoi*, native militia, to Cyrene. He is defeated and forced back to Egypt.

570   Khnemibre Ahmose (Greek: Amasis), a general in the army of Haaibre, uses the reversal at Cyrene to usurp the throne; defeats Haaibre in battle near Memphis. Haaibre escapes and flees to the court of Nebuchadnezzar at Babylon. Ahmose earns the name *Philhellene* ('Greek-lover') for his patronage of Greek colonists and soldiers.

569   Pharaoh Ahmose makes the town of Naucratis (established as a trading post under Wahibre Psammetichus), near Sais, the epicentre of trade between Greece and Egypt. Anti-Greek sentiments flare up among the *machimoi*; Ahmose is forced to garrison Memphis with Greek troops to prevent a native uprising.

567   Urged on by Haaibre, Nebuchadnezzar invades Egypt and is repulsed by Ahmose and his armies. Haaibre is slain in battle; Ahmose recovers his body and gives him a state funeral. In Tyre, Hasdrabal Barca is born to Gisco, a merchant-prince with strong ties to Egypt.

565   Phanes born at Halicarnassus, in Caria.

562   Nebuchadnezzar dies; he is succeeded by a series of weak rulers. The great Chaldean Empire begins to erode. In Cyrene, Ladice is born into a noble family.

560   Peisistratus usurps power in Athens (the first of three times); though a tyrant (the Greeks used the word *tyrannos* to describe a king rather than a despot), Peisistratus was known as a patron of the arts and literature, and embarked on a programme of public building and beautification.

559   Kurush (Greek: Kuros, Cyrus), a prince of the province of Anshan in Persis, deposes the Median king Astyages and seizes the throne for himself. Birth of the Persian Empire.

556   Nabonidus, an ageing antiquarian and former statesman under Nebuchadnezzar, becomes king of Babylon. The lyric poet Simonides, who would later go on to compose the epitaph to the fallen Spartans at Thermopylae, is born on the island of Keos.

555   Callisthenes born at Naucratis.

550   Darius, son of Hystapes, born in Persia. In the Shara Mountains of Arabia, Jauharah is born to a family of mixed Bedouin and Nabatean descent.

546   Battle of Pteria. A coalition of states – Lydia, Egypt, Babylon, and Sparta – cross the Halys River to invade Persia, hoping to squash the rising power of Cyrus. The battle proves inconclusive; the coalition forces return to their respective homelands. Cyrus, though, pursues the Lydians and their king, Croesus, defeating them in battle at Thymbra and sacking the Lydian capital of Sardis.

542   Pharaoh Ahmose marries Ladice of Cyrene, his third known wife. The union makes Cyrene an ally of Egypt.

538   Cyrus conquers Babylon. Nabonidus slain. The Persian is hailed as a liberator by the Jews of Babylon, whom he allows to return to Palestine, thus ending their Babylonian Captivity. Cyrus' eldest son, Cambyses, is named governor of Babylon.

530   Cyrus slain while fighting the Massagetae people near the Caspian Sea. Accession of Cambyses. Plans laid for the Persian invasion of Egypt.

527   In Athens, the tyrant Peisistratus dies; his
eldest son, Hippias, becomes tyrant. At
Babylon, Cambyses begins mustering his invasion force.

526   Phanes of Halicarnassus defects to the court
of Cambyses of Persia. Battle of Memphis.
Later in the year, Khnemibre Ahmose dies.
His eldest son, Ankhkaenre Psammetichus,
becomes Pharaoh.

525   Battle of Pelusium. The Twenty-sixth
Dynasty ends as Egypt falls to the Persian
Empire.

BIBLIOGRAPHY

Adamson, Stephen, Ed. *The Way to Eternity: Egyptian Myth*. London: Duncan Baird Publishers, 1997.

Adkins, Lesley and Roy A. Adkins. *Handbook to Life in Ancient Greece*. Oxford: Oxford University Press, 1997.

Bares, Ladislav. 'The Shaft Tombs of Abusir.' *Archaeology Odyssey* (May/June 2002): 14–25.

Braun, T. F. R. C. 'The Greeks in Egypt.' *Cambridge Ancient History* 2nd ed. Vol. 3 (1982): 32–56.

Bunson, Margaret. *A Dictionary of Ancient Egypt*. Oxford: Oxford University Press, 1991.

Butler, Samuel. *Homer: The Iliad*. New York: Barnes and Noble Books, 1995.

Clapp, Nicholas. *The Road to Ubar*. New York: Houghton Mifflin, 1998.

Cook, J. M. *The Persian Empire*. New York: Barnes and Noble Books, 1983.

David, Rosalie. *Handbook to Life in Ancient Egypt*. Oxford: Oxford University Press, 1998.

DeCamp, L. Sprague. *Great Cities of the Ancient World*. New York: Barnes and Noble Books, 1993.

DeSelincourt, Aubrey. *Herodotus: The Histories*. New York: Penguin Books, 1996.

Dodson, Aidan. *Hieroglyphs of Ancient Egypt*. Barnes and Noble Books, 2001.

—. *Monarchs of the Nile*. Cairo: The American University in Cairo Press, 2000.

Fagan, Brian M. *Egypt of the Pharaohs*. Washington, D.C.: National Geographic Books, 2000.

Glueck, Nelson. *Rivers in the Desert*. New York: Farrar, Straus and Cudahy, 1959.

Grant, Michael. *A Guide to the Ancient World*. New York: Barnes and Noble Books, 1997.

Hanson, Victor Davis. *The Wars of the Ancient Greeks*. London: Cassell, 1999.

Hawass, Zahi. *Valley of the Golden Mummies*. New York: Harry N. Abrams, 2000.

Hendricks, Rhoda A. *Classical Gods and Heroes*. New York: William Morrow, 1978.

Hitti, Philip K. *The Arabs: A Short History*. Princeton: Princeton University Press, 1943.

Hooke, S. H. *Middle Eastern Mythology*. London: Pelican Books, 1963.

Houtzager, Guus. *Complete Encyclopedia of Greek Mythology*. Edison: Chartwell Books, 2003.

McDermott, Bridget. *Decoding Egyptian Hieroglyphs*. San Francisco: Chronicle Books, 2001.

Oates, Joan. *Babylon*. London: Thames and Hudson Ltd, 1979.

Ray, John D. 'Egypt, 525–404 BC', *Cambridge Ancient History* 2nd ed. Vol. 4 (1988): 254–286.

Rohl, David. *Pharaohs and Kings: A Biblical Quest*. New York: Crown Publishers, Inc., 1995.

Shaw, Ian, Ed. *The Oxford History of Ancient Egypt*. Oxford: Oxford University Press, 2000.

Silverman, David P., ed. *Ancient Egypt*. Oxford: Oxford University Press, 1997.

Stephens, John Lloyd. *Incidents of Travel in Egypt, Arabia Petraea, and the Holy Land*. New York: Harper and Brothers, 1837.

Whiston, William, A. M. *Josephus: The Complete Works*. Nashville: Thomas Nelson Publishers, 1998.

Wilkinson, Richard H. *Complete Temples of Ancient Egypt*. London: Thames and Hudson, Ltd, 2000.

—. *Reading Egyptian Art*. London: Thames and Hudson Ltd, 1994.